Here's what readers and reviewers are saying about

THE LEGEND OF THE FIREFISH

Book One in the Trophy Chase Trilogy....

"Swashbuckling is the best way to describe Book One of the Trophy Chase Trilogy. Without wasting time, Polivka's first novel drops readers into a fantasy world filled with action, where chivalry is alive and well, and sword fights are frequent....With the nonstop action that cuts between multiple story lines, readers will be flipping pages eagerly."

—*PUBLISHERS WEEKLY*

"A ripping yarn with the feel of the open sea and glimmers of eternal wisdom."

—KATHY TYERS,
AUTHOR OF *SHIVERING WORLD*
AND THE FIREBIRD TRILOGY

"*The Legend of the Firefish,* first in the Trophy Chase Trilogy by George Bryan Polivka is a winner....This is a story filled with action, adventure, danger, intrigue, surprise, suspense. It will keep readers turning pages to find out what will happen next...The characters Polivka created are fresh and interesting...A must read for fantasy lovers and a highly recommended rating for others who want a good story."

—REBECCA LUELLA MILLER,
A CHRISTIAN WORLDVIEW OF FICTION WEBSITE

"I must confess that *The Legend of the Firefish* is not a book I'd normally pick to read. I mean pirates are not my usual cuppa cha. But as I began reading it, I got hooked.... The book is filled with adventure, action, pirates, intriguing plot and gore. Yes, gore. Blood spilling fights. It all had a purpose. Polivka brilliantly portrays the horror of life, sin, evil and carefully weaves the beauty of mercy into his story. That to me is what Firefish is really about...I really should say no more. You just need to read the book. And I'd especially recommend it for men and for boys. How hard it is to get our teen boys to read. Maybe this will lure them in. It did me—and I ain't no pirate person."

—JANEY L. DEMEO,
AUTHOR OF *HEAVEN HELP ME RAISE THESE CHILDREN!:*
BIBLICAL DIRECTION FOR PRACTICAL PARENTING ISSUES

"This was one of the most amazing reads!...I have to put this up there as one of my favorites!...It's been a very long while since I've picked up a book that I literally could NOT put down. My family was clamoring around me for milk, cookies, dinner, but no, all things had to wait because I could NOT put the book down."

—BETH GODDARD, AUTHOR OF *SEASONS OF LOVE*

"I cannot say enough how much I enjoyed this read. Besides the excellent storytelling, I actually found my faith strengthened as I followed hero Packer Throme as he was forced to rely completely on God's strength, time and time again. Polivka managed to do this so convincingly—without coming off as preachy or trite—by creating a genuine character. There were no cheap, quick fixes. He played his character's faith out on hard reality over and over. If you haven't read this story, you must. I would rank Polivka's novel with the elite in Christian fantasy and sci-fi. His is unique, but I enjoyed it just as much as C.S. Lewis' *Narnia,* and just as much as Walter M. Miller's *A Canticle for Leibowitz."*

—**BRANDON BARR,** CO-AUTHOR OF *WHEN THE SKY FELL*

"George Bryan Polivka has effectively created a lush and rich world of life on the high seas. Filled with disreputable characters who would slit your throat without a second thought for a few silver coins, he brings the reader into a world where the hero of the story struggles to reclaim his relationship with God. Filled with vivid descriptions and engaging dialogue, George Bryan Polivka masterfully weaves a story that draws the reader into this mythical setting from page one."

—**MIKE LYNCH,** CO-AUTHOR OF *WHEN THE SKY FELL*

"This book is not like anything I've ever come across before. It's an absolutely unique mingling of real biblical Christianity with a fictional, historical-type fantasy world. Take a look. You won't regret it."

—**GRACE BRIDGES,** AUTHOR OF *FAITH AWAKENED*

"Packed with authentic and crusty characters, duels that literally ring off the pages, and the most amazing creation known to fantasy literature—the Firefish—Polivka has achieved his own niche in Christian fantasy fiction. *The Legend of the Firefish* gets five out of five bookmarks from me!"

—**BLOG REVIEWER DEENA PETERSON,**
DEENASBOOKS.BLOGSPOT.COM

And praise for Book Two in the Trophy Chase Trilogy,

THE HAND THAT BEARS THE SWORD

"Polivka's characters are real. He makes these people come alive; gives them adequate motivation; shows their struggles, failures, successes, fears, hopes....The plot is full of action and suspense, twists and surprises...There is an unending list of what to like in this story. But don't lose sight of the fact that it is the middle book of a trilogy, meaning that at the end, we are far from THE END. This is good news, in my opinion, because it means I have another great read to look forward to."

—**REBECCA LUELLA MILLER,**
A CHRISTIAN WORLDVIEW OF FICTION WEBSITE

THE BATTLE FOR
VAST
DOMINION

George Bryan Polivka

HARVEST HOUSE PUBLISHERS

EUGENE, OREGON

All Scripture quotations are taken from the King James Version of the Bible.

Cover by Left Coast Design, Portland, Oregon

Cover photos © Tai Power Seeff / The Image Bank / Getty; Karl Weatherly / Digital Vision / Getty

This is a work of fiction. Names, characters, places, and incidents are products of the author's imagination or are used fictitiously. Any resemblance to actual persons, living or dead, or to events or locales, is entirely coincidental.

THE BATTLE FOR VAST DOMINION
Copyright © 2008 by George Bryan Polivka
Published by Harvest House Publishers
Eugene, Oregon 97402
www.harvesthousepublishers.com

Library of Congress Cataloging-in-Publication Data
  Polivka, Bryan.
  The battle for Vast dominion / George Bryan Polivka.
    p. cm. — (Trophy Chase trilogy ; bk. 3)
  ISBN-13: 978-0-7369-1958-6
  ISBN-10: 0-7369-1958-9
  1. Packer Throme (Fictitious character)—Fiction. I. Title.
  PS3616.O5677B38 2008
  813'.6—dc22

                              2007028420

Printed in the United States of America

08 09 10 11 12 13 14 15 / LB-SK / 11 10 9 8 7 6 5 4 3

For the joy of the Lord

NEHEMIAH 8:10

CONTENTS

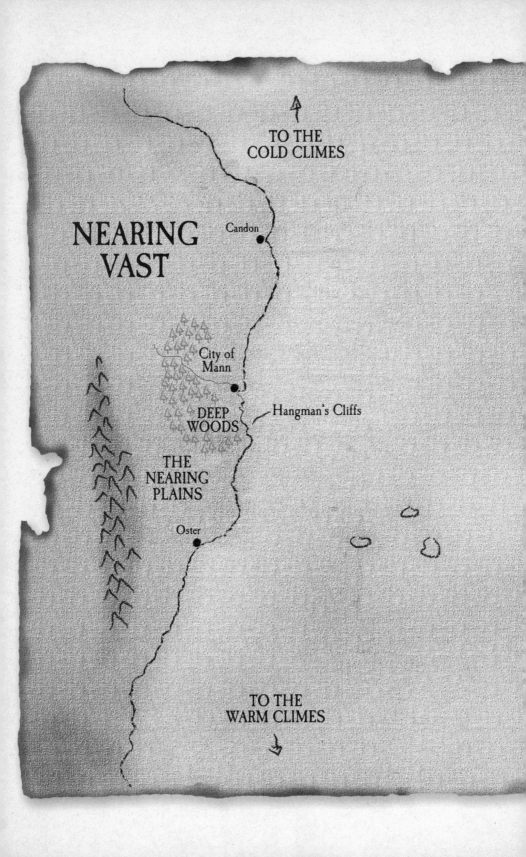

ACHAWUK
ISLANDS

UNCHARTED

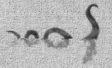

THE
VAST
SEA

TO URLAH

Hezarow
Kyne

KINGDOM OF
DRAMMUN

TO SANDAVALE

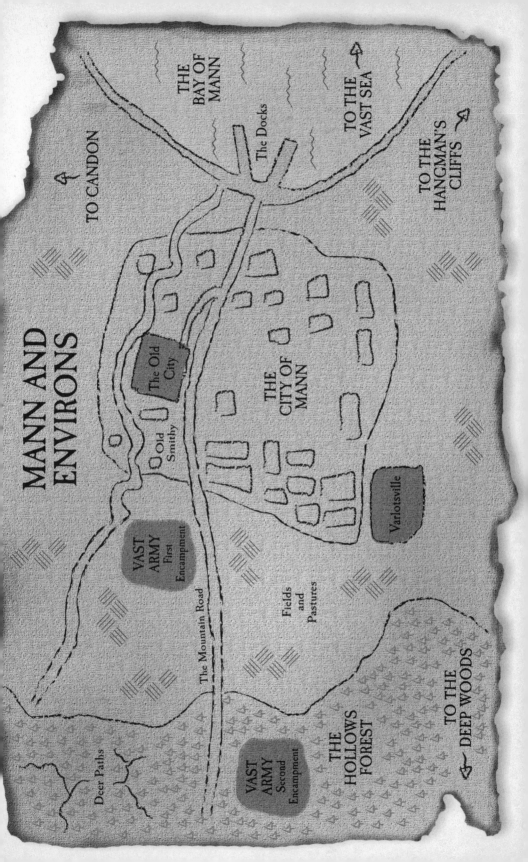

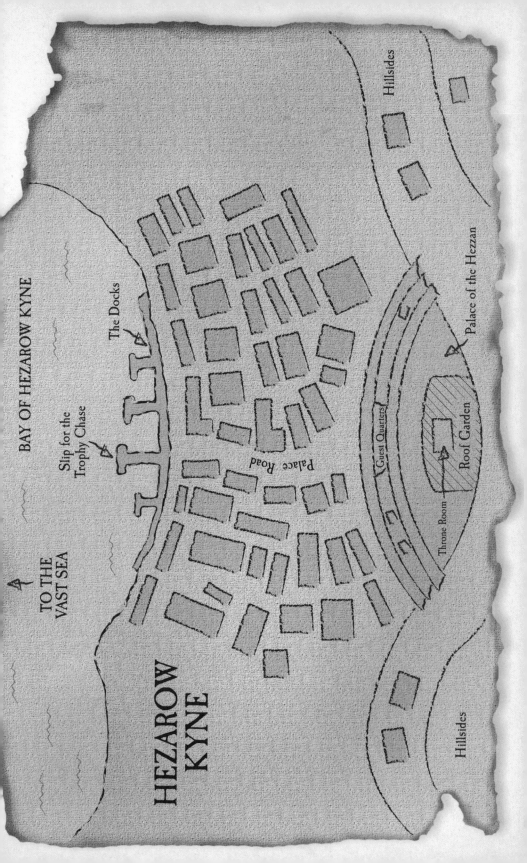

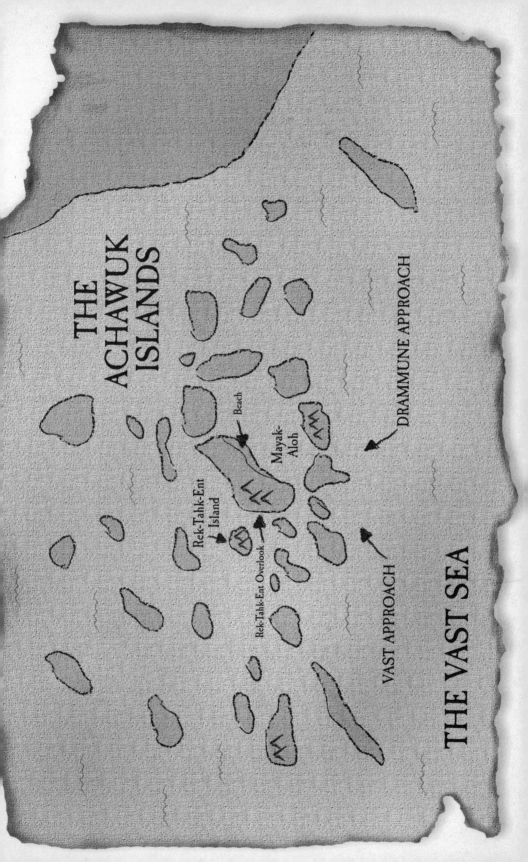

As Our Story Opens...

The great ship *Trophy Chase* is at sea, commanded by Admiral John Hand. But this admiral has no fleet. His navy was sunk by the Drammune in the opening salvo of war, and now Hand's desperate mission is to transform a handful of merchant vessels into a fighting force. As he contends with recalcitrant captains, the monstrous Firefish awaits, looking for the sleek ship it calls Deep Fin, and the enthralling, maddening presence that lives aboard.

The invaders own the capital of Nearing Vast, the City of Mann, having routed and humiliated the Vast army. But victory is not assured. The hanging of Packer Throme for war crimes against Drammun turned inexplicably to triumph for the rabble remnant of the Vast, pirates and priests and brigands, and led to the escape of their yellow-haired hero.

Across the sea in Drammun, the Hezzan Skahl Dramm has received reports that the Vast have trained Firefish to attack on command. She knows a single beast could destroy an entire fleet of ships. She believes the Vast have learned the secrets of the Firefish and she must learn those secrets in order to dominate the world.

The Vast army, regrouped within the Hollow Forest outside Mann, is now learning that Packer Throme, the fisherman's son, has been made King of the Vast. And his new bride, Panna, the principled daughter of a village priest, is now his queen. God is with them, the Vast believe. So certainly, victory will now be theirs.

But can an inexperienced king and queen, an outnumbered army, a tattered navy, and a single unpredictable Beast triumph over Drammune, and Achawuk, and the Firefish?

With Thee on board, each sailor is a king
Nor I mere captain of my vessel then,
But heir of earth and heaven, eternal child;
Daring all truth, nor fearing anything;
Mighty in love, the servant of all men;
Resenting nothing, taking rage and blare
Into the godlike silence of a loving care.

—GEORGE MacDONALD, *DIARY OF AN OLD SOUL*

CHAPTER 1

The King

Word got out.

"Have you heard?" Father Mooring asked.

Dog winced. The needle flashed in the lamplight as the priest slid it deftly through the old fisherman's torn flesh, restitching his chest wound, black thread pulling tight his wounds once again. *It shouldn't hurt this much,* he thought. *Tiny little thing.* He lay on his back under the stars with one big, calloused fist squeezed tight and trembling at his side, the other gripping the wire handle of the kerosene lamp.

"Heard what?" he asked through clenched teeth.

"Just the most amazing news. They made Packer Throme king." The priest said it with great warmth as he knelt over his patient. His needle went deep, searching out sound flesh beneath the ragged, torn skin.

"Ow!" Dog's empty hand came up and swept the little priest away, knocking him back on his haunches. "You tryin' to kill me?"

Father Mooring was unperturbed. He had stitched, sawed, sewed, pressed, and bandaged so many soldiers and citizens now, with nothing to dull the pain, that no reaction surprised him. Dog had a particularly deep gash, the same honorable wound he had stuffed with dirt and gravel to stanch the bleeding, and that had taken a long, painful process to clean. Now the stitching had been stressed past breaking by the stubborn man's long walk here through the dank tunnels from the Battle of the Green. And by his insistence on behaving as though nothing much had happened to him.

"Mr. Blestoe," the genial priest said, still smiling, but with a sense of command not even Dog could ignore, "you are a proud man. A strong man. But your wound is deep. It will kill you if you refuse the only ministrations that God has, in His mercy, sent you."

Dog grimaced, his eyes clamped shut and his face twisted in pain. The agony caused by his own sudden movement far outstripped the pinpricks from the needle. "All right. But what in blazin' glory are you goin' on about?"

Father Mooring grasped Dog's left hand, the one with the lamp, and maneuvered it back into position. "You just popped three stitches. Three of my better ones, I don't mind saying. This isn't exactly embroidery I'm doing here."

"No, I mean..." he couldn't bring himself to say the boy's name, "the king. What did you say about the king?"

"Oh, that!" Father Mooring brightened immediately. "That's what they say. Packer's been named king. Isn't that something?"

"King of *what?*"

"Why, of Nearing Vast. King of us all." The priest bent over the fisherman-soldier once again, needle poised. "King of you. Now, if you'll just relax and—"

Dog lowered the lantern again. "Of all the confounded, ignorant rumors..." Words failed him. "What blame fool would make a fisherman into a king?"

"Well, I believe God would be your fool there. He's been known to do such things. Did it with a shepherd once, and a carpenter another time." The priest positioned the lamp again, squeezing Dog's hand firmly. "Hold it there," he ordered. Then he stitched away as he spoke. "And I believe it was you who told me Packer wasn't much of a fisherman anyway. And he couldn't be a priest. So perhaps he's finally found his calling." Dog flinched, and the pain of his own movement again seared through his chest. "Listen now, Mr. Blestoe, if you continue to resist, I can't help you."

Dog stewed. It just couldn't be true.

"Now be still. This is medicine, not torture."

Dog begged to differ.

The soldiers of the Army of Nearing Vast were deeply enfolded by the Hollow Forest, hidden by its trees, protected by its hills and its undergrowth. For the moment, they were safe from the expected Drammune onslaught. Orders prohibited campfires, and so soldiers huddled together or bivouacked under cold moonlight. The first light of dawn revealed clear skies but brought no additional heat. They gathered together for warmth, regulars in near-pristine uniforms alongside recruits wearing now-ragged civilian clothes, interspersed with the irregulars, the already-storied veterans of the Battle of the Green. And they talked.

They talked of victory. They talked of hope. A thousand recitals with a hundred thousand details would not have been enough to quench their thirst for details about how the dregs of Vast society, the undisciplined and unwanted and infirm yet unintimidated, had overcome the most vaunted warriors alive. They wanted to hear of the charge of Bench Urmand, the prayer of Packer Throme, the sacrifice of Prince Mather, the surge of the Vast, the retreat and defeat of Fen Abbaka Mux.

Spoils of war were admired and coveted, Drammune swords and pistols and helmets and hauberks. These irregulars, most of them unaccustomed to being treated with even a sliver of honor, now spoke humbly, in hushed tones and solemn terms, to reverent audiences. "Seemed like we had to fight, is all. Like the sea rammin' up against the shore." "Never did think about winnin' or losin.' Just fought." Back in the City of Mann, the Rampart stood, protecting the conquerors of Nearing Vast. But here in the wilderness walls had fallen.

And now, they said, Packer Throme had become their king. Prince Mather had sacrificed himself, and a peasant stood at the pinnacle of power and prestige. If that were true, then they all now lived in a world in which anything could happen. Anything was possible. Anything at all.

The couple lay together in the tiny farmhouse, fully clothed, under a thin blanket. They had talked deep into the night, unable to sleep, unable to rest. The candle had long burned away, its wax melted and running over the brass cup that was its base. The pale light of morning peeked through dingy windows. Packer was content now just to listen to Panna breathe. His wife's breaths were soft and sweet, like a soloist's intake just before a first, pure note.

He could hear, too, the woods around them awakening. Soprano melodies of songbirds replaced the baritone of night owls. Bass bleats of bullfrogs rose, supporting the tenor hiss of insects. But there was another sound too—a distant-sounding hum that Packer didn't quite recognize—something familiar, not quite katydid, not quite cicada, a low rumbling tone from somewhere outside the farmhouse that came in waves, soothing, then growing urgent and tense, then fading away again.

Panna's breaths shortened as she came fully awake.

Her thoughts were her own for a long time as she remembered the conclusions she had drawn during the night. Now, with the world coming alive, she felt a great sense of confidence surge through her.

"Packer?" she finally whispered.

"Yes," he answered gently.

"We can do this."

Packer turned to look at her. As determined as she was, her face looked delicate in the pale light. She was lovely, all shadow and light, a strand of dark hair lying across her cheek, her dark eyes sharp and purposeful. He shook his head. "I don't know how to be a king."

"But God wants it." She sat up, leaning on her right elbow, facing him. "'God hath chosen the foolish things of the world to confound the wise,'" she quoted, "'and God hath chosen the weak things of the world to confound the things which are mighty.'"

He said nothing, but looked up at the dark ceiling above him. It had been his father's favorite verse. Dayton Throme had been thought a fool for his devotion to Firefish. It had always seemed a bit sad to Packer that his father had found so much comfort in the sentiment of that passage. And yet it was Dayton Throme's foolishness that had led Packer to the feeding waters of the beasts, deep in the Achawuk territory. And there they had discovered enough Firefish to control the destiny of the world.

Packer closed his eyes. His heart sank like a stone, drifting down to a sandy floor in shimmering waters. His choices had all gone awry, and had led to bloodshed and war and then, somehow, to a throne. It made no sense. The stone that was his heart came to rest on an ocean floor, light from above dancing on the rippled sand around him. He could not succeed. But it seemed he was called to try anyway. And somehow, that was a peaceful thought. And then he remembered.

"You're smiling," Panna said, relieved to see it.

He studied her. She was still propped up on one elbow, the angle of her shoulders acute against her neck, her dark hair drifting down. She was so beautiful. So certain. "I was remembering Senslar Zendoda," he told her, "and his turtle."

"The one that hatches on dry land and then crawls to the sea?"

"It doesn't know where it's going or why. It just has to go there."

"And you feel like that turtle."

"Oh, I *am* that turtle."

She felt a flood of warmth for her husband, for the way he suffered under so great an honor. She took his hand, looked at the hardened, callus-like burns on his palm, the round white circle at the base. She ran her fingers over them gently. Then she turned his hand over and looked at the royal signet on his forefinger, the blue gem set within the Vast crest, the intertwining N and V pierced by a sword. Suddenly she laughed.

"What?"

"Packer Throme, King of the Vast." She put a hand to her mouth.

He shook his head. "Well, if I'm the king, you're the queen."

Panna blanched. That fact sobered her considerably.

Packer again heard the hum from somewhere outside. Closer now. Perhaps right in front of the farmhouse itself. He rose from the bed, Panna following.

And as he opened the door Packer understood the source of that rising, falling hum. It was definitely not cicadas, definitely not katydids.

There, in front of the house, a large crowd had gathered and had been talking quietly among themselves, hoping for this very moment.

"It's the king!" someone called.

"The king and queen!" came from several others.

The crowd, released now from its strained effort to keep quiet, erupted. Amid the cheers a small band, a single fiddle and three drums, struck up "Long Life to King and Kingdom," immediately drowned by voices singing as loudly and as passionately as they could, tune and tone not primary concerns.

Panna's hand slipped into Packer's once again. They glanced at one another in wonder. Then they waved.

Word had, most definitely, gotten out.

The falcon flew from Talon's leather-gloved hand up into the morning sun, under a perfect blue sky. The flap of wings grew fainter with each beat as the bird rose, circled once to get her bearings, then bore its handwritten burden eastward over the Vast sea.

"They will think your message a grave mistake."

Talon, now overlord of all Drammun, turned to face her chief minister, Sool Kron, who stood behind her in the roof gardens high atop her palace. His long, thin beard was perfectly groomed, his new blood-and-gold robes glimmered in the sunlight. Talon narrowed her eyes. "You fear a roomful of Drammune politicians? You have never seen the Firefish."

"True, I have not. But I have seen the Quarto. They lead the Zealots, who in turn lead all who oppose you. I fear we have made a deal with the devil." He used the Vast word for the archenemy of God.

"I thought you might believe it is they who have made that bargain."

"I do not doubt your abilities, Your Worthiness. You were masterful in swaying them to our cause. But even so, you have ushered bears to a beehive. They will be harder to shoo away once they've tasted the honey."

"Even a bear must learn to respect the hunter." She snapped her head around, drilling into Kron's eyes. "Or it will die with its greedy paws buried in the honeycomb." Kron swallowed hard. He had made the same bargain, and for the same reason, and she did not want him to forget it. "I will show the Court of Twelve what power is," she said at last. "I will teach the ministers to fear."

"It is always prudent to remind subordinates where they rank..."

"Yes. Submission becomes underlings." She continued to stare at him.

He dropped to a knee, and then lowered his forehead to the paving stones.

She watched him a moment, trusting him not at all. "Call the Twelve together," she said. Then she turned and walked away.

Prince Ward had arrived at the small farmhouse along with the eggs and bacon and coffee he'd ordered sent over for the royal couple. But he needn't have bothered. Well-wishers from the crowd had placed baskets on the porch, packages full of freshly baked breads and biscuits, butter and jam, sausages, quarts of buttermilk, all for the king and queen and all prepared, amazingly, without benefit of campfires.

"This is way more than we need," Panna said, alarmed. She and Packer had made it back into the farmhouse after much shaking of hands and waving and calling out greetings. Now they stared at the table weighted down with this bounty. "This should be feeding the army."

"Ah, but they're a ferocious lot, and will not be deterred." Prince Ward said it with his usual easy good humor. Outside the window parcels were now being checked by guards along the picket fence, twenty yards from the already crowded front porch. Ward's coffee cup steamed under his chin as he watched. For himself, he had little stomach for food this morning, feeling stretched and wan after a long and restless night without his accustomed liquid sustenance. He wrapped himself around his coffee mug as though it held salvation.

"Couldn't we..." Packer began, now looking out the window as well. A woman in a red-checked apron pressed some baked goods on a familiar huge dragoon. "Couldn't we ask them to stop bringing all that?"

Ward shrugged. "Not me. You're the king."

"How would we...how would I do that?"

Ward rubbed his neck. "Well, I'm not much at public speaking myself. But if it were me, I'd step out onto the porch and raise my hand, and then say something like, 'Good people of Nearing Vast, thank you for your kindness. We have more than enough. Please take this nourishment for yourselves, and for our troops.'"

Packer pondered. Seemed simple enough. He put out his hand to Panna, who took it. With a sense of crossing a new threshold, they stepped together outside the farmhouse, onto the porch. Packer raised his right hand in preparation for his first pronouncement.

Fully five minutes passed before the crowd allowed themselves to be waved to silence. Even the guards along the picket fence faced Panna and cheered along. But only once did Stave Deroy crane his neck around to see his king and queen. Panna recognized him and waved, then pointed him out to Packer. The big dragoon waved his fingers, turned red, then turned back to his duties and redoubled his efforts.

"Good morning!" Packer said at last.

"Good morning!" the crowd thundered back in unison.

Packer felt keenly uncomfortable in the pause that followed. "Thank you for your kindness, but please, feed yourselves!" Their silence was a large rock poised on a precipice. Packer felt panic. They wanted something more, but he had no idea what. So he concluded with, "We want all of you strong and healthy. We have a war to win!"

The crowd exploded, the rock falling into the ocean with a satisfying *ka-thunk*. The cheering continued as Packer and Panna re-entered the house and sat back down to a considerably colder breakfast.

Packer looked to Ward in amazement. "Is it always like that?"

"I think you should expect that level of enthusiasm for a while," Ward told him.

"No, I mean, do they always know just what they want? When I spoke to them, it wasn't like I was leading them. It was like...they were waiting for me to say just the right thing, and they weren't going to be happy until I did."

Now Ward nodded. "They do have certain expectations of the Crown."

Packer looked to Panna. "But sometimes people need to hear things," he said to her, "that they don't want to hear." He was thinking about Mather, and how he had deceived the people about the destruction of the Fleet. He was thinking it might be a lot harder to tell the truth than he had supposed.

Just then, the crowd outside launched into a familiar Vast anthem.

> *Long life to King and Kingdom!*
> *Our fathers' land and ours!*
> *From regal throne*
> *God's will be done*
> *In honor and...in power!*

Ward sighed. "The House of Sennett seems a distant memory to them already."

"What of Mather?" Panna asked. "When will he be buried?"

"Already done. We had a small honor guard. An unmarked grave."

"That's not right," Panna shot back. "He was the king if only for a day."

Ward waved a hand dismissively. "Contingencies of war. We can see to proper ceremonies at a less anxious moment. For now I thought it prudent to focus on General Millian's plan of attack."

"Attack?" Packer's pulse rose.

Panna saw the fires flare up. Packer had said he put away his sword forever, and she was sure he'd meant it. But that didn't change his nature.

Ward lowered his coffee cup. He spoke with an unaccustomed authority. "Right now your people will tear down the Rampart walls with their bare hands to get at the Drammune. They will follow you, Packer, to the grave and beyond. You are considered by them to be invincible. The Firefish, the Achawuk, the Drammune at sea, all have been beaten by you."

Packer looked down as Ward's gaze grew intense. Panna was poised like a hawk ready to pounce on any sign the prince might be trying to manipulate her husband. Packer watched the floor, noting that the leather of his left boot was coming loose from the sole, just inside the big toe.

"A prince died for you," Ward continued. Now Packer looked him in the eye. "Do you think these people would do less? I would recommend, as your generals surely will, that you strike now and with the greatest possible force, while we may still surprise the enemy." Here Ward's voice softened, and he sounded more like himself. "And, I might add, without first bringing to our people's attention small, inconvenient items like the demise of the Fleet, or the loss of the king's gold. What will such trifles matter if we take back the city, and drive the Drammune into the sea? And then again, what will they matter if we risk all and are defeated?"

Panna stared, unblinking. "The king's gold?"

Ward tugged at an ear. "Well, yes. The bank has been…overdrawn. By the Drammune. Bad news, I'm afraid."

"You mean there's no money? At all?" Panna asked, dumbfounded.

"Well, there is money. It just happens to be in the possession of the Drammune. At the moment."

"But how?" she asked. "Weren't plans made to protect it? Hide it? Carry it away?"

"Yes, but those plans were made by my dear brother. He may have repented in his last moments, but I'm afraid he could not undo damage he'd already done."

"He gave the king's gold to the Drammune," Packer stated flatly.

"How will we pay the troops?" Panna asked. "How will we feed them?"

"We hope to get it back," Ward answered. "You might say our battle plan doubles as our financial plan."

Packer rose and walked slowly to the door. He walked out onto the porch as the crowd began the fourth verse of their hymn to the Crown of Nearing Vast. Their vigor was not lessened by a noticeable lack of agreement on the words, these lyrics coming so deep into the stanzas:

> Hail to the population
> The great people of this land
> Who shine and glow
> And in good works grow
> From meek to great to grand

Drawn by their exuberance, Packer walked down from the porch, out to the crowd, reaching out to those who reached out to him. At first he was uncomfortable with all the attention. Then he realized that these soldiers, these citizens, wanted something greater than he had to give, and his embarrassment ebbed away. Yes, of course they wanted more than he could give. They wanted the same things he did. They wanted hope. They wanted the setting right of wrongs, the return to peace, to pride, to prosperity. They wanted to be part of something larger than themselves, and to know that it was good, and that it would last.

Packer then determined that every hand he shook would be a promise, every eye he met an affirmation of his intent, that with whatever power God would give him he would work to set whatever wrongs he could to rights.

Panna watched from the porch. She knew how badly every grip of his damaged hand must hurt him. But he seemed to welcome the pain. That wound, somehow, Panna now thought, that circular scar and the hardened skin of his palm…she couldn't quite get her mind around it, but it was as though…as though he had lived all his life with that same wound, invisible and internal, until it had finally worked its way out in life. Now his damaged body mirrored his torn, rent spirit.

The crush around Packer grew until he couldn't be seen at all. Panna felt alarm, and straightened. Then suddenly there he was, his head popping up from the sea of faces, slightly dazed but seeming in one piece, and she realized he was now riding on Stave Deroy's shoulders. The big dragoon pushed his way through the mob toward the farmhouse with the mob following. Chunk, who was not so nicknamed without reason, at last reached the porch and deposited the king at the foot of the steps. Panna saw anger on Chunk's face, and felt the wild, raucous glee of the unruly crowd.

Packer stepped up onto the porch, turned back, and waved. Panna did her best to smile and wave, and the two ducked into the farmhouse. The door closed behind them; they looked at each other with eyes wide. Then they noticed Ward Sennett, who leaned casually against the side table and stirred his coffee, passive, distant, but utterly aware. "Like I say," he offered, blowing on the coffee to cool it, "they're a ferocious lot, and will not be deterred." He sipped once, found the drink still unsatisfactory, and blew on it again.

CHAPTER 2

The Opposition

The beast had not eaten for days.

It had tasted no meat since it had feasted on the fat ship storm creature, obeying the command of the Deep Fin. Then it had been sated, delighted, and it had followed the Fin all the way to the seashore, following from behind and below, as the Deep Fin outran the enormous pack of storm creatures that held it in pursuit.

The beast had been joyous, alive with a fire that knew no bounds. But the great and sleek storm creature went all the way to the shores and left the beast behind. Deep Fin slid into the high shallows, way up among the rocks, venturing into those thin, warm waters, sheer and invisible, where small fish teem and flow like darts of light. Here the beast could not follow.

And so it waited, circling slowly. And an empty place grew within it. And then…the great pack of storm creatures arrived. The beast fled farther. The pack stayed along the seashore, hunting and waiting. The Firefish circled, deep below. It waited, too. It watched.

But Deep Fin was gone. And the empty place grew, and grew, and became cavernous. And then, the darkest of thoughts worked into its murky mind…*Deep Fin had forgotten.*

The beast turned away from the shore, from the high shallows. It swam down. It swam far. The empty place inside now burned like lightning that never stopped, hot in its brain, in its empty belly. The memory of Deep Fin bit deep, and deeper. A great and mournful loss.

The beast swam deep, deeper down into darkness than ever it had swum before, pushing, fleeing downward until the sea was as cold as the faraway ice, until the waters pressed in thick black darkness and squeezed and squeezed, until all sounds echoed in emptiness and all was as cold and hollow as the cavern within.

And there the loss turned to anger. The anger was aimed at no prey, no enemy, no object at all. And then anger became hunger.

It wanted to feed.

"Stop where you are!" shouted the Captain of the Guard, and the young priest candidate reined his horse to a halt thirty yards away.

"I have a message for the Most Holy Reverend Father!" he shouted back. He wore the green robes of a novice still in school. His voice was thin. He sounded young, or exhausted, or both.

"Who hails us?" the captain called back.

"I am a lowly messenger, in service to Father Usher Fell, elder of the Seminary of Mann!" He had approached at full gallop as dusk settled over the long, dusty road. Eight dragoons had turned as one, protecting the two coaches ahead of them. Four horsemen, dragoons in civilian clothes, quickly blocked the road, pistols drawn, while four more dismounted, unholstering long rifles and taking cover in the ditches. The drivers of the two royal coaches shook their reins, each putting his team into an easy canter toward the Mountains, visible on the distant horizon.

The benign figure spoke plaintively, but the dragoons did not lower their weapons. "Approach slowly," the captain ordered.

The rider was in fact both young and exhausted, but his bright eyes held no fear. The horse foamed, and stumbled once as it bore its rider closer. He was allowed to fish a parchment from his pocket. The captain ordered him to dismount, and then required him to stand alone in the road as both the parchment and the horse were taken from him. Still the dragoons did not waver, but aimed their weapons and scoured the countryside for accomplices, as though the unarmed seminarian might become an army of Drammune warriors if they so much as blinked.

Once the driver of Reynard Sennett's coach had reined his horses in, the folded sheaf was handed up into the dusty compartment. The High Holy Reverend Father and Supreme Elder, Harlowen "Hap" Stanson, accepted it. Briefly he met the eyes of the man he still believed to be the king of Nearing Vast. Reynard's big jowls trembled.

Princess Jacqalyn watched both men with a comfortable, contemptuous smirk across her narrow face. Queen Maeveline watched with single-minded apprehension. Stanson examined the seal, saw it was unopened. He broke it, unfolded the sheaf, and read the note silently. Then he let his hands fall onto his lap. He closed his eyes. "Is this true?"

Reynard sniffed. "Would you like me to guess the contents?"

Hap Stanson shook his head. When he opened his eyes, his usually sunny visage was hard as a diamond. He glared at the former king. "You gave your kingdom to your son."

"Ah. Then he's announced it!" Reynard's heart leapt. The former king had been little more than a large lump on a padded cushion the entire trip, distant to the point of unreachable, his face pale and his puffy eyes blank as his enormous folds of flesh were bounced about mercilessly on the dry, rutted roads. Now he was animated. "I would not have kept the matter so close, but he swore me to tell no one but those present at the moment. And I felt I must obey because, well, those were orders from the king—my son, the king." The big man's tone fairly boasted. "Is he well? What news of the war? Speak!"

Queen Maeveline and Princess Jacqalyn looked at one another. Neither treated herself to anything like the large helping of hope Reynard had just dished up for himself. They had been "those present at the moment," the two witnesses required by Vast law, chosen by Mather as witnesses to his ascension because they were handy and they were headed out of town. "The moment" itself had been dreadful. The prince was ill-tempered, the king energized and impatient, the queen fretful, the princess draped in more than her usual disdain. In fact, that moment mirrored this one precisely, except that now the cleric stood in for the prince.

The look in the churchman's eyes only grew colder. "I need a horse."

Now a shadow fell over Reynard's heart. "What for? What news? What of my son the king?"

"You should have told me," Hap Stanson said, grim as death. "I could have prevented this." He climbed down out of the carriage with his small leather travel bag in hand, and called for a mount.

The Captain of the Guard usually accepted the cleric's orders as though they came from the king himself, having learned that Hap Stanson was universally granted whatever he wished. But there were no extra horses to give. "Yes, sir," he said, and spurred his own horse back to the dragoons behind.

Hap watched him go. The leader of the Church of Nearing Vast was a big man, both tall and heavy-boned, with waves of auburn hair and bright, pale-blue eyes. He wore a dusty blue robe for traveling, unadorned but for the ever present inverted chalice that hung from a gold chain around his neck. His demeanor was always one of confidence. He always knew what needed to be done.

"The message!" Reynard croaked. He meant it as an order, but it came out a plea. Hap handed the parchment back up into the compartment. Princess Jacqalyn snatched it up with sharp fingernails. She read silently as all looked on, all but Hap, who peered down the road impatiently.

"Dear God," Jacqalyn said aloud. It was not a prayer. She kept reading, and then said it again. She looked up at her father, then at her mother, folding the parchment slowly and deliberately. Even though the news vindicated her cynicism, and even though she generally relished the role of delivering such, she now had trouble finding her voice. Eventually, she chose her words the way a hunter chooses his arrows. "Daddy, your favorite child apparently managed to remain king for only a day. Then he, too, abdicated."

"Abdicated?" Maeveline asked, her mouth agape.

Reynard's mouth dropped open, then clamped shut, his head and jowls shaking back and forth. It was not possible.

"Yes, and quite publicly. Just before that dreadful Mux hanged him." She managed to toss it off as an afterthought.

"Hanged him? Hanged who?" Reynard asked, unable to grasp the meaning of the words.

"Oh, Lord!" The former queen put her hands over her mouth. Her words were, in fact, a prayer.

The king closed his eyes, let his head fall back, back into the blackness that rose up around him. "Who was hanged?" he asked from the darkness.

"Your son the king. Well, no, not the king. I suppose he died without any title at all. You see, our dear Mather gave the kingdom away. To that heroic young man whom the peasants adore."

This opened Reynard's eyes. He searched Jacqalyn's face. "Not Packer Throme."

"The very one. King Packer! And doesn't that have a ring to it? The fisher boy now wears your signet." All eyes looked at Reynard's right hand. With his thumb he turned the ring on his finger around, and they could see that it was not the king's signet at all, but a similar-size ring of no particular distinction.

Jacqalyn looked at the written message again. "Ah, finally some good news here at the end. All this activity has been embraced by the general populace with the greatest possible enthusiasm. Out with the old, in with the new, and long life to king and kingdom! Nice work, Daddy. A proud ending to an illustrious reign." Her words were a plunged knife that her cold smile twisted.

"Packer Throme..." Reynard repeated, as though unable to make sense of the name. His eyes were open, but he saw nothing. Reynard had abdicated so as to avoid any more errors on this scale, on the scale of sending the Fleet to its demise last year. But his abdication itself had now become an error of even greater proportion.

Jacqalyn took a long look at her father and then rolled her eyes. "What did you expect, Daddy?" Now her bitterness was unrestrained. "Mather was a shipwreck searching for a shoal. And now the palace, the Mountain House, this carriage, even the clothes we wear belong to that pockmarked little boy." Her eyes went wide and distant. "And to his pugnacious little bride." She shook her head at the thought. "They'll turn everything to righteousness and ruin. I can only imagine what they'll do with us." She envisioned Panna, fists unfettered, battering Sennetts at will.

Hap Stanson was listening. "I believe the Drammune will have something to say about who owns what," he suggested dryly. He watched the captain bring a saddled horse toward him.

"The Drammune!" Jacq exclaimed. "Well there's our hope, then! I'd far rather die at their hands with the dignity due me than bow and scrape before that..." images filled her head of Panna Throme dressed in the princess's own fabulous finery, ordering a rag-clad Jacqalyn to scrub her woolens. It was simply too painful for words.

Maeveline broke into sobs. Her son was dead.

The Battle for Vast Dominion

The Captain of the Guard climbed down from the saddle and handed Hap the reins of the horse. "We have no horses to spare, Your Holiness. This belongs to one of the dragoons, who will need to walk or be left behind, unless..."

"Unless what?" Hap asked irritably.

"With your permission, the messenger came on horseback. If he were to return afoot..."

"Yes, of course." The High Holy Reverend Father and Supreme Elder Harlowen "Hap" Stanson took the reins and climbed aboard the big bay gelding. "You should have told me, Reynard!" he called out. "None of this needed to happen." He maneuvered the horse up close to the carriage. He peered in, now at eye level with all three of those within it. His eyes suddenly sparkled. "But fear not!" His famously sunny disposition was back. "Where the State fails, the Church is ever ready to step in."

"And do what, pray tell?" Jacqalyn asked, her voice dripping disrespect. "Is there something here to annul?"

"My dear Princess," he answered, unperturbed, "certainly you know that the Sennett family was ordained from on high to rule. Passing the crown to a fisherman's son—why, that is simply an affront to all that is right and holy. But errors of this sort are often made in the confusion of turbulent times. And battlefield promotions need not stand once the battle is won."

"Won?" Jacqalyn asked.

"Oh, don't doubt that our young hero can rally our troops. We should all pray for his swift success. I suspect that this is precisely the divine purpose at work here. But thankfully, the Almighty has put in place His instrument to calm human storms, so that we all may walk unharmed across troubled seas. And," he added with an extra twinkle, "as Providence would have it, that instrument is me."

"But I don't understand. What will you do?" Jacqalyn asked in a tone that seemed quite close to sincerity. "Who will be king?"

"Do you want your crown back, Reynard?" Hap asked the enormous, dejected hulk.

Reynard looked as if he had seen a ghost. "No." He said it quickly and vehemently. The others blanched. He had not sounded so certain about anything in months.

"Very well," Hap said easily. "There is another male in the Sennett line with due rights to the throne. And we must follow the laws of God rather than those of man, am I correct?" His face was now positively beaming.

Jacqalyn did not share his confidence, or his enthusiasm. "Ward," she said, as though the word were a curse. "You'll replace the hero with the drunkard. Oh, the people will be so pleased when you reveal to them God's will."

The sparkle dimmed. "Fortunately, power is not given by popular acclaim."

"Or the Church would never have any at all," Jacq said coldly.

Hap stared at her just a moment, then laughed breezily. "You forget, Princess, that the pockmarked boy, as you call him, was once a student at my seminary. He was expelled for reasons our enthusiastic populace knows nothing about. Public opinion changes with the weather. And so! I must go now, and bring a little sunshine where dark clouds loom." He peered more deeply into the compartment. Maeveline was sobbing silently. Reynard was gone off into his own private hell. Jacqalyn was morose and bitter, but at least she was paying attention. "And dear Princess, if Ward will not or cannot be king, there is certainly a Sennett here who might be queen."

Her eyes blazed. Such words were a match to the dry tinder of her soul.

"Continue to the Mountain House," he said gently. "If it is within the power God has granted me, be assured that the House of Throme will be put down, and the House of Sennett shall rise again."

And then he rode off in a cloud of dust.

Princess Jacqalyn sat back in the carriage, stunned at the vision that streamed through the window the cleric had just flung open. She began to consider for the first time the value that might come to her through a personal commitment to the Church. For the first time, she felt she understood the whole point of religious conversions.

She read the message in her hands once more. The last words written there were, "The boy who delivers this message fought the Drammune on the Green, and shares the kingdom's current passion for Packer Throme. Just a word of warning." The note was signed, Fr. Usher Fell.

Hap Stanson rode up to the young seminarian, who now stood by himself in the road. The young man went unsteadily to one knee, and bowed his head.

"Rise," Hap said, towering over him from atop the gelding. "Where is your knapsack?"

"I was told the message was urgent," the boy said, his heart ablaze. He had never met his High Holiness. "I didn't stop for provisions."

"No provisions?" Hap asked, pondering his options. "How long have you fasted?"

"Two days now, sir."

Hap nodded appreciatively. He pulled a bladder from his own knapsack. "Take some water." He watched the boy drink, then accepted the bladder back and returned it to his own bag. "You are a student at the seminary."

"Yes, sir, name's Lester Mine, apprenticed to Father Usher Fell, Your...Worship."

"Do you know the contents of the message you brought?"

"No, sir. I know only it was about the new king, Packer Throme. May he live forever!" The fire within the boy leapt up, singeing the clergyman's sensibilities.

"Indeed. Your return walk is long. It will test your spirit."

The boy's eyes dimmed. "Sir?"

Hap's voice grew thick with compassion. "God has appointed you a task, my son. You have begun a fast that will end only when you return to the seminary."

"But...the Drammune, sir. They hold the city."

"Here is your mission and your purification. Speak to no man. Drink nothing. Eat nothing. Fast and pray until you have knelt at the altar of the Seminary Chapel. Stop on your way. Pray on your knees four times a day. For two hours each time. Ignore all men, all women, all children. This mission will purge you of politics, of devotion to mere men, and prepare you for His service."

Hap watched the change come over the boy. The seminarian swallowed the words like they were doses of bitter medicine. But he swallowed them. It was a spiritual journey now, entirely. "Yes, Your Holiness."

Hap was genuinely pleased. "God bless you, son." And the High Holy Reverend Father and Supreme Elder, Harlowen "Hap" Stanson, rode off, trailing clouds of dust. Hap gave Lester Mine no further thought. He had his own mission to worry about.

Huk Tuth sat hunched over a table in the library of the conquered palace, his white hair hanging in wispy strands over a carefully plotted map of Mann, and of the Hollow Forest. The Supreme Commander of the Glorious Drammune Military was an old man, but thick like a gnarled tree trunk. He had just dismissed his spies, two men and one woman, who looked for all the world like Vast natives. Tuth did not like spies, even his own, especially those who could so easily pass for enemies, and so he tended to treat them as though they were trying to hide something. But he had wrung from them all they knew about troop movements, and the preparations the salamanders now made for attack. They had told him of the hasty fortifications of the Vast eastern perimeter, their vulnerable left flank to the north, the exposed rear to the west, and the impenetrable, rocky, thickly wooded hills to the south. They had told him of the ascent to the throne of the yellow-haired warrior, who had escaped the Drammune noose. Now Tuth brooded over his options, anxious to destroy those unworthies.

"General Harkow!"

His most experienced field commander entered immediately. Tuth rubbed the stubble of his bare chin and spoke. "The Vast are out of food and their position poorly defended. They will move quickly. What news of the tunnel?"

Harkow was a tall man, taller than most Drammune, and he summoned his full height. "None, sir. Our engineers have not yet penetrated the doorway."

Tuth took out quill and parchment and began to draw up formal orders. "We will attack as soon as you can get your troops to the Hollow Forest."

By nightfall of their third day in the encampment, the Vast battle plan was in place and the armies of the new king were ready. Reorganizing the troops, ensuring that each platoon, company, and battalion had enough men and a suitable commander, had been the easier part of the job. In spite of the shameful disarray during and following the rout that was the Invasion of Mann, Bench Urmand had actually done an admirable job of organizing his army. When the initial shock of cowardly defeat wore off, a sense of discipline began to return. Soldiers found their units, the dead or missing were noted and reported, the next in rank stepped up to take their places, and the chain of command held. The Vast became an organized force once again.

Provisioning, however, had been more difficult. In the past twenty-four hours, barely half the troops had had a meal, and not much more than half a meal at that. The army's chief quartermaster, a tobacco-chewing, oath-swearing, utterly competent barrel of a man who lived in a constant state of frustration, managed to find and load wagons some fifteen miles away to the south and east, in a small community on the outskirts of Mann. He put his chuck wagons in a field outside this village, one of no particular note, undistinguishable from a hundred towns just like it scattered across the Kingdom of Nearing Vast, and there he awaited orders.

But war has a way of thrusting the modest into sudden and unexpected immortality, picking this man over that, this location over that one, and sometimes for the most mundane of reasons. A host of grumbling stomachs and the silent decisions of one profane army cook would, through the impenetrable mysteries of the workings of Providence, forever mark a simple town called Varlotsville.

Packer Throme sat on the porch of the farmhouse, staring up at the stars, pondering. He felt the burden of his new responsibilities, but the weight seemed less impossible now that he'd done it for a day or two. It felt like good, hard work. So far, at least, the job consisted mainly of making decisions, yes to this plan, no to that one. Some came easy, others less so. But now as he stopped to consider, he had to ask himself how many lives rested on each yes, and each no? What sort of future would his decisions bring?

He could hear Panna inside the farmhouse talking to Father Mooring and the bright young general, Zander Jameson. They were finishing up the long-neglected organization of the chaplaincy. That was comforting on many levels. At Packer's right sat Prince Ward, cradling his coffee once again, trying to keep his mind off a mug of ale that hovered somewhere just outside his reach, just inside the door of a nearby tavern, or just over that hill in the darkness where faint traces of laughter could be heard. He'd been fine during the day. But when night fell, the prince heard the call from everywhere.

On Packer's left sat General Millian, resting with his head on the high back of a rocker, his eyes closed, a wispy plume of smoke rising from a pipe loosely cradled in his hand. Packer heard a snore and turned to his left. General Millian's mouth dropped open as he drifted off. The young king gently removed the glowing bowl from the old soldier's hand and set it on the table before him.

"He deserves a rest," Ward said quietly.

"It's a brilliant plan," Packer said with a nod. Risky, he thought, but brilliant.

"He thinks quite highly of you, as well."

Packer shot Ward a questioning glance.

"It's true. He is well content to have leadership that understands no plan can succeed without divine intervention."

"He said that?"

"'That young man understands,'" Ward quoted, imitating the general, "'that a horse can be made ready for a battle, but only God can win it.' Or something like that."

Packer laughed. "Victory comes from the Lord."

"Yes, that was it! 'Victory comes from the Lord,'" he repeated in General Millian's deep voice.

The general snorted, then snored gently again.

"It's from the Book of Proverbs," Packer offered.

Ward nodded. "I assumed it was from something I haven't read."

Then Packer looked again at the general, now snoring peacefully, his head lightly bandaged. Packer marveled. Even in sleep the commander was ramrod straight, head up, shoulders back. Like he was born at attention. "I thought he'd believe me too young," Packer said. Now he looked at Ward. "And I thought you might believe me too ignorant, or too inexperienced."

"Well, you're older than me. And as for experience, there are a handful of people I'd trust with my life, and none of them are princes or princesses, or even nobles. In fact, most of them are simple soldiers. Or sailors. Like you."

Packer was thoughtful for a moment. Then he said, "You should know that I made a vow never to pick up a sword again."

"You did all right yesterday without a sword in your hand."

"*I* didn't do anything," Packer said firmly.

"Look, if it's a theological discussion you're after, I can tell you I won't be drawn in willingly. It was a subject I slept through at the Academy."

Packer took a deep breath. The Academy. Senslar Zendoda had had much to say about when and where to fight, but Packer had paid attention only to the how. He might as well have slept through it. "I had a teacher there who once asked me, What makes God laugh?"

Ward grinned back. "'Men making plans,'" he quoted, doing an impression of the precise wording, the intense eyes of a character quite familiar to Packer. "I had the same swordmaster," Ward confirmed. "I did manage to stay awake in Master Zendoda's classes. Not that I wanted to. It was hard to sleep with so many sharp objects moving at such high speeds."

Packer laughed, then looked up at the stars. "I'm going to take a walk," he announced.

Ward gestured toward the spot where a big dragoon stood in the shadows near the picket fence, his back to them, pike in hand, his head swiveling with every motion, every sound. "Let that enormous fellow over there tag along, won't you? You are the king, after all. And it's still a job I don't want."

Packer looked at Stave Deroy's back. "I'm not sure I could make him stay behind."

Packer and Chunk walked side by side through the camp. All was quiet now. All personnel had been ordered to get as much rest as possible, and most were dutifully obeying. No lights burned, and the quarter moon was low in the sky, so the king and his guard were all but invisible as they picked their way toward the woods.

"Have you ever been in battle, Chunk?" Packer asked when they were far enough away from the camp that he was sure they would not be overheard.

"No, not a real one. Unless you count puttin' a pike through that Mux fella's neck."

Packer nodded. "Actually, I would count that, yes."

"Nah. He was facin' the other way."

Packer paused. "Well, taking him down was a great service, regardless."

Chunk pondered that. "I didn't know that then. I just knew he wasn't one of us. And he had you by the hair." Packer could feel the ire rise in his big companion.

"Thank you again."

"That's my job."

They walked a few more steps. Then Packer said, "It's a funny thing when a man's job is killing other men. That was my job, too, on board the *Trophy Chase*."

"You did it good, from what I hear." He was proud of his king.

After a while, Packer asked, "Have you ever seen a miracle, Chunk?"

The big dragoon thought hard. It was his duty to answer honestly. "One time. One time when I was little I dropped a whole gold coin through a hole in my pocket, on the way to market. I thought I was in for the whippin' of my life. So I prayed the whole way home, walkin' back the way I come. And there it was, stuck in the mud. I just saw the edge gleam in the sunlight." He paused, remembering. "I thought then, *That's a miracle.*" He paused again. "I never did tell nobody about that before. Specially not a king."

"God answers prayers, Chunk. That much I know for sure. He has to."

"He has to?"

"It's His nature. If we pray to Him. If we love Him, and if we ask like a child. He has to answer."

After a pause, Chunk said, "That's a lotta 'ifs' to try and remember."

Packer laughed. "Maybe. But when you're hurting and you don't know where else to turn, and you ask God because you just want things to be right, it doesn't really seem very complicated. Like a child crying out for his mother."

After another long pause, Chunk said, "You're real different from the other king."

CHAPTER 3

Surrounded

Packer stood and brushed away the twigs and dirt that clung to his knees. He looked up again at the stars, and past them to their Creator. He knew now what he had to do. It was not the easy path, nor the safe path. But it was the right path.

As he walked back to where Chunk stood guard, he saw another figure in the dark. It was impossible to tell who it was, but he seemed formal and at attention, while Chunk seemed relaxed and at ease. This was not someone whom Chunk felt was dangerous.

"Beggin' your pardon, Your Highness," the big dragoon said, squaring up as Packer approached, "but this man here wants a word. Says he's a friend of yours. I can send him away easy enough."

Packer could now see the height of the man, how stiffly he held himself. Gray hair, big hands. "Dog?"

"Aye, Packer. It's me." He sounded glum.

"What is it?" Packer worried that Dog had some grim news, perhaps from home.

"I came looking for you to tell you..." he trailed off. Then he hooked a thumb toward the big dragoon. "You suppose I could say it without the threat a' death here?"

"Chunk, please let us talk a minute."

"Yes, sir." Chunk immediately crunched away through the woods, stopping just out of earshot.

"How is your…injury?"

"Fine." Dog sniffed. He hadn't come here to exchange pleasant-ries. "Look, it's just this. I been talkin' to that priest. Always a bad idea if a man don't want to face himself. But lyin' there with him stitching me, there wasn't much way to run. Anyhow, I know I been hard on you all your life." He went silent. Packer waited. "We fought a couple times," Dog managed. "I won once, you won once. So I figure we're square as far as that goes."

"It's in the past."

"Yeah, but all of a sudden, now you're king. I had some time to think, thanks to your robed friend, hoverin' around…helping." He said the word as if it were a fly to be swatted. "He seems to hold you in high regard."

"Well, I don't think he knows me all that well."

"That's what I told him. Anyways." He cleared his throat. When he spoke again, it was in a resonant tone, overly paternal. "I know I didn't treat your father well. All his Firefish talk, all that nonsense. And your priest school, you know, I thought that was just a load of slag, too. Then I thought you'd killed Duck and Ned, I turned you in. But that was an honest mistake." He paused, waiting for an affirma-tion Packer didn't offer. "So now you're king of everything and all, and so I'm thinking I just need to tell you, you know, as regards all that…" he sighed deeply. "I want you to know that I don't hold none of it against you no more."

Packer nodded slowly, then said, "Thank you, Dog." If that was all Dog could manage, Packer wasn't going to get picky. Such a state-ment was in fact a long, long haul from where he'd been.

"You're welcome. There's one other thing." Now Dog's voice soft-ened just a bit. "It's that I hope you're a real good king." The old man paused as he felt a stab of bitterness rise, then fall, then dissipate. "And as long as you are, I'll…I'll do my duty by you. You and the queen." Dog did not add, "especially the queen," but he thought it. And Packer heard it.

"Thank you," Packer said again. Then he added, "As long as you're here, I could use some advice."

Dog waited. "About what?"

"A lot of things. How much should we be asking the new recruits to do? How good are they? Do they have enough training? What about the irregulars? They fought on the Green, and we're treating them as part of the army. Women, as well as men. Does that make sense?"

Dog scowled. "The new boys are every bit as good as those festerin' fancy-suited stiffs that like to sit around and smoke and give us orders. They're treating us better, now, now that we've seen 'em run. And if women can kill the Drammune, I say let 'em kill the Drammune. Lotsa men couldn't do it. And I think most everyone feels the same way."

"Well, that's very helpful."

"That? Anyone coulda told you that."

"But they didn't. Dog…May I call you Dog?"

"It's my name, ain't it?"

"Dog, would you agree to be an advisor to the Crown?"

Dog felt his pulse go up, and as it did the blood pounded through the wound in his chest. He ignored it, not wanting to seem too eager. "What would I have to do?"

"Speak your mind."

"To who?"

"To me. Me and Panna."

His eyes went wider. "That's it?"

"That's all."

Dog rubbed his chin as he thought hard about this, looking for the loophole. "What does it pay?"

Packer pondered. "At least as much as soldiering, that I can promise."

It seemed reasonable. Dog's eyes narrowed. "I won't bow down to you. Nothin' like that."

Packer shook his head. "I won't ask you to."

"Do I have to sit around with all your muckety-mucks who know everything about everything?"

"Well…yes. I'm asking you to become one of those muckety-mucks. I don't want people around me who just tell me what I want to hear."

Dog spoke quickly now, seeing reason in the boy, some promise that he might turn out all right if he just had people to steer him away from his natural boneheadedness. "I promise you, Packer Throme, I will never do that. I'll never tell you what you want to hear. You can count on that."

Dog said it with such confidence that Packer didn't have the heart to point out that Dog had just contradicted himself. He put out a hand. Dog looked at it, then shook it. The big man's paw seemed softer; his grip looser than Packer remembered.

Dog felt the hard, scarred hand and the firm grip, saw the iron in Packer's calm blue eyes. Then he turned sharply and walked away.

The armies of Huk Tuth moved all night in the dark, carefully laying a trap. The Drammune generals had been adamant about troop placements. They did not want the Vast rabble to run again, and so rather than accept Tuth's orders as written, a full assault from the north, the left flank, with all due speed, they argued with him. "We must bring our forces in from three sides: north, east, and west," General Harkow insisted. "The tangled terrain to the south will become the anvil against which the hammer of Rahk will crush the Vast once and for all."

Huk Tuth was the ranking officer and in absolute command. But though he thought speed more important than position, he was a naval man and inexperienced with ground warfare. Harkow's plan won the day.

The first shots were fired by the Vast, at the eastern front. Drammune troops had crept in darkness to within twenty yards of the Vast trenches and redoubts. The first rays of dawn revealed that the floor of the little valley had become an army in the night, an army arrayed against the Vast, poised and ready. A single command was shouted, and the Vast opened fire.

It was a meager effort. Rain on a tin roof would have been only marginally less intimidating than the scattered gunfire the Drammune presence teased from the woods. The fits and coughs from behind felled trees and timbers piled as redoubts were unimpressive, and even those that found their targets also found Firefish-scale armor. Shots ricocheted away harmlessly.

The return fire, when it came, was merciless. The Drammune were five lines deep, five thousand foot soldiers on their bellies, each a marksman with plenty of ammunition, all ready to drive hard into the forest. These soldiers were backed by artillery. The cannon lining the farmland behind their ranks were mostly eight-pounders, with a few of the big guns, sixteen-pounders with eight-inch barrels, brought in to help open up the woods a bit.

A Drammune general on horseback watched from among the larger guns, waiting for the thunder of Vast cannon that would allow him to aim his own. The crack and plink died away, however, without so much a single bellow from a big gun. He uttered a single word—"Charnak!"—and the woods were shot through in an instant with thousands of rounds, a flashing of fire and thunder followed by billows of black smoke that blew from the field into the forest. Great trees toppled, felled by the cannonade. When the barrage ceased, not a single Vast weapon answered.

The general called the charge, and the horde went in uncontested.

The Drammune soldiers were soon cursing, however. They knew as quickly as their general that the Vast army had chosen not to hold this front. Climbing over redoubts and through trenches that lined the woods for miles, they knew this was no rout. The front had been abandoned. The real fighting would be on the flank, and to the rear. The Drammune pushed harder, hoping to catch the Vast from behind.

But this Drammune frontline assault was also a feint. This was not Harkow's main point of attack. The great majority of his troops moved on the cue of gunfire from the east. They were already deep within the woods, having spent the better part of the night creeping into position, close enough to the Vast outposts to hear the troops laughing and talking among themselves.

Now the Drammune appeared in the dark shimmer of dawn beneath the canopy of the woods, emerging from behind trees, materializing from the mists that floated up from the winding creeks, arising from the underbrush like spirits from the grave.

If the Vast resistance had been weak on their eastern front, it was hardly noticeable on the north, their left flank. The attackers easily overran Vast outposts and stormed through the woods, hoping to meet up with their fellow attackers coming in from the east and west. They would together crush the Vast against their southern perimeter, where the terrain grew rough and rocky and impassable.

Tuth knew his enemy now, and distrusted reports that the southern woods were impenetrable. He feared the Vast would somehow disappear again. So he had planned to cut off all escape. He dressed his deadliest fighters in black, those trained to kill in silence hand-to-hand, and sent them to infiltrate the forest to the south, cutting off all hope of retreat into the underbrush. These were the Nochtram

Eyn, handpicked by Fen Abbaka Mux, and named by him. They were "Death from the Darkness," silhouettes with special skills, men and women, mortach demal and assassins who, it was said, could appear and disappear at will. Five hundred Nochtram Eyn had infiltrated the forest, discovered paths into the woods. With crossbows, daggers, and flying knives they eliminated entire platoons of the Vast, and blocked the paths with their bodies. Then they waited for the inevitable flow of fleeing Vast salamanders.

With five thousand Drammune coming in from the east, and ten thousand down from the north, General Harkow's main forces now poured in from the west. Twenty-five-thousand soldiers came on from the least likely direction, a massive movement of Drammune military might, intent on crushing the Vast armies here once and for all. The mortar into the pestle. And so in a brilliantly planned attack, perfectly prepared in the dark of night, expertly executed at dawn, the Vast were surrounded.

The Drammune came on, and kept coming. They crushed all the troops they encountered. The Nochtram Eyn held the southward exits, picking off all the Vast troops that fled that way, dropping them in their tracks.

An hour after dawn, it was over.

An hour and ten minutes after dawn, Supreme Commander Tuth wandered through an abandoned farmhouse. His men, searching it upstairs and down, reported back to him what was obvious. It was empty. It had been left in perfect order. Beds were made with clean linens, dishes were done and put up in cupboards; even the table was set with napkins and spoons and forks. All the knives, however, as one officer noted, were gone.

Tuth walked out onto the front porch, stood beside a worn rocking chair and looked out over the picket fence. He frowned at it. It was broken down in several places. The house was left pristine, but the fence was in disarray. Why? Beyond it, his men patrolled the camp of the Vast, finding the occasional misplaced shoe or hat, but nothing of any significance. It was all wrong. Tuth knew it; the men knew it. It had been too easy, once again.

"I want a body count," Tuth said aloud. When his generals just nodded, he shouted the order. "I want a body count *now!*"

They bolted into action.

The Battle for Vast Dominion

An hour and twenty minutes after dawn, Huk Tuth had his number. He knew how many Vast had died at the hands of his army.

"Three hundred and forty-three," he said, looking at his generals, one by one. "Three hundred and forty-three Vast dead."

The generals were mortified. Each had assumed that the real fighting had taken place on someone else's front. Now it was obvious they had been outwitted once again. There had been no real Vast resistance. They had faced only feints and delaying actions. They had destroyed only the rear guard of the Vast armies, while the main body had already disappeared. Somewhere. Somehow.

The Vast had vanished once again.

The Army of Nearing Vast, ghostly flickers in the darkness, had in fact disappeared into the thick brush. They had been on the move since long before dawn. Troops that had bivouacked in a state of readiness had been rousted at three in the morning and given simple orders—march south in a column four abreast, and keep marching. None but the generals, the king and queen, and a few handpicked officers had known this order was coming. No spies could have reported it, unless they had been within the farmhouse as the plans were laid out to a few carefully chosen guides well after midnight. As the Vast column reached the heavily wooded area, they had followed four divergent paths, each one led by a guide, a man familiar with the territory. Between midnight and three the guides had marked these paths, strung ropes for handrails, positioned lanterns at the darkest spots; all routes carefully shielded by miles of thick growth, trees, and rocky hillsides. The Vast army slowed, but it never stopped. Thousand of troops disappeared into the woods. By dawn the Hollow Forest had lived up to its name, leaving only the rear guard behind, with orders to resist as best they could, and block pursuit by the main Drammune troops with their lives.

The rear guard were true Vast soldiers. They knew their duty. They understood their role. They recognized that obedience meant, in all likelihood, death. They were committed to their country, and their king. They fought, and they died. With honor.

A red-helmeted lieutenant ran up to the porch and bowed deeply.

"Speak," Tuth ordered.

"They went south. The road diverges quickly into various paths, which can be traveled only in single file. It looks as if they have divided their forces in order to escape. Shall we give chase?"

"Give chase?" Tuth was incredulous. His drawn face was dour and cold. "A bold idea. Don't you think so, General Harkow?" He turned on the man standing to his right. Harkow turned beet-red. "Your troops were in perfect position today. What was lacking was boldness. So tell me now, should we follow the Vast armies single file through unfamiliar woods?" Tuth goaded him, his eyes slit, as though daring the taller man to answer.

But the general knew he must speak. "I…would not recommend it, sir."

"'I would not recommend it, sir,'" Tuth repeated. "Yes, General Harkow, the opportunity for boldness has come and gone. We might as well shoot ourselves right here as follow them in there. At least, if we shot ourselves, we'd be given a decent funeral pyre." Harkow's face now emptied of blood, and took on the pallor of death. The others stepped away. Tuth nodded once, then turned his back.

Behind him he heard the telltale scrape of metal against leather, a pistol being unholstered. He heard a hammer click. He did not turn to face his general, but kept his back to him, and waited.

"I freely give my life," the general said, his voice a rasp, "to save and protect one more Worthy than myself. By the Law of Transfer, I offer my life to my supreme commander, Huk Tuth." There was a pause. Tuth crossed his arms and waited.

A single pistol shot cracked through the woods. It was a satisfying sound in Huk Tuth's ears. He turned to find the corpse of his general sprawled in the dirt, blood from a head wound pouring into the Vast soil. Tuth's mind went immediately to the glories of General Harkow's past, the medals of honor, the successful strategies of campaigns won. *He was a good man,* Tuth thought. It was a harsh reality that good men fell in battle.

"Put him on the porch, and speak the words of the Law over him. He is Worthy," Tuth announced. "Then torch the house." He pointed to the outbuilding. "Burn that shack as well." He looked around him. "Then set fire to the woods. We're pulling out."

Tuth was in a hurry now. He sent his scouts on horseback to the edge of the forest, what had been the eastern front of the Vast defenses. He ordered them to skirt the forest heading south, and to look for signs of an exit. The Vast were headed back to Mann, he knew. They would come out of these woods on this side somewhere. He ordered half his troops to trail the scouts, and sent the other half straight back into the city, in case the cowards had already found a way through tunnels back to fight at the Rampart.

In spite of what he had said to the late General Harkow, Tuth sent four of his best assassins into the woods, one on each of the paths found there. They were not to engage an army, but to scout and spy.

The situation was maddening, angering, like a thorn pressed up through his foot. The miserable Pawns had disappeared again, and this time they had lured fully two-thirds of his troops almost twenty miles from the Rampart. This morning, he'd had them outnumbered. But with his troops split...He hated these salamanders. And he had no idea where they were.

He now needed information about the tunnels, desperately. But there was none to be had. His men had soon enough discovered the secret doorway within the prison, through which the Vast dregs had disappeared from the Green. But the Drammune had to get through that door if they were to map the passages. And at this very moment his best Drammune military engineers stood before it, within the prison's torture chamber, scratching their heads. The façade had been torn away, revealing a block of solid steel as strong as the blade of any sword, set in solid bedrock. Picks, hammers, and even the small explosives they had dared to use underground had so far managed only to mar the surface and chip the granite.

Supreme Commander Tuth controlled a burning rage. He had not yet even fought them, army against army. The Drammune would win any forthright battle, he knew, on any ground, under any circumstances. Huk Tuth yearned, he lusted for a straight fight. He wanted to see the strength of his troops rushing across a field, banners flying, headed toward the strength of theirs. He wanted to watch his men cut their troops to ribbons, and then stand victorious as Vast blood drained into Vast soil. His men were Worthy. He wanted to give them the victory they deserved.

But while he thought these things, his scouts scouted and his generals pulled out, backtracking. It was humiliating; it felt like retreat. He cursed the Vast and their cowardice, their ignoble tactics that were made all the more vile by their success. *Schemes without courage.* They had made the yellow-haired warrior their king? That was fitting. He was the chief of the shrewd cowards, the bumblebee on the decks of the *Trophy Chase,* a man who would stab other men in the back again and again, man after man. And the Vast called it heroism.

Now he imagined Packer Throme leading their entire Army through some secret passageway to stab Huk Tuth's entire army in the back. The Supreme Commander of the Glorious Drammune Expeditionary Force climbed up onto his horse. He proudly wore the armor of the Drammune, the tunic and the helmet, crimson and shining in the sun. It was the best armor in the world, and proof in his mind of his nation's superiority. But still he felt vulnerable.

He spurred his horse toward the Rampart. He could not let the Old City be retaken by the Vast.

But the Vast soldiers were not underground. Nor were they advancing on the Rampart. Nor were they lying in wait along the way, to ambush Tuth and his divided troops. They were streaming toward Varlotsville, looking for a hot meal.

As they arrived, they found their quartermaster's wagons and fell on them with the single-minded purpose of an attacking horde. Their quarry: huge kettles of seasoned meat and potatoes boiling over open flames, buckboards loaded with bread and butter, and covered wagons filled with barrels of ale. Soldiers attacked the grub until their hunger was sated, until each had a belly full of such glorious battle. They praised their quartermaster profusely, granting him honor second only to Packer Throme. But Major Bustian Harmey, Quartermaster, shaken by the plunder of his provisions, took each compliment like it was a round of live ammunition fired over his head. He responded in his accustomed fashion, with an artillery barrage of invective.

A solitary scout found Huk Tuth deep inside the city, marching with the contingent of men whose goal was to protect the Rampart. He clattered up to the supreme commander on horseback. "My lord, we've found their army," he told the commander breathlessly.

"The whole of it?"

He nodded. "Tens of thousands. They're gathered in a small town at the edge of the forest south of here, just over ten miles away." He dismounted, stood beside Commander Tuth's horse and showed him the enemy position on an extraordinarily detailed map.

"Tens of thousands, here?" Tuth asked incredulously. It was an indefensible protrusion, a finger of civilization reaching out to touch the forest, a space of meadow or farmland surrounding it. They were inviting attack. "What are they doing now?"

"Taking food and rest."

Resting from what? Tuth wanted to ask. But he knew it was not what they rested from, but what they rested for that should concern him. What was their plan? They could have flanked the Drammune, if they had but seized the opportunity. They could have beaten Tuth back to the Rampart. Instead, they gathered together in an unprotected village to *dine?* His first instinct was to order an attack, now, while his own army was on the move and ready to fight. But these cagey cowards had him off his guard, and he second-guessed himself. Was this another Vast ploy?

Perhaps, he thought, perhaps they didn't even know the position of the Drammune army. Perhaps it was not a feint at all, but simply hungry soldiers feeding themselves. No, then why leave in the dead of night? Perhaps, he thought again, they gathered at the mouth of that infernal secret passage, ready to escape at any moment.

And with that thought, his decision was made. He had to move, instantly. His generals could get their men into position as they arrived. He would use the troops who had been skirting the forest to begin the assault.

He would catch the Vast this time. He would fight them army to army. He would finally and forever crush them.

At this obscure little spot on the map labeled Varlotsville.

Gathered were all the king's counselors, or almost all, around a worn table in a small, dark tavern that had become the Army's Varlotsville headquarters. The council consisted of a queen, a priest, two generals, and a prince. The latest addition, the old fisherman, was gone to visit the surgeon after having fallen twice on his trek through the woods, reopening wounds that required more stitches and fresh gauze. This time, he would receive them from someone other than Father Mooring, who rightly assumed Dog would be pleased for once to have surgery without a sermon.

"The soldiers are ready, sir, to enter the tunnels." General Jameson spoke the words to General Millian.

"Are you prepared to lead them in?" Millian asked Ward Sennett.

"Ready and willing," the prince replied.

"Excellent. Order them in, General."

"No, not yet."

Both generals reacted to Packer Throme's words as though small-arms fire had broken out in the next room. They pivoted toward their king. Ward squinted and cocked his head, trying to recall some conversation that might explain why the king countermanded the general at this late moment. But there had been no such conversation, not at this table.

"Sir," General Millian said to Packer carefully, "we have delayed all we can already, just feeding the troops."

"I understand," Packer answered. "But I want to speak to them."

"But…now, sir?" Jameson asked, something akin to both pain and panic in his voice.

"Yes. Immediately."

The room went silent, all eyes boring into Packer. Until this moment the mood had been focused but serene, even light, with the unusual exception of a rather melancholy Ward Sennett.

Ward had dismissed all attempts to determine the source of his discomfort, but it was no mystery. Just being here made Ward feel like the lone teetotaler at a Queen's Day celebration. The place smelled of ale. It reeked of strong drink and good smoke and endless nights of laughter and camaraderie. He inhaled its atmosphere, tasted its character. He absorbed its entire history through his pores, taking in everything except the one substance his mind and body craved most. But with a simple statement, the king had driven the prince's inner turmoil from every mind but the prince's.

Panna was watching her husband's eyes and the distant fire burning there. "What will you say to them?" she asked softly. She already knew the answer, but it was still a fair question. The others needed to know.

Packer didn't respond to her. Instead he asked, "Have we heard any reports from the rear guard?"

"No, Your Highness," General Millian answered slowly, leaning forward and choosing his words carefully. His hands shook visibly. "But regardless, the Drammune must know we are here by now.

We are outnumbered, indefensible, in broad daylight. We must enter those tunnels." He saw no change in Packer's determination. Millian cleared his throat. "Sir, with all respect and honor for your absolute authority, luring them here was only a wise move if we are not actually found here when they arrive."

The silence was now palpable. Packer looked down at his own scarred palm. "It's time to tell our people the truth."

Millian's voice turned to a plea. "Let us trust God, Your Highness. But let us do it with wisdom. Let us not put Him to the test, so that He must undo our own foolishness."

The others held their breaths. Had the general just called the king a fool?

But Packer had been called that before, and worse, and he didn't resent it. He stood and walked away, toward a greasy window half-covered with a stained and discolored curtain. His resolve wavered. He had prayed. He had been completely assured of the goodness, the rightness of this decision. To address the troops, that was required. The people must know. They must be given a choice. He had agreed to this on his knees. But now the act of presenting to them their choices seemed to be dooming them, giving them no choice at all.

Could he have been mistaken? Should he have gathered the troops last night, in the dark? That did not seem reasonable then. Or should he have spoken to them over their dinner? They were famished, and gorging themselves. They would not have listened. Perhaps the time had not yet come—maybe there would be another, better time to speak to them. But once they entered the tunnels, they could not be gathered.

Perhaps Millian was right, and the opportunity was past. He had missed it. Perhaps they should just get underground now, stream into the Old City, and fight for their lives and their king and their kingdom. Let God choose the outcome. But Packer knew that sending them to fight would mean taking the usual path, trusting God to bless the sword.

He turned to face the group. When he spoke, he sounded as pained as he felt. "I...believe I was made king for a reason, and I know it wasn't because I have the best mind for military strategy." He lowered his eyes. "I just know I need to speak to the troops."

Still, no one moved. The question suddenly formed in Panna's mind, and then in Packer's, as to whether the generals would obey him. Packer stared at the floor, but Panna watched the generals as they cut their eyes to Prince Ward. She knew what was happening. *Do something*, their eyes said. And the new queen had the distinct impression they would be glad, at this moment, if the prince simply asked Packer to hand over the ring.

"I remember once, I chose to take the long way home," Father Mooring said quietly, as though continuing a conversation no one else had heard, "because it wound through a part of the city I hadn't seen in some time. I stepped in a hole. Twisted my ankle badly, which kept me from traveling to Oster the next day." Packer and Panna listened carefully. The other men glanced around the table at one another impatiently. But no one spoke. Father Mooring continued. "Then I remember another time when I agonized over a decision, prayed for days and nights, fasted, and finally determined the will of God. I asked the young woman to marry me."

"We've all made difficult decisions," Ward said without his usual cheer, but with no trace of condescension. He was more accustomed to dealing with fools than anyone else at the table, though in his experience such fools were generally inebriated. "But I believe the decision on the table—"

"The decision on the table," Father Mooring interrupted, not unkindly but not backing down, "is a decision much like any other. We all make them, and none of us can know where they will lead. On that trip, the one I did not take, my companions caught influenza and two of them died. The woman I wanted to marry said no, and left town the next day with a good friend of mine. I believe they have seven children now." A shadow crossed his face. "Or is it eight?" He touched seven of his fingers, then reported, "Seven. Seven children." He looked wistful, and proud in a distant sort of way. "So now, the king has a choice to make. It's his choice. And we don't really know of which sort it is, life or death, or inconsequential, though it may seem very much like one and not the other. So, gentlemen," he looked to Panna, "Your Highness, it is now, as always, the *heart* of the chooser that matters." He glanced around the table, looking serene, apparently oblivious to the fact that his audience still hadn't the least idea what he was suggesting.

"Your counsel then, to the king, is…?" Millian finally asked.

"Counsel? No, no, no. I have no counsel. I only have a point." He would have to be more direct. "Our last sovereign sent the entire

Fleet to Drammun, following a heart bent on dominance and intimidation. The Fleet was lost. This king is on his knees before the living God. His heart instructs him in the path of service to that God. So…which of you wants to be the one who successfully persuades Packer Throme to get up off his knees and behave like Reynard Sennett?" The priest waited for an answer, now looking each of the king's counselors in the eye, one at a time. When his eyes met Packer's, the priest's right eye winked.

The gratitude in Packer's heart, the affection he held for this little priest, suddenly knew no bounds.

"Are you certain?" Millian asked Packer. It was a question, but the tone was one of resignation. His own decision was made. "Are you absolutely sure this is from God?"

"'The king's heart is in the hand of the Lord, as the rivers of water,'" Bran Mooring quoted. "'He turneth it whithersoever He will.'"

Millian ignored the priest and stared hard at Packer.

"Gather the troops," Packer said softly. "Those are my orders." He said it without a trace of doubt, but he did not mean it as it sounded. He did not mean to say that he was now giving the general those orders, but rather that he was a man under orders himself, and these were the orders he'd been given. Both generals, however, took it as a powerful appeal to their simple duty as military men, and both now felt their king's certainty. It boosted their own confidence.

Jameson saluted. "Yes, sir." Packer returned it, and the newest general in Nearing Vast went to make it so.

Prince Ward now looked around the table and pursed his lips, his jaw clenched. Wasn't the obvious lesson of the Fleet's demise that a king should not rashly put his troops in jeopardy? Ward had been ready to ask that question. But it was too late. Now, if somehow the kingdom survived this latest royal stupidity, sound advice would be banished until further notice, replaced by blind faith in a God who gleefully rescued fools from their own well-meant lunacy.

Strangely, Ward found relief in his silence. The day would now unfold as it would, and he would have no further role to play. There was no mountain left to climb. If none of them survived this, then it would all end as it would. If they all survived, then the celebrations of divine intervention would be extreme, and he could quietly take his leave to seek another crevasse, cool and dark. And amber and wet.

CHAPTER 4

Varlotsville

The square of Varlotsville was half the size of the Green, but the number of people gathered outnumbered those who had gathered at Prince Mather's hanging by at least four to one. The five streets leading away from the village center were packed. Soldiers climbed up on rooftops and into trees. The dais chosen for the king was atop the general store, not the highest but definitely the flattest roof facing the square.

Packer could see them all as he stood in the warm sun, waiting, watching the last battalions join at the farthest points. He had ordered them all here, every last soldier. They were a grizzled lot, not as varied in skin tone as the crew of the *Trophy Chase*, perhaps, but far more diverse in dress and age and gender. Drammune helmets and tunics, Vast uniforms, peasant shirts and skirts and breeches, priest's robes. And except for the priests, who had now been sworn to uphold the peaceful duties of the chaplaincy, all held weapons of one sort or another. A few even carried Achawuk spears.

Behind him were several blocks of homes and businesses, and behind those were the fields where the food wagons stood empty and alone, but for one sullen quartermaster taking stock of the bare cupboard that was once again his duty to refill. Behind those fields, a little more than half a mile away, the ground rose up into hills which were topped by a wall of great pines and oaks, a finger of the Hollow Forest.

But now specks of crimson began to appear on that hilltop, set against the deep forest shadows. These were figures on horseback.

The Drammune commander arrived and rode to a stop beside his generals. From here the gathered Drammune leadership looked across the empty field to the tiny town and watched the gathering at the square. From this distance it seemed unimpressive, the numbers puny. Huk Tuth took the telescope offered to him and twisted it into focus.

"How many, would you say?"

"Fifteen thousand at least. Perhaps as many as twenty thousand. They are fish in our net."

"How long have they been here?"

"They began gathering an hour ago."

"What do you suspect is their purpose?"

"I believe the yellow-haired one is about to address them."

Tuth scanned with the telescope, focused it more carefully, searching for Packer Throme. He found the tiny figure in his telescope, facing away. Yes, the yellow hair did seem to be speaking to his troops. "Where are their lookouts posted?"

"We have seen none."

Tuth frowned. He scanned the buildings. It couldn't be. But his pulse rose. "How long will it take you to bring your armies across this field?"

"To surround them? An hour. Maybe two."

"Not to surround them," Tuth said angrily. "To attack in force."

The general shrugged. "We could attack within minutes."

"Then do so," he commanded. "Move as quickly and as silently as possible across these fields. As soon as enough companies are in position, we will attack."

"Yes, lord. And how many companies will be enough?"

Tuth glared at him. "I will decide that from here, and signal the charge." His voice dropped. "I want Vast blood shed on that square before their king finishes his speech." His emphasis on the word *king* dripped with contempt. "Now go!"

"Yes, Your Worthiness." And the general rode off at a gallop.

"Good people of Nearing Vast," the king said to his troops. As his voice echoed and fell silent, he despised the sound of it. It was not the tenor of his voice he hated, but the phrase he used, the pretentiousness of it. He was play-acting, trying to sound like a king. He paused, considering his next words and the heart from which they must come. The crowd shifted uneasily.

"The Drammune call us Pawns," he told them. "They consider us worthless."

Grumbling and anger grew from below him, pikes and swords were shaken.

Packer clenched his jaw. "But that is what we are!" he shouted. His voice now boomed, and even those farthest away heard him clearly. "We cannot decide where we are born, who our parents are, the shade of our skin or our hair, how long we will live, or when we will die. We are not masters of our own fate. We are, in fact, pawns. But we are not pawns in the hands of the Drammune. We are pawns in the hands of God!"

The troops shifted uneasily once more, still awaiting the martial speech.

Packer took a deep breath. The words he knew he needed to say would seem harsh, unnecessary. Perhaps cruel. Finally he spoke. "But you should not be pawns in the hands of your own government. There are things you should know. All has not been well. You have been deceived."

Prince Ward had been squinting up from the ground in front of the general store, shading his eyes from the sun as he watched and listened. Now he looked down at his shoes. Panna, standing beside him, watched this reaction. Bran Mooring closed his eyes in prayer. General Jameson held his breath, eyes sharp and focused on Packer. General Millian stood like a statue, expressionless and waiting. Chunk guarded the wooden ladder that led up to the rooftop, ever protective of his king.

Packer was loath to say it, but he must. "You should know that King Reynard sent not just a few ships to Drammun, to answer the assassination of our swordmaster. He sent the entire Fleet of Nearing Vast. The Fleet was destroyed there in a single day. King Reynard and Prince Mather hid this from you."

Stunned silence. The rumors were true then.

"That was the reason for the call to arms. That was the reason for the king's proclamation. We no longer have a Navy. Our enemies have known it, but you have not. We have in fact only a few merchant ships equipped with cannon. We have the *Trophy Chase*. And we have you."

The Battle for Vast Dominion

Now the uneasiness found a voice, and grumbles could be heard—questions, even curses.

"I am telling you the truth because you need to know it," Packer shouted. "You need to make a choice today!"

"We want to fight!" one man called out, raising his sword. "Give us the Drammune! We beat 'em on the Green, didn't we?"

Others cheered these words, martial words they longed to hear, even if they were spoken by an anonymous citizen. The gathered Army of Nearing Vast held high their swords, their muskets, shook them in the air. If the king wouldn't inspire them to battle, they would inspire themselves. All, it seemed to Packer, were quite prepared to ignore the dark words of their king. They would simply leave all these thoughts behind, if only he would shut up and lead them on to battle, on to victory or death.

Packer tried again, his voice ringing like steel against steel. "Here is your choice! You may fight, or you may let God fight for you! King Reynard chose to fight, and the Fleet was sunk. Prince Mather chose to fight, and the City of Mann was lost."

"You fought the Achawuk!" someone called out. "You beat 'em!"

"You whipped the Firefish!" another called out. "We will fight with you!"

"No!" Packer shouted back, stopping another bout of raucous cheering before it could begin. "God defeated the Achawuk! God sent the wind, and the wind saved us! God sent the Firefish to defeat the Drammune! God sent the rain to us at the Battle of the Green!" Their silence was deep and ragged. "You are brave soldiers and sailors, and yes, you can swing your swords and shoot your muskets. You can vow vengeance and curse your enemies and fight to the death. You can look for blood and you will have it, by the gallon! But you—can't—win!"

The crowd was dumbfounded. Their king was telling them they were hopeless. That they were not capable. Wasn't it a leader's job to make them feel good about themselves? That's what Prince Mather had always done. That's what King Reynard had done.

Now Packer spoke into the silence. "We cannot win without God. We do not have the power."

After a long pause, someone shouted again, "We will fight *with* God!"

Now the troops cheered lustily. "Fight with God!" someone else called out, trying to get a chant started. "Fight with God!" Others picked it up, and then the whole army was chanting, raising their swords and pistols and pikes and maces and fists, pounding them rhythmically into the air: "Fight with God! Fight with God!"

Packer lowered his head. The words were blows to his heart, to his spirit. What he heard was not a vow to fight alongside the Almighty, but to fight *against* Him. They were choosing to *pick a fight with God.*

The Drammune armies crossed the fields like a torrent, a crimson flood. They came from the north, where they had marched along the forest's edge. They poured into the little field at a dead run, filling it like a steady stream of liquid fills a platter. They heard the Vast chanting. They gripped their muskets, pistols, pikes, and swords more tightly as they approached.

"What does it mean?" they asked one another.

"They call on their God," was the answer passed around among them.

Bustian Harmey lay inside one of his wagons, his wide body wedged tightly between two empty drums of ale. He had been inside the wagon when the first troops approached, and he had quickly decided to stay hidden there. Between the side boards of the wagon he could see a horizontal sliver of the activity around him. He saw an endless sea of gathering Drammune troops, a pinched panorama of impending doom. He heard the Vast army chanting something from the square, but their voices sounded tinny to him. They could not drown the stamp of Drammune feet, the rustle and clink of Drammune clothing, Drammune armor. He smelled their sweat and their anger, the foreignness of the food on their breaths. He felt the chill of death sweep through him.

He spit tobacco juice onto the floorboards in front of his face and swore silently, a streak of profanity that started strong but soon ended as more pained petition than imprecation. He put his forehead onto the floorboards, heedless of the juice he had just expelled there.

The chanting died away, but the Vast stood defiant, swords held high, fire in their eyes. They were ready for battle.

Packer watched as his people cheered him. Someone started chanting, "Death to Drammun! Death to Drammun!" Swords waved and clanked in the air. Bloodlust reigned.

Packer walked to the ladder. He had tried. They had chosen. They had not humbled themselves, but had worked themselves up into a lather. Might as well take them into the tunnels. He looked out over the crowd once more, and asked God to spare them anyway.

Huk Tuth sat on his horse where the hill met the woods. In his hand was the shaft of a flagstaff; at the end of it was the blood-red flag that bore the Skull of Drammun. Beside him on his left and right a company had placed his artillery, guns that had been brought from the Hollow Forest, now carted to this spot. His troops below blanketed the field, in position. Drammune warriors stood shoulder to shoulder, each with a weapon in his hand, every eye focused on the village square.

As each commander put his company into position, that commander raised his company's flag. Tuth saw them rise, one, two, three...a dozen, two dozen silky multicolored pennants fluttering lazily, high in the breeze that blew toward him. Each commander looked back toward the hill, toward the lone horseman that was Huk Tuth, their leader. They awaited his sign. When Tuth raised the red flag of Drammun, they would attack.

"May I please have your sword?" Father Mooring asked General Millian.

The general had it unsheathed in a moment, handed the hilt to the little priest without question.

"Excuse me," Father Mooring said to Stave Deroy, padding up to him. "I need to see the king."

"Sorry, Father," Stave said. "I have orders— "

"Let him up," Panna said quickly.

"Yes, ma'am." The dragoon stepped away, and the priest climbed.

Father Mooring's round face beamed as it topped the ladder. "Here, hold this, please," he said, grunting slightly as he handed Packer the sword. It was heavy and awkward in the priest's hands. Packer took it easily but held it gingerly, as though it might burn him. Then he gave the priest his free hand, and helped him onto the roof.

"Perhaps they will listen to me," Father Mooring said. And he turned to face the crowd, calm and fearless.

Packer couldn't imagine what the little man might say, but neither could he imagine saying no to Father Mooring. He raised his hand, and his army went silent. "Listen to the priest!" he said. He turned to Father Mooring. "They're all yours," he said gently.

"Thank you." Then Father Mooring turned to the crowd. "Packer Throme is your king!" Bran's tenor voice carried surprisingly well. "He could order you to your knees, and you would obey. But that is not his intent!" Now the priest held the general's sword up, gripping its hilt, aiming its point skyward. "When you raise a sword to fight, you point it at God!" He looked up at the point as though to say, sure enough, it was aimed heavenward. "When you raise a cross…" and here he flipped the sword upside down, held it by the blade, hilt high, like a crucifix, the point aimed at his own heart, "…you point it at yourself. By this you say to God," and now he spoke looking heavenward, "You have all the power, and may do as You please with me." He looked at the crowd. "So, your king asks you to choose this day. Raise your sword, and trust yourselves! Or, raise the cross, and trust in God!" He lowered the sword, set the point on the ground. "Choose one or the other! But your king has warned you. The victory you seek today will come only from God!" He thought for a second and then concluded with a simple, "Thank you."

Bran Mooring seemed particularly happy with his performance. "They were just confused," he said to Packer with a shrug. Packer looked out over the crowd. Their swords were lowered. Their eyes were open. They were waiting on him. Packer shook his head with a sense of joyful disbelief. Had Father Mooring succeeded where he had failed? Without wasting another moment, Packer called to the crowd, "Choose now! Raise your sword again, and you raise it against God! Kneel, and you surrender to Him alone! But choose!"

His troops stood stock still, unmoving, each one lost in his own thoughts. Packer was quite sure now, however, that they were paying attention. They knew exactly what they must choose between, and what each choice meant.

A wide-eyed soldier ran up to General Millian and spoke in his ear. The general stepped back, his head jerking as though he had been shot. "Are you sure?" he asked aloud.

"Yes, sir."

Panna watched the exchange and stepped in, her back now to Packer. "What is it?" she asked.

"The Drammune have filled the fields just to the west," the general told her.

"How many?"

"Their entire army, it would seem. We must move into position now. We must fight now, or be crushed here. The king must be told."

Panna's eyes went wide.

Huk Tuth squeezed the flagstaff in his hand. He looked one more time up and down the valley. All was ready. He drew up his arm.

But wait—one of the pennants in the fore, right at the edge of Varlotsville, dove. One of the leading companies was not ready. Tuth quickly lowered his flag. It had risen only to the top of his horse's ears. He waited.

Packer looked down quizzically at Panna. He looked to General Millian, who stood stock still, staring up at him, his sword still in his hand. "Your Highness, we must—"

"No," Panna said, interuppting the general.

"A sign!" the priest called out. He looked up to the heavens. He pointed upward, behind Packer.

Packer turned and looked up. A thick plume of dark smoke could be seen to the northwest, the direction from which they had come this morning. The Hollow Forest was burning. Packer turned back to face his troops. "Choose now!" he repeated.

Mack Millian turned to Ward Sennett for help. "The king must be told *now*," the general said to the prince. "He will move the troops into position if he knows."

Ward blew out his cheeks, the mountain now rising before him once again, in the shape of a ladder leaning against a wall just at the edge of a storefront. Of course, they needed to fight. That was obvious to any idiot. Of course, this king was not just any idiot. Ward looked up at Packer, considered calling out to him. But the crowd would hear him. He would then become the voice of the people, countering the king, taking up a mantle he had laid down. No. He raised a corner of his mouth and said darkly, "And so God laughs."

"The Drammune!" someone called out. The crowd swayed as the news spread, ripples of wind through ripe fields of wheat. Packer looked out over them, saw the movement, sensed the fear in it. The rumor swept through the crowd, and the troops were suddenly on the verge of panic. He turned around, looked toward the hills behind him. He could see the glint of the cannon, the crimson flecks in motion there on the hillside. He could not see the Drammune troops in the field, but he could see their battle flags raised high. He knew instantly what his own troops were whispering about. The enemies of Nearing Vast had gathered in force to attack.

"The Drammune are upon us!" someone shouted.

"There is no more time!" Packer demanded. "Choose now! Draw your sword and fight against God, or kneel and surrender to Him!"

Packer knelt, his eyes closed tightly. But he could not pray. His heart boomed within his chest like a bass drum; his pulse crashed in his ears like cymbals. What was happening? He knew last night as he prayed that God had led him to offer this choice, and it had seemed so simple and clean then. Fight the Drammune or surrender to God, and in surrendering, let God fight. But now he was asking his troops to bow their heads, to fall to their knees just as the Drammune were poised to attack. God seemed distant, but slaughter was near. Had he just sentenced all these people to death? Was he willing to sacrifice them for his own faith? He could sacrifice himself, but could he sacrifice a nation to God? That did not seem fair at all. It felt…arrogant. Presumptuous. Wrong.

He tried to throw himself on the mercy of God, to let God choose the outcome, to find the protection he had known that long ago day when he had stowed away in a barrel to board the *Trophy Chase,* or find the calm resignation he had known in his walk to the gallows on the Green. But he felt nothing, sensed nothing, heard nothing. Certainly not the voice of God.

Huk Tuth waited impatiently. The pennant at the fore rose again. His companies were ready. He gripped the flagstaff, and raised it slowly. In the silence, a bird cried out a chilling call.

Packer kept his eyes closed and did not dare to look. But he heard the bird, heard the movement of his troops, the rustle of clothing, the whispers, the shifting of balance, the shuffling of feet. He hoped that

The Battle for Vast Dominion

what he heard was the movement of God in the hearts of men. But it sounded to him like an army, departing.

Then there was silence. In that silence a bird cried out, a lone falcon or a hawk, releasing a long series of short calls that sounded like cruel laughter, or desolate sobbing. And then, feeling the heaviness of the weight of the world, Packer raised his head. His eyelids were leaden. He forced them open.

Below him on the square, in the streets of the village of Varlotsville at the edge of Mann, at the verge of the Hollow Forest, where civilization met wilderness, at the very brink of both, he saw his troops, the Army of Nearing Vast.

They were kneeling, every one of them.

Their heads were bowed, their swords sheathed or laid before them in the dust. Hats and helmets were held over hearts.

They had not fallen as one. Prince Ward had watched them. So had Panna. A few had simply followed Packer's lead, kneeling when the king did, *because* the king did. Then the priests knelt. Then the more devout officers, with a solemn sense of the consequences. Their charges followed suit. And then the decision seemed made, and all knelt, even the most reluctant, simply, to get it done and get on with it. The meekest had been first, the strongest, last.

Huk Tuth raised the flagstaff only to the level of his horse's head, and paused again. He cocked his head to one side, watching the falcon.

Father Mooring had not been looking at the smoke in the sky. The sign he had seen was something else entirely. It was this bird, a great predator that circled high overhead. Many eyes—both Drammune and Vast—were drawn to it.

Huk Tuth squinted. That falcon's call was familiar to him. It took him a moment longer to be sure. But yes, this was his own falcon, the one he had sent to Drammun with a message for the Hezzan. How could the bird have found him here? Even if she had made her way back to the great capital, Hezarow Kyne, and even if by some chance the Hezzan was now returning a message to him, this bird would have sought out his ship. Not him.

Mux pulled a leather glove on his right hand and held it up. He leaned the flagstaff against his saddle, but it fell to the ground.

Movement, by the trees! The falcon turned her head, and her sharp eyes locked onto the source. And then she saw him…He beckoned. Could it be? He held up his claw, covered with the familiar skin of long-ago prey. She circled once more to be sure. Yes…yes! Somehow, here he was! Her heart soared high as her body descended on rushing wings, fleet to the hand of her master.

At the back of the Drammune forces a sailor from the *Kaza Fahn* cursed his fate. He held in his hands an open cage, and he scoured the skies for the missing bird. *Take the falcon to Huk Tuth.* That was the mission. It was a simple thing; row the bird to shore and find the supreme commander and hand him the cage, with the bird in it, with the message still tied to her foot. How hard was that? But he had dropped the cage, and it had sprung open, and now the winged thing was gone, lost against the smoke that filled the sky to the west, down to the western horizon. He shook his head, wondering why he ever left a ship for shore, and why everything he ever did on land always turned into disaster.

Tuth watched her as she glided down and landed on his outstretched fist. The commander stroked the bird, clucked to her, spoke to her, told her how impressed he was with her. Then he held her low as a lieutenant rushed up and untied the scroll from her leg. Tuth took the opened parchment as it was handed up and read it silently, still holding his falcon on his right hand.

His face twisted as he read. He crushed the parchment in his left fist, and looked up in wrath at the miserable army holed up in this tiny town across the field. The Hezzan could not have known when these orders were penned that the nation of Nearing Vast would be one command away from total ruin. One command. Huk Tuth's command.

Packer Throme watched the falcon, saw her light. He saw the cannon spaced across the hilltop, aimed at his army. But he watched only the horseman atop the bluff. Even from this distance he recognized the crimson color. This was a Drammune commander, no doubt, overseeing his troops, preparing to attack.

Packer waited for what seemed like ages, watching that commander, expecting he knew not what, the answer to his prayers or the proof of his presumption. And then, finally, he saw the flag go up, on the end of a flagstaff held in the hand of the enemy commander.

Huk Tuth raised the gray Drammune flag of parley.

Packer walked briskly through the field of Drammune soldiers. He did not look at them, but kept his eyes forward, focused on the man on horseback ahead. The Drammune warriors, however, watched Packer very closely. They moved out of his way, turning in unison as he went by.

The Drammune were not the talebearers that the Vast were; they did not start rumors that built into legends within hours. But they all knew by now who this beardless man with the yellow hair was, a young man barely more than a boy. This was the one who had defeated Fen Abbaka Mux not once, but twice. This was the one who had called forth the Firefish to destroy their ship, the *Nochto Vare*. This was the one who had been granted the Ixthano on the gallows, and had thus become both the King of the Vast and at the same time a Drammune citizen. This was the one who had led peasants to victory at the gallows, and then caused them all to vanish from the city, reappear in the wood, and then vanish again and reappear here.

This unlikely king was dressed as a peasant, but his bearing was altogether regal in their eyes. Their own commander wanted parley— and that was as sure a sign of his stature as any they could imagine. As he walked by, they saw his eyes, blue as the sea, burning now with fire. He was a true king, and more than one warrior fought back the impulse to bow. This was a moment they would each remember, they knew…the time when the King of Nearing Vast passed so close they could have touched him, spoken to him. Or killed him.

Twenty yards behind him trudged one of their huge, blue warriors, pushing aside the Drammune who had closed in behind the king. He was one of their dragoons, they knew, the ones who could fight, and he wore a fierce scowl on his face. He met eye after eye, and looked as though he would be quite content to ram his pike through any who gave him the slightest opportunity. Behind him was a tall, angular man of some obvious importance, trying to act as though he wasn't terrified. Behind him was a stubby priest wearing an idiotically blissful expression.

Whatever positive impression they gained of the Vast through the regal qualities of their king quickly dissolved at the sight of his court.

The Vast quartermaster sat up and peeked over his barrels of ale, silently surveying the Drammune from within the shadows of his wagon. They had grown restless. Something was happening. Then he saw Packer Throme and his heartbeat quickened. It was a parley! There was a chance he might see sundown after all.

And then he felt a sudden, sinking feeling. What if there was a pact, and the king ordered him to feed all these Drammune as well as his own troops? That would be just his luck. Major Harmey spit once more, then clamped his mouth shut in a successful effort to silence the torrent of oaths that welled up within him.

CHAPTER 5

The Alliance

As Packer topped the hill, Huk Tuth dismounted. The boy seemed even less a threat now than he had been on the Green, when manacled for hanging. Then, at least, he had seemed dangerous, a criminal who if let loose might turn violent. Here, unarmed, wearing the commonest of Vast clothing, he seemed all out of place to lead even a single platoon. Much less an army. Much less a nation.

Packer was taken aback by his first encounter with Huk Tuth. In spite of his small stature, the Drammune commander seemed somehow to be a very big man. He was short but thick; his white hair was long and thin, straggling down to slumped shoulders that at one time surely had been broad, and that still tapered into long, thick arms. His brow below his helmet was heavy, his nose flat and broken and hooked, his skin creased and leathery. He had no beard, which was unusual for the Drammune. His dark eyes were hard and distant, eyes that had seen things that would turn most men to stone. To Packer, the bent old commander seemed like something from another age, hard and weathered, as inscrutable as he was foreign. The two stood face-to-face and worlds apart, both silent.

Then Tuth's face grew bitter with disgust. He was repulsed by the measure of the man before him, and by the message he must now convey. No Devilfish would fear this man. Any Drammune intelligence officer could wring out his secrets, given an hour and a cheap whip. This Vast king wouldn't make it through the first day of military training in Drammun; he'd die in the Opening Mayhem. And yet Tuth must deliver a message of peace to him, as though he were to be feared?

But that was his duty. "Do you speak Drammune?" Tuth asked in his native tongue.

Packer grimaced. "Do you speak Vast?" he asked hopefully, not aware that he asked the mirror-image question.

"Little," Tuth answered.

"I'll translate," Prince Ward offered cheerfully, now topping the rise, and relieved to have made it across the field alive. Packer turned, surprise in his eyes. Chunk and Father Mooring flanked the prince. Packer did not realize until now that he'd been followed.

"Father Mooring could provide the same service," Ward explained, "but Vast priests are not held in high regard by the Drammune military." The priest nodded his contentment with this arrangement, and the prince repeated his offer in Drammune for Tuth's benefit.

Tuth had his own translator in one of the officers standing nearby, but he did not reveal that fact. Instead, he wasted no time launching into his terms, speaking directly to the tall, skinny Vast native who spoke Drammune, ignoring the king.

Packer listened, uncomprehending, to the Drammune commander and his own prince. Tuth's tone was argumentative, and sullen. Prince Ward was patient, furrowing his brow as he listened, holding up a hand once or twice to ask clarifying questions. Ward surprised Packer by making some sort of demand, and then Tuth showed him the wrinkled piece of parchment, pointing toward the bottom of it. Packer could see the axe-and-skull insignia at the bottom, the official seal of the Hezzan of the Drammune, but the rest just looked like scratch marks. Ward studied the document for a moment, Father Mooring peeking at it from behind. Ward asked a few more questions. Finally both the prince and the Drammune commander went silent. Huk Tuth crossed his arms and looked away as though wholly uninterested.

Ward turned to Packer, who by now was anything but uninterested. "Well," Ward said, trying to pull all this together. "My Drammune isn't perfect, but I think the gist is that the Hezzan has, by way of that falcon we heard screeching overhead, sent this message..." it was still in his hand, and he tapped it with the back of his fingers, "one that may have saved us all a whole lot of trouble. It contains terms for peace."

Packer was dumbfounded. He looked at Father Mooring, who nodded, beaming again. The priest had certainly gotten the gist of it. "Terms...how? Why?"

"Well," Ward continued, "as you might imagine, I had the same questions. But it seems that our happy little commander here," and Ward jerked his head in Tuth's direction, "witnessed your performance with the Firefish at sea, you and the *Trophy Chase*. He immediately thereafter sent a report to the Hezzan about it. By falcon. How they've trained falcons to carry messages is a question the commander does not seem anxious to answer, by the way. Regardless, the return message dropped from the heavens at just the opportune moment."

Ward glanced back and forth between the priest and the king. There would be no stopping these two now. They had their miracle. "The result being that this war is over, and we are now fast friends with the Drammune, who apparently are not willing to have their Armada destroyed by Firefish, which as we all know by now, attack at the beck and call of the Vast. Your beck and call in particular." He said it with wry humor. Now he handed Packer the sheaf. "So...if you'll comply with a few demands, they'll simply pack up and go home."

Packer's mind reeled. He looked, uncomprehending, at the parchment. "The war is over..." He looked up into the sky. He looked down at Father Mooring. He looked over at Chunk. He shook his head in astonishment. Then he looked back to Ward. His heart was in his throat. "What are the demands?"

"There are three."

"Which are...?" Packer was suddenly impatient to get this done.

"First, we must immediately dispatch an emissary to write a formal pact. Send a diplomat, a plenipotentiary with full powers to treat with the Drammune on behalf of the king."

"Done!"

Ward glanced quickly at Huk Tuth, then stepped closer to Packer. "If you don't mind, I will wait until you have heard all three conditions before I convey any of your answers to our delightful new friend here. The others are not quite so simple."

Packer nodded.

"The second is that you send your emissary to Hezarow Kyne immediately, aboard the *Trophy Chase*."

Packer frowned. "The *Chase?* Why?"

"No particular reason given. But I see you're beginning to get the bigger picture here. The third condition, the revealing one, is that you must also send the leaders of the Vast Firefish trade on the same voyage."

Packer's brow furrowed further.

"Yes." Ward nodded. "This will be the sign of our goodwill toward our new allies. We will teach them our trade secrets regarding the Firefish, and they in turn will teach us all their trade secrets regarding their more mundane, but still highly lucrative, fishing industry."

Packer brightened a bit. "They'll teach us their harvesting techniques?"

"Yes, they'll even send us a boat, brimful of the leaders of their own fishing industry."

Packer looked at the glowering Huk Tuth, then back to the prince. "Hard to refuse."

"I'm sure that was the plan. But there is one other small item."

Packer felt a chill at the back of his neck. He had seen this act too many times before, from Ward and from his brother. Now would come the bad news. "Let's hear it."

"The message names names, those leaders of the Firefish industry who must sail aboard the *Trophy Chase* in order to meet these terms. I demanded to read it myself." He pointed to the wrinkled parchment in Packer's hand. "Sandeman Wilkins, also known as Scatter. John Hand. Lund Lander...and Packer Throme."

Packer's jaw fell. He didn't know where to begin. "Scat and Lund are—"

"Yes, Commander Tuth is willing to make allowances for the small inconvenience caused by their demise."

"But me? How do they know me?"

Ward shrugged. "Spies, perhaps? You've been a hero in Nearing Vast for quite a while now."

Packer looked at the parchment, and Ward pointed out the names. They were impossible to read, but that didn't stop Packer from trying. Giving up, he looked back over the field, toward the village. He saw figures on the rooftop of the general store, watching. He knew that one of them would be Panna—no one could have kept her from climbing up for a better view. He wanted to talk to her before answering. But only one answer seemed possible. If it was a choice between all-out war and sailing aboard the *Chase* to Drammun, how was it even a choice? God had answered his prayer, and the prayers of his people. God had saved His people, who had chosen to bow the knee rather than raise the sword.

"I don't see how I can reject these terms," Packer said earnestly.

Ward hesitated. He rubbed his chin. "You know, Packer. Your Highness. The way these things generally work is that you ask for a bit of time to prepare a response."

"Okay, good. How much time?"

The prince turned again and spoke to Tuth. The commander's eyes glinted as he spoke a few words, pointing first to the stand of trees nearby and then toward the town.

Ward mirrored the gestures.

"Until the shadow of these trees," he pointed above him, "strike that village." He pointed to Varlotsville.

"Agreed," Packer said, nodding, looking at Tuth.

Tuth made another statement, his eyes boring into Packer's.

"There seems to be one more thing," Ward offered. "And he seems fairly adamant on this point. If you move your troops off that square, that will be taken as a refusal of the Hezzan's terms. He seems particularly concerned about tunnels, for some reason. If he detects any movement of the troops, the Drammune will attack immediately."

Packer had not taken his eyes from those of Huk Tuth. The man had the light of battle burning there now, and this Packer recognized. It was neither distant nor foreign. Packer wanted to give some equally martial response to show Tuth he was not intimidated, but he did not have one to give. "Agreed," was all he said. And then he turned his back and walked away, back toward Varlotsville.

From the woods behind the Drammune commander, the two brothers lowered their muskets. Dall and Stub Hammersfold looked at one another. Dall nodded. They had no orders to be here, but without a commanding officer they had no orders to be anywhere else, either. After the Battle of the Green, they had traded in their smart uniforms for their more accustomed gear, the leather breeches and jackets, the wide-brimmed felt hats of the woodsmen that they were—that they had been until Bench Urmand found them, learned their mettle, and made them his deputies.

But Bench was dead, and they didn't particularly like any of the other officers they had met. So they had worked their way through the woods on their own, as scouts, following the Vast armies from a distance, secreted by trees and terrain of their home territory. They were now the only Vast soldiers who knew what had happened to the Vast rear guard, but they did not feel much need to report it to anyone. Soldiers had done their duty, and died doing it. This was not news.

They had been here waiting, watching, for only a few minutes. But they had determined when they arrived that, should there be an attack on the Vast, the short old Drammune general would not live to see it. This was soldiering more to their liking, and they felt it worthy of the legacy of Bench Urmand.

But now, having overheard a good bit of the prince's conversation with Packer Throme, they decided they would let Huk Tuth live.

"What now?" Stub asked.

"Stay and watch," Dall whispered back. "It ain't over yet."

Stub nodded. "You think there's any more of them furrin ones sneakin' around our woods?"

"Mebbe," Dall offered. "But if so, they ain't close by here."

Stub nodded. "They can put up a fight." He fingered a bruised cheek and a cut lip. "But they ain't much at sneakin'."

Dall said nothing more; he just watched Huk Tuth as Stub scanned the woods behind them. Two bodies lay here, their throats slit. Two more lay dead beyond the far ridge. All four wore the black uniforms of the Nochtram Eyn.

The High Holy Reverend Father Harlowen "Hap" Stanson reined in his horse as he topped the hill. The winding road before him led down the valley and into a thick forest. And the forest was ablaze. Thick black smoke poured from the mouth of the roadway as though from the barrel of a smoking gun. He had been watching this blackness fill the sky for hours now, fearing at first that it was the City of Mann burning to ash. But it was the Hollow Forest burning, from the road here as far south as he could see, and it was spreading northward, to his left.

His horse stamped and whinnied, fearful of the smell, the sound of crackling flame. The next road through the forest to the north was perhaps thirty miles away, and to get there on established roads he would need to backtrack twenty miles or more.

He pondered. He didn't want to waste that much time. He could try to skirt the forest, going north until he could find a path through the woods without following a road. That would be dangerous. He was no woodsman, and he had an unfamiliar horse. Or he could wait until the fire burned out. How long would that take? He didn't know. An hour? Days? A week? That was not acceptable. What might Packer Throme do to consolidate his power in a week? There was no opposition a king could not crush, no institution not under his direct control, with the exception of the Church. The Church could not be ordered about by any king. And every king of Nearing Vast therefore must make his peace with her. Packer Throme would be no different.

Hap Stanson patted his horse's sweaty neck, then rubbed his hand on his robes. *Throme.* That name had been a splinter in the thumb of the Church for too many years. First Dayton, and now Packer. If the elder Throme had not saved the life of Mather Sennett, rescuing him from the sea years ago, how different the recent history of this kingdom would be. The younger Throme would never have been schooled at swords, would never have stowed away on the *Trophy Chase,* or if he had, he would have been killed. Senslar Zendoda would be alive. There would have been no war, no abdication, no hanging of a king, no passing of the crown.

It could all be traced back to that shipwreck with young Prince Mather on board. And what had caused the flagship of the Fleet to sink in the dead of night, on simple maneuvers, with the crown prince aboard for nautical training? No one knew. Hap suspected Firefish. So did Dayton Throme, and that had created quite an awkward situation for King Reynard. Throme, simple fisherman that he was, just couldn't shut up about it. As long as he stayed in his own village and talked only to other fishermen, he was just a fool, ignored even by fellow fools. But once he had gained access to a king, through the rescue of a young prince, he gained confidence. And once he started telling stories around the fireplaces in the pubs, not in fishing villages but in Mann, his seeds started finding good soil. People had listened. Then people had started bringing him information.

Throme had been unraveling the secrets. He had learned that Scatter Wilkins might have met and might even have conquered a Firefish. He had gotten close to connecting the notorious pirate with the respected king. And in those days, secrecy was everything...

But the Crown had an obligation to Throme, and so the usual routes of silencing fools did not seem practical. The Church had stepped in. Hap Stanson had done it gladly back then, sanding down rough edges for Reynard Sennett once more. But the Church had picked up this nasty splinter in the process; and it had festered unseen for years as the Throme boy grew. And now, all of it had led to this loss of the Crown, the amputation of the Church's right hand. The Sennetts were many things, but as long as they were compliant, or at least pliable, they were quite acceptable leaders.

Now, the Church's influence was in jeopardy. The Thromes, of all people, held the power of the State. Packer had the ears of the people, and worse, he had their hearts. If he learned now what had actually happened to his own father—no, that could not be allowed to happen. It would cause no end of trouble. Sanding rough edges would not be enough this time. A crosscut saw would be needed to fix this one.

But so be it.

His decision now made, Hap Stanson spurred his horse to the left. He would travel along the forest wall until he could find a trail that might lead him through the woods ahead of the flames. He prayed with confidence that he would find a path through this tangled, burning wilderness his well-traveled road had suddenly become. God had always opened doors for Hap Stanson, even if a few hinges had needed oiling, or a few stuck jambs had needed a shoulder to aid the process. There was no reason to believe anything had changed, or would change.

He was the High Holy Reverend Father and Supreme Elder, after all.

The woods were burning.

No beast anywhere is drawn to the raw smell of wood smoke; it signals danger, only and always. And so the animals of the Hollow Forest, large and small, were on the move. The quick would live, the deer and the rabbit, the antelope and the fox, so long as they kept moving and did not allow themselves to be trapped in a clearing, or panicked into running off a cliff or into a pocket of flame. Possum and porcupine and groundhog, these were slow, and the slow would die, unless they were made of stuff that could take to the water. Turtles and otters and frogs and raccoons. Others, those neither fast nor slow, those that could scamper but could not fly, would need luck, or aid in some form, to prevent the firestorm from overtaking them. Among these were squirrels and chipmunks and badgers.

And bear cubs.

A fully grown redclaw bear could move almost as fast as a rabbit. But her cubs could not. And a fully grown mother redclaw would not leave her charges behind. She would lead them, nudge them, even carry them by the nape of the neck, to get them away from danger. She would be in no mood for distractions.

She would have no patience for predators lying in wait as she fled.

The High Holy Reverend Father and Supreme Elder Harlowen "Hap" Stanson had misjudged the difficulty of traversing the woods, even on a clearly defined deer path. Now he lay bruised and broken and bleeding, directly in the path of the approaching flames. He saw the deer and the rabbits as they ran by. There was nothing he could do now but pray, and wait.

How had he gotten into this predicament? He had had a revelation after an hour and a half of following the winding trail, his horse squeezing through thickets that the much thinner deer could manage easily, thorns tearing at his thighs as he ducked branches that the much shorter deer never needed to consider. This revelation came to him long after he had made several choices where paths crossed, choices he was sure he could not retrace in reverse. His realization was this: Deer had no intention of traversing the Hollow Forest. It seemed obvious, too obvious once it was formed that way in his mind. Why he had assumed that a pathway into the woods on one side would inevitably lead out of the woods on the other now completely escaped him. Deer, he now understood, for reasons known but to God, wander aimlessly on paths that lead nowhere.

He lost track of direction. The woods were hilly, and the paths meandered through and around the hummocks and knolls and ridges. The sun overhead was nearly straight up, and he couldn't see it much of the time anyway for the dense canopy. The position of the sun would be a help within a few hours, but he did not have time to wait for it to tell him which direction was west, and which east. He needed to make it through the forest while there was still daylight, before the fires spread further north. He did not want to be traveling here after dark. So there was really no way to be sure he was going in the right direction.

Until he smelled the smoke and heard the flame.

He knew, or thought he knew, which direction the fire came from. It came from the south. Since he needed to go east, he angled away from the flames, in a direction he judged to be northeast. He left the trails. This line of reasoning was not illogical. But now, as he thought it through, he had another revelation: He had assumed that fire traveled in something of a straight line. This, too, was a fallacy. He knew this because now he could hear the crackling of it approaching him from two sides.

What he didn't know was that he had not been traveling northeast at all, but southeast, between two fingers of burning woodlands. He had been riding his horse closer and closer to the oncoming flames. He was headed toward a dead end, toward the webbing between two enormous fingers of fire. He was riding into a trap.

His horse knew it. The big bay sensed it. He snorted and pranced, bobbed his head up and down, whinnying as Hap smacked him alongside his neck with the loose ends of the reins and spurred the miserable, stubborn beast with his heels. The bay broke into a canter.

And then a fox shot out of a thicket just in front of him, racing away from the flames. The horse panicked and bolted into a full gallop. Hap held on for a while, dropping the reins and gripping the saddle horn. But the speed of the horse through thick woods, and his own horsemanship, passable at best, presaged the worst.

He did not experience the worst, but close. He hit a branch, not a solid stem of oak that might have killed him, but a huge and springy pine branch that bent, then tensed, then slung him out of the saddle. He landed in a heap on a rock outcropping, the left side of his head banging hard, his left shoulder popping out of the socket as he reached out to soften the blow. Then he rolled off the rock and down an incline, wrenching his right leg, and finally coming to a stop wedged into a rocky crevice in the slope.

He was bleeding from the left side of his head. His right leg from the knee down was pinned under him, the knee torn and twisted. His

The Battle for Vast Dominion

left arm was broken in two places. He couldn't move. He was in a crack that broke the otherwise smooth decline of the hillside. He was only six inches below ground level, but he couldn't raise himself. He was stuck. He was invisible. And he was in extreme pain.

He lay that way for a long time, wondering what God intended to do with him, quite sure the Almighty would not let him die this way. He was, after all, Harlowen Stanson, High Holy Reverend Father of God's own Church. He was the Supreme Elder of every congregation large and small, in every neighborhood and every village in the kingdom. No, this was not how the Almighty took His appointed workmen home.

And then the bear cubs appeared. They clambered over the rocks and rolled down the hill in a playful heap without even knowing he was there. They stopped almost on top of him. Hap laughed, amazed that such cute little things, not much bigger than puppies, could appear from nowhere without a care in the world. One of them noticed him, and sniffed the air nearby. Hap reached out a hand to give the little thing a pat. Here was God's handiwork, and more than that, God's message, telling him that all would be well, that the Almighty was in control of His creation yet, and He watched out for all living things. Hap would not be abandoned.

And then came momma.

"Gentlemen, please rise!"

The Quarto looked at one another, faces grim. Slowly, all twelve men in the Great Meeting Hall of the Hezzan rose to their feet. They had prepared as best they could for their second encounter with the woman Talon, but they had learned caution from the first. They had intended then to sentence her to death, but instead had made her the empress of all Drammun. Now, as part of her Court of Twelve, seated within the power structures of Drammun, their real drive for the throne would begin.

"The Hezzan Skahl Dramm!"

Talon flowed into the room. She wore new leather robes, rich brown edged with oxblood and fur. Her straight black hair was no longer ragged; it had grown to cover the scarring of her scalp. Not yet long enough for the traditional braid, it was trimmed closer on the right side than on the left, where she wore it tucked behind her left ear, the flat of which bore the triple earring of the wife of a Hezzan. The heavy battle scar that fell from her left eye down her cheek and onto her neck was set off by her crown, a delicate braid that wrapped her head at a line just above her eyebrows, three fine strands of precious metal loosely interlaced, one gold, one silver, and one brass.

"Welcome," she said, as she remained standing behind the Hezzan's chair at the truncated corner of the table. "Please, sit. We have urgent business regarding the war." She watched the peevish Pizlar Kank, the leader of the Quarto, take his seat opposite her. Beside him was the bookish but bloodthirsty Zekahn Irkah, and next to him the solid, ruthless Dorn Rodanda. And next to Rodanda sat the newest member of the Quarto, Tcha Tarvassa, a small, lizard-skinned man with a patchy beard and narrow eyes that peered out from heavy, red-rimmed eyelids.

"A significant development requires your earnest attention. Vast warcraft has improved considerably. They have outstripped the Drammune in one important regard, which will prove our undoing unless we address it."

Brows furrowed, questioning looks were exchanged.

Talon's dark eyes pierced each of her ministers as she looked at them in turn. Her eyes lingered when they met those of Tcha Tarvassa. Behind his thick eyelids was a subtle mind constantly in motion. He had until recently been the highest-ranking official of the Infiltrators, and Talon knew he had been chosen by the Quarto to help counter the cunning of Sool Kron and his yet more cunning mistress. Her eyes also lingered on Zan Gar, the young cannonball Zealot who had been her husband's minister, and who had been the first to join the conspiracy to murder her. Gar had been released from the royal prison just this morning, and just for this meeting. She saw unbridled hatred in his eyes. This was good. She returned the look without emotion, a predator measuring her prey.

"More than two years ago," Talon began, "a Vast merchant came secretly to Drammun with goods to sell. The Hezzan bought. These goods are now a standard part of our best warriors' uniforms." She clapped her hands once. Vasla Vor, the General Commander of the Hezzan Guard, he who had been the first to side with Talon, returned with two folded hauberks on his outstretched hands, the top one of which she took. She held it up for all to see.

Puzzled looks were exchanged. The Twelve were prepared to overlook Talon's disregard for ceremony. Speeches and invocations could be dispensed within times of war. But for this? Was Drammun government business now to be centered on martial fashion, now that a woman warrior held power?

"This armor is not of Drammune manufacture, as you may suppose. It is made by the Vast."

Now the Court could not hold its peace. "No, this cannot be!" "What sort of nonsense is this?"

Talon watched and waited while the murmuring died away. Zan Gar was agitated to the point of rage. Talon stared at him coldly until he rose from his seat, put his hands on the table, and leaned in toward her.

"You are new to Drammun, having lived most of your life among the salamanders. Perhaps you are unaware that the Drammune forges of Rahk Kyne have been producing our armor for centuries. The light mail they manufacture is the best steel armor in the world. No Hezzan would stoop so low as to buy merchandise from the Pawns. Certainly not the Hezzan Shul Dramm."

She looked around the room, saw only blank stares. No one cared enough to call him back from this precipice. Excellent. "Commander Vor?" He stepped closer, and held out the second hauberk. "Show this to Minister Gar." Vor walked around the table and put the garment before the minister, who sneered at him as though he were no more than a trained monkey. Gar glanced down at the two ornate pistols in the General Commander's belt. Vor looked him in the eye and dared him.

"Thank you, General Commander." Vasla Vor broke eye contact, nodded at Talon, and stepped away. "Is this the highest-quality light mail in the world, Minister Gar? You'll want to be very sure."

The cold warning of her voice caused him to study it carefully. He looked at the tiny crimson-painted links, flexed the material, checked the workmanship. "This is Drammune craftsmanship, from the City of Rahk."

"And what is this, then?" She tossed him the other hauberk, which slid across the table and came to a stop before him. Distrust in his eyes, he studied it as well. "I do not know what this is. It resembles mail, but…" He looked up. "It is not the product of Drammune forges."

"And yet our best troops wear it. It is the superior merchandise of which I speak. It comes from the Vast."

"You lie."

Breaths were held.

"General Commander Vor," Talon said in a purr, "would you please put on the Vast hauberk?"

The disdain in Zan Gar grew palpable as Talon's monkey reached for the garment, picked it up, and pulled it dutifully over his head.

"And you, Minister Gar. Put on the Drammune armor."

Gar looked at her, aghast. His lips pursed and fire glowed behind his eyes. "To what end?" He said it with evident venom.

"To demonstrate your obedience to your Hezzan, of course."

Now the hatred in his eyes blazed. He whipped around to look at the Quarto, but Pizlar Kank was impassive and none of the others showed a trace of encouragement. He ground his teeth and looked back at the woman, this widow of the Hezzan who had slithered into his throne. He saw satisfaction grow just behind her blank stare. She knew she had cornered him. If he claimed here and now she was not worthy to be Hezzan, he would need to appeal to the Quarto. And they had put the woman in power, in exchange for their seats at this table. He knew, as all did, that they would like to take her throne away. But they hadn't done it yet. If he refused to obey the direct order of the Hezzan, she could banish him to prison or worse.

Gar looked around the room one more time, but found no help. Jaw clenched, he obeyed.

With both men wearing the loose-fitting vests, Talon walked over to them and stood them side by side, at the corner of the table nearest Pizlar Kank. She positioned herself beside Zan Gar and addressed the assembly. "Only a careful examination, such as the one Minister Gar has made, could tell them apart. The majority of our troops actually wear these Drammune steel hauberks and helmets." She put her hand on Gar's shoulder. He twitched. "They even feel similar." She ran her fingers over the material, looking into Gar's eyes. She saw no fear in him, only disgust and hatred at full boil. "Our officers," she continued, "our elite troops, and the sailors and soldiers who support them, wear the Vast merchandise, though we are striving to outfit all of our troops with this superior protection."

Gar grimaced. Talon was not tall, but he was shorter than she, and he hated looking up at her. More, he hated her praising the Vast, bragging on them, and by doing so bragging on herself and her own degenerate past.

"And it is in fact superior," Talon continued, looking at the Twelve but leaning ever so slightly into Zan Gar, her hand still touching his shoulder. "Infinitely so. Drammune armor cannot nearly compete. The Vast have outstripped our technical prowess—"

Gar snorted through his nose, gritted his teeth, and glared at her.

She pretended just now to notice his misgiving. "What is it, Minister? Speak your mind."

Gar squared his shoulders to her, pulling his shoulder from under her hand. "You demean your own nation," he growled.

"Do I really?" He was so easy to manipulate, it was hardly sport. "I believe I speak only the truth. But perhaps you would like some proof?"

"Without proof your statements are treasonous."

Now she grew serious. "Treason is something you would understand, Minister Gar. I believe that is the charge on which you were imprisoned, and sentenced to die. Treason, for the assassination of the Hezzan. My husband." Neither said a word for a moment, and then Talon called out, "Commander Vor, are you ready?"

"Yes, Your Worthiness." Vasla Vor, still standing beside the enraged Gar, took the two pistols from his belt and handed both their carved handles to Talon.

Talon stepped away from the two men, walking back toward her own chair, cocking the pistol in her right hand as she did. Then without pausing she turned and fired, a direct hit to Vasla Vor, midchest. The explosion was deafening and echoed in the high vault above them, ringing in their ears. The General Commander of the Hezzan Guard, Talon's most loyal supporter, took several steps backward, putting both hands to his chest. But when he lowered them, there was no damage.

Talon looked around the table. A blue haze hung before her. Amazement, fear, and relief filled the faces of the Twelve. "Vast merchandise," she said. "There on the floor you will find the slug," she added, to Vor.

The commander looked down, and then picked up a round, flattened piece of lead. It was hot, and he bounced it from hand to hand, then set it on the table. After a moment Pizlar Kank picked it up carefully, blew on it, then passed it around so each member of the Twelve could see.

Talon raised the pistol in her left hand and cocked it. Now she looked at Zan Gar, the satisfaction of the kill already pulsing through her, evident to all in the room. "What do you think, Minister? Is Drammune armor worthy, or is it not? Who speaks treason, and who speaks the truth? Shall we find out?"

Zan Gar hated this woman with every ounce of energy within him. She wanted him to show fear. But he would not give her the satisfaction. "You demean your ministers with this show," he snarled, his voice a ragged whisper. "You defile the office of the Hezzan. You praise the Pawns and slander the Drammune. You are Unworthy. Our people, our weapons and, yes, our armor are superior in every way—"

She raised the pistol and fired. The gunshot ripped through the room as had the previous one, leaving a trail of blue smoke and an ear-shattering echo. Zan Gar took two steps back, his hands over his chest, an identical reaction to that of Vasla Vor. But when Gar looked at his trembling hands, blood covered them.

"Superior in every way, perhaps, but one." She turned her back on Gar as he slumped to the floor with a moan. She nodded at Vor. "Thank you, Commander. You may remove the minister. His services will no longer be required."

Vor clapped his hands and two guards entered, wearing crimson hauberks. He waved them toward Zan Gar. They stood over the minister as he twitched once, then lay still. They picked up the lifeless body and carried it away.

"Now," Talon said, taking her seat for the first time at the head of this table. She put the pistols, one of them still smoking, on the table before her. "I would like to explain precisely how the Vast managed this achievement."

She had their undivided attention.

Momma bear was angry. And she did not have the least bit of respect for her fallen predator's spiritual accomplishments. She came at a run, over the crest of the hill faster than the fastest man could run, huge forelegs and massive hind legs covering as much distance in a stride as a cheetah, four-inch claws ripping up the earth. She roared her fury with teeth bared, spittle flying.

The High Holy Reverend Father could only cower, flattening himself to await the end. The bear hit him with an explosion that sounded like rifle shots and felt like a thousand pounds of muscle, bone, claw, and tooth. It was nearly that.

And then it rolled over him, sprawled onto the ground, and lay still.

Hap looked down at his chest, saw the gashes in his good travel robe, blood seeping through. He put his good hand on the wounds. They were not deep. He looked at the bear. She lay still, but she was breathing hard, wheezing. And then she exhaled once, and was silent.

Hap Stanson looked heavenward, at the dark canopy above him. What had just happened? Was it a miracle? How could the bear be dead?

And then into view came a man, a woodsman with a wide-brimmed felt hat pulled low over his eyes, a bushy moustache, and a plug of chewing tobacco in his cheek. He held his long musket in his hand by the barrel, stock down, like a walking stick. Smoke still curled from the bore.

"You alive?" he asked. Then he spit, not averting his cold, insistent eyes.

"Yes," Hap replied. "Yes, I'm alive."

Another man just like the first appeared. But he had no moustache, just a small bunch of hair at his chin. Neither man had shaved in several days, and the civilizing effect of their facial hairstyles was gradually disappearing. "Better'n I can say for the bear," the second man said. He also held a smoking long rifle in his hand.

"Looks like she hit the rock there instead a' you." The beast had careened down the hill and been shot from the side, two rifle balls to the brain. But her head had indeed hit a lip of rock, one of the two between which Hap was wedged. Blood and bits of brain matter dripped there.

"You better get outta here," the first said. "There's a fire headed this way, y' know."

"That would seem the prudent choice. But I'm injured here, and I wonder if I might ask for a little assistance."

"You just got it. But you want more, we can do that, too," the mustachioed man said. "Dall Hammersfold. This here's my brother Stub."

"Pleased to meet you, I'm..." somehow the whole lengthy title didn't seem appropriate at the moment. "I'm Father Stanson. You can call me Hap."

"Hap, then," Dall said, and spit tobacco juice again. "Let's get you gone."

Getting Hap Stanson gone took some doing. After taking a closer look at his injuries, Dall went to work fashioning a litter they could use to pull the injured man to safety, while Stub took care of the litter of cubs that played near their mother's carcass. He did this in the only humane way he knew. "Couldn't stand to have 'em burnt to death," he said afterward, wiping their blood from his big hunting knife. "Just a shame we don't have time to skin 'em." He looked longingly at the carcasses. "Great waste a' good meat. Whatcha think, Dall? Do we have time for a strip or two a' bear steak?"

"It'll take me another minute here," Dall answered, looping a length of vine around one of the two poles he had cut and then pulling it tight. "You think you can get a loin strip from the momma, you go right ahead."

That was a challenge Stub was clearly ready to tackle.

"How did you ever find me?" Hap asked.

"You left a trail like a stampede a' cattle," Dall answered easily. "We could tell you were no horseman, and seein' as how you was ridin' into the fire, 'stead of away from it, we figured you didn't know which one was the rear end a' your horse. Sorry to think such. Didn't realize you come by your ignorance of such things through devotion and study." Dall seemed not to mean any harm by his words. Hap had the impression he had no idea he'd even insulted him. "Also," Dall continued, "didn't know we'd find you laid up here, messin' around with a mother bear."

Hap was now nonplussed. "I assure you I was not messing—"

"Stub, how far do you think that horse is gone?" he asked his brother.

"Long gone. Miles."

"Let's follow her tracks, though. She'll know better'n us how to find a trail that'll keep us all from gettin' broiled."

"Okay, got the meat!" He held up a bloody strip as wide as his hand, just as thick, and about three feet long. Hap Stanson almost passed out.

"Good. Time to get gone."

And so the spiritual leader of the Church of Mann was painfully, without protocol or sympathy, picked up and laid on the makeshift stretcher. Then he was carried by two men with long rifles and loaded knapsacks strapped to their backs at a pace that was nearly a dead run, through the Hollow Forest.

For the clergyman, every step his rescuers took was painful. Every bounce was agony. And there were many, many steps and bounces ahead for the High Holy Reverend Father and Supreme Elder of the Church of Nearing Vast. Dall and Stub Hammersfold dropped him to the ground only once, spilling him from the stretcher while attempting to maneuver a slippery hillside at high speed. Then they stopped and tied him in securely.

"Does a whole lotta groanin', don't he?" Stub asked his brother by way of making conversation. "Do all priests do that?"

"Don't know. But I wouldn't worry. He'll pass out from the pain if it gets bad enough," Dall assured him.

And soon, Dall was quite right.

CHAPTER 6

The Unworthy

The tavern was empty but for the king and queen. Their counselors had left them: the generals to manage their growing list of discipline problems, Prince Ward and Bran Mooring to deliver their carefully worded document, just now drafted, to Supreme Commander Tuth. Panna and Packer awaited official word as to the end of the war.

Panna watched her husband pace, watched his eyes stare blankly out the window. Then she moved a chair closer to his. When he looked at her, she put a hand gently on the empty seat. She was oddly calm, and her gesture irresistibly inviting. He sat down beside her, and she wrapped his right arm around her own shoulders, then laid her head back on his chest. This was how they had sat together that day in the carriage when Packer had proposed marriage. It was how they often communed about things of importance, large and small. Packer felt instantly relieved, and he relaxed. He hadn't realized how tense he had been until he had a reason to let that tension go.

"You're going to Drammun."

"We have to. Don't you agree? It's the answer to our prayers."

Panna waited a few moments and then said, "Once Huk Tuth signs that parchment, I don't know how much time we'll have. I don't know how fast things will happen." Her voice was silvery and smooth, but it did not have that quicksilver, laughing quality that always reminded him of water over stones in a stream. It was the same sound, pure and true, but more melancholy now, as though the stream had grown deeper, and now moved slower.

"But this time, finally, you can come with me."

She was silent.

"It's a diplomatic mission after all," he added, expecting confirmation, "and not a battle. Besides, I'm the king. I get to decide these things now." Finally, here was some advantage to this title.

Still she was silent. She snuggled in closer. She took a deep breath, and he heard it catch. This alarmed him. "Panna? What is it?"

She waited a moment, then said, "Today when you were speaking, when word came that the Drammune were surrounding us...a messenger brought the news to General Millian. He would have stopped you. He would have sent everyone out to fight, right then."

"But you stopped him."

"Prince Ward would have gone along, too."

Packer didn't doubt it. They were both silent for a moment as each pondered what might have happened if the troops had not knelt, but rather had gone out to fight. Would the falcon have flown its message to Huk Tuth? Or would the sounds of muskets and pistols, the shouts of battle, have scared it away? They were both quite sure of the answer.

Panna sighed again. "Twice now, I have wanted nothing more in all the world than to go with you. And twice you have gone away without me."

"And twice, God has saved us both, and brought us back together."

"Yes. Now I can see the reason we had to be apart, even though I couldn't see it then. You learned to kneel and pray in the midst of battle, and to trust God for the outcome. I didn't understand until today, really, what that means. But now I do. God has been teaching you that. And he's been teaching me things. At least, He's been showing me things. I have learned...I have seen what happens when men trust only in themselves."

Her voice grew cold, remembering. "I have seen men order others around as if those people were put in the world just to serve them. Men in power acting as though the law doesn't apply to them. As though the rules of honesty and kindness exist only to help them manipulate people. I've seen powerful men kill the weak."

She looked up at him. "They kill the innocent, Packer. They kill the upright."

Packer knew of whom she spoke. "Your father was a good, good man."

She thought for a moment, looking away again. "Why would God take him? I still don't understand that. He would have been so proud of you. He could have helped us so much. The world needs men like that."

"Yes. But the world doesn't want them."

She thought about that, and knew it to be true. She thought of her father, that laughing bear of a man, and she pictured him in heaven, serving his Master, the Great High Priest of his order, never to be sad or hurt again. "But God does. God wants him." She shook her head. "And so the world is left to people like King Reynard and Prince Mather and John Hand and this Hezzan."

Packer was surprised by her tone. "But there is hope, Panna. God does work in the world. He takes away power, and gives power. He put us here. And even Mather, for all the bad things he did, repented in the end."

"'He hath put down the mighty from their seats, and exalted them of low degree,'" she quoted. Then she turned her head up toward her husband again. As he looked at her, she seemed saddened to her soul, empty, as he had seen her only twice before, each time just before he left her. "Packer," she said in a whisper, "if you leave, what good man will make the right decisions here at home? Who will protect the innocent? Who will trust God, and pray?"

"But Panna, I can't stay. You know that. The Drammune…they think I control the Firefish. I have been given this chance, this one chance to tell them, to teach them they have a Creator, and He alone controls everything, and if we'll just—"

"The Drammune are schemers, too," she interrupted, with tears spilling from her eyes. "They will deceive you if they can, Packer, the way Talon deceived me. Please, please be careful. Promise me you'll pray. Promise me you'll be careful."

Packer closed his eyes. Now, finally, he understood. "You're staying."

As she looked up at him through her own darkness she now saw the pain in him. His eyes were closed, and his face was pale. She suddenly knew how he must have felt in the Blue Rooms of the Palace, when she was sure she should go to sea with him, and he knew it could not be...or how he had felt back in her father's house on that bench, when he knew they had to part and she did not.

How terrible it was to be the one who knew.

"You are the king," she whispered. "If you order me, I will go with you. But this time, Packer, I know I need to stay. And this time I know why."

Packer, eyes still closed, now knew why as well. Who would he put in charge if both of them left, and what power would he need to leave that person? No, Panna was the queen. She would protect the helpless. She would keep the innocent out of prison and the guilty locked away, and she would act with mercy when she could.

Suddenly he felt her hand on the back of his head, then her lips on his, soft and gentle. He kissed her. And in that kiss was the sadness and the heartache and the longing that has been bound up for countless ages, deep within the fabric of the world, on the dark and dusty side of the locked gates of Eden.

Orders to the troops were simple: rest and remain quiet, and stay within the defined perimeter, the square itself and two blocks in any direction. A significant portion of the soldiers were quite content with these orders. That portion was quickly dozing on sidewalks or under porches or in the shade of the few small trees. But many others were too restless to rest. Some of these climbed buildings to get a look at the Drammune troops filling the fields, and were suitably impressed. Others pushed their way to the edge of the perimeter for the same purpose, only to be disappointed there was little to be seen. Once all the curious had their curiosity sated, the milling about became focused on the few shops here, in what after all was the main business district of the town.

All it took was a few soldiers emerging from the grocer or the miller or the chandler or the general store with a jar of preserves or a cake of honeyed oats or a sack of tea lights or a box of matches, and very quickly every store was packed, and then almost as quickly, completely cleaned out of whatever goods it stocked.

Shop owners were at first delighted, then dismayed, and then outraged, not so much by the lack of decorum but by the lack of any payment corresponding to the value of the merchandise. More than one shopkeeper waded out into the streets in a loud, complaining search for some officer who would restore order—defined as either returning merchandise or providing reasonable restitution. A third definition, less satisfactory but still acceptable, would be the arrest of the actual thieves, or short of that, any soldier who had about him or her anything that might perhaps have been inside a store at some point a very short while ago.

Captains and majors and lieutenants did their best to sort out the ensuing chaos. "Everyone was takin' stuff," these officers heard again and again from their remorseful troops. "I thought they was just givin' it all away. You know, patriotic-like." There were very few actual thieves among them, and so eventually most of the merchandise was restored, most of it mostly uneaten, unopened, or unbroken. And along with the merchandise, much, though certainly not all, of the goodwill between soldiers and shopkeepers was restored as well.

Eventually, tedium finally reigned, and troops once restless now grew listless. They dozed, played cards, and smoked and chatted, content to wait further orders. This glorious state ended abruptly when the prince and the dragoon and the little priest departed for their appointment across the field, document in hand. Everyone came awake, and the rumors started in earnest.

Some soldiers someone knew had very reliable information that the Drammune commander, a general named Hush Tuck, or possibly Hank Tush, or maybe Chuck Tooth, was coming to the square. One utterly authoritative source had it that the enemy commander would bow down to the King of the Vast and surrender unconditionally. This led to discussions about how best to colonize Drammun, and whether the Drammune should become citizens, or whether they had any beaches worth visiting, or if their ale was worth a trip across the sea. Another story, equally verifiable, said the Drammune commander would duel with Packer at swords, winner take all. This led to a discussion on the merits of broadswords versus rapiers, the inevitable conclusion being that the King of the Vast could be beaten by no one in the world, and the discussion about Drammune real estate and ale continued. A third story pooh-poohed both of those, claiming, on highly dependable information, that the Drammune general was simply being invited to have a drink and use a privy.

But regardless of which version of which rumor was heard or

repeated or believed, the stores were emptied of people, sleeping soldiers were kicked awake, some accidentally, card games were interrupted, and the population of the square swelled again with men and women on high alert, now awaiting the appearance of the notorious Drammune leader.

And sure enough, a squad of armed and armored Drammune warriors walked onto the square, led by Prince Ward and the priest and the dragoon. The foreigners eyed their gathered enemy with a great deal of animosity. In the midst of the contingent was a bent old man, thick as a tree stump, scraggly white hair visible under a crimson helmet. Four of the six Drammune warriors waited outside the tavern while the old commander and two others went in.

The Vast said not a word, but watched in fascination. The only sounds on the square were birds, the wind, and the clump and creak of the wooden porch under Drammune hobnails. And, just as Huk Tuth stepped into the tavern, one loud, long, and fertile raspberry.

Followed by gales of laughter.

Packer and Panna stood and collected themselves when they heard the silence outside and the footsteps on the worn planks approaching. Ward entered first, made sure his king and queen were prepared, then stepped aside to allow the Drammune commander to approach. Packer had explicit instructions, given by Ward before he left on this errand, not to bow or to speak, but to stand tall and await the appropriate acts of submission required of dignitaries visiting a foreign king. But the embarrassing sounds from outside drove everything from Packer's mind. He blushed and stepped forward, then bowed, saying, "You are welcome here, Supreme Commander Tuth."

Ward looked at the floor and rubbed his forehead. But when he looked up, the old warrior was bowing deeply. Ward was astonished. Apparently, the gesture from the Vast king was so generous that it left the commander little choice but to return it, and then some. Packer glanced back at Ward, not knowing what to do next.

Ward raised an open palm and shrugged. *You're on your own.*

Going on instinct and sheer fishing village etiquette, Packer walked up to Huk Tuth and extended a hand. "Glad to see you."

Tuth's own Vast was rudimentary, but he understood Packer's intent easily enough. He also recognized the gesture, the Vast sign of greeting, and of agreement between equals. Surprised but willing to go along, he put out his own hand in return. Packer took it, and shook it firmly. That bit of unpleasantness concluded, Tuth closed his fist and then rubbed his fingers with his thumb, managing to resist a strong urge to wipe his hand on his tunic. He was no Zealot, but that didn't mean he relished touching an Unworthy.

"Commander Tuth is willing to sign the document as written," Ward informed Packer, holding up the roll of parchment. "But he has a single question, which he will ask only you, and which apparently only you can answer."

Packer glanced once at Panna, who did not take her eyes off Tuth. "Tell him he may ask it," Packer said.

Tuth spoke, and Ward translated. "Your document demands agreement to details about returning your gold, and demands promises of safe passage in Hezarow Kyne, and that you be allowed to leave at any time you wish. These are foolish demands, to which I easily agree."

"Foolish?" Packer asked, not sure the translation was correct.

"*Silly* is perhaps a better word," Ward assured him, "but you get the idea."

"Why are our terms foolish?" Packer asked. Ward asked Tuth.

Tuth glanced at his translator, a lieutenant who was here to assure that the Vast cowards were not attempting deception. Then the commander shook his head. "If you think us less than honorable, why should we become honorable when words are written on a paper?"

"Your signature on that paper is a promise from you."

Tuth smirked. Then he looked as though he thought Packer a great fool. "You are a king, and yet you agree to travel to Drammun yourself."

This gave Packer a moment of misgiving. "I was named on the list sent by your Hezzan. Was I not?"

"Circumstances have made the Hezzan's terms contradictory," Tuth responded, "demanding only an emissary here, but the king by name there. Yet rather than negotiate the point, you chose to travel across the world and into the lair of your enemy to make peace. It carries with it the odor of desperation."

Packer was at a loss. He didn't need to go? He turned red.

But Panna spoke. "And what would the commander have done if the Vast had refused to send Packer Throme to Drammun?"

The Battle for Vast Dominion

As Ward translated, the old commander showed his gray teeth. "The woman does not know her place. But she knows more of diplomacy than her husband. You would have refused our terms, and I would have rained shells on your heads. And then cut your army into small chunks of salamander meat."

Packer swallowed, his embarrassment turned to anger. "What is the question you came here to ask me?" he demanded.

There was a long, silent pause during which Huk Tuth stared into Packer's eyes. It was a look as grim and deadly as any Fen Abbaka Mux had ever given him. Then the commander spoke. "Azu kark skovah Sankhar koos?"

Ward's eyes went wide. He had not been told what question Tuth would ask, and this one was dangerous, very dangerous. He looked at Packer, who waited darkly for Ward to translate. Still Ward said nothing. It would be just like Packer to speak the whole truth in answer. But any answer now except an ardent "yes" might undo everything—everything—right here at the end. There could be blood on the floor in this very room.

Ward felt suddenly parched, his throat constricted. He sucked some moisture into it and said softly, "He wants to know if you..." he glanced at Tuth's translator, knowing he couldn't shade this in any way, "he wants to know if you do in fact control the Firefish." Ward nodded slightly, eyes wide, trying to will a simple affirmative into the young king.

But Packer saw the trap clearly enough. He looked away from Ward, back to Tuth. The Drammune commander had wanted to fight rather than to treat, that was obvious all along. Tuth was looking for an excuse. At this moment, all that separated Nearing Vast from the bloody dominion of the Hezzan was Huk Tuth's belief that the Vast held the secret to dominating the Firefish. In fact, the literal translation of Tuth's question was, *Do you own the dominion of the Firefish?*

Ward was right to fear. Packer was not prepared to start lying now. He looked to Panna, who was still standing to his right. She had the same concern Ward did, the same unspoken question about what he might do. But she showed nothing but confidence in his answer. He looked at Father Mooring, who was serene as a cat on a sunny porch. Then he took the roll of parchment from Prince Ward's hand, and unrolled it. He held it up, his right hand at the top, a fist with his royal signet prominent.

"If you sign this document," he said softly to Tuth, but with great earnestness, "we will teach you all we know about Firefish, as friends. If you do not sign it," and here he rolled it back up, "then you will learn all we know about Firefish out at sea, as enemies." He stared calmly into Tuth's dark, deadly eyes, and held out the parchment to him. "You choose."

Tuth kept his eyes locked on the king's as his lieutenant translated the answer. The boy had some strength in him after all. Now in the commander's head images rose, their ship, the *Nochto Vare*, brutally, mercilessly, utterly annihilated by the beast from beneath the sea. At the beckoning of Packer Throme.

Ward could barely keep from grinning. The old tree stump could do nothing now but bow down before the green sapling.

Tuth took the document and unrolled it, then plucked the quill from an inkwell held out by his lieutenant. He scratched out his signature at the bottom. He looked at Packer one more time and said in Drammune, "Keep your salamanders away from my men, or we will skewer them and cook them for our dinner."

Tuth turned and left the tavern, followed by his entourage.

Out in the sunlight, the Vast army stopped and held its breath. On the porch of the pub Commander Tuth paused, put his hands on his hips, and stared at them all, meeting eye after eye, watching them recoil. They were such weaklings. They were such cowards. So *Unworthy*. He turned and walked away.

Behind him he heard raspberries again, this time in short bursts, in time with his every step, followed by howls of laughter.

"Storybooks," Talon said aloud. Her tone was derisive. Sool Kron sat across the table from her, deep within the Archives far beneath the palace. Lamps and candles lit the chamber, but could not ward off the chill, nor the sense of darkness barely kept at bay. Dust was heavy. Yellowed scrolls and ancient tomes sat along shelves, but on the table were only small, weathered, and aged parchments, hardly more than notebooks. "From the pens of madmen and poets," Talon concluded. In Drammun, the two words were variations on the same root, "sooma." *Insane*.

"Certainly nothing our best minds would ever study," Kron

agreed, rubbing his tired eyes. He had been poring over these tomes for hours. "But in spite of our fine show for the Court, we don't have much on which to build an industry."

She raised an eyebrow at him. After the demonstration with the hauberks, they had convinced the Twelve of the dangers of Firefish by reading from Huk Tuth's narrative, the destruction of the *Nochto Vare* and the *Rahk Thanu.* "That *show* will keep the Quarto in line for some time. Do you disagree?"

Kron was suddenly not the least bit tired. "Not at all. I was referring only to the statements I made regarding these documents."

She eyed him carefully. Yes, of course that was what he meant. Kron had then assured the Twelve that the Archives contained hidden secrets, formally deemed Unworthy, books that would be reopened so they would have their own knowledge of the Firefish, and not need to lean on the Vast.

Talon turned her eyes back to the table. It worried her, the killing of Zan Gar. Not that he didn't deserve it; he did, and all she had done was to add more drama to the moment than was customary at an execution. What worried her was that it presaged difficulties ahead. The Quarto could not be won over. She could intimidate them for a moment with shows of force, demonstrations of power. But she knew such actions would only inflame their hatred of her, drive it deeper, make them more determined to stand against her. And these four would be far more devious than the blunt and stupid Zan Gar. Perhaps they would even be as crafty as Sool Kron.

She needed to crush the Quarto. She needed the full strength of the army to do it. She needed Huk Tuth and the Glorious Drammune Military. She did not say that, however, not to Kron.

"We need the *Trophy Chase,*" she said instead. "And we need what the Vast have learned among the Achawuk."

"Yes, and most particularly, we need this Packer Throme," Kron added, glad to have skirted his mistress's ire. His finger ran down the page of a pamphlet in front of him, and he missed the flash of her eyes at the mention of that name. "He seems to have pulled all these strands into a single braid. Here, let me read this—" and he turned the pamphlet to its cover, "from something called 'Savage Religion,' a document officially deemed Unworthy over one hundred years ago. It was written by we know not whom, but the man claims to have traveled among the Achawuk." He flipped back to where he had been reading. "Here's what the madman says:

"'These people worship not the monster, though they paint the monster's image everywhere. Skin and bones and teeth adorn every home and every structure. Their god is a flow of water, an invisible fluid coursing through every living thing, giving life and energy, making alive the currents of the sea, and the currents of the air, and the soil deep under the earth, finding its highest form in two equal, opposite incarnations...' then he goes on and on about the meaning of the term *incarnation*, and here he concludes, 'the equal incarnations are monster and man.'" Kron looked up at Talon. "How would you interpret that?"

She shrugged. "They worship the forces of nature, which they visualize as a river. The two highest forms of this force are man, and Firefish."

"So I would read it, too. But there's more here than just nature, it would seem. It's nature as a sentient being, an intelligence."

"A god."

"One with a purpose." He ran a long, yellow fingernail along the document and read again. "'The river is leading to an ending. A great catastrophe will bring a new world, where all shall live in peace. They call this 'tannan-thoh-ah.'"

"Which, the catastrophe, or the peace afterward?"

He shook his head. "The term seems to apply to both. Whatever it is, it's the end of the world. And there's this..." He found a line. "'When the tannan-thoh-ah comes, man shall become the glory of the beast.'" He sat silently for a moment, eyes racing back and forth on the single line. "I do not know what that means."

But she was thinking about something else. "Let me read."

He handed the pamphlet to her. She went back, found what she was looking for. "'They paint the monster's image everywhere. Skin and bones and teeth adorn every home and every structure.'" She went silent.

"What is it?"

"Do you suppose this means they paint the image of skin and bones and teeth everywhere?"

"That is what it says. Is it not?"

"But how does one draw an image of skin?"

"I don't understand..."

She read it silently again. "What if this writer is saying that the monster's image is painted everywhere, *and* its skin and bones and teeth adorn every structure?"

Kron nodded. "Pictures everywhere, but also armor in abundance, covering every building. The place would be indestructible—and as valuable as solid gold."

She nodded. "If that were so, then these savages kill Firefish. Lots of them."

"And they've been doing it for a very long time. But can they tame them?"

Talon shook her head. Then she tossed the pamphlet back onto the pile. "We don't even know if these are the words of a scholar or of a lunatic."

"There is but one way to find out."

She stared at her chief minister. Then she nodded. "Prepare the ships."

CHAPTER 7

The Crown

Without fanfare and with little delay, the Drammune army marched toward the shore, where their tenders would begin shuttling them back to their ships. Packer had taken the words of Huk Tuth seriously, and gave orders to his own army that the Drammune were to be given wide berth. There were few incidents, and most of them involved citizens hurling stones or bones or eggs or epithets from upper-story windows down onto the receding red tide of warriors.

The war over, Ward sat in cool darkness, contemplating the full mug before him. This had been a long time coming. He had not yet tasted the blissful liquid within it, but he could smell it. He could feel it. His belly burned with warmth just looking at it. Still, he resisted, savoring the anticipation. This was a familiar place, territory he knew. This was home.

He had watched the king and queen ride away, trailing streams of splendor—the horde that was now the Vast Army. They were a ragtag bunch, and growing worse. Uniforms had become a badge of dishonor. Ill-fitting Drammune helmets and vests were the new insignia of honor, and they adorned both men and women, old and young. All the military regimens with which Ward was so accustomed, and to which he had always been attracted, had vanished overnight.

The little group of counselors left in that pitiful wake suddenly seemed to Ward to have absolutely nothing in common with one another. Millian and Jameson seemed to have left military thinking behind. Bran Mooring was his usual beatific self, and therefore unapproachable. Dog was surly and uncomfortable when he finally returned from his stitchings. They had nothing to say to one another. Everyone seemed to feel it. No one quite knew who, if anyone, should take the lead. At least that's what he told himself. It wasn't quite true, however. The fact was, the others immediately looked to Ward. And he just as immediately bowed out.

So Ward had taken a walk, looking for just such a spot. It was a short walk. This little dark dive seemed a perfect spot for thinking, and for not being found. There were only two other customers here now, a couple seated at a table across the small room, talking in low voices.

Now Ward turned the earthen mug around, just to look at it from all angles, and to feel the condensation on its sides. The liquid was quite cool. The head of light brown foam was slowly sinking, concave now across the top. It would be wonderful.

His problem was not with his fellow counselors, all of whom seemed fair-minded and decent men. The problem was that Ward could not shed this new feeling that the king's reign was going to end in disaster. Of course, it had already lasted three times as long as the last king's reign. Mather would forever provide the prime example of royal disasters in all of Vast history, surpassing in a flash even the tarnished legacy of the man he had replaced. But Ward had had nothing to do with Mather's ascent, or his demise. And Ward had had everything to do with this new king's fortunes. And so when Packer's royal ambitions and most likely his life were snuffed out, which the Drammune would inevitably do as soon he preached his version of the gospel on shores where no Vast uprising could save him, then Packer's demise would be Ward's legacy.

For a man who fled from responsibility as though it chased him foaming at the mouth and barking, this was an enormous weight. In contrast, the mug in his hand was light as a feather. He picked it up and poured a great, cool, drenching torrent down his throat, swallowing four times.

Aaah! Ward licked his lips, savoring every ounce of the flavor. The mug was half empty. That was a sad sight, as he had promised himself he would drink only one. But already, as he felt the liquid in his belly, warm and safe and comforting, he wondered why he would make such a promise to himself.

Packer had foretold his own doom. Ward had heard it. The king had said he would go teach the Drammune how the Firefish were controlled. *But you said you don't know how you controlled that beast at sea,* Ward had protested there in the pub, around that table where the king and his counselors debated policy and the strategies of peace. *I didn't control it. God did that.* Packer had stared into Ward's eyes while the prince had grappled unsuccessfully with this explanation. Then Packer explained: *I will go teach the Drammune about their Creator, the one who does control the beasts.*

So that was the plan. Convert the Drammune.

It was absurd. Not only would they not convert, they would be deeply insulted. Packer Throme, the Boy-King, Premier of the Pawns, coming to Drammun to speak out against the Rahk-Taa? A salamander trying to convert the Hezzan from the most ancient beliefs of the Drammune? It would have been laughable if it weren't so utterly hopeless.

But what could be said against such a plan now, now that the king, defying logic and deifying lunacy, had gotten his miracle? In such a kingdom, words of common sense were nonsense, or worse. They were faithless. Maybe heretical. The world had been turned upside down. He closed his eyes and raised his ale again. Maybe if he turned his mug upside down enough times, it would all make sense. It was worth a try.

But the mug did not reach his lips. Something tugged at his sleeve. Ward jerked involuntarily, almost sloshing the ale onto the table. A figure loomed over him, dark under a heavy hood.

"Excuse me," a soothing voice said from within that darkness. "I didn't mean to startle you."

"No?" Ward asked in something short of his usual good manners, his heart still pounding. "Too bad. I could have complimented your success."

"Terribly sorry. It's just that I just couldn't help but notice you were drinking alone, and I felt this was somehow not right for one of your...stature. So I thought you might like company."

"Who are you?" Ward said, squinting. He could now make out the wrinkled flesh within the circumference of the hood.

"My name is Usher Fell. Father Usher Fell, Elder of the Seminary of Mann."

Ward took a deep breath. Another cleric to show him the pathway

to God. *Sure, why not?* "If you're drinking, you're welcome here."
Here at least was a good excuse to have that second ale. "Sit down.
Have a pint."

It was a bittersweet tour. Neither Packer nor Panna were in a hurry,
feeling that every moment they had together should be savored. The
king and queen walked through the huge building, now their home,
with a gaggle of servants in attendance, all of whom had rushed back
as soon as the news made it to them. Which was, of course, almost
instantly. Stave Deroy was here as well, ever watchful, unsure what
ill intent might hide in the hearts of old men and women and young
servant girls.

Packer absorbed it all, memorizing, wanting to be able to picture
Panna in each room as he thought of her over the days and weeks
to come. He asked many questions. He wanted to know what would
happen where, when, and who would be involved.

Panna answered carefully, with only occasional help from the servants. It allowed her to imagine herself in charge, making these decisions. The conference rooms, the suites for royal visitors, the counsel
chambers, the courts where the people's petitions were heard by
judges, then appealed to the Crown...all of these were known to
Panna, but she had never thought about them except in terms of
distant processes of government. Now she had to think about them
as responsibilities, her own responsibilities. And the burden seemed
unbearable. By the time they finished the tour, the two were side by
side, hand in hand, painfully aware of the enormous gap between
their own experience and what was required to manage a palace, a
city, and a kingdom.

More than once, each of them wished that Packer were staying.
Together, it seemed as though it might be possible to learn all this,
to become comfortable with the complexities and the uncertainties
of government. By herself, though, it seemed overwhelming, and
Packer sensed it. More than once, each of them wondered where
Prince Ward had gone. As long as he was here, so long as he would
counsel them, there would be at least one person who truly knew
how to navigate these waters.

But countering the royal couple's grave trepidation at running
the machinery of government was the warmth that now filled the
place, flowing from the household staff. Panna had started her tour

by guaranteeing employment to all those who wanted it—even those who were uncertain about this stark change in the occupants of the palace. Several of the younger housemaids and servants, particularly those who had been so skittish with her when she had been confined here, confessed they had secretly been proud of the way she had stood up to Prince Mather. They had simply been too afraid to let any of that be known. The older servants likewise let down their guard and dared to tell both Packer and Panna how difficult life had been under the Sennetts, how Panna had been a fresh breeze through the place.

"Oh, child…rather, Your Highness," said Millie Milder, the elderly maid who managed the household chores, "how bad we all felt for the way you both were treated. How we prayed for a miracle. And when you broke His Highness's nose, we just praised God." Her gentle eyes twinkled.

Any heartfelt emotion put the cold marble and polished brass, the high arched windows and thick woven rugs, in a very different light. Neither Packer nor Panna had many pleasant memories to associate with these walls, but now they saw that it was, in fact, a beautiful place. And if it could be a source of light for the entire kingdom, a hearth from which justice and rightness warmed the nation, the pot-bellied stove of the kingdom, then there truly might be hope for a new era.

Then they entered the throne room. The servants all held back, refusing to cross the threshold. Packer and Panna walked in gingerly, hands clasped. It was not an enormous room, though the high, vaulted ceiling, the pure white walls, and the polished white oak floors made it feel spacious, even cavernous. The king's chair, however, actually was enormous. It was velvet-covered and sat on a single-stepped white-marble dais. The seat cushion was deeply dented, as though Reynard had just this moment stood up from it and walked away.

Beside the throne was a glass-fronted cabinet. Within the cabinet was the king's crown, a heavy, jeweled circle of gold. Beside it was a scepter, three-and-a-half-feet long, flared and fluted at the top where was set a single blue sapphire the size of a ripe plum. Beside the scepter was the queen's crown, smaller, narrower, but also jewel-encrusted gold.

Packer looked around for a few moments, not venturing closer.

This room felt like a museum to him. The royal jewels seemed like ancient artifacts, strange emblems from some distant past. They carried history and weight, and he knew that they were immensely valuable, both monetarily and in the power of their symbolism. But none of that connected, in his mind or in his heart, with leading the people he knew. He turned and looked at Panna.

And at that moment Panna saw something in Packer she had never seen before. She saw now a man every bit as big as the priceless pieces in this room. She saw a heart that was bigger than all this, that found meaning in things far higher, more noble. She saw, for the first time, a king.

She squeezed his hand, and then they turned and walked together out of the room.

Prince Ward looked hard at the craggy old man across the table from him. "You look familiar," he said. Actually, it wasn't Usher Fell's appearance that triggered Ward's memory as much as it was the voice. Or maybe it was the aura that surrounded him. Regardless, Ward couldn't place him.

"You took lessons with me once, many years ago. Theology."

Ward shook his head, still not remembering. This man was not one of his teachers. He remembered all of those quite distinctly; each name and face always came to his mind with a gauge, a ranking based on how thoroughly he had abused them, how thoroughly he had disappointed them. Usher Fell was not among that honorable, dishonored brigade.

"Father Stube was ill," the priest said, looking through yellowed eyes that hovered above sagging lower lids. "Dyspepsia. I filled in for two class sessions."

Now the memory came back. "You let me off taking an exam," Ward nodded. And the aura of the man returned. He'd had a tender look and kind words that somehow created dark misgivings in the young prince.

"I did just that," Father Fell nodded, appreciating that he was recalled. His voice grew more melodious. "Though it was only a quiz."

"Still," Ward answered, "that happened rarely in my academic career."

"I felt you had earned it," the old priest explained. But before he could elaborate the barmaid brought him his own pint. "To your royal youth," Father Fell offered.

Ward nodded. "Cheers," he said simply.

"I have followed the events of the past days with great interest," the priest began when he had wiped his mouth. "As have all those in your kingdom."

"Not my kingdom," Ward corrected.

"So it would seem. A very unselfish move, which many would applaud."

"So it would seem," Ward echoed, taking a short sip. The two men looked at each other until Ward dropped his eyes to his mug. Then he raised them again to search Father Fell's face. "Who, by the way, would *not* applaud?"

Father Fell gave Ward an appreciative look. The prince may have been a poor student, but he was not without intelligence. "There are a few of us who believe that the divine right of kings should not be usurped by mere men. Theology." He waved his hand dismissively.

"Usurped? Packer Throme usurped nothing. This was thrust on him."

"Oh, I did not mean to imply that. I'm sure that's quite true. The usurper would be the one who chose instead."

Ward's throat went dry. "You accuse my brother?"

Father Fell laughed easily. "This is not an accusation, my dear Prince. It is a theoretical discussion. But let's look at it, since you're interested. God chooses kings through family lines. This has ever been the case, both in Scripture and in our own humble practice in this poor kingdom. There are exceptions, of course. King David, notably. But those exceptions were accompanied by the clear voice of God speaking through His prophet, as He did with Samuel. Perhaps I simply wasn't close enough to the current situation, but it seemed that your brother's rash act could have been, should have been, undone. Packer Throme sought to relinquish what he knew in his heart was not his to take. And yet the crown was thrust upon him anyway."

The aura of Father Fell now engulfed the prince like a shadow. He remembered it fully. The smooth voice dragging him down into some hidden, shameful wellspring deep within. "You're talking about me. You're saying I did this selfishly."

"I wasn't there. And I can't pretend to know your motives."

Ward went dry as dust. He poured ale into his parched mouth and swallowed it, with no appreciable relief. So he did it again.

Father Fell leaned in. "I do not mean to trouble you. I am one who would always give you a pass on difficult tests, were it in my power. I am a simple clergyman and only mean to speak what is in my heart, praying it will help guide you aright."

Ward didn't know what was in Usher Fell's heart. He barely knew what was in his own. But whatever shred of understanding he did have told him that this old man's message meshed seamlessly with his own strong foreboding that Packer's reign would end in disaster. It also told him precisely why he preferred to drink with military men.

"You have been told by others that you did an unselfish thing," Usher Fell continued, driving deeper into that vulnerable place he now saw as clearly as an archer sees a bull's-eye. "But 'the fining pot for silver, and the furnace for gold; so is a man to his praise.'"

"Sorry, I have no idea what that means."

"It means that a man is tested by the praise he receives. A slathering of flattery produces either a puffed-up sense of self, or a melancholy sense of remorse."

Ward's eyes dropped to the tabletop.

"And I see in you the latter. You feel in your heart that what you did was not unselfish." Now the priest's smooth voice was a mellifluous, penetrating instrument, a device both musical and surgical. "You feel something within that whispers to you, saying you did not act to save your nation, but to protect yourself. To hide from your responsibilities."

Ward's eyes were withdrawn and distant. He was listening, and as he listened he looked deep within and found only a vacuum. It was as though all his thoughts were being pulled into that vortex, which led down into the seat of his greatest fears about his own nature.

Usher Fell continued. "What does it mean to act unselfishly? Does it not mean to bow to the will of God and the laws of man? To allow one's own shortcomings to be tested in the light, to be burned away in the fiery furnace of trials, trials which one was born to bear? To humble oneself before God and man and accept the mantle of responsibility, knowing the Almighty works His will through the institutions He has established on earth? Would not this be truly unselfish?"

Ward's eyes were closed as he took these arrows to his heart.

Usher Fell continued to fire his darts. "Selfishness on the other hand, wraps itself in its own fears and protects itself in dark places, soothing itself as best it can…in dark places such as this, perhaps."

Ward came back to the moment, and looked at his mug of ale. It had lost its allure. Life was so much simpler when the will of God was not a part of it. He thought about Packer speaking from the top of the general store about what God could do, and would do. He wondered what it would be like to have that kind of faith. And then that thought startled him awake. "Wait, though," he said to Usher Fell. "Packer Throme is clearly God's man of the hour. Don't you think? I mean, surely you saw what happened today. What happened three days ago on the Green."

"A man with sensitivities to divine leading is a rare man," Usher Fell said, as though he were agreeing. "And yet God's ways, while mysterious, are not impossible to understand. One must study His mysteries, drink deeply of them. Packer Throme was unable to do that. He did not complete his studies at the seminary. He barely began them. Did you know that? He was released from the Seminary of Mann because he insisted on taking his own path, refused to submit to God. In fact, he was defiant in the face of Church discipline."

"I heard he was expelled," Ward said, trying to make it sound like this was just another conversation over a mug of ale. "I never knew why."

"But I can tell you precisely why." The priest hesitated for full effect and then began the tale. "Packer Throme came to the Seminary of Mann hungry to make himself great. He understood the words of Christ, that the greatest are those who serve. This was his motivation for entering the priesthood. He was looking for a path to greatness. But the path of humility was not one he could walk. He would not submit. And as his life has proven from that day to this, he is a man of action, taking what he wants."

"But surely there was some offense? This wasn't a summary judgment against the true nature of his soul."

"Of course. He attacked a priest. An old man who had no hope of defending himself. And he did that in order to divert attention from his own sins. He had conspired to cheat on an exam. Again, unable to accept that he was unprepared, unable to humble himself."

"He hit a priest?" Ward suppressed a smile. That took some gall.

"He hit me."

Ward's amusement vanished.

"I found him out, you see, and cornered him. He had conspired with another student. The other student had a young wife who worked at the seminary as a cleaning woman. This is not unusual. She entered my cottage to clean it. Or so she said. I returned unexpectedly, and found her writing down the answers to the next day's test. Packer Throme was the lookout, and when he saw me enter my own cottage and heard me accusing her, he rushed in. From there, it got very ugly. But suffice it to say that rather than submit and repent, he struck me, once, in the jaw. He knocked me unconscious. To this day he has not shown remorse for his deed."

Ward looked at his mug, shaking his head. It was hard to believe. In fact, it was almost impossible to believe. And yet, Packer had certainly been expelled for something. "I think he's softened quite a bit in that regard," Ward suggested. "I don't find him ambitious in the least. In fact, I believe he would give up the crown in a moment, if I asked him."

"That would be good news," Usher Fell assured him. "Very good news indeed. I wonder, though, should he not prove so flexible, what you will do?"

"What do you mean?"

"What role might you play? What career might you choose for yourself?"

"Career?"

Furrows appeared on Father Fell's forehead. "I mean, should things stand as they are, what would you do, no longer being a prince?"

"No longer being..."

Father Fell's look was sad and cruel at the same time. "You are a Sennett, my dear man." Fell was the essence of patience. "Today you are no more a prince than your father is a king."

Ward took another long pull, but again paid the ale little mind.

"However, things need not stand as they are," Usher Fell confided. "All can be made right, with God's help."

Ward closed his eyes. Darkness was falling. The ale felt warm within him. He had been hiding, he knew that. He had been fleeing. He had turned the kingdom over to Packer Throme out of fear, not

The Battle for Vast Dominion

out of righteousness or selflessness. All these things were true. As the ale went to his head, a sense of familiarity, of comfort within the darkness fell over him.

He felt as though he were coming awake after a long, strange dream.

CHAPTER 8

The Flotilla

Though the *Trophy Chase* and her crew were unaware of the events ashore, their ignorance fell somewhat short of bliss. They prepared for war. But as battle formations go, theirs was not among the most threatening in the history of Vast naval engagements.

Their decorated admiral, John Hand, had entertained visions of turning these merchant ships into a small, agile squadron that could appear and disappear quickly, strike and retreat, led by the nimblest, quickest ship ever built. Over the last few days such visions had drained away like a keg of bad cider, leaving nothing but a bellyache and a bad stench. He could neither coerce nor cajole his little flotilla of ships into any type of synchronized action, much less a coordinated attack. So he came up with a new strategy: give up trying.

Instead of predators on the prowl, his ships would float like carved and painted ducks, decoys awaiting the Drammune. With a day or two of hard work, the *Chase* sailing back and forth madly, John Hand pacing her quarterdeck, fuming and cursing, his flagman sending signals until his arms ached, the trap was finally set. The Vast ships were positioned in an enormous U-shape, several thousand yards across, and double that distance from top to bottom. If they would but stay put and maintain a relative distance from one another, Hand could sail the *Chase* in search of the Drammune Armada, bait a ship or two, and lure them back within the U. Then, with fortitude and daring and a whole lot of luck, several ships of his hapless Fleet might manage to close in and do some damage.

This strategy had some strengths, and it had some weaknesses.

Among its strengths, standing orders were very simple: Sit and wait. Then, attack any Drammune warship that ventured inside the trap. Another positive: It also required that Hand's captains do nothing much that resembled skillful sailing. They needed only to heave to, matching just the right amount of canvas to the wind so as to minimize drift, and await the enemy.

Among its weaknesses, however, these captains were now expected to follow specific orders over a very long stretch of time. They were doing their level best to adopt a military mind-set, their admiral firmly believed, but such discipline did not come easily to Vast merchant captains. Careful analysis, decisive action! These were the hallmarks of command, the form and substance of a captain's pedigree. Blind obedience? That was for deckhands. Their admiral had put the utterly competent captain of the *Marchessa*, Moore Davies, firmly in command, but once the *Trophy Chase* disappeared over the northern horizon to range the seas, perhaps as far as the mouth of the Bay of Mann, there was no telling what might happen.

The other key weakness was that if the trap worked, his ships would, eventually, need to close in on an enemy. They would need to aim and fire their guns. Admiral Hand would not allow himself to imagine the heights of ineptitude that might be scaled when all his captains decided at once to move in, each taking his own tack toward eternal glory. So instead he worried, even as he sailed away, that those captains of more independent spirit were already planning to sail after Drammune warships themselves. And he worried about the distinct possibility that his little flotilla would be discovered and attacked in force while he was gone.

And that was in fact what happened.

It took the *Chase* twelve hours to find suitable quarry, a red-sailed vessel poking around the seas just off Hangman's Cliffs, well out of any formation, far from its Armada. The *Hezza Charn* was a small ship, and even though its name translated as *Firepower*, it was not built for fighting. John Hand knew instantly by her keel and her beam and her waterline that this was a scout ship, quick and light, built for reconnaissance.

He was not pleased. He could certainly lure the thing into his trap, but he doubted any ship but the *Chase* herself would catch her. Still, the thing was Drammune, and like a mother lion teaching her young to hunt, he felt a strong pull to take this prize back to his flotilla. Owning the weather gauge, he gave orders to fly into cannon range, fire, and flee.

But before his cannon could take the measure of his adversary, the flag of truce unfurled above the *Hezza Charn*'s mainmast, a gray silk triangle with a long, whipping tail that was unmistakable at almost any distance. Not only the admiral, but the officers and crew watched it undulate lazily above those blood-red sails, astonished. The Drammune at war, wanting parley? In all the history of naval warfare John Hand had ever heard, experienced, studied, or taught, he could not remember a single time when the Drammune had initiated a truce on open sea in time of war. They were known to honor white flags offered by their adversaries, though they distrusted the practice entirely, believing it a ruse ten times out of eleven. But to unfurl it first? That was considered Unworthy.

The deception of Scat Wilkins was still fresh in every crewman's mind, and the rain of Drammune grappling hooks raw in every memory, but John Hand was more dumbfounded than suspicious. He sailed his vessel within hailing distance.

Stil Meander, the bosun with the booming voice, shouted, "Do you surrender?"

"No, truce!" came the reply in broken Vast. "Orders peace!" The Drammune sailors lined the gunwales, watching impassively, as though those words were comprehensible.

The admiral exchanged glances with his first mate, the unflappable Andrew Haas. Then he ordered Stil to try again.

"Do...you...surrender?"

"Cannon no, ship yes!" came the call in return. "Shoot now stop not!"

Hand sighed. "Let me have a try." He didn't have the vocal pipes of Stil Meander or even Andrew Haas, but he had the vocabulary. He took a deep breath.

"Azu enahai?"

"Nagh!" Came the answer back. "Zai karchezz sko tachtai Drammun!"

John Hand stared hard at the ship. Waves slapped gently against the glittering scale-covered hull of the *Trophy Chase*. The men looked down from the rigging, up from the decks, waiting. "Lower the boat," the admiral said simply. "It's a parley."

"But what did he say, Admiral?" Andrew Haas implored.

"He says we're no longer at war."

"Now what?" Delaney asked no one in particular. Mutter Cabe and Marcus Pile were both within earshot, one on either side of him. The three stood in a row, perched like seagulls on the standing rigging along the foresail yard, the breeze rustling their clothing like flags, cutting through their hair, blowing Marcus's mop like dandelion seeds.

Mutter's bald head felt no disturbance, but his distressed look darkened further as he watched the admiral bobbing in the tiny shallop, two oarsmen sculling it into the shadow of the enemy craft. "No good will come of this," was all he said.

"This is a strange one," Delaney agreed. He didn't need to elaborate. Mutter and Marcus and every other sailor aboard understood instantly.

"Aye," Mutter responded. "Strange and evil."

"Not evil," Marcus corrected. "Just...odd."

They were talking about the voyage. It had gone bad from the beginning. Ever since they had shoved off from the docks of Mann in such a hurry, everything had seemed askew. The crew had fumbled for lines, misheard orders, and then almost run the *Chase*'s prow into a ship at anchor in the bay. A ship called *The Omen,* no less. Then there was the flotilla's complete incompetence, running aground, catching fire. No one ever felt at ease. Everything was harder than it should be. The porridge was rancid. Stitch Doreo, the surgeon, was ill with the ague. Even the *Trophy Chase,* the great cat, was not herself. She moved like lightning and leaped like no ship has a right to leap, but to veterans of her decks she seemed agitated, nervous, hard to control. The more superstitious among them, Mutter Cabe at the fore, believed her heart just wasn't in it.

"This ship wants that boy." It was not the first time Mutter had said those words. "Whatever spirit is in him, breathed by a witch or breathed by God Hisself, that's what she's missing."

Marcus swallowed hard and Delaney rolled his eyes. "Looky here, Mutter," Delaney said flatly. "You need to read your Scriptures more and your tea leaves less. Some prophet or apostle is always goin' on about how no stick a' wood carved by the hand a' man has life nor spirit in her." His brow furrowed. "I mean, in *it*."

"This ship," Mutter answered as though from far away, "misses Packer Throme."

Delaney shook his head, unconvinced. "He's just a regular man, Mutter. Sure, he learned some things when he went off to senem…to sermer…to priest school—"

"Sermonary," Marcus offered helpfully.

Delaney's brow furrowed. "You sure that's the word?"

"Aye, it is." Marcus looked hurt. "Sermonary. Where you learn to preach sermons."

Delaney nodded, convinced. "Anyhow, I don't think it's the ship that misses Packer. It's just all of us."

Mutter shook his head, watching the Admiral of the Fleet climb a rope ladder onto a foreign vessel. Just then a gust of wind slapped the sails of the *Hezza Charn*, and Admiral Hand's foot slipped. He held on tight, but his shoulder jammed against the red hull. Then the same gust rocked the *Chase*, and each sailor in the rigging tensed, gripping lines more tightly. Marcus hugged the yardarm in front of him.

"Tell me that was just all us, missing Packer," Mutter concluded, his eyes narrowed.

From far below the waves, from a darkness so deep that daylight was but a faint bluish glow high above, the Firefish came flying. It was alone. It was angry. And it was hungry. It spotted this pack of surface creatures, storm creatures like Deep Fin, and a strong pang shot through it. Coals now flared up, fire coalescing into memories. The longing returned, the pain of being left behind, watching at the high shallows, waiting at the shore. Hunger and longing merged. It watched, it circled.

But the Deep Fin was not among these.

Anger burned hot. It wanted to attack. But its instincts would not let it. These creatures behaved oddly. They banded together, but they did not move in a pack. They fanned out. They sat still.

The beast had no reference for this behavior, no point of comparison. Storm creatures were predators, and yet this behavior was not predatory. No pack gathered in a circle and then remained there, docile. The feel of them was not at all fierce. Not like the great pack that had chased the Deep Fin. Nothing like Deep Fin itself.

And yet their behavior was not like prey, either. A school of fish would travel together, tightly grouped for safety, always moving, ever ready to disperse, to flee. Rays would hide themselves for protection. But this group did neither. It sat, each distant from one another, too distant to aid. Never hurried. This had no precedent in the beast's mind. If it could have known about land creatures, it might have compared such activity to a herd, grazing. But as it was, the Firefish could not comprehend.

Was this a predatory arrangement, or was it merely an inconsequential grouping?

The same question had already formed in Moore Davies' mind. He would learn the answer soon enough. The flotilla's glorious flagship had been absent just over twenty-four hours when Drammune sails began appearing on the horizon to the northeast. Remarkably, the Vast ships were holding something close to the formation in which their admiral had left them. The more outspoken captains, conferring by signal flag, had decided to give John Hand's plan a day or two's test, to see what might develop. The U was a bit skewed now, as though italicized, and the spacing was not what it once was, with larger gaps here and smaller ones there, but it was still recognizable and it still opened to the north, and the *Marchessa* still held point on the upper right-hand extremity.

Captain Davies heard the shout from the crow's nest. "One, two, three, four...seven ships in all! Sailing abreast, from the nor'east!" It was high noon and the weather was clear, with a light breeze steady from the southeast. Every sailor understood that these ships were sailing across the wind, approaching at maximum speed. To escape, they would all need to turn and run the same direction.

"Signal the others," Davies ordered his flagman. "Seven Drammune warships, northeast! Stand by for orders!" He had fifteen ships against their seven, but Davies found no comfort in the math. At seven abreast, the enemy formation was almost as wide as his own fleet's. Worse, the Drammune weren't headed into the mouth of the U. The *Marchessa* and the two ships just south, *Gant Marie* and *Forcible,* would take the brunt of the attack, three against seven. Three

Vast merchants against seven Drammune warships. They would over-whelm the trap. Like pouring water from a bucket into a shot glass.

As signal flags flashed and word passed from ship to ship down the line and around the horn, Davies considered his options. Finally he decided on the only prudent course of action. He would collapse the U, and order all the ships in the right-hand arm, the entire right flank, to turn and run to the west. Let the Drammune give chase until the sides were more equally matched. Once the fleeing ships passed those waiting to fight, they could turn and fight also.

Davies prepared to give orders. But he paused. It was a complex set of instructions for this lot, and he needed to get the wording right. If he began with "Flee..." they might not wait for the rest of the message. "Front line ships sail to the rear," was obvious and simple, but he was not sure his captains would know whether they were, in fact, front line or rear. At the moment they all faced away from their attackers. So he decided he'd better order them by name.

He began the message, his flagman's arms spelling it out as quickly as possible: "*Gant Marie, Forcible, Blunderbuss...*" fate would have it that his slowest ship was among these, he thought, "...*Wellspring, Windward...*" and here he wondered, not for the first time, what idiot ship owner would name a vessel after a common sailing term, begging for a lifetime of confusion, "...*Gasparella...*" he felt himself starting to sweat; this was a long message already, and no orders had yet been conveyed, "sail west past the far line of our ships, then come about. All others, stand and fight!"

But his message was sent to no avail.

The orders were indeed a long time getting to the point, but even had they been concise, they would have been useless. The final phrase of Davies' very first message, given upon sighting the Dram-mune, had been dropped by *Gant Marie,* just one ship away. What she passed down the line left an ellipsis where "Stand by for orders" should have been. The result was that bold sea captains did what bold sea captains do. They analyzed the situation and took decisive action.

Anticipating orders, or courageously acting in a warlike response or, in the case of *Blunderbuss,* simply maneuvering for a better view, all the ships on the eastern perimeter began turning toward their attackers. This motion not only broke ranks, it focused them on the fight, and not on their commander. Davies' second communication did not make a clean hop from ship to ship to ship. It did not make it around the horn. In fact, it did not make it past the gunwales of the *Marchessa*.

Unheeding of anything but the fight at hand, Vast sailors went scurrying to battle stations. They manned cannon, measured and poured powder, loaded and tamped cannonballs. They locked in headings and freed yard upon yard of sailcloth. All the ships in the Fleet, not just those on the right flank but the entire formation, now either sailed toward the point of attack, or turned slowly, coming about, intending to do the same.

As the formation dissolved, Moore Davies stood in awe. He shook his head, wafted on tidal waves of sheer, stupefied disbelief. Every captain of every ship, the entire Vast Navy, such as it was, had just reacted to its commander's direct orders by doing precisely the opposite.

"What now, Captain?" his first mate asked.

Davies pulled absently at his beard as he scanned the seas. The set of the impending battle was wholly against him, and wholly out of his control. The *Marchessa* was flying west, away from the attackers, but she was the only one. Just south of him the *Gant Marie* had turned almost ninety degrees clockwise already so her prow faced north-northwest. *Forcible* was almost all the way about, the needle of her bowsprit now pointing due north. *Blunderbuss* had, for reasons known but to God, turned counterclockwise, into the wind rather than away from it. She was now facing south, the wind at her prow. She was in irons. Dead in the water.

Davies estimated that with the speed at which the Drammune were closing, they would be firing on *Gant Marie* within five minutes, *Blunderbuss* in no more than ten. He shook his head once more. If he repeated his orders, requiring yet another maneuver, the Drammune would certainly run up on them all mid-turn. They might yet anyway. But who was he kidding, thinking they'd bother to obey orders now?

Moore Davies was not a man prone to mood swings. He swore seldom, and was known to keep his head in the highest seas, the heaviest weather, the fiercest fight. But right now he hovered on the edge of an angry outburst. He mastered that urge, took a deep breath, exhaled through his nose. And then he said, reluctantly but resolutely, "Come about, boys. We'll be needing battle stations."

The Drammune warships approached like a jagged row of bloody teeth. Their triangular red sails were full, their heading direct and unswerving. Their military precision alone was enough to intimidate the Vast Fleet seamen, who now saw, and with utter clarity, what John Hand had tried to teach them. Sailing side by side in a straight line was not silly at all. Not the way the Drammune did it.

Pulses raced. Palms sweated. Knees wobbled.

But resolve did not. Fifteen ships of widely varying sizes, shapes, speeds, and capabilities, similar only in that their square sails were as white as their crews' knuckles, now sailed or attempted to sail directly into the blood-red maw of highly regimented destruction.

"Hold steady, men," or similar orders, were given by every Vast captain. Oaths were sworn. Prayers were prayed. Muskets and cannons were inspected. Stomachs were emptied. Breeches were filled.

And then, much too early, shots were fired. The Vast crews, too raw and too undisciplined and ultimately too afraid to await their orders, opened up with all they had.

"We should see them by now," John Hand told his gruff new Drammune allies.

He stood on the quarterdeck of the *Chase*, telescope scanning the horizon ahead. He was being watched by two Drammune naval officers in full-dress uniforms flanking him, behind. Neither man so much as grunted. One turned, using his own telescope to confirm that the *Hezza Charn* was still in sight. It was, just as Admiral Hand had promised. It was far back in the haze of the horizon, but it was visible.

Under their captain's orders, the crew of the *Trophy Chase* now held the great ship in check, tightly reined. But she longed to run ahead, more restless than ever. The parley had been a study in frustration. The *Charn*'s captain, Tchorga Den, had been tight-lipped even by Drammune standards. He had showed Hand his orders, and a hastily scrawled parchment with the Vast royal seal, confirming the end of hostilities and the requirement for the *Trophy Chase* to return to Mann immediately. If the Drammune captain knew more details, he wasn't telling.

John Hand studied the parchment carefully, looking for any trace of forgery or deception. He could find none. And the message was signed by General Mack Millian. It got tense for a moment when the Vast admiral refused to return to Mann without his flotilla, but it was Tchorga Den who offered this compromise: The *Chase* and the *Hezza Charn* would together sail back for the Vast flotilla. These two armed Drammune officers would be welcomed aboard the *Chase* as guests. Friendly reminders to the admiral of his promises.

But to the *Chase*'s commander, every minute now felt like an hour, and every hour like an open grave. Tchorga Den had alluded to another flotilla, this one of Drammune ships, that had set sail on a heading that would lead them straight to the Vast. The disaster that loomed should those two squadrons meet…the military machine against merchant mariners with no Drammune language skills, no understanding of battle. He worried that none but Moore Davies would even recognize a Drammune flag of truce.

And sailing with the Drammune had slowed the *Chase* dramatically. Hand could have sailed directly to them, or nearly so, some twenty-five degrees from the headwind. But that angle could not be matched by the *Hezza Charn*. It would put the Drammune ship in irons. So the admiral needed to sail south, and then turn eastward across the wind, at an angle the *Charn* could handle. It seemed to the admiral that time itself was becalmed.

Right now John Hand longed to raise his confused little fleet on the horizon; he would be delighted to find them in disarray. He wanted more than anything to see the chaos of his captains striving for some modicum of competence…just so long as all fifteen ships were afloat and no Drammune were near. But it was hard to hope. Too much had gone wrong already. He had tried to attack a Drammune warship only to be brought into parley. And then that parley had thoroughly thwarted him. Now his own crewmen's resentment was palpable. They felt hobbled, as if they had been manacled, and all because two Drammune guards held them prisoner. Or so they saw it. The pair certainly strutted and posed as if they were prison guards.

But there was a deeper fear that gnawed him. He seemed to have lost his feel for riding the current of time and human activity. He felt like he had no control. Every stride was a limp, every limb was out of joint. Every decision led to a dead end. The men knew it, they sensed it. And they believed the voyage was snakebit because Packer Throme was not aboard. They thought him a talisman, a charm that could keep disaster at bay and order all things for good.

The Battle for Vast Dominion

Though the admiral rejected that belief out of hand, nothing he did or said seemed to penetrate it. If he addressed it directly, as he did once in frustration, he built walls between himself and his men, walls he would later need to break down with an apology. As he had in fact done. The reality was, they believed more in Packer Throme than they did in John Hand.

The Firefish sensed, before it saw, the approach of the pack. The docile storm creatures began moving, the circle breaking up as each creature turned toward the intruders. And then, amazingly, their aura changed. The beast felt a charge to these creatures now. There was ferocity here. These were predators after all.

And then the storm began.

It was unclear who fired the first shot. Some would say it was a cannon on the *Gant Marie* that let loose the first volley, but others would swear that it started with small arms from *Forcible*. But wherever it started, it was not to be stopped. Inexperienced Vast captains ordered inexperienced crews to open up on their trained and battle-hardened Drammune foes. The Vast fleet fired at will. Abandoning small arms quickly, they blazed away almost exclusively with cannon, the armament with which they were least familiar. Black smoke choked the decks as blast after blast cracked, splitting the air, rocking the ships. They learned as they went, but this did not slow their efforts. No power on earth was going to separate these men from their powder, their shot, their appointed martial duty, their inevitable eternal glory, now that the battle was joined.

Cannonballs splashed into the sea, struck hulls, ripped through sails. Splinters flew. Men fell. The Vast sailors, fired upon for the first time in their lives, redoubled their efforts, fearlessly reloading and firing with abandon, burning themselves on hot muzzles, scrimping too much on powder here, watching cannonballs flop pitifully into the sea a few feet from the hull, or overdoing it there, shattering a breech with disastrous effect to their own life and limb. But they were focused on the three square feet of deck before them, the single piece of real estate within their control. They fought. And they believed... no, they knew for certain their own lives and the lives of their families and the future of their nation depended on the speed and sureness of their hands at this moment—delivering this shot into this cannon, and then moving it quickly out again with a yellow flame and an ear-ringing explosion.

Though he wasn't present to see it begin, John Hand's sense of foreboding proved accurate. Their inexperience with these weapons led the Vast crews to begin firing far too soon. The cannonballs they launched flew at targets far out of range. The Fleet of Nearing Vast came under fire, yes. But unfortunately not from the Drammune.

"What are they doing?" a puzzled first mate asked his equally puzzled Drammune captain, the commander of this squadron.

The commander shrugged. "They seem to be shooting at one another."

And indeed they were. It occurred to very few Vast sailors on the six lead ships now engaged in battle that the cannonballs whizzing overhead or splashing short or occasionally crashing into their own ship's timbers represented friendly fire. Those who did notice made little headway getting anyone else to notice.

The Drammune captain watched, perplexed, trying to find a military reason for such strange behavior. He had passed the Drammune leadership tests and survived Drammune training regimens. Whether he understood the activity before him or not, once the Vast were within five hundred yards the mystery became a menace. He had a duty to perform.

"Ahn skova, Hezz Zaya?" asked his first mate. *What orders, Captain Zaya?*

The commander of the Drammune squadron gave the order, and up went the flags of parley, seven gray pennants streaming from atop seven mainmasts, so obvious as to be impossible to miss, impossible to ignore.

Or so he thought.

The mind of Captain Zaya's opposite, Moore Davies, marveled at this breathtaking display of nautical ineptitude. His resignation sunk into despair. This was his, his alone as commander, to claim forever. He ordered his flagman to signal the cease-fire, utterly confident that not one of his captains would pay the least bit of mind. He ordered all his men to the ship's rails, and then into the rigging, with whatever white or nearly white cloth they could find. They all went and waved their towels and rags and shirts frantically, not at the Drammune, but at their fellow Vast ships.

But the fierce Vast ships sailed on, firing as they went. Moore Davies' men might as well have been signaling the cannonballs as they flew past.

The Drammune commander pondered this silently. Commander Zerka Zaya had fought the Vast before, and recently. His ship was the *Karda Zolt.* He had given chase to the *Marchessa,* and had steered clear of the flying spectacle that was the *Trophy Chase* as she passed by with sails alight, accompanied by the glowing sea beast, the one that had destroyed the *Rahk Thanu* and the *Nochto Vare.* The Vast were better than this.

But as Zaya watched through his telescope, a cannon placement of the *Gant Marie* exploded, bodies and body parts flying as it was struck by a projectile from *Forcible.* The Drammune commander could now draw but one conclusion. He shook his head. No matter, in another moment they would be firing on Drammune vessels sailing under a flag of truce. If the *Trophy Chase* was not among them, and that certainly appeared to be the case, Zerka Zaya would destroy them all.

The Vast ships did reach the Drammune, and pass in and among them. The aggressors did not slow the pace of their cannonade, but almost to a ship, increased it. They fired on clearly flagged Drammune vessels seeking parley. And the result was an order from the Drammune commander that was obeyed instantly.

Disciplined, precise, and deadly Drammune cannon answered the wild Vast barrage.

CHAPTER 9

Disaster

"Ship ahead!" came the call from the crow's nest of the *Trophy Chase*. "Ten points off the port bow!"

"Finally," Admiral Hand said aloud, searching the horizon.

But before he could find them, the lookout called again. "Fully engaged!"

"Ahhh!" Hand seethed, teeth bared. He lowered his telescope, squinted with naked eye at the horizon, then raised the scope again. Now he saw the tiny vessels, looking semitransparent, like ghost ships, in the haze. He saw a flash, and then another. Then ten more, and then twenty.

He turned angrily to the Drammune behind him. "There's a fight underway, and I'm going to stop it," he told them in Drammune.

The admiral looked up at the set of his own ship's sails. "Mr. Haas! Main, maintop, maintopgallant, full!" he ordered, shouting it out in a rhythmic cadence so every syllable was clear and audible all the way to the crow's nest. "Mizzen, mizzentop, full! Foresail, drop three points! I want the port gunn'l in the water! Let's fly, gentlemen!"

Sailors did not need to clamber anywhere to obey. They were already positioned across the yardarms in the rigging, awaiting just these orders. They loosed canvas almost simultaneously. The great cat leaped, the breeze from starboard just afore the beam snapping the canvas full instantly. Both of the Drammune officers on the quarterdeck stumbled, then regained their balance and put hands to pistol grips, fearing attack.

But no Vast sailor seemed the least bit concerned. The snap of canvas had done it all. Now the deck pitched, the port rail descended lower, and then lower, and then lower still as the *Chase* pulled away from the *Hezza Charn*, until it seemed a certainty the ship would capsize. The two officers reached for the rail of the quarterdeck simultaneously, steadying themselves. But again, not a single Vast sailor blinked. The ship now raced through the water, deck splashed lightly by crested waves whose spray overtopped the port side gunwale. The Drammune looked at one another in astonishment. Then they grinned, unable to contain the energy they felt pulsing through the ship, through the decks, and through themselves.

Surely, the *Trophy Chase* was a new and glorious thing in the world.

The Drammune cannoneers fired cautiously and aimed carefully. Self-defense was hardly needed. The Vast projectiles were not aimed well, most in fact not aimed at all, and therefore most flew harmlessly overhead or splashed equally harmlessly into the sea. The Drammune were able, at an almost leisurely pace, to shatter Vast rudders, cripple and then sever Vast masts, puncture exposed expanses of Vast hulls, and blast Vast cannon placements. It wasn't much more dangerous for the Drammune than being on maneuvers, taking target practice on decrepit vessels destined to be scuttled.

For the Vast, however, casualties mounted. Earnest men devoted to king and country were blown down by explosions, lacerated by splintered rails and decking, cut deep by shrapnel. Fear filled every corner of their beings, numbing fingers and loosening joints, pouring cold sweat out every pore. But pain and anger fired this fear, heating it into a desperate, combustible emotion, fueling bloody hands and aching arms and straining backs as these men loaded, and fired, and reloaded, and fired again. Sweat ran in rivulets from faces, down necks, down backs, combining now with blood that poured from wounds of every description, red and slick onto the decks.

The living pulled the dead away so one more cannonball might be loaded, one more round fired. Those who stopped to help the wounded were shooed away angrily by the wounded themselves. "I'm done, leave me!" and "Fire the cannon!"

And they fought on. They were mistaken and misguided, partially trained and poorly disciplined, but they fought on with grit and tenacity.

But the Drammune were mercilessly accurate, ruthlessly efficient. *Gant Marie*'s hull was quickly torn open in three places, the two lower of which drank in water at such a rate that the third highest wound, four feet higher up the hull, would be doing the same within minutes. She was doomed. *Forcible* lost her foremast and her mainmast almost simultaneously, and sheets of canvas billowed down over the decks and were then held fast by a web of rigging and lines, rendering her unable to fire her guns, unable to free herself. Roped and tied and blindfolded, she was hammered again and again and again. She too would go down. *Wellspring* had no rudder and had suffered under a particularly bitter broadside to her cannon placements, leaving the crew decimated and unable to return fire. She was crippled at sea, but she would survive the pass. *Windward,* however, would not survive; she was burning.

Only *Blunderbuss* made it through unscathed. This was because at the crucial moment, as the Drammune came into range, she quit firing her cannon. The crew had run out of ammunition. Deckhands looked around at one another, baffled, and then began to discuss the problem. Their captain wandered down to the main deck, considered the issue, and suggested he may have left several crates of ammunition unopened in the hold. Men volunteered to search. The crates were located. The lack of a cargo crane was noted. A mate suggested that a bucket brigade be formed. The captain assigned crewmen to spots along the companionways. The lack of a crowbar was noted. A crowbar was found. The crates were opened. Eventually, individual cannonballs were passed, one by one, up to the deck. By this time, of course, the pass was long over and done.

The pass complete, the Vast now assessed the situation. Finally, captains raised their eyes to find their flagship. They saw the *Marchessa* waving more white linen into the wind than the royal hospital on wash day. They saw their commander's message, signaled frantically again and again by an arm-weary flagman: "Cease fire. They flag truce."

But even this became distorted in the retelling. Davies' unequivocal statement became, after but one or two re-transmissions, "They have surrendered!"

Cheers rose.

Then chants, then songs of martial glories praising the prowess of Nearing Vast. The king's Navy celebrated what they now fully believed to be a great and historic victory. The Drammune commander lowered his telescope, his amazement turned to incredulity. Zaya had seen threescore battles fought and won, fought and lost, but he had yet to encounter anything quite like this. He looked at his first mate. "Vastcha anetho soomay?" *Have the Vast gone mad?*

The sailor answered dutifully. "Seyk, hezz." *Aye, sir.*

Vast casualties were heavy. But thanks in part to Vast ineptitude, in part to Drammune restraint and accuracy, and wholly to the sheer, unmerited mercy of God, most wounds were not mortal. Almost all of these humble fishermen, these common sailors, these men of peace in peacetime, would live to tell the tale. But they would live to wish this tale were never told. Their hearts were as true as any hero's, but their errors were simply too egregious.

Commander Zaya looked around at the steely eyes of his men, who now awaited his orders. He saw sullen looks, simmering anger. They had been attacked by a people without honor, and now the salamanders sang and reveled as though victorious. They mocked the Drammune. The Drammune wanted blood.

Within minutes the Drammune ships had moved into positions of power over those six who had dared to attack under parley. As the Drammune closed in, the seas went silent. The noise of celebration died away. Vast captains, doing the honorable thing, quieted their crews and prepared to accept the unconditional surrender of their foes.

The *Karda Zolt* slid in alongside the *Marchessa,* now hove to nearby. This Vast crew was anxious and intimidated, rags of truce now hanging limp in hands. They alone seemed to know the grievous nature of their error, and the penalty Commander Zaya was preparing to impose. They could not help but eye the Drammune cannon now positioned and ready, aimed so as to sink the *Marchessa* in a single volley amidship, at the waterline. The *Marchessa*'s captain quickly had a ship's boat lowered. Zaya watched Moore Davies without emotion as he bobbed about on the way over for parley, four men rowing him in the tiny shallop. His head was up, his chin high,

but his mouth was drawn down and his jaw clamped tight. He would come aboard of his own free will but would stay aboard in chains, and he knew it.

Such was Commander Zaya's design, and to that end all events flowed. But for Zaya, for Davies, as for all souls that bob and skitter across the surface of earthly seas, currents shift. Winds bring change with astounding speed. Ships appear on horizons. Monsters arise from the deep. This day was destined to be remembered for far more than the deeds or misdeeds of a score of obscure ships that had found and scraped the bottom of the Vast nautical barrel.

The beast's skin sizzled, flaring yellow. Within it was kindled a matching fire. The long fin angled downward, the sparkling skin reflecting light as it skimmed quickly across the surface of the waters…this could be only one creature, only one! The Firefish rose from the depths where it had circled far beneath the stormy battle, and now it swam with all its might, with all its heart and mind and soul, toward the object of its devotion, its desire.

Deep Fin.

Deep Fin had come. It had come for the Firefish.

Deep Fin *remembered!*

"Hahn!" cried the Drammune lookout. "Enmenteras!" *Enemy ship!* He then called out the compass point, and commander Zaya wheeled about, scanning the seas to the northwest of the *Karda Zolt*. Through the scope he could see that the approaching Vast vessel was heeled to port at an impossible angle. It could be but one ship, the one last seen when the *Nochto Vare* went down. Then, she was fleeing. Now, she attacked.

"Chekah Kai," the commander said softly. *Trophy Chase.*

The Firefish broke the surface moving at its fastest speed, an all-out sprint upward toward the light. It flew from the water. This was an enormous leap, not over the bows, but straight into the air a hundred yards from its great Deep Fin, well over a hundred feet into pure, dazzling, invisible daylight. It shot almost straight up until its tail left the water and it was airborne, a flying fish, a porpoise. Eyes alight, its hide gleaming and glittering in the sun, it rotated in the air, its entire long, lithe body spiraling gracefully, once, then again, and then a third time. And when it smashed down into the water on its dorsals, it soaked the *Trophy Chase* with a wild wall of joyful seawater.

And the men aboard roared their approval. Their ally had returned!

But just as quickly, the roar died away. All eyes turned to John Hand. All hearts and minds registered the same question at the same moment.

The admiral did not join in the outburst. He barely glanced at the Firefish. He watched his men. He watched their reactions, listening as their cheers turned hollow, then went silent. He saw all eyes turn toward him, one by one, as he knew they would. He knew what they were thinking. They looked to him for the answer to one question, and none needed to speak it aloud.

With Packer Throme not aboard, who will now command the beast?

The Admiral of the Fleet had a choice to make. Finally, here was a decision that did not feel foregone, nor pre-scripted. He had three options. He could set his face like a flint and sail on, ignoring the Firefish as though it were nothing but the natural oddity it most certainly was, no more noteworthy than the surfacing of a whale. Or, he could treat the thing like the dangerous predator it also most certainly was, and order up the sides of beef he'd salted away in the hold, get men to the longboats, load the lures, and kill it once and for all.

Or...he could behave as though the beast was the trained animal his men believed it to be, the circus act it quite certainly was not. He could take up Packer Throme's mantle, his place at the prow. To John Hand, the professor of nautics, the rider of the waves of history, this came down to a simple matter of strategy. Which path gave him the best chance of success? Which path could win him back his ship?

He knew what he needed to do. But he hesitated. The series of failures that had marred this voyage taunted from the back of his mind, conjuring up images before his eyes, like bones jangled on a witch doctor's amulet way down south in the Warm Climes. His failure to command his own fleet, his poor decision to leave them all alone, his would-be attack that ended with armed Drammune officers aboard his own ship watching his every move...all these spoke out against him. He needed to sweep all that away somehow. He could either throw those bones into the fire, show the men that such drivel was powerless, or...he could put them around his own neck and use them to his own ends.

Either choice would be the right choice, so long as it worked.

The men waited. John Hand set his jaw. Decision made, he walked silently, without word or expression, to the stair of the quarterdeck. He descended to the main deck, crossed it, and climbed to the foredeck. All eyes still on him, he climbed to the forecastle. But when he grasped the stays that ran up from the bowsprit, and then stepped up onto that wooden beam, the men cut their eyes to one another, sharing a wonder, a fear, and a deep misgiving.

The admiral looked at the bowsprit beneath his boots. It was thick as a man's torso where he stood at the base, and tapered to the width of his forearm fifteen feet from him, at its farthest point. There he looked out over the seas, calmly, serenely, in the very spot where Packer Throme had stood. And then he waited for the Firefish.

"That now," Mutter Cabe said in a hoarse whisper to Delaney, who stood beside him on the standing rigging along the mainmast yard, "that just ain't right."

The sea coursed by, flowing directly underneath them. With the ship heeled as far to port as it was, the water was closer to Delaney and Cabe than was the angled deck, now down and to their right. In the blue water directly below them, just under the surface these sailors could see the Firefish swimming, its lean body snaking alongside the ship at their precise speed, just below the waves. It was a great yellow streak of flame and power. It moved forward now, toward the bow, toward John Hand.

Delaney worked some moisture into his mouth. "Mutter, don't get all shocked now. But for once, I think I agree with ye."

The Drammune commander had seen the Firefish leap, from a thousand yards away. He had seen the beast shoot out of the water, twist, and splash back down into the sea. He waited now, expecting to see a lunge, hoping to watch the Firefish take down the *Trophy Chase* as it had done the *Nochto Vare*.

But the beast did not lunge, did not destroy...instead, it rose alongside the ship's prow.

John Hand felt a creeping dread. The specter of all his recent poor decisions rose once again, dark in his mind. *This was not the right*

choice. Everything in him now screamed it. But it was his choice. He had made it knowingly. He made it because he believed the beast was but a beast, acting according to the laws of its nature, according to ebbs and flows that could be measured like tides, according to instinct and animal reflex, all predictable. Lund Lander had measured these things, reduced the hunt to a series of calculations.

It occurred to the admiral, in a small bubble of clarity that rose up within his dark doubts, that Lund Lander had ultimately been unable to calculate these monsters. He had died in the maw of one of them, and on this very ship. But John Hand pushed that stray thought back down from where it had come. Accidents happen.

When the Firefish rose, John Hand turned to look at it. He had seen these things before. From a distance, yes, but not a great distance. He knew what they looked like. He knew what to expect. He would not be surprised by anything he saw here.

But he was surprised.

As the Firefish closed in on the bow, still racing below the surface, flying alongside the Deep Fin, it remembered. So clearly, so cleanly, so vividly, as if it had happened just now...the beaming light, the wonder, the rows and rows of eyes, the joy of the Deep Fin! Yes, the source of it, the mind of it, right there at the front, at the creature's head. And it rose, ready to bask in that same glow, to look the Deep Fin in the eye once again, to know its power once again. To obey its command.

The Firefish, too, was surprised.

The Drammune commander twisted the outer sleeve of his telescope, focusing it. The head of the beast was now up out of the water, at a level even with the prow of the *Trophy Chase.* And someone stood there, up on the bowsprit. What was this about? Could it be that the stories were true?

And then the Firefish opened its mouth. Its jaws just seemed to unhinge, dropping down like an inverted portcullis, until that figure, whoever it was, could have stepped in.

What had shocked Talon in her encounter with one of these beasts more than a year ago was the intelligence of the thing. Packer had seen the same intelligence, had been able to read its thoughts in the creature's eyes. And now those huge, wet eyes pierced John Hand, focused on him so crisply, so deeply, that they seemed to penetrate his very thoughts. He had been proud and aloof, coolly surveying this animal, disdaining fear, knowing he and his men could slay this monster if need be. Those had been his thoughts. But what John Hand saw in the beast, what surprised him to the core of his soul, was the beast's deep, deep disappointment.

This beast, somehow, found John Hand wanting. The admiral blanched, his bravado gone in an instant. Then the beast's discontent melted into anger. And just as quickly that anger grew into rage. The transition in that enormous face, within those eyes, the emotion that exuded from that scaly, misshapen thing, its jutting jaw, its bristling, skewed teeth, could not possibly be misread. Had there been an audible click accompanying the shift to anger, like the cocking of a firing mechanism, it would not have seemed out of place.

The beast's jaw dropped as its eyes widened. Hand felt the wave of heat emanating from the fiery yellow scales.

He knew now the beast would attack him.

The beast had come within the presence, there at the head of the creature. But this was not the presence of the Deep Fin. Not remotely. Here was a shocking darkness, where before was light. Here was suspicion, where before was empathy. Disdain, where there was honor. Where once light glowed and pulsed outward, now darkness pulled. Here was intelligence, yes, but without an embrace, without warmth, without the fire that burned and glowed and charged through all, that invited, that inspired.

Was this truly Deep Fin? Yes. But the presence, the mind of it was not same. Here was the look of a predator. The eyes of a killer. The Deep Fin was a storm creature, and the storm creatures were hunters. But in these eyes now, the Firefish was the prey. The animal instinct John Hand had expected took over, but not in the manner he expected. This instinct allowed a simple choice, an either-or, to flee or to fight. The beast clicked through this process in an instant. And locked into *fight*.

That's when the beast's jaw dropped.

It would kill. It would kill now.

The admiral's jaw dropped also. His eyes went wide just as the beast's narrowed. His instincts also kicked in, and the same two choices fired through his mind. He chose *flee*.

But his legs would not move. The beast's jaw was wide, its eyes fiery yellow, its lunge imminent. He had to move. He let go of the forestay with his left hand, the one closest the beast, in a jerky effort to turn and leap off the bowsprit back onto the forecastle deck. But as he did, he lost his balance and started to fall backward toward the water, away from the beast. Instinctively, he swept his left hand and arm up and behind him, where his hand struck the other stay. He grabbed desperately for it, found it in his grip, then let go with his right hand. Now he faced astern. He found his feet again, and bent his knees to leap to the deck.

But the Firefish struck at that moment. The admiral put out his right hand to fend the thing off, and as he did, he cried out in sheer terror.

The rage within the Firefish demanded it attack. And so it attacked. But when it saw the movement, saw the awkwardness of this bit of flesh, this ungainly motion from the very place where the intelligence emanated, out of which the dark aura flowed, another thought darted like a sparrow through its brain. Even as it lunged, as its teeth snapped down, other images flashed through its mind, and its memory. As it had swept the seas clean of morsels after killing the crunchy storm creature, some of those morsels behaved precisely as this dark, fleshy presence did. Those morsels had flailed their little fins and whimpered and cried, just as this bit did. And deep within the beast, an awareness took hold...

This was a morsel.

The morsels were creatures. The storm creature was a creature of creatures.

And in that brief flash of insight, the Firefish adjusted its attack. It snapped not at the Deep Fin, but at the morsel, at the awkward fleshy thing, to pluck it away, to swallow it as it had swallowed many others.

To rid the Deep Fin of this dark presence.

The crew watched in horror as the jaws of the lunging Firefish closed on their admiral. But the beast's adjustment was not precise. It did not take the whole of John Hand. It took his arm at the elbow, severing it instantly with an explosion of electricity that flashed like smokeless gunpowder. They heard no crack of powder, however, only

The Battle for Vast Dominion

a crackling, like the sizzling of a pinecone in a fire, or the crinkling of brittle paper in a flame.

And then the beast was gone.

John Hand stood on the bowsprit still, his knees still bent, his left hand squeezing the taut line for all it was worth, his right arm gone. He watched the beast disappear. He stared after it, unseeing. Then he held what was left of his right arm up before his eyes, and stared at the stump that remained.

Crewmen ran to him, grasped him by the legs, the belt, trying to pull him down. But he would not let go of the line with his left hand. Finally a sailor climbed past him and unwrapped his fist, one finger at a time. Then they took their commander, their captain, their admiral, and laid him on the forecastle deck, hovering over him like lion cubs nosing and whimpering around their wounded mother.

"Stand back, you ham-handed lot—you'll kill him! Give him air!" Andrew Haas pulled men away, pushed them back, cleared a space around his fallen captain. Then he knelt beside him. He looked closely into his eyes. "Admiral?"

No answer.

"Where's Stitch?" Haas asked without looking up.

"Right here, sir," the frumpy old surgeon answered. He had come up from sick bay when he heard the whoops of the crew. Blowing his nose as he came, he had pushed through the crowd, and now he knelt at John Hand's right shoulder. He emptied his sack of tools onto the deck: a few clean rags, a saw, a file, a needle and thread, a hammer, a pair of pliers, tin snips, a role of baling wire, and a jug of malt whiskey. All the implements of his healing craft.

But he would need none of these, save the whiskey. And that he would take for himself.

"Can you stop the bleeding?" Haas asked, still focused on John Hand's pale, sweaty face.

"There's no bleedin'," Stitch said, carefully peeling away what was left of a sleeve. "The lightning...it closed everythin' off, like." He was mesmerized by the soft white color, the smoothness of the stump, as though the skin had simply melted. It looked like a round of smooth, white cheese. "No surgeon coulda done it better."

Now Andrew Haas leaned over to look. The cloth of both shirt and coat was cut through, ripped, and blackened. But sure enough, the stub was cauterized. "What about burns?" he asked.

Stitch just kept staring at the stump, then cautiously reached out to touch it. He pulled his hand back before he did. "I can still feel the heat of it."

"I mean other places!" Haas' irritation was evident. "From the lightning goin' through him. It'll have come out somewhere."

"Oh, right." Stitch checked the admiral's feet, legs, torso, his remaining hand. "Nothin'," he announced.

Haas sat back on his haunches. "Went through him clean, then. That's a mercy. I don't think he's really even hurt. 'Cept for his arm." He pondered a moment, then felt the need to add, "Which is mostly gone."

Stitch pulled the stopper from the jug of whiskey, took a pull, then lowered it toward the admiral's mouth.

Smelling it, John Hand blinked several times, as though coming around, although his eyes had remained open all this time. Stitch took the liquor away and drank again.

"What happened?" the admiral asked.

"You don't remember?" Haas asked right back.

He thought for a moment. "No."

"Firefish ate your arm," Stitch offered, wiping whiskey from his stubbled chin. "But you're okay." He sneezed loudly.

John Hand looked at the stump of his right arm, ending at the elbow. Then he laid his head back on the deck and closed his eyes, pondering the surgeon's words. The two statements did not fit together very well, in his mind.

The beast circled lower and lower, brooding. The morsel...the morsel...the image of that small, predatory face stayed, hung before its eyes, even as the taste of blood remained in its mouth.

The beast looked up, watching the Deep Fin fly on, wrinkling the gleaming water behind it, as though nothing had happened. But something had happened, something dark, something brutal. The Firefish could not understand it, did not comprehend it. The seas themselves had turned cold and dark. The taste of the morsel, tiny though it was, lingered, warm, tender...it fired a deep and angry hunger.

The beast needed to feed.

But what was the Deep Fin now? Master...predator...

Or prey...?

The two Drammune officers aboard the *Chase* looked to one another. Their hearts were in their throats. What had they just witnessed? The Vast commander had called forth the Devilfish somehow. And it had come. He had walked away from them proudly, to the prow of the ship, to command it. But then…what was the meaning of the attack? Why did it bite the commander? They conferred among themselves, but could only agree that they did not understand.

John Hand was helped up to a sitting position. He also did not understand. He felt sick, dizzy. His right arm ached and burned, all the way to the tips of fingers that were no longer there, that in fact felt nothing at this moment, being in the gullet of a beast far under-water. He looked at the faces of his men. They were blank, a slate on which he could write the explanation of his choosing. But he had nothing to write there.

"Firefish," he said at length. "I liked it better when all we had to worry about was killing those yellow sons a' mothers."

The men laughed softly, relieved to hear such an earthy sentiment at a terrible time such as this. One or two even slapped him on the back. John Hand was not Packer Throme; he had just proven that. But that was okay. He was one of them, and he was alive, and he was on their side. And at the moment that felt at least as good.

"Can you stand, Admiral?" Haas asked gently.

"I think so."

"Help him up, boys," the first mate ordered, and multiple hands helped their captain to his feet, all taking care not to get too close to that bloodless white stump.

Once upright, John Hand took a deep breath, then looked up at the quarterdeck. The Drammune officers looked across at him, staring right through him. "Guess I better explain this to our guests," he said aloud.

He started walking toward them. He would give them an explanation. He had about twenty paces to figure out what it would be.

The Firefish circled tighter and tighter, lower and lower, preparing to fly upward at its prey. It had made its decision. Its mind was now focused only and solely on its target. Yes, yes…now was time to feed. Time to crush, time to kill, time to destroy. The beast was a predator. Storm creatures were prey. All of them, all of them were prey.

It turned, eyed the creature's heart, opened its mouth in a silent roar, and hurtled upward toward the surface for the kill.

The Drammune officers narrowed their eyes at the pallid figure of the Vast admiral who climbed unsteadily up toward them. They could read easily enough that he was uncertain. He had expected to command the beast, and he had been attacked. But this commander had fight in him. That they could also see.

John Hand managed half a smile as he topped the stair to the quarterdeck. He looked each man in the eye. "Dangerous beasts," he said in Drammune. Then he turned away from them to face the prow, and put his good hand on the rail to steady himself. He sniffed once. "Takes a little practice dealing with them." He looked at his two guests again, one after the other. "I'll be glad to give you some pointers if you want to give it a try."

Two Drammune jaws clenched and two faces went white. "Nagh," one of them said, shaking his head and raising a hand to ward off the very thought. "Oma skayn aziza." *We will learn from you.*

The little meaty lump had a predator's face. The Firefish hated the little meaty lump. It made the Firefish fearless, reckless, wanting to kill. The darkness of that little face was a hard mystery, a cold question that cut deep, like sharp teeth into soft flesh. The Firefish had attacked the dark lump. But where was the beaming source of light, the joy that was truly Deep Fin...? Where was the radiant morsel? Where was the presence?

Gone...replaced somehow.

Hunted!

And that thought rocked the Firefish into action. Deep Fin was in danger, some strange danger, a danger from within. The small dark lump was not the presence, but had hurt the presence. It had hunted the presence!

Bloodlust rose, the desire to kill. But the Firefish could not attack Deep Fin. Not now. Frustrated, maddened, frenzied, it flew toward other prey, toward the nearby storm creature, the one toward which the Deep Fin ran.

And then, as it approached, it saw its entry...and rose.

Moore Davies was facing the *Karda Zolt*. His men had turned the jolly in an effort to put the stern against the hull so their captain could more easily climb up. He felt the dark rumble from under the water before he saw it. And then saw it before he heard it, barely before, the briefest yellow flash just under the surface. But when it struck, he heard, saw, and felt it as though it had come up through the bottom of his own little boat.

Drammune sailors were lining the gunwales with pistols and muskets raised, all aimed carefully at the approaching prisoners. The Drammune captain was looking down on the Vast captain when the beast crashed upward through the decking just behind him. A solid yellow pylon rose up, up through the sails, into the rigging. The captain and the well-armed sailors around him did not look back. They did not have time. The floorboards beneath them rose, pulled upward at the point of impact but still fastened to the beam ends at the gunwale. The planking rose at a sudden, severe angle, and it simply hurled them over the rail and into the sea.

There they splashed heavily, half a dozen ungainly bodies flung into the water mere feet from Davies' boat. One or more of them might have landed within the jolly, had it not been for the fact that the Vast sailors at the oars did not hesitate, but pulled for all they were worth the instant the Firefish struck. They were all veterans of Firefish battles, having escorted the *Trophy Chase*, lowering long-boats full of huntsmen to kill their quarry. Two of the four had been huntsmen, original killers of the beasts. The sight of a Firefish did not freeze them in terror, but it motivated them strongly to remove themselves from its presence.

They pulled for their lives.

Commander Zaya came up sputtering along with five of his men. He was facing away from his ship, which was already taking on water, and toward the rapidly fleeing shallop. He did not understand what had just happened, but he was sure these Vast had done something underhanded. Somehow they had set off an explosion, they had fired some sort of missile. His anger flashed. "Azo nochtram!" he shouted, spewing seawater and crashing his fist into the ocean. "Azo nochtram!" *Kill them!*

But his men, those still aboard ship and those treading water around him, paid no mind. A shadow fell over the water, and Zaya saw the faces of the Vast turn upward, craning their necks, their mouths agape as they pulled on the oars. A chill shot through him now, like ice water down his spine. He feared what he would see before he turned to see it.

And now he understood.

The *Trophy Chase* did command the Devilfish. The Vast had ordered an attack. These were his last thoughts.

The full weight of the Firefish, a hundred feet long and fifteen feet wide at its widest, came crashing down, smashing, crushing, and burying at sea Commander Zerka Zaya and his men.

The beast did not fall on top of the jolly. It missed Moore Davies and his crew. The wave the beast created actually pushed the shallop away. The thing had not fallen like a tree trunk, stiff and straight, but like a length of rope coiling into a barrel. It did not create an enormous sinkhole followed by a mountain of water, the sort that had soaked the *Trophy Chase* just minutes ago, or the sort that had taken Stedman Due and Gregor Tesh down in their longboat. Instead, it pushed a wave of water before it, a swell of only eight or ten feet.

The speed of the shallop, pulled now by blistering hands and arm muscles that were knotted and balled like monkey fists, allowed the small boat to skim down the surf. The rounded hull fled downhill from the beast on a wave, like a sledge down a snowy hillside.

Moore Davies felt elation.

John Hand felt a sharp and deep distress. He closed his eyes. He couldn't watch. He had not sent the Firefish to attack the *Karda Zolt*, of course. He couldn't command the thing. But he had just now made the Drammune think that he could. He shook his head, cursing yet one more evidence of his bad luck on this voyage. How much worse could it get? He had lost his arm. And now he had apparently just attacked a Drammune flagship sailing under flag of truce, with the most powerful weapon the Vast possessed.

He turned slowly to look at them. Their eyes turned just as slowly from the destruction of the *Karda Zolt* to look at him. John Hand saw what he expected—condemnation, accusation, and rising anger. The admiral shook his head.

"Eyneg skove zien sankhar koos tachtai." He had ordered it not to attack. "Azo seydem nochtram," he told them with a shrug. *They like to kill.*

"Sko sankhar koos!" the Drammune officer demanded. He had his pistol out, and though he didn't point it at John Hand, the admiral had no question about the man's intentions. *Stop the Firefish!*

Pistol hammers clicked back all around and above the quarterdeck. The admiral held up his left hand, his only hand, and glanced around at nearly a hundred armed sailors ready to pick off two overbearing Drammune brass. "These are our guests, gentlemen. We are not presently at war."

He turned to his guests and shook his head. "Sankhar koos zien tcho," he told them. "Azo tacht hezz." *Firefish are not dogs. They are difficult to command.*

And with that he walked right back down the stair, across the decks and up to the bowsprit. The men watched him in amazement, but they lowered their weapons.

"Give me a hand here," the admiral said under his breath, in a voice that sounded like a curse. Andrew Haas, still standing on the forecastle deck watching the dual spectacle of the Firefish and the one-armed admiral, took hold of his commander's right arm just below the armpit and helped him back into place, to the same spot where he had tempted fate and lost not five minutes before.

John Hand felt pain shoot through his torso from his armpit, and sweat broke out all over him in a flash, as though he had suddenly been thrust into an overheated smithy after running a mile. He cursed under his breath, but he knew what he was doing and why, and once again he was determined to go through with it. Only this could undo the damage.

"*Stop!*" he called out, bellowing the words with every ounce of command he could muster, as though the Firefish might actually hear and obey. It was all show, of course. But a necessary show.

Up in the rigging Mutter Cabe shook his head once more, his sense of foreboding appeased not one whit. "His name is Hand. And that's what the beast took."

Delaney shot him a glance. "His arm, more like."

The old sailor seemed to be speaking from far away, from inside a dark pit. He spoke with absolute certainty. "He can't live. It took away his name."

"It did not!" Marcus responded, quite shrill. "It didn't take no name!"

"Anyways," Delaney chimed in, "he's got his left one yet. Admiral will do fine, you watch." But Delaney watched closely himself. What John Hand was doing, climbing back up to that perch to face that beast again, struck Delaney as either the bravest or most foolish thing he'd ever seen. Maybe both.

Moore Davies turned away from the destruction of the *Karda Zolt* when he heard the admiral's call. He looked at the *Trophy Chase*. He couldn't figure out why Admiral Hand was standing at the prow. He couldn't fathom to whom he was calling out, who or what might obey an order of that sort, presented in that manner. *Stop who? Stop what?* The command seemed senseless.

But the Firefish heard the call. It did not understand it, but it felt the urgency, the command within it. It was an animal sound, barked with the assurance of the vicious. This was the howl of an animal not to be denied. The beast turned, and faced the approaching storm creature.

The dark morsel was on the prow. The little meaty lump called out a challenge!

The beast swam toward it immediately, keeping its head above the water. It locked eyes with the lump once again. It now sensed both fear and anger. Its anger was the root of its viciousness. This was not cornered prey. This was a wounded predator. This was the enemy of Deep Fin!

John Hand saw the thing turn. A thrill of terror went through him as he realized he had, in fact, beckoned it. He had challenged it, and it would accept the challenge.

Without turning, as the thing approached he gave another order, more urgent even than the first, but this one for his men and not the beast: "Get me a lure!"

CHAPTER 10

The Darkness

The admiral stood on the bowsprit, propped up by his deck-hands, who held him from behind, who grasped his belt, his knees, his ankles. He looked back at the lure being handed up from behind. "Light it," he ordered. Focused now on death, either his own or the beast's, his voice quavered not at all. It was the essence of command.

Andrew Haas pulled the brass box back down, dutifully opened the hatch at the end, and with trembling thumb flipped the flint wheel. Sparks flew. The fuse caught. Haas slammed the door shut, pressed it tight against the wax that sealed it, then handed it back up.

The Firefish came face to face with the darkness again.

This time, it would crush the dark, angry lump. But now the darkness was powerful, more powerful than it had been before. It pulled light into it; it drew energy from the air, away from the beast, depleting the Firefish of its rage. But the beast would not be overcome. Its rage doubled. It would tear this tiny fury away from Deep Fin.

Its eyes blazed as it opened its maw. Its jaw unhinged, dropping low, white teeth bared to swallow the darkness.

John Hand could feel the heat from the Firefish, smell the stench of death on its breath. He reached back with his left hand and accepted the lure from Andrew Haas. He looked into the maw, saw splinters of wood, bits of cloth stuck in its teeth. He saw a Drammune helmet punctured through by one white tooth, a serrated blade protruding through a flattened, mangled, crimson skullcap.

John Hand did not look the beast in the eye this time. He had seen enough. He hurled the lure into its mouth.

"Chew on that!" he roared. The lure struck the back of the beast's throat, and its concrete jaws closed around the brass box reflexively.

Lightning shot from the Firefish to the bowsprit, exploding the wooden beam under the admiral's feet. The spar cracked, split—and the carved figurehead fell away into the ocean. At the same time, the beam itself broke, snapping just under the admiral's feet. The severed spar flew upward, the pressure from the taught guy lines slinging it toward the sky. The crewmen holding their admiral pulled him back now into the ship, back to the safety of the forecastle deck. There they all went down, falling backward in a heap.

Above them the foremast creaked and groaned. Two thirds of the bowsprit now dangled from slack guy lines above them, gyrating like some crazed puppet.

"Uh oh," Andrew Haas managed, clambering back to his feet.

"The devil's in it now," Mutter Cabe said, looking down at the same sight from his perch on the mainsail footlines. "Never shoulda kilt that one."

Delaney said nothing, but once again he was prone to agree. "Gotta strike the foresail, or the mast's a goner." He said it as he navigated the standing rigging, forward toward the creaking, cracking mast.

"You'll just go down with 'er!" Cabe called after him.

But Delaney had made up his mind. He would try to save the mast. All the sailors on the foremast were scrambling down, or across lines to the mainmast, anxious to get away from the danger. All but one. One man who had been stationed on the foremast now clung to the yard of the foretopgallant, fear clawing away inside his chest like a small, frightened animal.

Marcus Pile.

Haas rose to his feet, peering only above him. He could see clearly now that the foremast was bent backward, like a bow. Creaking and cracking sounds came from up and down its length. Without the tension provided by the forestays, and with all the pressure from the sails in the wind, it was just a question of where it would snap, and when. The other sailors on deck stood now as well, looking upward. Most of them had seen a mast go before. This mast, like the others, was fashioned from three separate timbers in rough thirds, joined with an open mortise and tenon drilled through with two-inch dowels. One of the two joints would give. They cursed and prayed, watching Delaney climb out to Marcus Pile while all the others escaped with their lives. If the mast snapped low, the two men would plummet into the sea. If it snapped high, it would flick them like spitballs far into the ocean.

The explosion came with precise timing. It came from port side aft of the ship, raising the water in a rounded white bubble twenty yards across as the *Chase* sailed away. Lund Lander would have been proud.

Delaney flew across the foremast yard, sword in hand, hacking away the tie lines that held the sail fast. With each cut the tension eased, but with each easement the mast gave another agonizing groan, until the foresail was gone, and the foretop sail, and only the foretopgallant was left. Delaney cut the ties, working his way across the yard high up in the rigging, until only one corner remained attached.

At the end of the foretopgallant yard he reached Marcus Pile, holding the spar with both hands, hugging it tightly to his chest. Under him was the nock, and the last tie line left unsevered. It was the one that would set the foresail free. The great sheet of canvas snapped and whipped below them, a huge banner snapping in the wind, shaking the yard and the mast and the two men, like a shark tearing at a hunk of flesh.

Marcus's eyes were wide, and the shock of wheat that was his hair blew crazily as the yard whipsawed. He looked at Delaney.

"You have to let me cut it!" Delaney told him, firm but gentle.

Marcus Pile did not move. His eyes were open and focused, but he saw nothing.

"The boy's clutched again, Admiral," Andrew Haas said, still looking up, a deep sadness in his baritone. "Clutched again."

But John Hand did not hear.

When the first mate finally looked for his captain, the Admiral of the Fleet, he found him still lying on the deck. He saw the bloodless gash, the indentation in the forehead, just above his right eye. John Hand's eyes were open, but he too saw nothing.

"Stitch!" Haas screamed out, his voice little more than a yelp as he knelt by the pale body. Tears stung his eyes. "Stitch, ye blaggard, where are ye?" That blow, that dent—Haas knew it; he recognized it. It was a crushed skull. Between pirate battles and Firefish fights, he had seen it too many times before.

But once again Stitch was already there. He knelt beside the admiral, saying nothing. He sniffed and wiped his nose on his own shoulder, then pressed his fingers against the clammy skin of John Hand's neck. Stitch shook his head. He put his cheek near to the admiral's mouth. Then he sat up, and gently closed the captain's eyes. "He's gone, Mr. Haas. Admiral's gone."

"No!" Haas breathed out. "It can't be." The other men stared in shock, uncomprehending. They all had precisely the same thought. It couldn't be. John Hand was the admiral. He knew everything a whole navy or a single sailor ever needed to know. He always knew. He was unconscious, that was all. He'd come around in a moment.

But John Hand would not come around.

The last thing he had seen on earth was the splintered bowsprit, this broken bone of the *Trophy Chase* as it rushed up to meet him, and the severed figurehead of the lioness falling away, as though her spirit fled downward into the sea.

"You gotta let me, Marcus!" Delaney shouted. "You gotta let me cut the line!"

But Marcus didn't budge. The yardarm blew this way and that as the sail strained for its freedom in the wind. The mast creaked and groaned like the grating of an enormous rusty hinge on some monstrous iron door.

"All right, you just hold tight," Delaney said, resignation in his voice. He never should have let Marcus come up here. The boy was a carpenter's mate. He was in the rigging because he had to take his turn. But he didn't need to have taken it now, not when the ship was running hard, looking for a fight. The boy wanted to prove himself. Delaney took his knife's edge to the white canvas and sliced at the hem itself, rather than at the tie line that ran through the grommet. He was cutting the sail around Marcus. He had barely ticked the bolt-rope that was sewn into the tabling when the whole of the sail ripped away. It went so quickly and with such force it sounded, and felt, more like a gunshot than a tear. The yard ceased its crazy gyrations almost instantly. Calm suddenly descended on them both.

"There. Not so bad, eh?" Delaney asked.

Marcus looked around him. He had good footlines under him, a firm yardarm in his hands, and a friend beside him. The sun was shining. A light breeze blew. They sailed past silent ships, sailors watching the *Trophy Chase* glide by. All seemed well.

"You see?" Delaney said, sadness pouring through his bright eyes, "It all goes easy if you just do what you need to do."

And now Marcus understood what had just happened. He had not done what he needed to do. His heart sank. "I clutched again." He said it softly, searching Delaney, looking for a denial he knew would not come.

Delaney nodded, gentle. "You did." And the old sailor and the boy both knew what it meant. Marcus had now had two chances. He had clutched twice. Marcus Pile would never sail on a tall ship's crew again, not on any vessel in Nearing Vast.

"I'm sorry, Delaney. I don't know why…" but his voice trailed off.

"None of us hardly ever do know," Delaney picked up for him. "Like you say. We don't never know what God's doin'. Ain't that so?"

"Aye," Marcus admitted, grateful for his good friend's kindness. "I guess…we hardly ever do."

The two Drammune officers honored John Hand. They removed their helmets as the crewmen approached, carrying the body of their admiral, taking him to his quarters.

"Is he dead?" one asked the other in Drammune.

"They carry him, and themselves, as though he is," the other observed.

And as the body passed them by, the strangers saw it for themselves.

Ugly glances and grimaces were directed at the Drammune, these whom the Vast sailors believed were, somehow, to blame. If not directly, then certainly indirectly. This war, that was reason enough to blame the Drammune. And if not the war, then the truce.

But the enemy officers ignored all these looks. They understood them. Instead, the pair saluted in the Vast tradition, as the Vast admiral was carried by them.

"He is one of the bravest men I have ever seen," the first offered.

"He commanded the Devilfish. And he destroyed the Devilfish. Such deeds…"

The second man said no more, but the words that came to his mind, words heard clearly in the silence, were these: *Such deeds are Worthy.*

The men of the *Trophy Chase* did not understand Drammune. But they understood a salute, and they understood the respect behind the gesture. And because the Drammune gave it, the crew of the *Trophy Chase* returned it. They had lost their captain and their admiral, but the Drammune had lost a whole ship. And yet they saluted their enemies. These were men of honor.

There would be no animosity on the *Chase*'s sad, slow return journey to the Port of Mann.

Before they sailed, the Drammune and Vast together fished sailors from the sea. They took up the Vast who had abandoned ship, those who lately had crewed the *Forcible,* the *Gant Marie,* and the *Wellspring*—two ships already sunk and the other fully aflame, pouring black smoke into the sky and sizzling embers into the sea. They took up the sobered and chastened Drammune who had survived the destruction of the *Karda Zolt.* The truce held. The ships were made ready, and all turned for the Vast harbor.

Cheers rose as the *Chase* drew near to her slip, but they petered out amid whispers. The last time she had come to port, shot up and splintered, trailing grappling lines and lost lives, she had looked somehow regal. It wasn't just her pristine hull but her posture, the pouncing cat at her prow, the pride with which she had carried herself. This time, even though she had seen no battles and lost but one life, she looked beaten. Her nose was broken. Her foremast was bowed backward and bare of sailcloth. All the damage still unrepaired from her last trip was weathered now, and it made her look old and in disrepair. And her figurehead, that lioness in full pursuit, clawing her prey at the moment of triumph…was just gone. The crowd sensed it. She was wounded.

And then as she docked, even before her mooring lines had her tied tightly to the pier, word came down from the decks that Admiral John Hand was dead. Killed by a Firefish, they said, one that first took off his right arm. He had killed it right back, though, all were assured. And yes, in answer to the next question, it was that same beast Packer Throme had tamed, the one that had attacked the *Nochto Vare,* winning the war for the Vast. All were sure of it.

The feeling of gloom deepened. Something was deeply wrong. All this was not just bad news, but a portent, somehow. The crew of the *Chase* looked hollowed out, tired, as though they had been gone for months. And then the crowd saw the two Drammune officers standing proudly aboard her, as though they belonged. As though she belonged to them.

And they would take her away.

The mood in the crowd, already dark, started to turn ugly. But no one spoke a word to address the crowd's grumblings—no officer, no sailor, no Vast prince or Drammune conqueror stepped forward to explain, to give them words either to fire their anger or assuage their sense of loss. The king and queen had not come to the docks, and no one knew why. But they all knew the royal pair would be here soon enough. One would sail away with the Drammune, and one would stay.

Then the body of Admiral John Hand was removed. The anger melted back into dread, and sorrow. Four sailors carried a simple stretcher down the gangway, the admiral's remains covered with the flag of Nearing Vast. With respect but no ceremony, the body was loaded silently into the back of a military wagon and driven off to the Old City.

So the great ship was back. Repairs began immediately. Within a week at most, as soon as her mast could be repaired and her bowsprit replaced, she'd sail again. After a while when nothing more happened, just seagulls squabbling and waves slapping, when it began to dawn on the crowds that they were watching the ordinary activities of a ship at port, longshoremen loading and unloading, ship's carpenters hammering and sawing, common sailors cleaning and polishing, the conversations died away. The crowds thinned, fading to nothing.

Packer and Panna stood hand in hand beside a fresh mound of

earth in a little clearing in the woods atop the Hangman's Cliffs. The stone marker there was a beautiful piece of white granite, polished and carved with a relief image of a cross, sun streaming from behind it. On the stone were engraved the words:

Will Seline

Husband
Father
Pastor
Friend

Beside the brown earth were a manicured patch of lawn and a matching polished marble stone, this one with the image of a descending dove, brought here from Mann to replace the rough-hewn wooden cross that had weathered here for almost a decade as Tamma had awaited her husband. It read:

Tamma Seline

Wife
Mother
Daughter
Friend

The service ended, all the townspeople, Cap and Hen among them, paid their respects and left the couple here alone. Panna's tears had been flowing freely, in both joy and sorrow, but now she stood looking at the two plots thoughtfully, damp handkerchief in one hand, Packer's scarred right hand in the other.

"I can't help but think of all they've missed here, and all they will miss."

Packer thought a long while and then said, "I pray...I pray that what we do will honor them. They were all that men and women should be on this earth."

Panna thought of her mother, who had been orphaned young and raised by an aunt. She thought of Tamma's dark moods, her intro-spection—her great spirit that overcame all in ceaseless work and bottomless generosity. She thought of her father, who had lost his wife and then had almost lost his daughter. She thought of how he had lived his whole life for God and for others. And she could not disagree with her husband.

As they departed from the graves, they stopped at the marble memorial to all those *Taken by the Sea.* Packer ran his finger across the name of his father, Dayton Throme. Here, too, was a good man gone too soon. "I wish he could know how everything he started has turned out. He never saw any of it amount to anything." Then he swallowed as a tear stung his eye. "He never saw me amount to anything."

Panna looked at her husband, the king. "He always knew who you were."

Packer saw the utter confidence in her eyes.

The two walked, hand in hand, back to the little village high on the cliff. This voyage would be different, and they both knew it. Neither was quite sure that Packer would return this time. But neither had the heart to confess that doubt to the other.

The *Chase,* refitted and repaired, would sail for Drammun within the week. Her bowsprit would be rebuilt. Her foremast would be tested and found fit and stable. It would not need to be replaced. "That's western hardwood," a grandfather would be overheard telling his grandson as they looked up from the docks at the great mast. "From the Farther Forest. You can bend it, but you can't hardly break it." And this time, he would be right.

Cabinetry would be repaired or replaced. The best craftsmen in the kingdom would work day and night to restore her to her glory. "Can't have the king sailing off in anything but the best," the workers told one another. "This here's for Packer Throme." And, "We'll show the Drammune what a real ship is all about."

But the mood remained somber around and aboard the *Trophy Chase.* She had no figurehead. She had now killed off two captains. One of them—Scat Wilkins—had conceived her, the other—John Hand—had designed her. And the man who built her, Lund Lander, the engineer who oversaw every timber, all the deadwood and the decking and the pine deals as each piece was laid and hammered and fit into place, he had died aboard this ship, too.

Now Andrew Haas would take his turn at the helm. If he worried about these things, he didn't show it. This was his first voyage as a captain. He didn't focus on the darkness of the night just past, but on the light of dawn ahead. Packer Throme, the stowaway king, would be aboard. So she'd had a difficult voyage. If anyone could recapture her spirit, if anyone could voyage out to sea and return in honor, it was King Packer of the Vast. And it couldn't hurt that Father Bran Mooring was aboard. God would surely have the keenest of interest in protecting this voyage…or so the people prayed.

As the hour of departure neared, the darkness of the parting cast a deep shadow, until at last it was a palpable pall even Andrew Haas couldn't shake. Everyone knew what this voyage meant to the kingdom, and yet no one could guess the result. Would the Drammune turn and be converted, as the king hoped, or would they turn and destroy the king, as many feared? Would they take the hand of friendship, or would they take the *Trophy Chase* by force and then come back for the rest of the Vast? Would any Firefish obey the king's command again, or would one kill him, as had happened to John Hand?

But with stark inevitability, the king took his leave of the queen, and the greatest ship ever built sailed from the Port of Mann late in the afternoon of a late spring day, out into the bay under a setting sun, and on into the dark Vast Sea. Every man, woman, and child knew that the future of the kingdom, of the world they knew, hung on this voyage.

The people watched in silence, wanting more, knowing there would be no more. They drifted off, and the crowd thinned. Words were few, and voices were low. And then, here and there, groups gathered and bowed their heads. Then men and women sank together to their knees. Without fanfare, without the leading of any single person, without being organized or preached at or shamed, the people of Nearing Vast prayed. They prayed for Packer and Panna and the kingdom and themselves. They confessed their fears. They asked for hope they did not feel, and they asked for faith they could not summon. None of them knew what the Drammune would do. No one knew what the Firefish would do. Not one man or one woman on the shores of Nearing Vast could predict either victory or defeat. But they could kneel and pray, as their king had done, as their army had done.

And that they would do.

Across an ocean, the Hezzan of the Drammune sat on her throne overlooking the city and the sea. The sun had almost set, and ribbons of red glowed on the horizon like flames from a dying brush fire. It was a fire she imagined burned now in Nearing Vast. As she sat, as she contemplated, she drew power to herself. She absorbed it like a sponge soaks up water. She did not fully understand her ability to extract power from those around her, through circumstances, through acts of the will and the mind, through any and all means. She did not understand it the way she did the healing arts or the way of the sword. But she knew she was good at it. And she was still learning. She had fought for so long, using only nerve and skill and ruthlessness. But now she had become a student of power, ever since her first encounter with Packer Throme.

And now, she was drawing him to her. He would come. He would bring the knowledge he had gained. He would wrap it in his religion, give it the name of his God, but he would bring it to her. He would bring her the greatest power imaginable. She would absorb it, soak it up from him. Take it from him.

She knew what he would say to her. He would say that she must lay down all her claims and devote herself to his God. She must let this God's crucified Son rule her heart and mind. Then and only then would power, God's power, be granted to her. But she did not want God's power, not at such a price. She had pondered that severe cost over the body of her dead husband, and many times since. But those thoughts always led to the same place. She could not entrust her unborn child to that God's care, the God who slew his own children. What power He might give, should she choose to serve Him, no longer interested her. What power He had given Packer Throme, that interested her very much. This was a power she could take, and use to her own ends.

The red glow across the horizon winked out like an eyelid closing. She knew Packer Throme's weakness. It was the weakness of every man, woman, and child who followed, sincerely followed, the bleeding Messiah. She would need only to convince him that she truly, desperately needed his help. She would need him only to believe that he, Packer Throme, was the one sent to help her. And then he would give his help freely. He would give up his own power.

He would have no choice.

CHAPTER 11

Madmen

In Drammun, Talon waited eagerly for the arrival of the King of the Vast. On the docks of Mann, prayers went up from worried Vast citizens. And half an ocean away, another prayer vigil was ending. This one was solitary, a lone man who offered up words he had repeated so often and for so long that sometimes all his concentration was required to remember the meaning of them. He raised his head, his shaggy hair falling to his shoulders. He pressed his palms down into the soft and sandy soil, pushed himself up, then sat facing the setting sun, feeling the breeze on his face through his ragged beard. He wrapped his arms around his knees, laid his cheek on one of them. It had been years. Five? Seven? More? The days here were the same, the seasons almost the same, ranging from warm to cool. Sometimes now he went for weeks, even months, without thinking about what day it was, without putting any label on a day, whether a number or a name. Now when he did think of it, it seemed very odd.

And what had changed in all the time he had been calling out to God for deliverance? Nothing. Precisely nothing.

No, he had to admit, that was not quite true. *He* had changed. He had become a part of this place, these people. Or rather, this place, these people, had become a part of him. They had grown into him like ivy into the ruins of an old castle. He had ceased to think like the Vast, like all the people on that distant shore far away, far to the west, where the sun fell into the sea. He could remember things. Things like money and reputation. He could remember striving for them, or against them. But he couldn't remember why. He could remember he had worked extremely hard at a trade he hated.

Yes, he had certainly changed.

He remembered tables. He remembered, distinctly, polished wooden tables covered by colored cloths, which were in turn covered with steaming dishes—trays of sliced turkey, puddings and sauces, gravy and stuffing. Pickles and potatoes. He remembered pies—sweet potato, pecan, cinnamon apple. And he missed them.

But he missed his family far more. He missed his wife and son like a dull ache that never went away, like a hollow place in his soul. But that had changed, too. What once had been a sharp stabbing, day and night, a regret that probed an open wound, was now a deep sadness tinged with the distant joys that once were his.

His life in Nearing Vast seemed odd to him now. He could have had his family without tables, couldn't he? Without the striving, without all the backbreaking, frustrating work? So what was all that for? Were tables full of food the goal of all toil? Was that why men ached and sweated and risked their health and their lives and wore themselves out day after day? Why they robbed and stole and lied and cheated? For a table covered with a cloth, and a cloth covered with dishes filled with food?

Perhaps it was.

There were sweet, sweet days among his memories. His wife and son, seated around such a table. Too few days, too little food. Too much fish. But the laughter, the walks with his tender, sad-eyed wife, the dreamy yet excited eyes of his son seated high atop that cliff, wondering about the meaning of it all. These were memories he never wanted to let go, and he worked hard to keep them clear of cobwebs, fresh and clean.

The boy was just becoming a man the last time his eyes had taken in that sight. Was he well? And what of his wife? Did they prosper without him, or did their lives grow harder and leaner yet? He prayed for them, ached for them, prayed for them again, longed for them. He could still see their faces, but he could no longer hear their voices.

He had a hard time recalling his village. He remembered the buildings, the general store, the pub, the church. But when he thought of the services inside the church, or the conversations inside the tavern, his mind took a strange turn. He would be inside the building, or sitting on a beach, or on a hilltop overlooking the sea, just as he was now. And then the memories would fade and he would be alone, just as he was now. And then he would be back here.

Remembering life indoors…that had become quite strange to him. Why did his people spend so much time hiding from the world, from the weather? He used to know why. The weather was harsher there, that was certainly true. But men gathered in pubs all year round, rain or shine. They chose to be inside whenever there was no need to be outdoors.

Outdoors. The very word assumed that surrounding oneself with wood or brick was normal. Why would any people call the great world "the outdoors"? Only if they preferred their cramped, dark hiding places. He shook his head. He was less and less Vast. He spoke in this foreign tongue now, exclusively. He dreamed now in the Achawuk language. And his thoughts ran slower than they used to. Even now, the stars were out and shining across a great expanse of sky, and the last rays of the sun were gone. He had been sitting here praying and thinking for how long? Hours, perhaps. A long, slow time.

But time meant little here. These people found meaning in the changes of the wind, in the flow of currents, the rise and fall of tides, the chatter of chipmunks and the scurrying of spiders, in the schools of fish that danced in the sparkling waters, in the great rays that flapped their wings slowly across a sandy ocean bottom. And this, he now understood. These were nature's creatures. They had meaning given by their Creator.

But the meaning of a gold coin or a silver tea set, or a fish market, or closing time or starting time for meetings and for church, these he no longer understood. And yet, it was ironic. He had come here to bring meaning to these people. He had been put on a ship just as it sailed, without saying goodbye to his loved ones, sent on a ship full of missionaries as a missionary. He was one of a dozen. All the others had been longing to reach out to the Achawuk for years, praying, beseeching the church authorities for such a chance. But he had been interested only in Firefish.

The High Holy Reverend Father had sent him here. A golden opportunity, he'd said. The opportunity to learn of Firefish from the source of all such knowledge. And Harlowen Stanson had been right. The Achawuk did know the secrets of the Firefish. But those secrets belonged to the Achawuk alone. They were not willing to part with them, and would kill any who tried to learn them and would feed their bodies to the beasts. True, he had been spared, but he had often wondered if perhaps that was a mistake. Perhaps he was supposed to have died like the rest, and God had overlooked him, glanced away at just the wrong moment. And now here he was, all these years later, a pariah and a misfit, a madman to be watched and studied. He was neither Vast nor Achawuk. God sent him here with some purpose in mind, perhaps. But then God had lost track of him.

Better to have perished with the others.

Dayton Throme had sought knowledge of Firefish. That desire had consumed him for most of his life. Now he knew far more than he cared to know.

"I'm sorry we aren't meeting under better circumstances," Panna said, taking a seat at the bedside of the High Holy Reverend Father. She felt awkward, not knowing how to address such an august figure in what must be quite humbling circumstances for him. His left arm was wrapped in a splint, as was his left leg under the bedclothes. His head was wrapped lightly, but a thick wad of gauze padding protruded fully three inches from his skull above his left ear. "How are you feeling?" she asked.

"Quite well, considering," Hap said sunnily. "Not as well as I hope to feel tomorrow, but better than I felt yesterday. Your hospitality has been outstanding."

"Thank you," she said, wondering vaguely why she was thanking him rather than the other way around. But the way he paid her the compliment was so rich and warm, she felt honored by it. "That is the purpose of a hospital, as I understand it," she added.

"Hence the name," he said easily.

The royal hospital was little more than five spare bedrooms on the ground floor of the palace, with tall, wide windows facing south to let in the light, and doors that opened onto the palace gardens. It was the place where physicians worked with royals and dignitaries and other people of note when they came down with chills or fever or the bellyache. It was where young queens gave birth to infant princes and princesses, and where aged kings struggled through their last brittle hours of life.

"You are kind, and gentle," Hap assured her. "A good Christian woman."

Panna could not answer. His praise was again lavish, and she felt flattered. But how could he know her? She knew she must be on her guard, and now knew it would not be easy to guard against such flattery. But she had not forgotten the words of Father Mooring, who had assured her Hap Stanson would not help her in her hour of need, but would side with the power of Prince Mather.

They had met before, of course, on the decks of the *Trophy Chase,* but only briefly. And that was just before that terrible series of speeches designed to convince the people that Packer Throme and the *Trophy Chase* could win the war single-handedly. A slight shadow crossed Panna's face as she suddenly realized it had turned out almost precisely that way.

Hap Stanson continued to beam light and warmth. "I hope to be fit and walking within a week or two, if these surgeons know anything at all about their craft. But I couldn't wait that long to have an audience with you. I'm so glad you answered my call. There are things you should know, in your new position. And a few questions I'd like to ask as well."

The way he said "your new position," with that little nod, it was flattering again. Panna felt a small pinprick, a warning to her heart. "As you wish," she granted him.

"You are new to the dealings of government, and I understand that. I would like to help. The relationship between Church and State is, and must always be, one of give and take. After all, the king cannot have total sway over the Church, to order her to do his bidding."

Panna saw the logic in that.

"Nor can the Church run the government, for its kingdom is not of this world."

Panna saw the logic in that as well.

"And so we have come to a place in Nearing Vast I like to call a 'position of mutual service.' A Christian monarch should honor the Church, and serve her to the best of his ability. In the same way the Church should honor the State, and to the fullest extent possible serve the king of the realm. And the queen. If that happens, there is harmony. Much like in a marriage. Do you agree?"

Panna nodded, but she was thinking of something else. She now understood her reaction to his words, now that he had said them again. He had given her that same extra twinkle as he added those three words "And the queen." It made her think of Queen's Day, the annual Vast holiday in which one woman from each village was chosen to be queen and was treated as such as she went around ordering things as she would like them to be.

It was a fun holiday, but with a practical purpose. The women of the village could finally accomplish those things the men never seemed to get around to doing...removing the rotting tree stump from in front of the schoolhouse, repainting the stoop of the pub, or even replacing some poor farmer's wagon wheel. The women had learned, of course, to conspire in advance of the choosing ceremony about what deeds might be done, and to focus on those things that could not well be undone the very next day. But what Panna remembered now was the tone in which the men always addressed the "queen." They showed great deference, playing along. Hap Stanson sounded just like one of those men.

"Excellent," he said. "Then we shall have a very fruitful relationship."

"There are rumors," Panna said, not unkindly but with steel. "There are rumors that you would put King Reynard back on the throne."

His easy demeanor didn't change, but his eyes backed away. "Rumors? From what possible source?"

She watched him carefully, and realized he would do almost anything to avoid answering a direct question along these lines. In fact there *had* been rumors. The palace was full of them, as were the pubs. Such was to be expected when so many days had gone by without any statement at all from the Church regarding the change in power. She chose the most direct question she could frame, and asked it. "Do you see the ascension of Packer Throme as legitimate? I ask only because the fruitfulness of our working relationship would of course depend on that."

Hap scratched his neck. He had heard that this one was the more forthright of the pair, but he hadn't quite expected this. She forced him to make a choice. Either he had to lie to her to win her trust, or he had to show her his hand. "You don't let a conversation meander, do you? I respect that. I must admit I came back into the city doubting. You can imagine the shock of it, having been gone only a few days. But as I've questioned witnesses to the passing of the ring, I have no doubt that all the laws of man were followed—"

She interrupted him. He was not answering a direct question directly. And he was admitting to having investigated Packer's legitimacy. He might have begun with that, rather than with nods and happy little confirmations about fruitful mutual service. So she cut him off by asking another, even more direct question.

"And what of the laws of God? Were they followed, or were they broken, do you believe?" She asked it kindly, but this time the steel in her words was sharpened to a gleaming razor's edge.

Hap hid it, but inside he was surprised and angered that she would choose to corner him like this. This went well beyond mere forthrightness. This was a total lack of decorum. It bordered on hostility. It also made it impossible for him to shade the truth. If he said yes, the laws of God had been followed and Packer was the rightful king, he would give up his leverage. More to the point, he would feel like a fawning puppy dog to this young queen, and that was a posture he refused to assume. If he said no, then lines would be drawn and he would be engaged in a battle he was not yet prepared to fight. But she would not so quickly get the better of the High Holy Reverend Father and Supreme Elder. If she wanted swords unsheathed, then so be it.

"And if I say the laws of God were broken," he answered breezily, "will you then renounce the throne?"

Panna sat back and blinked.

He suppressed a laugh. "I think we should be friends, Panna. Your father and I, God rest him, had a great mutual respect. I'm sure he would want you and me to have the same respect as we work through the intricacies of earthly power."

She knew better. She knew that Hap Stanson had no time for priests with tiny congregations out in the middle of nowhere; she knew it from experience. But she also knew her father would demand she show respect for this man's office. So she waited for an explanation.

"Let's reason it out. You fear that I do not acknowledge your position with regard to the throne. Fair enough. And yet you just proved you will not acknowledge my authority in important spiritual matters, such as the working of God in the succession of kings." He watched as she grappled with the implications. "Now, perhaps, you are beginning to learn about the need for a position of mutual service. What would the people do, or say, should they find out that you do not respect my authority? That you have refused to obey, or even to befriend, the Church?" Hap seemed to grow sunnier as he spoke. "Or worse, what would happen if in the first days of your reign, with Packer gone to return who knows when, the Church took an open position against you? Questioned your right to rule?" He waited again, watching such a possibility work its dark way through her imagination. "The people expect me to bless your reign, and I have not yet done so. We really should be friends."

She could see the truth in what he said. But what he did not say, and what she felt most forcefully, was that she was, in fact, pretending to be queen until he said otherwise. And that he felt quite comfortable in his position, which if she could state it for him, she would put this way: *No little girl from the backwoods is going to take away my authority.*

What he presented to her was open, sunny, happy blackmail. It was every bit as sinister as Prince Mather's crude attempts to win her favor, but Hap wasn't playing for dinner and the wearing of fancy gowns. The stakes were the kingdom. This wasn't crude at all. Hap had yet to make any demand. He was simply opening negotiations from a position of power. Here was someone who knew how all this was done.

He waited patiently, pleasantly, watching with serene satisfaction as the reality of Panna's predicament enfolded her. She had no choice but to work with him. She was a strong girl, and she wasn't stupid. But how smart was she, really? He would find out now.

"Packer Throme did not ask to be king, nor I queen," Panna said at last. "God has put us in these roles."

"As He has put me in mine. He could easily have taken me home to heaven, right there in the woods, but He saved me from that bear, and from that forest fire, for a purpose."

She paused for a moment, then continued. "And so God may take the kingdom away, however and whenever He chooses. He may use you to do that, and I will accept it as coming from His hand." Her voice now grew hard. "But with all due respect to you and your office, I will not play your game." She stood up. "Please, by all means, tell the people we are not legitimate, if that is what you truly believe. Not that you need my permission, but you have it anyway. If, however, you decide that the right thing to do is to add the blessings of the Church to the obvious blessings of God, then by all means, call for me again. Until then, I wish you only the best, and a very speedy recovery." She curtsied, and left the room.

He sighed and shook his head. She was headstrong, and that would create problems. But she wasn't very smart. She wouldn't see the end coming until she was flat on her back, wondering what hit her.

Dayton Throme looked around him now, down at the village illumined by cooking fires. Its structures were not even huts; they were made of treated hides, Firefish hides stretched over frames made of wood or fashioned from huge, round bones. The ribs of the beasts. These were lean-tos, more shields than buildings, and like shields they were painted with the fiercest images of Firefish Dayton ever could have imagined, far more vicious than anything the Vast could conjure. That little sign above Cap Hillis's pub was a drawing of a child's toy in comparison.

Now, with the sun set, families gathered around fires, surrounded by such images. Evening songs were being sung, chants that were short on melody but long on soulful harmony. Men prepared food and cleaned up alongside the women. In fact, men shared all duties with women except for actual childbearing. Women sat at family councils, war councils. They ate and drank with men. They hunted, they worked. Women shared all duties with men but for actual warfare.

No fences surrounded this village, no lines marked one family's area from the next, or one man's possessions from another's. The only barriers at all were these framed huts…and the rather dramatic ring of spears at the base of this hill. Dayton Throme's hill. Hundreds, thousands of spears, standing upright side by side, leaning this way and that like the jack-o-lantern teeth of the Firefish from which each spearhead came. They pointed toward the stars, standing ready at a moment's notice to be taken into battle. Until then, they were the fence that symbolically kept the madman at bay.

But it was only symbolic. Dayton had no chains on his hands or on his feet. He could walk freely through this or any other village. He spoke with the Achawuk casually as they shared their food and he shared in their labors. And yet every evening he returned to his own small lean-to atop this hill, to be by himself until morning.

Shackles would be meaningless anyway. There was no place for him to go. The island was full of villages just like this one. If he took a canoe or swam to another island, he would find more of the same. The few ships that ventured near over the years were destroyed, overrun just as his own ship had been, every man, woman, and child killed without so much as a blink. Everyone but him.

And every ship had been destroyed except that singular one, that sleek and beautiful craft that had escaped a year or so back as the wind blew into her sails and rocked the warriors from her hull and rails. He had watched. He had been standing ashore, face painted. He was glad the ship had escaped. The Achawuk had questioned him about it, as though he had somehow freed it from their grasp. They spoke of it as if it were a sign. But of course, to them, everything was a sign. He himself was a sign, the madman on the hill.

He recalled again the terror of being aboard ship as the Achawuk closed in. He felt the fear anew every time he remembered. He looked down now at his bare chest, his ragged vest open, and at the single white blade that hung around his neck. He held it up, looked at it again. It had saved him. He had pulled it from around his neck to fight, to use as a weapon. The Achawuk had recognized it immediately, of course. They had taken him ashore to safety in one of their canoes, even as they burned his ship, even as they killed all his companions. He didn't understand what was happening to him then.

Soon he knew. When he had arrived, a stranger brandishing a Firefish tooth, using it as the weapon it was, they believed it to be highly significant. He had stepped into a mystery, an ancient mystery. He was to them a holy man, to be revered and protected. But he was not a prophet, not like the prophets of the Hebrew Scriptures. The Achawuk cared little for his teachings, and nothing for his God. They listened with some interest to stories he told about the Son of God, sent into the world as a man. But they did not believe them.

Dayton Throme had come to understand that he was considered not a prophet, but a prophecy. He himself was a remarkable event, and he would be followed by a more remarkable one yet. He was a precursor to cataclysm. They no more needed to reason with him than they needed to converse with a bolt of lightning, or a storm, or a Firefish. And so he was a pariah, a prisoner, and a portent, all at once.

A holy madman.

Over the years, they had softened toward him, as he learned to speak with them. But they never wavered. He was not Achawuk. But he was theirs, and would be until the great event occurred. Or until they all died waiting for it.

This is the Lord's doing; it is marvelous in our eyes.

That phrase, that scrap of Scripture, careened around inside Bran Mooring until it overflowed, and he said it aloud. Everything around him was utterly marvelous. The warm wind on his face, the angle of the decks on which he stood, the thud of the waves as the prow crashed through them right under his feet, the snap and billow of canvas above, the squawk and career of gulls behind, and all the scrambling activity of men up and down the masts and the rigging, orders being shouted, piped, ship's bell ringing out the hour…it was powerful, and pristine. And marvelous. But more marvelous still was the meaning of it all, clear to him as the morning sky. God's hand was steering the ship of state toward a glorious destiny.

Above, in the rigging, Smith Delaney paused to look down at the odd little priest at the prow, as did all the other men. Frequently.

"What'll one of those big Fish do if it finds that one standing there?" Mutter Cabe asked, jarring Delaney from his thoughts.

Delaney felt the brooding within his superstitious companion, then looked down again, scanning the seas for any sign of the beasts. He saw none. He looked back at the little figure, brown robes flapping behind him, hands gripping the rail for dear life, head on a swivel, taking it all in with a palpable sense of delight. "It'll laugh at him," Delaney decided.

Cabe grimaced, but one corner of his mouth rose. All the men assumed that Packer Throme had sent the priest there, but he had not. Bran Mooring was simply drawn to be in that spot, finding it the place he preferred. But the men didn't mind. The happy little priest seemed like a cleansing agent, a purifying spirit. Sure, they were being escorted to Drammun, and Huk Tuth himself was below deck somewhere, but light and life were returning to the *Chase*. The ship seemed lighter in the water, swifter in the wind. She sailed easy.

And why shouldn't she? Packer Throme was aboard. That fact alone was enough to turn the men's thoughts toward better days. The stunning news about Packer's ascent to the throne had, of course, taken them all off guard. But only for a moment. It had been almost instantly accepted as his due, his right.

And so the men stole glances at Packer even more frequently than they did at the priest, heartened each time they saw him. He stood on the quarterdeck, a step behind Captain Haas, wearing a satin shirt and breeches.

"Why don't he wear robes and a crown?" a sailor asked once.

Delaney sniffed, looking down at his royal friend. "Well, he has no need for such as that. He knows who he is."

The sailor thought a moment, then nodded.

"Still," Mutter Cabe grumbled. "A little cape or something couldn't hurt."

Delaney pondered, but shook his head. "That one there, he's a king on the inside. He don't need a costume to show it. Look at 'im now," Delaney pointed out, "talkin' to a regular captain who's more gussied up than himself is." They all watched Andrew Haas, who stood proudly in a full naval dress uniform, speaking with Packer. "But it ain't hard to say who's the king among the two." The others had to look for a while, but eventually they could see it. Or at least they thought they could.

"Now look 'round about ye," Delaney continued. "Who's leadin' who? I tell ye, even *they* know." The others looked across the ocean at the scores of ships that accompanied them. The *Trophy Chase* was the only one with white sails, those sails billowing, her Firefish armor intact and glistening on her hulls. Behind her and to port and starboard, stretching out beyond the horizon off both rails, were crimson sails, crimson hulls, Drammune warships and troop ships. The entire Expeditionary Armada of the Glorious Drammune Military, all aligned in a flying wedge that went on for miles, and the *Trophy Chase* at the point.

Word spread through the City of Mann that Packer Throme had once been expelled from seminary. He had refused to submit to church discipline, they said, even after he had been caught cheating. Everyone seemed to know someone who knew someone who had seen his official transcript, shown to him by a priest. And unlike most rumors, this one turned out to be extraordinarily easy to

The Battle for Vast Dominion

confirm, particularly for anyone who ventured onto the seminary grounds.

But even those citizens who found it troubling—and most did not, preferring to view it as an amusing and youthful indiscretion or the sign of a healthy young man in an oppressive environment—even the most pious agreed it would have little import on his ability to be a good king. Except, of course, that it did suggest he might need to show a little extra contrition and humility now that he was in the seat of power.

Another rumor followed quickly, however. This one was completely unverified and much harder to confirm, but so close on the heels of the first that it shone with reflected authenticity. This one said that the High Holy Reverend Father and Supreme Elder, Harlowen "Hap" Stanson, had made repeated efforts to meet with the new queen, and she had rebuffed him. She had refused to visit him on his sickbed, preferring to wait until he was well enough to come to see her. She demanded the respect due the throne.

Many discussions were held over many mugs of ale as to who was in the right here, the queen or the cleric. But all agreed that things would take an ugly turn if those two didn't work out their differences. And by the way, the Church had been strangely silent regarding Packer's ascension, hadn't it? What happened to the coronation ceremony, led by the Supreme Elder himself? Packer had sailed off without so much as a tip of the ecclesiastical hat. Wasn't that odd? Yes, they all had to agree, that was very odd. But these things would be settled in due time. Packer and the Church, why, they played on the same team, didn't they?

But over the next few days, things became less settled. New rumors began to spread. These were darker, spoken in whispers, phrased in questions, concerning the inexperienced young woman from the fishing villages and what she was doing alone there in the palace. Wasn't it true that Prince Ward still lived there? And wasn't he a notorious drunk, and a womanizer? And so why hadn't she kicked that lecher out? And what of this story that she had actually lived at the palace with both Prince Ward and Prince Mather while Packer was gone the last time? Was there something the Church knew, after all, that kept the Supreme Elder from blessing the new king? Perhaps the problem was the new queen. She was young and attractive. She was without her husband...

The Battle for Vast Dominion

As the rumors grew, Hap Stanson's pain subsided. He rested well. He ate well. He slept well. The number of visitors in and out of the palace hospital rose. Among these were many priests, and among the priests the one most often seen was Father Usher Fell.

CHAPTER 12

The Mission

"God is moving," Usher Fell assured Ward Sennett, speaking as loudly as he dared, wanting to be heard over the raucous strings and drums of the tavern band, but not overheard by unwelcome ears. "He is moving, and He is maneuvering, and when it is all over, you shall be king."

Ward's eyelids blinked lazily. Even when opened, they were half-closed. He licked his lips slowly. "You're quite sure of that, are you?" His tongue was thick but articulate. He had much experience managing the affects of alcohol.

"Oh, yes!" Usher Fell was only slightly abashed by the current state of the prince. The tavern was crowded; it was past midnight, but the dancing and singing were not winding down. Ward looked over Usher Fell's shoulder and winked, slowly and methodically, as though thinking the action through as he performed it. The priest did not turn around to see the object of the prince's momentary affection. He had seen enough of them already, just getting across the floor to this booth where he now sat across from the prince.

"The High Holy Reverend Father—" but a sudden whoop of laughter and then applause drowned out the rest of the priest's message.

"What?" Ward asked, his hand cupped to his ear.

"I said, the High Holy Reverend Father and Supreme—" but another round of laughter cut him off again.

"Who?" Ward asked.

"Hap! Hap Stanson!" Usher Fell fairly shouted. "Hap wants you to know he cannot be public about it just yet."

"Public about what?"

"His support for you! But his message is this: Do not lose heart, or faith, no matter what you may hear."

"I will try not to lose…anything at all," the prince replied, numb and thick. Then he looked confused. "But what might I hear?"

"Rumors, that's all. Just rumors. Ignore them. All is as it must be."

"All is what?"

"As it must be!" As Usher Fell nodded assurance, a barmaid fell into his lap. Ale went everywhere, three mugs spinning across the table and onto the floor. Usher Fell pushed the girl off him roughly. Her apology came from deep inside a laugh. She didn't try to hide her amusement as the old robed figure stood, hands held out to his sides, looking down at the enormous stain that his robe had suddenly become. The ale quickly soaked through to his skin, cold and uncomfortable. She dabbed at the table with her towel, saying things like, "I declare, a priest! My luck. Probably go straight to hell for this!" But she never lost the wild glimmer of glee. She looked up at him, towel poised to help him dry himself.

Usher Fell snatched the towel from her hand and started blotting at his own robes. He pulled several items from his pockets, a handkerchief, a scrap of paper, a few pennies, looked them over, then shoved them back where they came from.

"Thank you," Ward said, standing. He shook the priest's wet hand. He looked at the priest's sodden robes. "Say, that's quite a mess there." He shook his head solemnly. "But ignore it, won't you? It's all as it must be." He fairly shouted the final words.

Usher Fell stared and blinked, unsure if he was the butt of a joke. But the prince seemed to say it without spite. "Quite. Well, good night."

Usher Fell made it to the door before the laughter from the back booth rang out through the pub. The priest could not tell for sure whether Ward Sennett had joined in, or whether in fact they were laughing at a poor old priest's expense. And he preferred not to know. He did not look back.

"I'm so sorry! Here, this is probably his," the barmaid said, still giggling, handing the prince a folded piece of parchment. "Found it down there." She waved generally at an indistinguishable patch of wet wooden flooring. "Might be something he wants."

"I'll be sure to take that right to him," the prince said with a knowing look that assured her he was quite, quite thankful.

But he stuffed the paper in his pocket.

"We have found the one you seek, Your Worthiness," Sool Kron purred, with a nod.

The Hezzan Skahl Dramm stood up from her throne. "Who? Where?" Talon had been seated here high above the city, looking out over the sea. She liked being here; this was where she belonged. Her eyes could see only her capital and the blue waters before it, but from this vantage point her mind could envision her entire empire, and watch as it expanded far beyond the horizon.

Kron saw the light in her eyes. "I searched the kingdom, as you requested, leaving not a pebble undisturbed. I found him. He is a slave, or was, aboard a slaver, nearing the end of his useful life. Another week and we might have been too late."

"Where is he now?"

"He waits in your prison."

Her eyes turned dark. "Prison? No…he is a guest! Free him, feed him, bathe him, clothe him in crimson! His life is worth more than a hundred thousand Zealots to us now."

Kron grimaced. He should have guessed this. "Yes, Your Worthiness, immediately."

"When he is rested, bring him to me here." She thought a moment. "No, not here…put him in my personal guest quarters, and when he is ready, I will go to him."

"Of course. All shall be prepared." Kron turned to make it so.

"Minister Kron," Talon said, her voice a dagger. He hated that she had this ability, that she could run him through with her voice alone. But she held that power over him. She had it ever since the day she had shot Zan Gar down during the meeting of the Twelve.

He turned slowly, bowed his head. "Yes, Your Worthiness?"

But her look was one of gratitude. "I was confident that if one Achawuk man, woman, or child existed in my realm, you would find him. Well done."

He felt genuine relief, and bowed deeply. "My life is yours, and you are Worthy to serve." Then he turned and left.

His fears instantly alleviated, he now felt old and weak, and he cursed himself. What had she done to him? He was becoming the lapdog he pretended to be. The woman had power over him, that was certain. But he was sure he had won her trust. And he had a play in him yet. Didn't he? Yes, if he could make it quickly. But if he delayed, he might truly grow too old and too weak to care.

A steady breeze from the southwest meant that ships headed east-southeast would sail across the wind, making excellent time. The sea was calm, and the sun shone through a sky strewn with small, high clouds. At night the moon wandered slowly through a milky path of stars. Packer Throme spent much of his time on the afterdeck, appreciating now why it was also called the "weather deck." It was the highest deck of the ship, and with no sails above, no covering of any sort, it was open to the elements. And on this voyage, that was delightful.

It was odd, traveling as the king. He had no specific duties. He tried to pitch in once, grabbing a mop just to feel productive, but the sailors didn't take it well at all. They just froze in place, and stared at him.

"What?" he had asked to their blank, almost sorrowful faces.

"Sir," one stammered, looking at the wet decking and at the mop in Packer's hands. "If we ain't doin' it to yer satisfaction, you jes' tell us. We'll work harder. We'll get it right."

He handed the mop over, and complimented their work.

Then he got smiles. Actually, it was the same smile, over and over, the one he started to think of as the *royal grin*. It greeted him almost everywhere he went. Crewmen ceased talking, quit singing, stopped working when he came by, and they grinned. They were just delighted to see him. Always. And, he knew, they were just as delighted to see him go.

He had come quickly to the realization that a king was simply not welcome in the ebb and flow of ordinary life. It was strange, but it was so, and there seemed to be nothing he could do about it. He had never had more responsibility, and had never had less to do.

So he spoke little but thought much as the hours poured by.

He thought of Panna as he looked west, back toward Nearing Vast. He prayed for her, his heart welling up with a strange mixture of pride and longing. He knew she would be a great queen, and he prayed that the people would see it quickly. If he never returned, he hoped she had a long and prosperous reign.

He thought of the Firefish. He could not help but feel a great loss when he remembered the face of the beast, the questioning he saw there, the yearning, the joy it so clearly felt. Had it obeyed his command? It had certainly seemed that way. Though now with John Hand killed and so much time having passed, he doubted it was so.

And then Packer thought of his mission. It was a crystal thing in his mind, a bright white light that shone down on his path, like the silvery trail of moonlight across the sea at moonrise. To take the knowledge of God to a nation of the godless. What higher calling was there? For this, he could believe he had been made king. He had no illusion he would somehow convince the Hezzan, much less an entire nation, that suddenly they should leave their traditions and believe in the God of their enemies. But he knew his role. It was simply to speak the truth. They wanted the secret of controlling the Firefish. He would give them the mysteries of God, and let come what may. Would the Hezzan care to hear? He prayed that he would. He asked God in fervent pleas that the Hezzan would have an open heart, some shred of sensitivity. A weakness into which he could speak, perhaps. A secret fear that could lead to the protection and security, and ultimately the love, of God.

He felt content that he had been given this opportunity to speak the message, and then to let God unfold the rest. He had been made king, it would seem, that he might speak to a king about the King of Kings.

Talon saw the line of ships approach. Her Hezzan Guards had watched day and night through the powerful telescope she had placed atop the palace. She was determined to be the first to know of the return of Huk Tuth and Fen Abbaka Mux. She scanned the seas, unable at this distance to determine which ships were which. Except for one. There in the center, enfolded that it might not escape, were the white billows of the *Trophy Chase*. Surely Packer Throme was aboard. Now it began. She would consolidate her power. And then she would rise to heights undreamed of by any Hezzan, even her late husband. She felt his pride. Yes, she would fulfill his vision, and then some.

She called for Sool Kron and Vasla Vor.

The docks had been made ready. The red sails of the Drammune warships filled the bay, then filled the sky. As they approached the docks, each ship sailed toward its appointed slip, then dropped sail and was rowed by tug to its moorings. In this manner the *Chase* slid into the slip at the farthest end of the longest pier.

"Sure keepin' us a long way out," Delaney commented. He pulled at his collar, then scratched under an arm. All the men were on deck in their war whites for the occasion. They itched and twitched as they watched with fascination the big oar boats expertly maneuver the *Chase* to her moorings, one boat at her bow and one at her stern. Delaney stood at the rail to Packer's left, while Captain Andrew Haas stood to his right. Huk Tuth watched from the afterdeck, finally making an appearance.

"Almost like they know the depth of our keel," Haas said, "keeping us in the deep waters like this."

Packer pondered that, but couldn't imagine how the Drammune knew much about this ship.

"Rather a sorry welcome, I'd say," was Delaney's next observation.

On the dock stood a handful of soldiers, the Hezzan Guard, in crimson vests and breeches. Two dignitaries, one an old man in fancy crimson and gold robes, the other a sturdy general, stood waiting at the end of a crimson-carpeted gangway.

"That may be their Hezzan there," Captain Haas ventured, gesturing toward the ancient Sool Kron.

"No, the Hezzan is not present," Father Mooring noted. "See how the soldiers stand with their backs to him? They would never do that to a Hezzan." After a moment he said, "I would guess that the truce is not popular here. They don't trust their citizens to come greet us, and the Hezzan is not prepared to be seen in public with the Vast. This arrangement is likely for our own protection."

"Comfortin' thought," Delaney muttered.

As the gangway was rolled into position, there was a conversation in Drammune between Tuth at the rail and the general, who was Vasla Vor, on the dock.

"Can you make out what they're sayin'?" Delaney asked.

Father Mooring nodded. "They only want Packer. They've come to take him straight to the Hezzan."

"What about everyone else?"

"Confined to the ship."

"That ain't right," Delaney said, as the two dignitaries strode up the gangway followed by the Hezzan Guard.

"I won't go alone," Packer said. "You tell them I need my translator. That's you, Father. And I won't go without my bodyguard." Here he looked at Delaney, whose chest swelled as he rose to his full height. Which was barely an inch taller than the small, round priest.

Talon had orchestrated this arrival carefully. She needed one thing from Sool Kron and Vasla Vor, and one thing only: that they bring her the Supreme Commander of the Glorious Drammune Military. She assumed this was still Fen Abbaka Mux. He would be given one fair chance to serve her. If he swore allegiance, as the Quarto had done, then all the power was hers. If not, she would appoint his successor.

She knew she could not venture to the docks herself. She was wary of an assassination attempt, but that she would have chanced. More important was that a Hezzan must summon her subordinates. To go to him, to appear at the docks herself, would smack of desperation and carry the deadly whiff of weakness. She needed Kron and Vor to stand together and vouch for her absolute authority, her total legitimacy. This she was confident they would do. Vor, she was sure, was loyal as a hound dog to her, as he had been to her husband. The death of Minister Gar was a display for the Court of Twelve, but was also designed to assure Sool Kron that Vasla Vor would happily kill a traitor.

But just to be sure, she had kept the general commander suspicious of Kron, feeding him subtle evidence that the chief minister was looking for a way to undermine him, and her. And she let Kron know that Vor was watching him. She was confident. The two of them would bring her the supreme commander.

CHAPTER 13

Drammun

At the foot of the ramp, a carriage waited. It was squared-off in shape, and the color of dried blood. The interior was well-appointed, with dark leather seats and velvet curtains, and a small keg of ale embedded in the wall between the front-facing seats. A leather mug hung from a strap beside each seat. Delaney had hardly gotten settled before he eagerly tested the Drammune ale, which he found strong and harsh. Much to his liking. Father Mooring and Packer declined to partake, which troubled Delaney so much that Packer then agreed to have a taste. He found it bitter.

Packer looked at Father Mooring. His eyes were far away. He was listening to a conversation outside the carriage.

"They disagree," he said. His usual sunny visage clouded over.

"Who?" Packer asked, alarmed by the priest's reaction.

"Commander Tuth wants to accompany us. Well, you. And the other two, they want to travel alone with the commander."

"Why, do you think?"

Father Mooring listened for a while longer. "The Hezzan Guard is going to take us to the palace. They've convinced Tuth he needs to ride with them." He paused, looked at Packer. "It's some news having to do with the Hezzan."

"Bad news?" Delaney asked.

"Bad or good, I can't tell. But it's big."

"Big news is most always bad news," Delaney said, finishing off his ale. He looked at the spout with longing, but did not pour himself another. He hung up his mug and patted the golden leather scabbard on his belt—he wore Packer Throme's sword. Then he nodded, mostly to himself. He felt ready for anything.

The carriage door was closed, and then locked from the outside. The carriage rocked once, creaked, and began its trek to the palace.

In this conveyance, behind the clip of a four-horse team, they rode through the city streets of Hezarow Kyne. Delaney stuck his head out the window and craned his neck in an effort to see the sights. But Drammune guards rode on horseback, two abreast on either side of the carriage, blocking his view in their effort to provide security. Undeterred, Delaney thrust his shoulders and both arms out of the window, and by doing so managed to peer around the sullen Drammune escorts. He saw red-tiled roofs, dark wood, and red-brick walls with tiny windows, people dressed in dark clothes hustling about with little to say to one another. Everything was different; everything seemed odd. The stones in the streets were darker, somehow, and odd-shaped. Wood was wood, but somehow always the wrong color. Chimneys were squat where they should be tall, and tall where they should be squat. Even trees and shrubs seemed strange, green and leafy, but not nearly the right shade or shape.

And then there were things he'd never seen before. He saw iron rods bent and twisted into symbols, fastened on rough wooden planks in front of buildings, or just free-standing. It took him a long time to understand that this was ordinary Drammune signage, written in a language and presented in a manner utterly foreign to him. It seemed to him impossible that anyone could ever get used to this enough to think of it as normal. But there was more to it. Something behind it all, some quality that made everything seem so…not-Vast.

When they finally stepped out of the carriage at the foot of the winding stone pathway up to the palace, Delaney forgot where he was and let loose with a long, low whistle. The palace was an enormous structure, ten times the size of the meager little dwelling of the King and Queen of Nearing Vast. It was built into a steep hillside, and it towered up and up, story after story of concentric rings, each story smaller than the one on which it rested. It had dark stone masonry, blood-red, and crimson tiled roofs. There were parapets, and places where broad porches jutted out, and where walls jutted in.

"The Hezzan lives there?" Delaney asked. "It's like a whole screamin' city."

"It is," Father Mooring said, his hands clasped behind his back as he peered up at it, suddenly both professor and student. "It is quite the equivalent of the entire Old City of Mann, all under one roof."

"You been here before?" Delaney asked suspiciously.

"No. But I read."

"No one cain't read this. Ye have to see it."

"I won't argue."

"Looks like a big red snake, don't it? Kinda all curled up and sleepin'." Delaney studied the porches and porticoes another moment.

Packer felt severe misgivings as they started up the broad walk. The dignitaries were nowhere to be seen. Tuth was gone. They were surrounded by guards. One of them grunted a command, and the three Vast natives walked in silence, more like prisoners than honored guests. Packer looked up at the building, and felt Delaney's description might be a little too accurate.

At the center of the roof garden was a portico, a rectangular structure supported by four columns, one at each corner. The windows of the structure were wide arches, one per side. Inside the portico was a marble throne. If one were walking toward it from the roof garden, as a servant did now, the throne appeared to sit within the structure, resting on a low dais just slightly higher than the level of the garden floor. But in fact, the dais rose up from the floor one story below. A falcon at rest on the sill of that arched window could flutter easily to the dais. But if the servant were to step over the low window ledge, she would tumble twenty feet or more onto marble stairs below.

To walk from the throne to the roof garden, as Talon was now doing, one would need to go by way of a marble catwalk, twenty-five feet long, three feet wide, and a foot-and-a-half thick. One catwalk protruded from the dais to the left of the throne, and one to the right. Everywhere else, the stairs flowed directly down from the dais into the Great Hall of Feasts below.

From the catwalk, Talon passed the servant. She accepted the cup of kathander, rejected the plate of fruits. The servant bowed deeply, then turned back with the tray, headed toward the back of the gardens from whence she had come.

Talon now walked through the gardens to the frontmost ledge.

Here she peered through her telescope, permanently bolted to the stonework. She saw figures far below climbing out of a dark carriage. Three men, surrounded by her guards. One of them had yellow hair. She recognized Packer Throme. A shorter man had dark hair. That would be the plenipotentiary sent by the king. And the third was a priest. She frowned. Where was John Hand? Lund Lander?

A second carriage pulled into view behind the first. In it would be Vasla Vor, Sool Kron, and the supreme commander. She waited. But the door did not open. The three Vast dignitaries began walking toward the palace. Alarmed now, Talon swung the scope to the carriage again and refocused. The door remained closed. Her heartbeat quickened. "Open!" she said aloud. But it did not. Suddenly, her future, her kingdom, all her power hinged on one carriage door. She told herself they just needed more time. There was more to be discussed. Kron and Vor would convince him; all they needed to do was gain his agreement to see her. They would exit in a moment.

But they did not. Instead, the second carriage pulled away, following the first.

She felt a stab of fear, and then of rage. She felt the sharp sting of betrayal. And as she turned from the rail she felt all her power, absorbed and extracted so carefully, from so many sources, over so much time, flow from her. Like water from a broken dam.

She put a hand to her belly, and wondered whether these three men had just taken the crown away from her unborn child.

Inside the carriage, Huk Tuth had cut through the veneer of manhood, the thin armor that each of the two servants of the new Hezzan imagined to be impregnable. He did it with two questions. The first was, "Which of you is responsible for bringing this woman to power?" He asked it through iron-gray teeth, with eyes as cold as death.

Tuth's anger, as he heard their story, had focused on the orders he had received via the falcon at Varlotsville. Had he known that the parchment came not from his Hezzan, but from Talon, he would have treated it as so much rubbish. The Vast should be his...*would* be his, but for her. He did not speak these thoughts aloud, however.

In the brief silence that followed, Sool Kron feared a checkmate in one move. If he tried to disavow Talon or his own actions in putting her on the throne, he would be denying the Hezzan he clearly served and thereby revealing his own treachery. Men like Tuth tended to regard loyalty as a higher virtue than the fine arts of policy that Kron had mastered. Yet if he claimed responsibility for enthroning her, he risked admitting to a crime that Tuth might well find unforgivable. He could neither confirm nor deny, and so he remained silent, searching for another option.

In that same brief pause, Vasla Vor had similar but simpler thoughts. He felt embarrassed to admit his own role to a man like Tuth, whom he respected greatly. But to deny his role would be Unworthy. Vor, however, had one small but significant advantage over Kron. While the commander of the guard had arrested the Twelve for their crimes, he had not brought her to the throne. That, he firmly believed, was Kron's doing, accomplished when the old man took her to see the Quarto and then invited that rat's nest into the Court of Twelve.

"I arrested the Twelve for their crimes against the Hezzan and his wife," Vor said. Tuth snapped his eyes toward Vasla Vor. "Sool Kron ushered her to the throne, with the help of the Quarto." It was an authoritative statement from a man known to value truth and integrity above all else.

And then Huk Tuth's eyes swung slowly back to Sool Kron.

Kron said nothing. He was trapped. Tuth had not threatened him, nor yet even stated his position on the matter. It would be cowardly to deny it. Possibly fruitless as well. He raised his chin. "It was all done according to the Rahk-Taa. The Twelve have confirmed it. She is the rightful Hezzan."

Huk Tuth glowered at him. Then he drew his knife, a jagged thing forged for the single purpose of bloody combat. And now he asked his second question. "And who will take that power away from her?"

The pause here lasted quite a while longer. In it, both Kron and Vor saw themselves dead. Vor imagined himself hanging from the Hezzan's rope. Kron pictured himself stabbed through the heart by Huk Tuth's knife.

But this time it was Kron who thought quickly, and spoke first. "Why, Supreme Commander Tuth. I do believe that would be *you*."

Dayton Throme stood on the shores of the "mayak-aloh." Its name meant *still waters*. He had heard it used to describe other, smaller bodies of water, and so in his mind it was akin to the terms for "lake" or "pond" in Nearing Vast. All bodies of water smaller than the great sea were mayak-aloh, and all were named after this place. This was not, however, a lake or a pond. Rather it was a part of the sea, surrounded by enough islands and hidden reefs that the waters behaved like those of a great lake.

It was here, the Achawuk believed, that the great event would take place, the tannan-thoh-ah. And looking at it, this open expanse of water in an imperfect circle of islands, with its various shades of blue—from shale here at the shore to aquamarine, turning to cobalt and then a deep royal blue in the center where the waters were deepest, it seemed as though this place was in fact created for some great event, something even larger than the ritual Firefish feedings that happened here. And those were certainly stupendous events themselves. Whatever the great event was—the cataclysm, the apocalypse—whatever happened and whenever it happened, if it happened, it just made sense that it would happen here.

"Ta-hohn shayn con-grahsa." Dayton looked behind him, saw the man called Zhintah-Hoak, *Red Spirit*, walking toward him. Though he was a leader among the Achawuk, it often seemed to Dayton that he treated his role as largely ceremonial, even somewhat of a nuisance. He would rather talk than almost anything else. Among the Achawuk, this was a noble trait. There was no small talk here. People spoke with meaning and of meaning. They spoke of life and what sustained it, physical and spiritual: food, the hunt, preparing meals, caring for the young, procreation. The river that flowed in all men and women, in all things. They spoke of Firefish, of death, joy, love, and friendship, and the future of the world.

Zhintah-Hoak looked like an aging dockworker who had been in one too many tavern fights, but he behaved like a combination of a friendly small-town constable and local freeloader. Like all Achawuk, he spoke slowly and deliberately, choosing every word with care and pleasure. *Everyone watches you these days,* he said.

"Ta-hohn shayn po," Dayton responded in the same, slow cadence. *Everyone always watches.*

"No," Zhintah responded. He paused. The fingers of his mind sorted through the fruit of his lush green lexicon, selecting only the ripest berries. These he chose to speak, one at a time, savoring each one. "Not like now. You grow restless. You sense the approach."

Dayton studied the man's face. It was hard and strong, but not at all unkind. His eyes seemed old and satisfied. Dayton looked again across the mayak-aloh. There was something to what he said. Dayton did feel a particular longing for home lately, and with that came a sense of restlessness. It did not seem to him that this portended anything except a personal bout of melancholia. He did not argue, however. "I hope that the tannan-thoh-ah comes soon, and that it brings with it my freedom."

After a while, Zhintah answered with certainty. "It will bring freedom to all."

Dayton stared at this man, as much a friend as he had here among these warriors. But he could find nothing to say in response to such an assertion.

Eventually, Zhintah spoke again. "The dreams have started."

Dayton had never known a people who put so much stock in their dreams. "And what do the dreams foretell?"

"The tannan-thoh-ah, of course."

"Of course."

Zhintah nodded, content. Their conversation had been a good one. Then he looked out over the waters again. After a while he put a hand on Dayton's shoulder, and asked in his calm, deliberate manner, "Shela hooyer taha-an?"

Do you have any dried fish?

Talon entered the Great Meeting Hall of the Hezzan, calm and erect, showing no sign of anything being amiss. Seven of the Twelve were here, in their places. Missing were Sool Kron and the Quarto. Also missing was Vasla Vor, who always sat in the visitor's dock behind her, in part to protect her from threat of assassination. His absence was not comforting.

The four Prefects of Justice stood, as did the three Prefects of State. They looked terrified. She strode to her chair and stood behind it. She stared at each of them in turn.

"Who called this meeting?" she asked them.

No one spoke.

"Who summoned you here?"

Mouths opened, no sounds emerged.

"Guards!" Three of the Hezzan's personal protectors entered the room. She took a pistol from the holster of the nearest one. She looked at the dregs of the Twelve. "Now. The last to answer me will die. Who called this meeting?"

The eruption that poured forth was easy to disentangle. The answer was the Quarto, and in particular, Pizlar Kank.

So, it had all come apart, just that quickly. The Quarto had made their move. They had gotten to both Kron and Vor. Talon cursed silently. She had missed her chance to turn the supreme commander, and now it was too late.

Then the obvious occurred to her. It was so obvious, she wondered how she could have missed it. The source of power was within her grasp. "Excellent, then," she said. "Carry on." She turned and looked at the three guards. She handed the nearest one his pistol.

"You three, come with me." And she left the room.

Delaney rubbed the back of his neck vigorously, trying to work the crick out of it. He'd been staring up at something or other, it seemed, ever since he got off the ship. The buildings, the palace. Now he was inside the palace, with its vaulted ceilings high overhead, shining in sunlight and lamplight, mirror-finished stone and highly glossed wood, with walkways and parapets… "It's like bein' outside when you're in," he noted. "'Cept in here the sky is made a' stone."

Even the guest quarters made him feel small. The rooms were laid out on three levels, like the last three steps of some huge, cascading stairway. And in fact, each was connected with a sprawling, ever-widening open stair. Across the rail at the farthest edge of each floor, one could look down over the next. The bedrooms were on the top level. The middle level boasted meeting rooms and banquet rooms, plus a kitchen stocked with wines and cheeses, breads, and all sorts of wrapped-up goods just waiting to be sampled. The lowest level was a sprawling recreational area for parties or for lounging, with cushions and low chairs and thick, square carpets, all opening out onto a porch that stretched the length of the apartment, more than two hundred feet across, with a panoramic view of the whole city and the sea.

"Appears to be set up for doin' nothin' at all," Delaney observed of the lowest level. "But I suppose those who get invited here are probably used to doin' a whole heapin' lot of that." He caught himself and looked at Packer. "Beggin' your pardon. I mean to say, others who may get invited here, and not you yourself. Sir."

Packer laughed. "Delaney. It's all right. I'm your friend." He managed to avoid adding "not your king," but he was feeling particularly small himself. All he could think was that whatever expectations the Drammune had of him, or the Vast for that matter, he was not likely to live up to them. He was still imagining formal dinners and formal negotiations, where unknown protocols and obscure customs might any moment reveal him for the fisherman's son he was.

Father Mooring ignored all else and went straight to the porch rail at the lowest level, and looked out over the world of Drammun and its capital. He stood there silently a while until Delaney and Packer flanked him. Then he said, beaming, "Isn't this just the most exciting thing?"

Packer swallowed, unable to speak his agreement. It was exciting, certainly, but it was the sort of excitement he had felt once when he was visiting a distant cousin on the Nearing Plains and was chased around a pasture by a bull named Furious Floyd.

The great square door of the guest quarters was crimson, with an iron slash across it dividing it into two blood-red triangles; it was the same pattern featured on the double doors of the Hezzan's own private chambers. In front of the door stood two guards. Flanking them were two more, four guards blocking the only way in or out of the chambers.

Talon feared the guards might already have been reached by the Quarto. She was prepared for anything as she approached. "Stand aside," she said easily.

They did, looking only mildly worried by her presence. She took one of them by the elbow. "You will announce me to the ranking Vast diplomat," she said.

"Your Worthiness…" he stammered. "I don't think—"

Suddenly she was behind him with his own pistol stuck under his chin. She watched all other eyes as she asked the one in her grip, "You don't think what?"

"Begging your pardon, ma'am. I was just going to suggest that I announce you to their king."

"Their king?" The other eyes confirmed it. Her mind reeled. No doubt, the dark-haired one she'd seen get out of the carriage…that would be Mather Sennett. So Reynard had died, or abdicated. She released the guard. "The rest of you wait here. Let no one in. If anyone approaches, warn me. Anyone at all. Do you understand?"

They assured her they did.

"...and so, O God, please honor our meager actions," Delaney prayed aloud, "which art as sawdust...on a plate...where we was hopin' for meat and such. And by Thine own hand make that sawdust come round to bein'...more foodlike." He paused, eyes still closed, not happy with the image he'd just conjured before his Creator and his king. "In a manner of speakin'," he added, and tugged again at his collar, wishing Marcus Pile were here to say a proper prayer.

Packer Throme looked up as the great door creaked open, one level above. Bran Mooring looked up as well, closing the leatherbound book on the table in front of him, quite sure that the time for prayer was coming to an end one way or another. He saw the armed guard appear at the top of the staircase. Delaney stopped mid-prayer and opened one eye, sensing the intrusion more than hearing it. Then he looked up to where his two comrades now looked, and said, "Amen, then." He was relieved to have wrapped that up.

"Hezzan Vastcha, Skahl Dramm rolhoi!" the guard announced loudly, stiffly, looking straight out ahead of him. "Skovah karchezz!"

Bran Mooring stood. "Here comes the Hezzan," he said simply. Packer and Delaney rose to their feet. "Step out here," Bran offered, gesturing for Packer to stand beside him. "No need to be shy. You're the king."

Packer obeyed, though his feet and hands tingled and his knees felt wobbly. He remembered how he had felt as a boy, readying himself to leap off one of the lower faces of Hangman's Cliffs into water far below. Delaney took his place beside Packer so that the three stood in a row, with Packer in the center.

And then Talon appeared at the top of the stair.

The Hezzan Skahl Dramm descended with a dignity and grace that any observer would have sworn came from noble birth and years of privilege. Her brown robe trailed a step or two behind her, its crimson borders, its cuffs and hems, its simple lines dramatic in the daylight. Her hood was up, obscuring her face, but the three men could detect that she was a dark woman, angular, with high cheekbones and piercing eyes, and a crown of three strands, gold, silver, and brass, elegantly wrapped around her forehead. She looked like a queen. She did not look at all like a ship's security officer. Or an assassin.

"I thought the Hezzan was a man." Delaney whispered, loudly enough that the Hezzan could hear him.

"There's your big news," Father Mooring said in answer. Then he added, "Packer, you stand, we bow." Bran Mooring went to one knee, then bowed his head. Delaney followed suit. Packer waited.

But halfway down the stairs, Talon stopped. Packer Throme she expected, but not like this. Not in this role. "Where is the King of Nearing Vast?" she asked.

"I am the King of Nearing Vast." Packer bowed.

She considered this absurdity for a moment and then laughed. It was a cold and ringing thing, and it went through him like a bitter winter wind. He had heard it once before, below decks on the *Trophy Chase* as he suffered at Talon's hands. This was that same voice. But even now, he assumed it was another Drammune woman much like Talon, another from the same nation, the same culture, who sounded like her. Talon was dead.

Bran Mooring and Delaney raised their eyes. The Hezzan was a woman; that was certainly true. But why would she laugh at the King of Nearing Vast? Then Delaney stood, and when Talon recognized him, she laughed again. Only minutes ago, she had mistaken Smith Delaney for a king!

The sailor drew his sword, Packer's sword, and advanced on her. "You've laughed your last, you scarlet witch!" he proclaimed. But he stopped at the foot of the stairs, the point of his blade trembling noticeably in the air.

"Delaney!" Packer cried out. He was sure his old friend had lost his mind. "Put that down. It's not Talon."

"It is, sir!" Then to Talon, "If yer wantin' to kill Packer again, then by God this time you'll go through me!" His voice cracked on the last syllable.

She seemed amused.

Packer fairly ran to Delaney, grabbed his arm, pried the sword from his fist. "I'm sorry," he said to the woman, looking up at her as she descended. She dropped her hood as he continued. "He thinks you're..." and then he stopped, his heart sinking into his stomach, his hands and feet tingling numb.

Her eyes pierced his.

"Hello, Packer Throme. So good to see you once again."

Packer raised the sword and held it straight out toward her, his body turning sideways reflexively, melting into the guard position. She walked down the final two stairs, to within an inch of the blade, its point hovering utterly motionless before her throat, as though locked there. All his training came back to him, all his experience, as though every minute, every hour of it had been packed into an open funnel and forced down into this one moment. His mind and body reacted to the sudden appearance of this threat with a thousand ways he could kill her, and a thousand and one ways she could counter. But underpinning all were desperate truths that ate away at his resolve. Talon was back from the dead. She was Hezzan of the Drammune. It was she who had had brought war on the Vast.

Talon shook her head. "The King of the Vast should not threaten the Hezzan of the Drammune. I have invited you here that we may be allies."

More realities. She was the one who had ended the war. She was the one who wanted to learn of the Firefish.

Talon took the blade point between her fingers and moved it aside. Then she released it and walked down the stairs past him, stopping in front of Delaney. She admired his dress whites for a moment. "And you, Smith Delaney—you look almost elegant. Has the stowaway king made you a prince of your meager realm?"

The sailor's face contorted with hatred and confusion. Mostly the latter. "I ain't no prince. I'm a friend a' the king! You just ask 'im! And if you want to kill 'im again, then I mean it, I'm your man."

"Are you? How delightful." She paused, then added, "But please. Relax. You are a guest here. And I should tell you that I was the one who saved Packer Throme's life. I didn't kill him then, though I wished I had. But that's in the past." She walked over to Bran Mooring, who was still kneeling. He now rose, a bit clumsily, to greet her.

"And who is this charming priest?" she asked. "The father of the lovely Panna Seline, perhaps?"

"Sadly, our worthy friend Will Seline is dead," Bran said in Drammune. "I, too, am a friend of the king. Your Worthiness."

She nodded appreciatively at his Drammune as she noted his brown robe. She knew him by such to be a teacher. "The king has so many highly placed friends!" she replied, also in Drammune. Then in Vast, to Packer, "I am sorry for the loss of Panna's father. Is she well at least, I hope?"

"The queen is quite well," he answered.

"The queen! My yes, haven't we all thrived since our last encounter. Congratulations to you both. Please give her my regards when you see her again."

Packer looked at the weapon in his hand, its tip now pointed toward the floor. "I swore I would never take this up again," he told her. "But I am sorely tempted to break that vow."

She laughed once more, this time less cruelly. She seemed to actually find humor in his statement. "The swordsman has given up the sword. This is a habit with you. The last time we met you would not avenge your swordmaster, nor your girl, nor the blood of innocent villagers. Then you were but a simple sailor on a ship. Yet as king, you are sorely tempted to assassinate the head of an allied state, while on a diplomatic mission? The Vast never cease to amaze me."

"You are guilty of crimes that a crown cannot cover."

"Well said, Packer Throme. Yes, I am guilty of many crimes. I may have started the war between Drammun and Nearing Vast. But you, Packer, you ended it. You tamed the Firefish, and taught it to attack." She watched his eyes, noted that he did not shrink from this assertion. This was good. Were it not true, a man as honorable as Packer would reveal it in his eyes. "Is this the glorious victory for which the Vast made you their king? The defeat of Fen Abbaka Mux and the Drammune Armada?" She said it in a slightly mocking tone, but she knew that if ever a crown could be earned for a single deed, that single deed would earn it.

Packer stared at her a long while, trying to piece it all together. And then the full weight of Talon's involvement, all this time, behind the war with the Drammune hit home. One more reality. "You knew I would come. You brought me here."

"Yes," she said simply. "Packer Throme has been summoned to Drammun to teach Talon the ways of the Firefish."

Packer closed his eyes and shook his head. All those miracles. The wind with the Achawuk. The battle with the Firefish. The victory on the Green. The ascension to the throne. The prayer at Varlotsville.

190

All of those led, somehow, back to Talon. All the good he'd seen, all that God had done…all the while, Talon had stood across the sea, scheming, reeling him back toward her. Twisting everything to her own ends. It was as though every miracle he'd seen was also part of her dark magic, as though the flip side of every gleaming act of God was the shadowy will of evil. It was almost enough to make him doubt the goodness of God. It was certainly enough to deflate him, and to make him feel smaller and more helpless than he had felt in a long, long while. And the last time he had felt this helpless? The last time he had stood before Talon. And yet, when he was helpless, that was when God seemed to work most powerfully.

He handed the sword back to Delaney.

She saw the act, and did not miss its meaning.

Packer looked at her again. His voice when he spoke was quieter, rasping a bit with the emotion he felt, but more serene. "How did you survive? You fell through the ship's floor and into the fire."

She shrugged. "The cabin into which I fell was not aflame. But I perceive the question in your heart is not how, but *why*. Why did I live?"

Packer said nothing.

"Perhaps it is because your God had other plans for me. And for you. Perhaps, this moment is a part of those plans."

Her voice was almost gentle. Her eyes sincere. But Packer had no trust in her. "Don't talk to me of God," Packer said ominously, remembering all her mocking words, all her contempt for the weakness of the Son of God, the weakness of His followers. "Don't speak of Him unless you can do it with respect."

Talon looked him in the eye. "But I have learned a great deal about your God since last we met."

The silence grew thick as the two stared at one another, Packer trying to see into her motives without being deceived, Talon wanting to convince him she was in earnest, and to hide away anything that would cause him to doubt.

Finally, Talon looked away, studied Bran Mooring for a moment, and then Delaney, whose dark look still spoke of death. She walked past them both and descended the stair to the lower level. The three men looked at one another, unable to find words.

"I must speak to her," Packer said at last. "It's why I came." He held out some hope that one of them would try to talk him out of it.

Neither did. "I'll go with ye," Delaney offered.

"No. Thanks, but this is my task."

"Watch her," Delaney warned. "I'll wager she didn't get to be Hezzan by askin' real nice."

"I know what she is," Packer said. But he didn't feel certain. He hoped she had in fact been transformed somehow. But he dreaded hearing her claim to have found truth, to be a changed woman. How could he ever believe her? "This isn't about swordplay anymore," he told Delaney, putting a hand on his shoulder.

Packer looked at the priest, then looked to where Talon had disappeared down the stair. "I don't think you can help much either, Father."

"I can watch and pray," Bran said, understanding Packer's thoughts.

"Thank you." But Packer recognized the reference, and it was not comforting. It was what Jesus asked the disciples to do, just before He was crucified.

CHAPTER 14

The Queen

Like Packer, Panna could not abide the idea of summoning anyone to see her while she sat elevated in regal splendor on King Reynard's elaborate, and far too large, throne. Crowns and scepters seemed to her an absurdly ostentatious show, a flaunting of power that couldn't possibly help her accomplish any good end. But she was sorely tempted now. Harlowen "Hap" Stanson had asked to see her. She wanted to speak to him, but she wanted that conversation to happen in some context other than a charitable visit to a wounded man's bedside. She needed him to understand that she was not play-acting. He must be made to understand that Queen's Day had come to stay.

She decided on a State dinner. She realized, as she worked through the details of the invitations and the seating arrangements, that she was beginning to think like a politician. She didn't like the feeling. She would rather talk to people casually, make them comfortable over coffee or a simple lunch. But Hap was a powerful and dangerous man, and he was far too slippery. She needed to speak to him where the lights were bright and there were no dark corners into which he could retreat, where his every statement would be known to all.

The topic of the dinner would be this: the deployment of the Fleet. He had sent her a strongly worded message, and she had read it several times over the course of several days. She could not tell if he really believed it, or if it was another ruse of some sort. But the subject was certainly worthy of discussion, and worthy of advice from all her counselors. The message read:

> *The kingdom is in grave danger. Bravely or foolishly, your husband has sailed away into the heart of Drammun. While we may hope and pray otherwise, we must assume that once the Hezzan knows all we know of Firefish he will return to our shores in force. We have a limited army, a joke for a navy, and we have sold all our impenetrable armor to the Drammune. But what we do have, Panna Throme, are Firefish. Not live ones to sic on our enemies, perhaps, but dead ones to use for armor. We have the ships to hunt them. We have the lures to kill them. We have the knowledge and the ability to process the beasts after we kill them. And while we may have no Navy, we do have a Fleet, one like none other on earth. Perhaps our sailors cannot shoot cannon, but they can certainly kill Firefish. You must refit our ships, and send them. Our Fleet must bring home Firefish flesh, skin, and scales if we are to have any hope of survival. We must use the time we've been given, time granted to us by God, through the wisdom and sacrifice of your husband. I pray you will take this advice to heart. I request an audience to discuss it in detail.*

> *Yours Most Sincerely,*
> *Hap*

Hap would sit at her right hand, in the place of honor. Ward Sennett would be seated to her left. He had been acting erratic lately, as though burdened with some secret he couldn't, or more likely wouldn't, tell. She assumed it was that he was drinking again, though frankly it wasn't much of a secret. General Mack Millian would sit opposite her, at the foot of the table, with Zander Jameson to his left. Her nation's oldest and youngest generals, both of whom had been unfailingly upright, honest, supportive, and wise, would be a tremendous help. To Millian's right would sit the new Admiral of the Fleet, Moore Davies. It would be his first foray into diplomacy. Rounding out the guest list would be Dog Blestoe. A representative of the people would always have a place at her table.

Panna planned everything carefully, from the initial soup course to the walnuts that would accompany the port and cheese after dessert. When the night came, she was ready. The dining room was prepared. It was all white linen and crystal. It was a State dinner; it was what royals do.

But, as it turned out, it wasn't quite the success Queen Panna had hoped for.

Talon stood at the rail, looking out over the city, out onto the docks. "My reign is at an end," she said.

Packer looked at her with a furrowed brow, but she did not turn to look at him.

"You see those soldiers in the streets, coming toward us?"

Packer looked, saw darkness filling the streets far away. If he squinted, he could imagine they were Drammune soldiers marching in columns. "Yes."

"They come from the docks. From the Armada. I ordered them to stay. But my enemies have turned them against me. They are coming for me."

He looked at her again. She seemed saddened, but not surprised. Nor was she angry, nor impassioned. "What happened?" he asked.

She shrugged. "I am a woman, and I took the crown my husband left behind when he died."

Packer hesitated. He couldn't help thinking of Panna, left behind now as well.

"I have made many enemies." Now she looked at Packer. "I suppose you are beloved by your people."

"Well. Not all of them."

She knew she was right. "I have killed my enemies, and now they will kill me. If they can." She watched his eyes, saw the brief flash of emotion. He was transparent as glass. "Your God demands sacrifice." She looked out over the streets again. "But not like the pagan gods of old. Those gods wanted goats or lambs or chickens, or the occasional virgin. Your God is greedier by far. He wants to swallow His followers whole. He wants their children, their titles, their lands. Their entire dominion."

Packer watched as the legions slowly approached the palace. He could tell now that these were indeed troops. "Yes," he had to agree. "But it's all His in the end, anyway. And He doesn't demand it for His own gain, but for ours."

She shook her head. That made no sense. But she was not here to argue with him. "And you have offered Him such sacrifices."

"I have tried."

"No, you have done it. You have given yourself up to Him, without reservation. This is the source of your strength."

Packer was uncomfortable leaving it there. "I have done that," he admitted, "but as for strength...I don't feel much of it very often."

"No, but your strength comes in the offering."

She did not look at him, but he searched her eyes, her face. Somehow he saw no coldness there now. She didn't have it right, but she was so close. "Talon."

Now she looked at him.

He searched her. "Do you believe? Do you believe in God?"

She searched him. "Do you command the Firefish?"

Packer's heart sank. He dropped his eyes. He had already thought through all the possible results an honest answer to that question might bring him once he faced the Hezzan. None of those imagined results were good. But he had come all this way, through all these trials, and God had put him here to bring the truth to the Drammune. And now here he was, speaking to the Hezzan. It wasn't how he'd imagined it, but here was his answer to prayer. He had no choice but to keep speaking the truth.

"Only God can command the Firefish."

She thought a long while, then she asked, "And did your God command the Firefish...to obey you?"

There was only one truthful answer. So he said it. "Yes. I believe He did."

"And you sent it to destroy the *Nochto Vare*."

"I gestured. And it went."

She was silent, remembering the beast's yellow eyes. The one she had killed was certainly intelligent enough to understand a command. But that one was a killer. What had Packer Throme done to align such a thing with his own will? The idea that such a thing could be tamed now seemed stunning. If a beast like that could change its nature...

"Talon, if you were to make that offering—"

She turned on him. "Your God cannot be trusted! He killed His

The Battle for Vast Dominion

only child. Why should He not torture and kill my child, when He will gladly do so with His own?"

Packer didn't know what had just happened. But behind Talon's anger he now saw pain. It was the same look of desperation he had seen on the *Camadan* as she fell through the flames. She wanted to reach out, but instead backed away. "Talon, His nature is always to…" Then he stopped. "Wait, did you say your *child?*"

She put a hand to her belly. Then she turned again to look out over her city, at the soldiers, still approaching, coming closer and closer. Her voice was hardly more than a whisper. "I carry the child of the Hezzan."

"Oh, Lord." He felt his head buzz. He realized now that he had assumed she had killed her way to the top. He had just assumed she had married for power, and…well, people near to Talon had a way of dying. But her position had come to her much like Panna's would if something happened to him. He looked down to the streets again, at the troops approaching, and suddenly he felt a need to protect Talon. Which he recognized to be quite absurd, but there it was. "What…what are you going to do?"

"I should ask you the same, King Packer of Nearing Vast, since those troops also come for you."

"For me?" Packer asked, newly alarmed.

"But of course. The men who seek my life are mad for war with your nation. When they succeed in taking my throne, they will undo our alliance without a thought. And they will have the King of the Vast as their captive."

Packer took a deep breath. He could hear the troops in the streets now, their hobnail sandals striking the stones in unison, like a distant snare drum. "So…what now?" He couldn't believe she was just going to let this happen.

"Come with me," she said, and turned away from the porch railing.

"You have a plan?"

She laughed once. "Of course I have a plan."

For the first time since he'd heard her name spoken in a hoarse whisper over a mug of ale in a pub in Mann…what seemed like eons ago…and in spite of all the events in which she had played a role since, all of which argued fiercely to the contrary, Packer Throme found himself relieved to know that Talon was plotting something, and that he was a part of it.

The Battle for Vast Dominion

"The Fleet is a key part of the military apparatus of the Kingdom of Nearing Vast," General Millian pointed out. "It must be drilled, schooled, and focused on warfare if it is to become a fighting force. Returning those ships to their merchant past, sending them to hunt Firefish, would mean we once again have no Fleet at all."

"We have no Fleet now," Moore Davies conceded, settling his spoon into his soup. "They certainly can't fight. I'm not sure they can hunt, either, but I can promise you they will hunt better than they fight."

"And so you suggest taking a Fleet that can't fight into Achawuk waters?"

"And you suggest taking a Fleet that can't fight to war. We know how to prepare for the Achawuk. They have primitive weapons, and are unaccustomed to dealing with large numbers of ships. We just need numbers. And we do know how to take a Firefish."

"Then how do we shore up our defenses?" returned Millian. "We are vulnerable here in Mann."

"What's the point of shoring up defenses that won't hold regardless?" Jameson interjected. "I say send the Fleet to Drammun."

All eyes turned to him, all spoons stopped moving. "To Hezarow Kyne?" Millian asked. "Why on earth would we want to tempt those fates again?"

Jameson shrugged. "Because the Drammune don't expect it. And if things go poorly for our king, we'll have help at the ready. If things go well, it won't matter where the Fleet is sent. But at least there, we'll be able to learn the outcome of the king's efforts and take some reasonable action."

"Reasonable action?" Davies asked glumly. "You don't know our Fleet."

"Well, it's the first thing I've heard that makes any sense," Dog offered, holding his soup spoon upright in his big fist. He stared at the tablecloth, a scowl on his face. He had been listening, unwilling to interject an opinion among such an august group. But finally he couldn't help himself. He caught Panna's eye, and she nodded, just the trace of permission he needed. He sniffed. "I say take the cork to where the bottle is." Cream chowder dripped from his spoon onto his fist, and he licked it off. As he did, more dripped onto his shirt front.

There was a pause, as all considered the man and his words. And his manners.

"Father Stanson, you haven't said anything yet," Panna interjected, drawing eyes to the sunny visage of the high holy one seated to her right. "I know you have an opinion in this matter."

"I do," he said. "And I am grateful to be asked to this table that I might share it."

Panna managed not to roll her eyes. "Please do."

At that moment the wine steward leaned in at the Supreme Elder's right hand, and he nodded appreciatively. The red liquid pinged perfectly as it poured into the pure crystal of the glass. Stanson swirled the wine, admiring it. But he didn't drink. He held it before him, resting it near his chest as he spoke. His left arm was in a sling, but his head was no longer bandaged, though a yellow-and-purple bruise was visible around his temple. However, his wavy locks covered the scab nicely. "I am a peaceful man, schooled in peacemaking and not in war. War is about dominance, and dominance is about power. The Church operates, as you know, on a very different set of principles in that regard."

Panna glanced around the table, but got the distinct impression that all these men believed him. All but perhaps Ward, who watched through narrowed and distant eyes. He had a look about him that seemed almost cunning. Satisfied, in some dark way. It was not a look she was accustomed to seeing him wear, and it was not one she liked.

"First," Hap continued, "from a spiritual perspective, I must observe that this war was never about which nation is stronger, but which is more Worthy. The Drammune lay claim to that title, of course, and have their own godless definition of it. But in the eyes of the Lord, worthiness is found in righteousness, which we may define as fearlessness, faith, and forgiveness. I would like to suggest that all three of those qualities may be proven by sending the Fleet to the Achawuk territory. Let's look at them one at a time." He touched his right forefinger with his thumb. "Fearlessness...I don't believe I need comment on that. It will take brave souls to sail into Achawuk territory, where the only knowns are also deadly perils."

"Courage must be measured by the yardstick of wisdom," Millian interjected, "wouldn't you agree?"

"Yes, very much so. But hear me out," Hap answered easily. He touched his middle finger to his thumb. "Faith. God may be trusted regardless of where the Fleet is sent. But to go where the dangers are so great will certainly test our faith."

He touched his ring finger. "And then, there is forgiveness, the greatest gift we are given, the greatest gift we have in our possession to give. Bear with me here, but the question I must ask is, how might we best forgive our enemies, the Drammune? And how might we best forgive those among the Achawuk who have slain our missionaries, attacked and burned countless of our ships?"

Dog shook his head, amazed. Forgive them? Were the military leaders of Nearing Vast seriously taking advice from a preacher?

Hap leaned forward, and his voice dropped. The others around the table leaned in to hear. "To forgive, one must have the power to forgive. We all know that Firefish armor is invulnerable to the best weaponry in the world. Imagine with me, envision a future, a very near future, in which Nearing Vast holds the key to such earthly superiority. God has given us the Firefish. Imagine that we harvest the things by the hundreds, drape all our ships in their hides, all our men in their armor. Imagine that we are invincible.

"Once the Drammune submit, what nation will stand against us? Imagine Nearing Vast with all the power in the world. Imagine we use that power to do good. With all the nations bowing to us, we can then teach them. We can reach them. Envision Judah under David, Jerusalem under Solomon. The City of Mann as the City of God. Imagine it, my friends. With the power God has given, we may teach them the ways of truth and help them to find forgiveness. We are talking here, gentlemen…" he nodded at Panna, "ma'am…we are speaking here of the means by which God may, if we have but the faith and the fortitude, let our fair city shine as a lamp on a lamp stand, a beacon to the heathen. A city on a hill that cannot be hid."

All were silent, envisioning just such a time.

Hap had them; Panna could see it. It was a dazzling display of… something. Leadership surely. Persuasiveness undoubtedly. He wove a powerful vision.

"Prince Ward, you have yet to speak," Panna interjected, breaking the spell and bringing the others back to the moment. Panna hoped he might offer a counterpoint, but what came forth shocked every guest, and her majesty as well.

Ward's dark look seemed to vanish in an instant. He looked at the wine in his glass, as yet untouched, then held it up. "I do have an opinion," he said brightly. "But first let me say this. I vowed to avoid this liquid until the war was won. I can't say that I upheld my vows religiously, but I gave it a good try. Still, I hereby declare victory, and if what we have now is not victory, I hereby declare that it's close enough for me." And he closed his eyes and drank the wine down in a single swallow, savoring the taste. He then beamed at those around the table, suddenly feeling a bit invulnerable himself. "Now, as to my opinion. Thank you for asking, by the way," he nodded at Panna, to his right. "Your Highness. Queen Panna." He bowed his head low toward her, then made a point of looking across the table at Hap Stanson. Ward was sure he was not the only one who had noticed that the High Holy Reverend Father, always eager to be draped in his own golden titles, could manage only to call Panna "ma'am."

"I have promised you, my liege," he said to Panna, "promised both you and the rightful King of Nearing Vast, your husband, that I would always tell you the truth as I see it. So here it is." He raised his chin. "I believe it makes not one whit of difference whether you send the Fleet or keep it near, or chop it up and sell it for firewood." He did not look at Moore Davies or either of the generals, but only at Panna as he spoke. "Because it is not a Fleet; it is a collection of merchant vessels with big guns stapled to their decks. If they can fish, let them fish. If they can hunt a valuable quarry, by all means let them do so. But we all know that the only way they could stop the Drammune is to double them all over in laughter."

Now he looked around the room. "Say, I'm particularly dry here," he interrupted himself, holding his glass toward the steward, who came running. "Ah, thank you," he said as the wine poured.

"Prince Ward," Panna said gently.

"You may order me to be silent, my queen, but short of that, I'm bound to give you my advice."

She held her tongue.

He swallowed half the glass. "Now, where were we?" He settled back in his chair. "Yes, the Fleet. Send it or save it, it doesn't matter. The issue on the table is not Drammune or Achawuk, armor or firepower. The subject at hand is not about these things at all. None of them. It is all about power, pure and brutal. Gussied up, as I believe they say in the fishing villages, or tarted up, as they say in slightly more refined circles, but still raw, cold power." Now he turned to

Hap Stanson. "The issue on the table is really your power, sir, to be more precise."

Now the table went dark, as though candles had been snuffed. Father Stanson blanched, then shrugged breezily, the way one might when singled out by a clown hired to perform at a picnic.

"Ward," Panna warned.

He looked at her. "I have not yet given you the truth as I see it. Nor have you ordered me to be silent."

"I ask you to consider your words carefully."

"Oh, I have considered them. Now, I would like you to consider them as well. I have watched my father do this man's bidding my entire life." He pointed at Hap Stanson. "I have seen this man pull secret strings on everything from taxes to the choice of tapestries that adorn these very walls. Why did my father care nothing for his throne, there at the end? Why did he sink into the soft comforts of lazy disillusionment? Because he had long ago lost his throne. He had lost it not to Mather, but to the High Holy Reverend Father and Supreme Elder of the Church of Nearing Vast!"

"My dear man," General Millian started.

"I will be silent for the queen, but not for you," Ward said, turning on him. "Nor for any other man here." He waited. No one spoke. Eyes darted, stealing glances at the queen. She was stony, but silent. Ward nodded. "And here he sits again, weaving visions of dominance, drawing us all in, so that we might follow along. And for whom does he do such things? For the king? No, he won't even call Packer Throme by that name, much less deign to bless his ascension. For the queen? Don't be ridiculous. 'Ma'am' is the best he can do when addressing his monarch. For the Church? Ha! For God? Think again."

"Ward..." This time it was Father Stanson himself who warned the prince. His tone was fatherly. "I beg you, don't say things here you will regret."

"Hap," Ward countered, imitating his tone. "I promise you, I will not regret anything I am about to say. Let me ask you directly. For whom do you seek power? No, I can't stand to hear you lie in front of these good people. I'll show mercy, and answer for you. You seek it for yourself." Now Ward looked around the table again. "Why did Mather not tell the Church that he had ascended to the crown? Why did my father not mention that little fact to the Supreme Elder himself? I'll tell you. They kept it from him because they knew what I know, that this man poisons everything he touches, as he drags it into his lair, and puts it under his spell, and calls the evil result holy."

"You poor man," Hap said gently. "In the words of St. Paul, 'Being reviled, we bless.' I forgive you for this delusion."

"I don't want your forgiveness. It is no delusion."

"But my dear prince, I have never harmed either you or this kingdom." Hap looked around the table. "I don't need to defend myself here." He looked at Panna, who did not come to his rescue. He grimaced. "I have always and ever advised kings and princes earnestly and with all the godly wisdom within my meager reach. My robes are spotless in this regard."

"Your robes." Ward shook his head. "Sir, you sent your henchman to me, to convince me to undermine the king and this queen."

"What are you talking about? I have done no such thing—"

Ward stood suddenly, angrily, banging the table with his thigh, knocking over his water glass. "Look me in the eye and tell me that Usher Fell is not your toady! Tell me he doesn't do everything you order him to do, good, evil, or in-between."

"Father Usher Fell is a respected teacher, and an elder of the seminary."

"And obedient to you."

"Of course, I am the Supreme Elder—"

"Thank you for not lying. He's your henchman."

"'Henchman' is a very strong word."

"Is it? He tried to convince me that you—no, that *God* wants me to take back the throne for the Sennetts." All eyes swung over to Hap Stanson, whose look was serene. Even sorrowful. *The poor prince,* Hap's demeanor suggested.

"And then you spread lies about me," Ward went on. "And that would be fine, because you could hardly make up enough of them to do justice to the many indiscretions of my life. But you went too far when you drew this young woman," he pointed to Panna, "your queen, into your web. Yes, I know all about the rumors you started, spread from your sickbed. While you were soaking up the hospitality of this fine, Christian woman, you were at the very same time spreading your disease among the good citizens of this city, convincing them that she was somehow…involved…with me."

"Ward!" Panna was aghast. She had not heard this rumor, and this accusation seemed preposterous. Perhaps Ward had come unglued after all.

But now the prince ignored her. "You would stain her good name in the vile ink of my own reputation. Tell me you did nothing of the sort. Go on. Tell us all."

"I did nothing of the sort, of course. Clearly, you wrestle with a guilty conscience—"

"And just as clearly, you do not, to your shame." He pulled from his pocket a scrap of parchment, folded over, stained with ale from the tray of a clumsy barmaid. He turned to Panna. "Here is his note to Usher Fell. It fell from that man's pocket during my last meeting with him. It was found after he left the pub, after he had bought me ale and assured me of his undying loyalty to my bloodline. Shall I read it aloud? Or should I pass it around the table so that all may read it from your own hand?"

Now the armor of the High Holy Reverend Father showed its first crack. "I know not what is written on that paper, but I assure you it is not from me, or if it is, there is nothing there to shame either myself or the Church."

"Perfect! Then I shall read it aloud with the confidence you are not ashamed of your handiwork." Still standing, Ward threw the last of his wine down his throat, and ran his fingers through his hair once. His hands shook. "'Father Fell, the rumors you have planted within the palace are succeeding in abundance, blessed by His Almighty hand. I have overheard workers here in the hospital say that the queen and the prince are secretly in love. If such is the talk in here, I can only imagine what they must be saying in the pubs.'"

Ward glanced at his audience. "'The rumors you have planted'!" he repeated. The expressions on every face were now of shock, or of disgust, as though some repugnant smell had just circulated through the room.

Ward continued reading. "'A further idea strikes me...you might remind the citizens of the many weeks our newlywed queen spent in the palace without her husband. Perhaps Panna's devotion to Ward, and Mather's resulting jealousy, would explain Mather's clumsy advances? But you know better than I how to squeeze all the juice from such plums. It is a God-given talent, and I am grateful that you employ it in His service. As always, burn this note immediately upon receipt. Yours, HS.'"

Stanson now sat upright, ramrod-straight. His face was almost as red as his wine. Ward held the note up. "For once, your toady did not do all you asked. The note survived. I think I shall pass this around the table now, sir, so that all here may see the flourish of your initials. They are a thing of beauty, by the way, the 'H' grand enough to stand for all of Hell, the 'S' for all that is Sinister." He handed the paper to Panna, and sat down heavily.

Panna looked at the note, scanning it quickly as though it might harm her if she lingered on it too long. She looked up, feeling ashamed, and not knowing why. "Did you write this?" she asked Hap.

He was silent, brooding. Ward took the note from her and passed it to his left, to Moore Davies. Each guest reread the parchment in silence. All waited for the High Holy Reverend Father and Supreme Elder to say something, either to confess his remorse or to counter the claims, but he did neither. He sat stock-still, sweat beading on his brow, waiting his turn to read the note as though he were but another interested party. But as each man looked at it, Moore Davies, then Dog, Mack Millian, Zander Jameson, they looked up at Hap Stanson with an air of condemnation, the likes of which the cleric was thoroughly unaccustomed to receiving.

"Do you admit that this is yours?" Jameson asked, turning to Hap on his left.

"I have not seen it," he answered.

Jameson held it out to him. Hap took it, and immediately put it into the flame of the nearest candle.

"You devil!" Ward exclaimed angrily, and dove across the table to wrench it from his hand, pulling the tablecloth, spilling wine and water everywhere. Once he had it in his hands again, he slapped the flame out against the tablecloth, and pocketed the paper.

Panna stood to avoid the spilled wine, now spreading with a surge across the table, staining all it touched. With the queen standing, the rest of the men stood as well. All except the churchman. He could have managed to get up, with great effort, but the injuries both to his leg and his reputation conspired to keep him down.

"God works in mysterious ways," he said serenely. "And so does the Church. I appeal to you men," he said, looking up at them. "Forget my methods for a moment, if you can. Look at the ends for which I have labored. Packer Throme is a good boy, I'm sure.

He's brave and humble. But he is in no way fit to be king. And this woman cannot even keep a dinner party from turning riotous. She is no queen. 'A fine Christian woman,' Prince Ward called her. And she may well be that, I do not know. But I would be surprised if the prince could recognize one. Most of the women he has known have been, shall we say, well known before."

"I will not allow you to talk like this—" General Millian began, but Panna cut him off.

"No, let him speak. Let him have his say." She didn't say it in mercy, however. She knew he was hanging himself. And if any others here by chance agreed with him, then they would hang themselves as well.

"Thank you…ma'am," Hap's voice dripped sarcasm. "As I was saying, this land needs a king who will rule, if not uprightly from his own moral sense, then at least by listening to reason, by taking good counsel from those who will respect God-given institutions. Those who will protect the Church." He pointed at Panna. "This young woman has refused to protect the Church."

"From what?" Ward asked.

Hap appeared to ignore the question, but in fact he only ignored the questioner. He also ignored the servants who now worked quickly between the standing guests to sop up wine and water with thick towels, and to remove broken glass. "Packer Throme lays claim to the blessings of God. Don't you see what that means? He has short-circuited God's holy plan, which He has laid out so clearly in His Scripture. Throme is not an elder. He is not a pastor. He has none of the gifts listed in our sacred texts. He is not even the lowliest of priests. He holds not one single credential that would justify his claims that God is with him. And yet he has the entire kingdom on its knees."

"If I recall, the same accusation was made against our Lord," Ward countered.

"And so the reprobate is now a theologian," Hap said dryly, then ignored him again. "The knees of our citizens should bow to the king in submission, and to God at the altar, guided by His appointed and His anointed. If the Crown usurps the power of the Church, as happened in Varlotsville, then the Crown will have the power to enslave the nation."

The servants now gave up on restoring order to the table, and began removing all the dishes, the candleholders, the centerpiece, and then folding the tablecloth up over the remaining mess.

"But the 'city on a hill' you just described," Millian interjected. "Jerusalem under King Solomon. What is that, if not the union of Church and State?"

"But God must do it, you see? God's man must be the king. And herein lies the problem. And the opportunity."

"Packer is the problem because he has no credentials?" Ward asked.

Hap nodded.

"But the opportunity...why, *you* could be king," Ward offered. "You are God's anointed, with more credentials than will fit on a scroll as long as your arm."

Hap said nothing. Millian nodded, as though finally understanding the situation. He looked at Jameson, who looked at Panna. Panna watched both men, and waited. "Excuse me," General Millian said, and left the room abruptly.

"He's seen many physical battles," Hap said, watching the general leave, "but apparently he hasn't the stomach for spiritual warfare. And that's what this is. God saved me from the beast and the fire for this purpose, gentlemen, marking my own trials," here he pulled aside his hair to show the nasty scar, still scabbed, above his left ear, "marking my head to counter the claims of that pretender and his scarred right hand. God did this that I may come before you now, and appeal in His name that you do the right thing."

"And what is the right thing, pray tell?" Ward asked.

Still he would not look at Ward. "Depose this woman and her absent husband. What say you, General Jameson? Admiral Davies? With your help, with the strength of your army, and what navy we can muster, tomorrow will bring a new day, the dawn of the City of God."

General Millian returned just then with Stave Deroy and two fellow dragoons. He stood silently as Stave walked up to Hap Stanson and took him by the arm. "You're to come with me, sir."

Hap laughed. He looked at the general, and his mirth vanished. "You wouldn't dare! I am the Supreme Elder of the Church of God!"

"Yes. And you are also under arrest for treason, and for conspiracy to commit treason." Millian said it curtly, with dignity. "Crimes punishable by death."

The Battle for Vast Dominion

Stanson went white. He looked at the hard faces of General Jameson and Admiral Davies. "No. I was saved for a purpose. God could have taken me. I was protected for a reason. It is the will of God that He rule through me! He saved me!"

"'Saved' is a very strong word," Millian responded, his thin form standing tall, his shoulders square and erect. "But I do not doubt that your life was preserved for a reason, and I do not doubt that this is it. If you had died in the wilderness, the world might never have known the depth of the evil in your heart."

"The world? Evil in my...but surely you can't plan to make any of this public? Surely we are men of standing here, who will work this out among ourselves. The dignity of the Church, after all, demands decorum."

"It is the nature of evil to hide its own deeds," Millian offered. "Yes, this will be made public. Your deeds, and the note you penned to prove them, will be made very public."

Stanson put his hand to his heart, then grasped the inverted chalice that hung there. "God will smite you for this!"

"Take him away, son," Millian ordered.

Chunk paused. He did not want to be smitten.

"I'll walk with you," Jameson told him. "If God wants to strike someone, He'll strike me."

The churchman was helped to his feet, and a servant brought the cane he had used to enter the room. Stave held him steadily, gently, as he hobbled painfully away, putting almost no pressure on his torn right leg. He spoke all the while. "I'm the Supreme Elder of the Church of Nearing Vast," he muttered, wincing. "I lead every flock in this kingdom. Every one of them. They will hear my voice. This is not over. I'm the High Holy Reverend Father, appointed by God. Fools, that's what you all are. Fools and puppets. This is sacrilege. We are now a nation that persecutes the Church. This government is persecuting the Church of God, and God will judge it! You wait..."

Eventually, his mumbled rant could no longer be heard, as the dragoon and the general led him out, flanking him. The remaining men turned to face their hostess.

Panna clasped her hands together. "I apologize, gentlemen. I hope you don't think ill of my hospitality."

"Not at all," they agreed.

"It was my fault entirely," Ward offered. But the three remained standing with their queen.

Panna looked down at the table and was shocked to find the cloth once again white and clean, the candles lit, the centerpiece in place. She had not seen a thing that the servants had done. And now, plates were appearing in front of her guests, hot slices of bread on them, a hunk of creamy butter melting in the center of each piece.

"Is anyone still hungry?" she asked.

"I'm famished," Ward answered.

"Utterly," agreed General Millian.

"Let's eat," Dog added.

A storm was coming. The Achawuk watched him now, more closely than ever. The clouds on the horizon were promising rain, but the clouds within the "rek-tahk-ent," the *One Who Comes Before,* were promising far worse.

Dayton Throme sat up, wiping the soft earth from his hands, then from his forehead. He looked down the hill, saw the people gathered around, looking at him. Talking quietly. They watched him as though he were a living barometer of doom. Zhintah-Hoak had said it. He was growing restless. The words had surprised him, but now he knew they were true. He was spending more time praying, more time walking the villages, less time sleeping. Memories were coming back to him, vivid memories of home, of the sea, of his Nessa, of Packer.

But how could those things have anything to do with the tannan-thoh-ah, the Mastery? That was about the end of the world, when the flow of nature would embrace all, and overwhelm all, and change all, and man would no longer strive with man, nor with animals. The literal translation, he had eventually realized, was not really about mastery, not like the Vast think of it. Not domination. It was more "mastery with knowing," or "master-knowing." As though each would know the other's secrets. And then there was this saying, that man would become, somehow, in some way no one could quite explain to him, "the glory of the beast." It was some sort of reversal of fortune, Dayton believed. Somehow men would serve the animals. It only seemed right, Dayton thought, after men had dominated animals, killed them, served them in dishes on colored tablecloths.

But the tannan-thoh-ah, if it was anything like a Firefish feeding, would not be pleasant. Dayton had watched their battles from the shore. They brought him to every Firefish feeding, hoping, he knew, that the next one might be the great one. Why people such as these would hope for the end of the world, he couldn't figure. Greedy and lustful and lying people loved their lives and would do anything to save their own hides. Yet these people, with all their noble traits, looked only for the end of it all.

"You know," Moore Davies said, almost dreamily, watching the smoke from his cigar rise to the ceiling. "The *Marchessa* is actually the most experienced Firefish-hunting ship on the seas."

Glances were exchanged, and a few throats cleared. The queen's guests had all retired to the parlor off the dining room, a place not unlike Mather's private sitting room, with a huge fireplace, polished floors, and comfortable stuffed chairs and sofas.

"Excepting the *Trophy Chase,* of course," Panna said, stating aloud what everyone else was thinking.

Davies raised an eyebrow. "Including the *Trophy Chase,* Your Highness."

Now he had everyone's attention. "The *Chase* is the finest and fastest ship ever built, I grant you that. And she was built to chase the beasts. She was our flagship, our standard-bearer. Yes, she had a couple of longboats and a few lures, and yes, she has maintained the spotlight for all her exploits. But it's the *Marchessa* that's carried most of the huntsmen, mostly all of the lures. The *Marchessa* has bagged scores of the beasts, scores more than the great *Trophy Chase.* And she was captained not by the infamous Scat Wilkins or the rightly glorified John Hand, but by your humble servant."

"But my dear Admiral," General Millian said, the light of a new respect in his eyes, "that would seem to make you the world's pre-eminent expert on the hunting of Firefish."

"Yes, well," he blushed, "perhaps."

"So how is it that you avoided sailing with the rest of the leaders of our fledgling industry to the land of Drammun?" asked General Jameson.

He shrugged. "I wasn't on the Hezzan's list. And I wasn't about to volunteer."

It was a light moment, but it sealed the decision. Hap Stanson was right about one thing. Nearing Vast had a distinct advantage over the Kingdom of Drammun in one regard, and one regard only: the hunting and killing of Firefish. Those captains who had drilled under John Hand for only a day or two in the art of war had been preparing for almost a year to hunt the beasts, and to hunt them in their feeding waters. This was the purpose of the Fleet, why Scat Wilkins had bought the ships, how he had outfitted them. Those captains who could not follow military orders would certainly make their own decisions under duress. Or at least, most of them. And seamen who were untrained in handling live ammunition were fully trained in lighting the fuses of Firefish lures. The same sailors who could not aim a cannon knew how to man a longboat. And the captains and crew who had fared so poorly in the sailing of warships to war were ready and willing to prove their mettle in the sailing of hunting vessels in pursuit of Firefish.

It was not necessary that domination of the world be the goal. Self-protection would do. So it was now clear

The Fleet would sail to the Achawuk territory.

CHAPTER 15

Snakes

"Go find and secure the King of the Vast," Huk Tuth ordered Vasla Vor. They stood inside the palace doors now, underground at the eastern entrance, where servants and supplies came and went. Their carriage clattered away toward the livery stables. "I will deal with the Quarto."

The General Commander of the Hezzan Guard hesitated. "You are Worthy, my lord. However, I am sworn to take orders only from the Hezzan."

Tuth stared at him. Then he reached up and put a knobbly left hand on Vor's shoulder. "I know you to be a loyal soldier. You have served your Hezzan and your nation well. But you have been deceived. A wife has no right to her husband's throne. The Quarto has no right to choose a Hezzan." Vor was unseeing as his mind whirred with the all the logic that put her in power, the arguments she made, the Ixthano she claimed, the dominion the Quarto had granted. Suddenly they all seemed hollow. Now Huk Tuth stepped closer. "You have done your duty as you saw it. No one will hold that against you. But I command the Glorious Military. And the rule of Talon is over. She cannot stand against my troops. Nor can you. For the sake of Drammun, go secure the King of the Vast. Keep him far from her."

Vor's chest expanded, then he let out a solemn breath. "I will do so. And thank you for your commitment to Drammun."

Tuth nodded, then turned and walked away, silently sheathing his knife.

Kron saw it. He hesitated, considering escape. Then he followed after. "With all due respect, Supreme Commander, you cannot simply walk in and defy the Quarto." Kron hated the pleading tone in his own voice, but he seemed unable to control it. "They have power, more power than you know. The Zealots, Your Worthiness! Many in your own military will follow them rather than you."

"Not if the Quarto are dead." He kept walking.

Kron shook his head, feeling desperate. "Especially if they are dead! Don't you see, destroying the Quarto will rend our nation in two! The Zealots will storm the palace."

"The Army will put an end to that."

"No, there is another way! I can introduce you, help you." The words echoed until they were lost in the sound of the unrelenting footsteps of the supreme commander, now pounding up the granite stairs toward the Great Meeting Hall of the Hezzan. Sool Kron was amazed at how fast the gnarled old man could move. He needed time, and time was slipping away. "The Quarto put Talon in place, true," Kron tried again, "but she is a stench in their nostrils, as much as she is in yours. Bloodshed can be avoided. They will welcome a claim to the throne from you. But it must be legitimate, and I can help you define such a claim. It's what I did with Talon, that's why they accepted her."

Huk Tuth shook his head, and kept climbing.

Kron was climbing, losing his breath, feeling like he was sliding downward. The words flowed from him now, and for some reason he could not take his eyes from the knife on the supreme commander's belt. "It's politics, Commander Tuth. No more and no less. You are new to it, but I am not. It would be my honor, my deep honor to assist you. To serve you." He stopped climbing. He sounded like a sycophant in his own ears. His chest heaved.

Now Tuth slowed to a halt, then turned and stepped back down to face Kron. He looked at him eye to eye. "You have aligned yourself with both Talon and the Quarto." He said it in a gruff rumble that struck fear into the wizened politician. The sound was like a lion's growl. "And you have convinced them all you are loyal. But you tell me you do not honor the legitimacy of one, nor the beliefs of the other. Now you would have me believe that you would honor and serve me?"

"I only did what needed to be done," Kron said quickly. He put his hands out to his sides, vulnerable, pleading, trying to keep his knees from shaking. But his voice quavered uncontrollably. He could not catch his breath "Our nation was headed toward open rebellion... There were riots in our streets, right here outside the palace. And...the military...you were across an ocean. I kept the peace. I brokered a union. It has held until your return. There will be riots again, and worse, if the Quarto is...if you...don't you see, I can help you!" He was pitiful, and he knew it.

Huk Tuth's eyes went cold and distant. The commander's pallor, his scraggly white hair, he seemed more skull than skin. And then Kron saw a left hand come up, felt it hard and clawlike on the back of his neck, clamped there in a grip he thought might snap his head from his shoulders. He never saw the blade, but the image of the thing hung before his eyes, cold and jagged and gleaming as it plunged, ripping through robes, cracking into his chest, slicing between his ribs, and into his heart.

Huk Tuth let the body slump down to the steps, and watched it roll limply, pathetically, down the stairs. "Politicians," he said aloud. Blood covered his own right hand, but the splatter was invisible on his crimson uniform. He wiped the knife on his shirtsleeve, his hand on his hauberk. He looked up the stairs.

Now, the Quarto.

Talon stepped outside the door of the guest quarters. Immediately, the hair on the back of her neck stood up, and a chill shot through her. Vasla Vor approached. He stopped, thirty feet away. Talon could read the General Commander instantly. He was a boy caught stealing apples. But he was no boy, and these were not apples he had come to steal. "Guards, take our guests back into their quarters," Talon ordered easily. Three went, while the original four, positioned there by Vor, hesitated. "All of you," Talon said with a hiss, not taking her eyes from Vor.

They obeyed.

The General Commander of the Hezzan Guard did not move, but watched silently as his seven soldiers took the Vast King and the meager entourage back behind the door. He stepped closer as Talon turned and locked the door, sliding the big iron bolt in place with a precise click. She turned back toward him.

When she did, he had his pistol aimed at her heart. "It's over," he said. "Supreme Commander Tuth is in charge now."

"You still want to follow her? Are you kiddin'?" Delaney asked. They had stepped far enough away from the Drammune Guard so as not to be overheard. "No, no, Packer. That was military brass, right there. Did you see his face? You hear her? They ain't on the same side, Packer. And I'll bet my rum rations for life he ain't standin' there no more when that door opens again. That's *Talon,* in case you forgot."

"I know who she is," Packer said. "But we came here, I was led here, to reach out to the Hezzan. And that's her. And now she's in trouble."

"She ain't *in* trouble, she *is* trouble! She's no more Hezzan than me," the sailor insisted.

Talon's gaze was deadly calm. "And where is Supreme Commander Mux?"

Vasla Vor cocked back the hammer of his pistol. "Abbaka Mux was killed in honorable combat."

She looked doubtful.

"By a Vast dragoon," he added. "So says Huk Tuth, and he is a Worthy man."

"Yes. Isn't he though?" Talon wanted to ask how such a thing could have happened to a supreme commander. But she did not ask. It no longer mattered. She was undone by it. Mux was a Zealot and would never have stood against the Quarto, nor against her once he knew that the Quarto had approved her reign. The Quarto was the key to Mux, and Mux the key to the military. Now the death of one man on a far shore at the hands of a single Vast soldier had ended her reign.

But it had not undone her power. This she firmly believed. So instead of asking questions, she informed Vasla Vor how the next few moments would unfold.

"For your disloyalty, General Commander, I will send you to the Dead Lands. There you and the honorable Abbaka Mux may trade stories about your mutual bad luck."

He shook his head. "You are a Worthy woman, and a Worthy warrior. But you hold no weapon. It is not right for you to die this way."

"All you say is true. And I find it fitting, Vasla Vor, that you should die with the truth on your lips. You served my husband well, and me also for a time. I am sorry that you chose so poorly, here at the end."

He could see in her eyes that she had no fear of him, that she believed she could defeat him. And yet she stood fifteen feet away, unarmed. But that stare, that cold calculation in her...was he missing something?

Talon saw the shadow rise in his mind, the doubt she had carefully planted there. It was all she needed. The corner of her mouth went up. She moved her eyes to a door twenty feet behind him, and nodded, ever so slightly. Then she looked back at him with a look of victory.

He knew as he turned away that he should not take his eyes from her. He knew her reputation as an assassin. But he could do nothing else. General Commander Vasla Vor, as Talon well knew, was a man far more accustomed to sending others to fight than he was to fighting himself. Feeling the essence of command in her, knowing she had the silent and deadly Nochtram Eyn at her disposal, all his senses told him that he was outnumbered, that a surprise attack awaited. Of course she would not leave herself so vulnerable. How could he have been so stupid? He looked away to assess the new threat.

She was in motion the instant his eyes left her. He looked over his left shoulder, and she darted to his right, immediately out of his line of sight. Her hand went into her robes as she moved, and came out with a long knife. Vor dropped to his knees a fraction of a second later. Her blade had pierced his throat, its point entering the base of his brain, severing his spinal cord. And then it was out again, wiped clean and back in its sheath before his lifeless body fell backward onto the cold marble, pistol skittering harmlessly away, unfired.

She stripped off her robe, revealing her black leathers underneath. She laid the robe on the floor, rolled the body onto it, and tucked the pistol into his belt. Then she dragged him to the doorway at which she had glanced, the entrance to another set of guest rooms. And she left what was once Vasla Vor, the dutiful General Commander of the Hezzan Guard, inside.

The bolt slid, and the door opened. Talon entered. "We must go. There is danger about."

All three men were shocked to see her in her forester's leathers, a long knife in a scabbard at her belt. Delaney stared holes into Packer.

Packer looked at Talon. Her eyes were focused, clear. She nodded her head once, urging him. It was the merest trace of a request, but that's what it was. It was not a command. It carried no venom. She needed him to go with her, and she wasn't forcing him. And he knew this was the answer to his prayer. He had asked God that the Hezzan would have some shred of sensitivity, even a secret fear. And though she looked like the Mortach Demal she was, she was being pursued and she needed him.

"We're going with her," Packer said to Delaney and Father Mooring. And he stepped past his grim bodyguard.

Delaney screwed up his mouth, and then his courage. And he followed. As did Bran Mooring, humming softly.

The slightest trace of gratitude crossed Talon's face, a momentary brightening of her eyes, a flash of appreciation.

"Guards, stay here," she ordered them in Drammune. And she closed them away, locking them once again in the guest rooms.

Delaney gritted his teeth, seeing the resolve in his king. He searched for something he could say that wouldn't seem disrespectful. "I humbly disagree," he managed.

"With what?" Packer asked.

"Dern near everythin'."

"Noted," Packer replied.

Talon pulled her knife and looked up and down the hallway, listening carefully. All was silent. "Draw your swords." Delaney quickly drew his, but held it out in the general direction of Talon.

With a glance, Talon studied Delaney, then Packer, and then the priest. She shook her head and heaved a sigh. Two of them were unarmed, and the one who had a weapon thought she was the enemy. Talon pulled a derringer from her boot and put it in Packer's hand. "Take this. Shoot only whom I tell you to shoot."

He accepted it before he thought. Now he looked at the small pistol lying on his scarred palm. He shook his head. "Talon, I can't..."

"What?" she asked, impatient. "You have given up the sword, fine. That is a gun."

Packer looked at Father Mooring for help, but the happy priest only shrugged. So he closed his hand around it, looked back at Talon, and nodded.

Talon moved down the hallway like a cat, her knife held down to her side.

"Any queen you know of does that?" Delaney offered in a whisper, ostensibly for the priest's ears.

"No," Bran offered. "But I know of one back home who'd do pretty well in a boxing match." His eyes twinkled as he padded along, trying to keep up.

Following Talon, they turned a corner and heard voices and footsteps. She quickly ducked into another doorway, a small anteroom. A squad of soldiers went by, maybe a dozen, the iron studs of their sandals clattering. When the sounds faded, Talon opened the door and peered out. "Wait here."

"Mightiest person in all the land," Delaney said in a whisper, "sneakin' around like she was robbin' the place. Strike you as peculiar?"

"Shhh," Packer glared at him.

"I can't help it. She's tellin' us wild stories, like she did your Panna. And remember how that ends up, with her killin' yer swordmaster."

Packer closed his eyes, the brute force of Delaney's accusation hitting him like a mule kick.

At that moment Talon stepped back into the room. "We are going up to the roof garden," she said. "It is at the highest point of the palace."

"Why *up?*" Packer asked, caught in his moment of doubt.

"They are searching for me. There is open rebellion in the palace. They will not expect me to go up to escape."

"So we go where there ain't no exits," Delaney said, darkly.

She looked Packer deep in the eye. "We have no time for debate. If you trust me, follow. If you distrust me, stay."

"Well, *I* don't trust ye," Delaney offered. "She's a killer," he told Packer. "Don't forget it."

She looked at Delaney. "Yes. But I only kill those who will not shut up."

Delaney's face twisted like he had gotten a mouthful of something awful. He didn't take his eyes away from hers. But he didn't speak, either.

She looked back to Packer. "Choose."

"I'm gonna kill her myself," Delaney said to Father Mooring, in a whisper all of them could hear. "You wait."

"You will not kill her," Packer ordered. Then he turned to Talon. "We will follow you, until you prove untrustworthy." He turned back to Delaney. "And you will follow me."

"What if she tries to kill you, Packer? What if she tries to kill someone else? Do I stand and watch?"

Packer heard the loyalty bound up in the sailor's frustration. He looked again at Talon, who seemed to watch and listen from an impassive distance. "Then that's different," he said.

Delaney pressed. "Permission to kill her if she tries to kill one of us, sir?"

Talon cocked her head, waiting for Packer's answer. Her look said she expected his response to be mildly interesting, perhaps even amusing.

"If she tries." He looked at Delaney. "Until then, you follow. No more questions."

"I got my orders, then." Delaney held his sword in a clenched fist, like a butcher holds a meat cleaver, anxious to begin the day's work.

Talon was, in fact, amused. "Excellent decision. Let us go." She ducked out the door and back into the hallway.

The party wound its way up several flights of stairs, avoiding voices, and found the great doors to the Hall of Feasts closed but unguarded. It took three of them to draw the bolt and pull one of the huge doors open wide enough for them to slip through one at a time. Delaney stopped on the other side to push it shut, but Talon tapped the top of his head with her knife blade. "There is no time!" she said.

Delaney whirled to face her, his sword clanging awkwardly on the door. She was already far out of his reach. Then he looked around him. He felt the familiar crick in his neck almost immediately. This one room was almost as big as the entire palace back in Mann. Marble floors, black and slick. Mahogany walls to the ceiling far above. A hundred chandeliers, each holding hundreds of lamps. At the far end of the hall, an enormous white granite staircase rose up to the ceiling like a pyramid, stairs on all four sides, and light pouring down onto it from above. Talon ran toward it.

At the top of the pyramid was the dais, twenty feet square, and in the middle of it, a few more steps rose to the throne. Sunlight streamed into the room as though it was not the Hezzan, but some relative of the sun who reigned from up there. Those in the great hall could see the throne only if they were almost on the stairway, and of course during royal banquets, the stairs were ringed with guards. Packer marveled. Being granted an audience with the Hezzan under such circumstances was guaranteed to raise one's heart rate. If only from the climb.

Talon reached the stairs and climbed them two at a time. The others followed. She did not stop at the dais, but walked across the catwalk to the right and out onto the roof. At the top of the stairs something caught Delaney's eye. He tapped Packer's shoulder and said, "Look up there."

Packer looked up to see a sword fastened to the wall, out of reach, but prominent. It was his own. The one he'd left on the burning decks of the *Camadan*, placed here by Talon where it could serve as an inspiration—or perhaps as a reminder of that dark day.

"Come!" Talon ordered.

They obeyed.

The view from the roof was spectacular. Unfazed by either the climb or the view, Talon sheathed her knife.

"This way," she said, leading to a small stone structure, a box no more than five feet high, and about as wide. She pulled a key from her pocket and used it to open a small, square, heavy wooden door. Inside was a tray, about four feet across. "Get in," she said to Packer.

"Whoa now!" Delaney reacted with full-scale alarm. "Don't you do it!"

Talon grimaced and climbed in herself. She turned back and held out her hand. "Get in. It goes down to the lower floors, to the kitchen and below. It is a mechanism used by servants for catering to the Hezzan. Now it will be our escape."

"But all of us can't fit," Packer noted.

"There are ropes here," and she pointed to them, two thin ropes that ran just inside the door on the left. "We will lower ourselves using these. Once we are at the bottom, we will get out and signal the others that they should pull it back up. Then they will join us."

Delaney went crimson. "No, no, no! There is no way you are

gettin' in that thing with the likes a' her. You're the heavin' *king*, Packer Throme. And that's Talon!" he said once more, as if repeating it often enough would finally force it into Packer's head. "And if you care to take a notice, she's got a big knife in there with her."

"And you have a gun," Talon said to Packer easily.

Packer moved toward the opening. "I've made my decision. I told her we'd follow."

Delaney grabbed his sleeve. "Until she proved herself not worth followin'! Packer, what's she gotta do to prove she ain't Hezzan? Murder?" His voice whined like a windlass spinning free. He pointed at the dark opening of the dumbwaiter. "She could slice you into stew meat before you knew she wasn't just stretchin' her arms to yawn!" He did not let go of Packer's shirtsleeve.

Packer set his face, spoke sternly. "Am I your king, or am I not?"

"Well, aye, ye are, and ain't that jus' my whole point?"

Packer looked at his sleeve, and Delaney let go. He looked glum. And then he brightened. "Hey, how about you just let me go with her?" Delaney figured he had solved it. "Then I'll send the devil-blasted thing right back up to ye!"

"No," Talon said from within the dark space. "I will not leave the King of Nearing Vast up here unprotected."

"I'll go, then," Father Mooring offered.

"I will not leave Packer here without protection," she repeated. She eyed Delaney coldly.

"Without pro—" he was red in the face now, and wanted to give her everything that was on his mind and in his heart, but he couldn't. There was too much. Like a herd of cattle trying to enter a squeeze-chute all at once, nothing at all got through.

Packer climbed into the small space.

"Pull down on the nearest rope," Talon instructed.

He set the derringer down on the wooden surface of the tray, and pulled. The platform creaked and moved downward. Delaney's forlorn look seared into Packer's memory. It was the look of a man losing his best friend.

The platform moved easily, lightly, and with a smooth speed down into the darkness.

Delaney looked at Father Mooring accusingly. "You coulda said somethin'!"

Bran shrugged. "His mind was made up."

"Ye could have told him God wanted him not to go."

"But I don't know whether God wanted him to go."

"Ah, what's a priest good for, anyways? I never had no need of 'em."

"Well, I could pray," Bran offered mildly.

"Pray?" Delaney said glumly, sitting down on the hard tile of the garden walkway. "Yeah, ye could. Ye could pray that we weren't the two biggest idiots who ever lived, standin' up here on top of everything in the world Drammune, waitin' for a murderer to prove she ain't worth trustin'. Ye could pray I wasn't the most worthless dunderhead ever stepped foot off a ship, pretendin' I had some business protectin' a king. Yeah. Ye could pray. Pray we had a king who didn't find it just a fine idea to climb down a rat hole with a rat. Ye could pray that."

Bran sat. "All right then," he said gently. "Let's." And he bowed his head.

Huk Tuth felt his first trace of misgiving as he approached the Great Meeting Hall of the Hezzan. His brisk step slowed almost imperceptibly. The contingent of guards stationed outside the door, six of them now snapped to attention, wore not the dress reds of their station, but battle crimson. For a moment, he thought they were his own men, somehow arrived from the ships already. But no, the halberds were Hezzan Guard. No matter, he was the Supreme Commander, and only the Hezzan had more authority. "Follow me, all of you," he said, and strode between and past them.

They obeyed instantly.

The Hezzan's chair was empty. Tuth's eyes cut back and forth among the four members of the Quarto. None of them stood. None of them recognized his presence, other than to cast haughty eyes in his direction. Because they did not recognize him, neither did any of the rest of the Twelve. His anger grew. He saw behind the Quarto, standing attention against the far wall of the room, two more members of the Hezzan Guard. Tuth drew his knife and approached Pizlar Kank.

"Stop this man," Kank said, a noticeable trace of alarm seeping through the cool exterior.

The two guards behind him stepped forward to block Huk Tuth's path.

"Stand aside," he ordered them. They did not move. "I am your Supreme Commander, and I order you to stand aside."

The Battle for Vast Dominion

Neither budged. Tuth's iron-gray teeth showed in a flash, but before his knife moved, before he spoke again, his eye caught the slight modification to the uniform, the telltale red triangle that was the end of a red sash, the belt of the Zealot, peeking out from the waistline of these two guards. He glanced behind him. The guards he had just brought with him, to help execute his wrath, wore the same. Their beards were ragged, their hair shaggy.

Now Pizlar Kank's eyebrows rose. "Did you have a message for the Quarto?"

"Do the Hezzan Guard now serve the Quarto, and not the Hezzan?"

"Not that this is any of your affair, but since you have proven your Worthiness many times over, I will tell you that even as you entered, we were debating a motion to declare the Hezzan Unworthy."

As the blood ran from his face, Huk Tuth considered how best now to counter this mockery of all that was Drammune. He didn't know where to begin to plumb the depths of this debasement. A self-appointed board of judges, daring to pass sentence on a Hezzan? A wife of a Hezzan, who set herself up in power by kowtowing to such conceits? A raft of Hezzan Guards, abandoning their one sworn mission, obeying these pretenders rather than direct orders from the military?

"You have approached the Quarto," Kank said, his arrogance fully returned. "But as you seem to have no business here, I will ask the Guard to escort you to your chambers, where you, too, will await our judgment."

Tuth spun around and saw it, felt it—the betrayal and treason these guardsmen were perfectly prepared to execute. He looked one more time around the table, saw the empty chair from which Sool Kron had brought forth this monstrosity. And then he knew what he needed to do. He turned back to Pizlar Kank. He scowled. Then he said, "I claim the Kar Ixthano, for an Unworthy man slain by my hand."

"And whose dominion would you claim?"

"That of Sool Kron."

There was a long silence. "He is dead?"

"You will find him sprawled on the stairs two floors below us."

Kank nodded to one of the guards, who disappeared out the door behind Tuth. "What are your proofs of his Unworthiness?"

A glimmer shone from Tuth's eye as he said, "He was a politician."

Kank cleared his throat. No one in the room dared even to shift his position. Kank sniffed. "Can you be more specific?"

"He said he would help me overthrow the Hezzan. He called her a vile stench. He also said he despised the Quarto."

Kank nodded. "We have known Sool Kron to be disloyal. And you could be very, very helpful to us." Kank looked at his compatriots, who nodded back at him. "The Ixthano is granted," he said breezily. "You may take your seat, Chief Minister Tuth."

The dumbwaiter, lowered by hand, passed the doorway to the Hall of Feasts, then no others for quite a while, at least four or five floors by Packer's reckoning. During this time he heard nothing but the soft banging of the tray against the sides of the chute, and the occasional creak of the ropes. His back ached from the awkwardness of the angle required to pull the rope downward. That ache reminded him of another time, not too long ago, when he was cramped in darkness and unsure of his destination. Then, he had listened carefully to the foreign and terrifying voice of Talon, who walked alongside a cart filled with barrels as he stowed away on the *Trophy Chase*. He was afraid of being found out by her then. Now she was in the barrel with him.

He remembered offering himself up to God then, putting himself in God's hands. A glow of satisfaction filled him, thinking of all he'd been through since then. He was surprised and pleased that the fear in him seemed to melt away. God still had him in His hands, and He could still crush Packer, or protect him, just as He chose. Talon might kill him yet. But even if she did, he knew now that it would somehow work to the Almighty's ends.

He saw light from the outline of a doorway.

"Stop here," Talon said.

Packer's disfigured right hand burned him, aching from the effort. He was glad to stop at the outline of the next doorway, and see the dim light seep in from the cracks along its edges. And now the faint smell of lye and ammonia reached him.

"Open it." Talon ordered.

Packer pushed. "I think it's locked."

"Move to your left."

He squeezed himself to one side. He sat still a moment as Talon shifted her weight, and then suddenly the door exploded, slamming open. Packer saw her leg extended for a fraction of a second, and then he saw a blur, felt a wisp of a breeze, and she was standing outside looking around the room. He was sure he had never seen anyone move so quickly, and certainly not with such precision and such power. Not even Senslar Zendoda.

"Are you staying there?" she asked, as though she had been standing there for several minutes rather than several seconds.

He climbed out into a small kitchen. It was no more than ten feet square in size. This couldn't be the kitchen for the entire palace. A few pots hung above a small counter, and there was a washing basin and a small stove, with a stovepipe turning at a right angle near the ceiling. A large cutting block jutted up from the floor to their left, an island built near the middle of the kitchen. Meals for a dozen or so might be prepared here, but not for the number of guests that could fill the Great Meeting Hall above them. Talon started for the door, outlined now in a brighter light. "This way."

"Wait," Packer said, remembering the pistol. He peered back into the darkness, felt across the surface of the tray, but he could not find it. "The derringer..."

"There is no time," she said. "Someone will have heard the noise."

The lip of the tray was only a half an inch from the edge of the chute. The clearance was the same all around its edge. He looked on the floor. It couldn't have fallen, he thought. Then he realized. Talon had taken it.

But he had no time to confront her. "Someone is coming," she said. Packer now heard footsteps approaching from the corridor. She took his hand, pulled him toward her, and then pushed him down behind the small island. "Stay there!" she ordered in a whisper. She went back to the apparatus and yanked on the near rope, raising the platform slightly. Immediately, it began to rise, as Delaney and Father Mooring took over from above.

In an instant, Talon was crouched beside Packer, and they heard the door to the kitchen swing open. The footsteps stopped. Then they came slowly closer. Packer could tell by the sound that this was a big man, but light on his feet. A trained warrior, most likely. The man stopped again, listening to the creak of the ropes as they raised the tray through the chute. He walked toward the open dumbwaiter door, now hanging from one hinge. Packer glanced at Talon, could see her in the shadows, crouched, gathered, waiting, her face a picture of calm, her eyes cold and distant. A predator. She had her knife in her hand. A chill ran through him. He hadn't seen her unsheathe it. It was just there.

The guard looked around the room once more, then edged closer to the dumbwaiter. He moved it slightly, examining the broken lock, its hinge. Then he put his head inside the opening.

Instantly, Talon was in the air, springing silently toward her prey.

She recognized him, this Hezzan Guard, as she came down on top of him. She could see his face as she grabbed his hair with her left hand, and snapped his head back. He had protected her. She felt no pity, however, as he took a quick breath in, reacting to the pain. Her right hand, knife held lightly like a surgeon, reached under his neck. She thought about how stupid he was to have put his head into that small, dark doorway. All the training he'd gone through under Vasla Vor, and he walks into a small room to investigate a loud noise, sees a small door with a shattered latch, and puts his head into it. These were her thoughts, flashing through her mind in the instant it took to bring the knife back toward her with a flick of the wrist. He flinched once, like a sleeping man when he dreams he is falling. Air rushed from his lungs through his open throat as he attempted to cry out. But the cut was well below his vocal cords. And then he was plummeting down the chute, head first.

"Let's go," Talon said to Packer, wiping her blade on her leather legging. She took Packer by the arm with her left hand, hauled him up, holding the gleaming blade aloft in her right. "More will come." She walked Packer toward the door that led out of the kitchen.

"But Delaney—"

"Yes! We must protect Delaney, and your priest." But she did not slow. Once outside the kitchen, she propelled Packer through a small corridor toward a larger door, with more light yet behind it.

He tried to understand what had just happened. She had moved like a cat. She had killed her own countryman without a trace of remorse, without so much as an acknowledgement of the deed, and now she pushed him toward...what?

He could fight her. But he feared he had nowhere near her speed, her agility. And he certainly didn't have her deadly calm. She seemed completely at home here in the dark, dealing out death, walking into unknown dangers. In fact, she was energized by it.

And then they were through the doorway and standing in a large, marble meeting hall. Lamps flickered upward toward vaulted ceilings, lighting twelve men who sat around a triangular table. One of them was Huk Tuth. Two guards stood to their left.

The four men seated nearest Packer turned in unison as he and Talon entered. On the end, on Packer's left, one man stood up hurriedly and turned to face them. He was a small man, with leathery skin and a patchy beard and heavy, half-closed eyelids. Another man, seated, spoke in Drammune, a sharp order in a cracking voice. Packer could not understand the words. But the meaning came clear as the pair of guards responded. They came toward Talon and Packer with halberds raised.

And then suddenly Packer's right arm was twisted behind him. Pain shot through his hand, up through his wrist, his elbow, his shoulder. Talon stood behind him, shielded by him, his arm folded like a chicken wing, her knife at his throat. He could feel its razor edge pressing into his skin, as he had felt it once before. She was speaking in Drammune now, pouring out a guttural string of words that seemed to freeze the room.

"Meht ema Kar Ixthano," she said. The room did not breathe. Eyes flashed from Talon to Packer to the lizardlike man. And then into the sickly silence she injected these words: "Kar Ixthano tah nochtram Hezzan Vastcha."

Packer understood Kar Ixthano, the *Right of Transfer.* He understood "nochtram" to be some form of their word for *death.* And he understood "Hezzan Vastcha." He knew that the death she spoke about was his own.

At this point Packer determined he could no longer safely follow wherever Talon led.

"Well, I can't very well save the kingdom on an empty stomach," Princess Jacq complained. "And I can't very well eat this…substance. Do they have a name for such a mishmash here in the hinterlands?"

"Well, actually they call it 'mishmash.' It's a slumgullion of sorts. And we are in fact inside the city limits—"

"*Slumgullion?*" She was aghast. "Do you mean to say these people serve gluewater? What the whaling boats cast off?"

"No, no, it's not literal slumgullion," Usher Fell tried. "It's a nickname." He had no idea how to get through to her. "It's just stew, Your Highness."

"Stew?" The princess laughed, a combination of derision and relief. "My dear Father Fail, I have eaten stew, and pretend as I might, I could never generate enough imagination to call *this* 'stew.'"

"Fell."

"Excuse me?"

"I'm Father Usher Fell. You said 'Fail.' And while I understand the food here isn't quite up to the standards of the palace—"

"Isn't quite? I can tell you that this mess of pottage does not even meet the standards of the Mountain House. Look at it. No, go on, look! I want you to see what you've served me."

He looked into her bowl, eyes downcast. Her Royal Highness, the Princess Jacqalyn Devray Arnot Sennett, had arrived in Mann incognito after leaving the Mountains on her own accord. Or at least, she thought she was incognito.

From the moment Hap Stanson mentioned the possibility of succeeding to the throne, the thought had hardly left her mind for a moment. By the time she reached the Mountain House she had decided to hold him to this veiled promise. But to do that, she would need to find him, and give him some guidance. So she traveled back to the city in a relatively ordinary, unadorned carriage, dressed in finery that was somewhat less ornate than she would generally deign to wear, and in the company of only two dragoons, both in civilian clothes. All of which seemed to her quite the equivalent of poverty. To an outside observer, however, she had dropped down maybe a single rung, from princess of the land to fine lady of wealth and means. She turned heads everywhere she went.

But the heads she wanted most to turn right now hid within clerical hoods. Spurred by her newfound religiosity, she went straight to the nearest church and demanded an immediate audience with the High Holy Reverend Father, Harlowen Stanson. The priest to whom she made her demands pastored a tiny church on the outskirts, and was unaccustomed to anything like the turmoil she caused. She ordered everyone about, sent meals back, demanded bedding and linens and comforts that many in town had never seen, and some had never heard of.

The priest made discreet and worried inquiries about what to do with this personage, inquiries made at ever-increasing levels of urgency, until eventually Father Fell was found and summoned. At the end of his first visit with the princess, her coach had left the church grounds, bound for the quiet inn that was still the base of Usher Fell's operations. At the time, Father Fell did not fully understand why the priest of the little church had seemed quite so elated as he waved her goodbye. Now he understood completely.

But at the moment, Jacq was not finished discussing her soup. "And what is *that?* Look at that piece of...something. Right there. Tell me what that is. Is it potato, or is it lard? Or is it something else entirely? Well, Father Fall, I can promise you that I will not be putting it into my mouth. I can live without finding the answer."

"Fell."

"Excuse me?"

"It's Father Fell. You said, 'Fall.'"

"Fell, Fall, it's the soup I'm talking about here, not you." She looked at him, saw he was crestfallen, and relented some. "Dear me, have I upset you? You didn't cook it, after all. I'm so sorry, dear man." Her voice took on a maternal quality that was highly patronizing, so much so that Father Fell immediately preferred the complaining. "You are only trying to help, aren't you? So why don't you take this away," and here her voice turned suddenly cheery, "and tell the chef I want to see him at once! I'll be happy to help him understand what is meant in Nearing Vast by the term 'stew.'"

Usher Fell faltered. Her talking to the chef would be a disaster. "The cook," he explained, "is actually the wife of the proprietor, Your Highness. And I must tell you that the situation demands a bit of delicacy. Not only would it be best if the proprietors did not know your precise identity, there is also a small matter I have been discussing with the innkeeper having to do with a horse."

"A horse?"

"The price of a horse, to be more exact. A horse that seems to have gone missing."

She looked into the stew again, aghast. She pushed it away.

"No, no—I borrowed it when I sent a rider to find you," the priest desperately attempted to explain. "I mean, to find the High Holy… that is, Father Stanson. I am in discussions now with the man about payment for the loss of his horse, and would rather not create more animosity—"

The princess rolled her eyes. "Money. Is that it? It's beyond me, really, the importance men attach to the stuff. It's really so tiring." She walked across the room to a large, fat purse, essentially a leather bag, that she had set on the dresser. "I would have thought men of the cloth would be above such things." She pulled open the drawstring, stuck her hand in, pulled out a fistful of gold coins. "Here. How many of these do you need?"

The priest cheered up considerably. "Four. Just for the horse, that is. One more for room and board. Though that's just paying what I already owe. I could prepay—"

"There, what's that, seven or eight?" She poured them into his hand. "Anyway, there's plenty more in the bag if you need them. As long as it helps get rid of those dreadful Thromes, one way or another, it's money well spent."

"Thank you, ma'am." He counted the coins quickly. There were ten of them. He closed his hand around them. "Under the circumstances, I would suggest we postpone questioning the chef, and focus on the mission at hand."

"Fine." She looked at her dinner tray, still worried that the horse had somehow wound up in that stew. She picked up the apple that accompanied it. She studied it carefully, picked off a small blemish with a fingernail. Then she looked at the old priest coldly. "So. What is the Church's plan for returning the Sennetts to power?" She bit into the apple. It popped, and she chewed it deliberately, staring at the priest, awaiting his answer.

Usher Fell blinked. He had ten gold coins in his hand, and an imperious princess with solid bloodlines at his table, one with the means and the desire to overthrow the current government. He had rumors, and the means to start more. He had God on his side, in the form of the High Holy Reverend Father and Supreme Elder. But plans? No, he had no plans.

The path before him, he was beginning to understand, would be strewn with obstacles.

Packer watched the faces of the men around the table. These were those who plotted against Talon, to overthrow her. She had come here to confront them, not to escape. But what good would it do, he wondered, for her to kill him now? They would still kill her. And that, he realized, seemed to be precisely the discussion now underway.

"Go ahead and kill him," Tcha Tarvassa said in Drammune, standing at the corner of the table. His lizardlike eyelids were half closed. He had joined the Quarto to engineer this very coup, to over-turn the perversion of the Rahk-Taa that had put the woman Talon in power. He was pleased to see she had arrived unsummoned, and had immediately proven her own Unworthiness. It would make this all easier. "Kill the King of the Vast," Tarvassa continued, "and you shall by right claim his dominion. And then when we find you Unworthy, we shall kill you, and claim both yours and his."

Talon scanned the room. Huk Tuth had taken Sool Kron's place. She knew what that meant. The look in his eye, though, said he detested everything around him; her perhaps most of all. "Kill the King of the Vast, and with him dies the secret of the Firefish," she answered.

"Give her some room," Pizlar Kank said to the guards. They obeyed. "She is Hezzan yet. Let her speak."

Talon's eyes moved from Kank to Tarvassa to Tuth as she spoke. "You say you care not whether I slay the King of the Vast in viola-tion of a signed treaty. That is dishonorable. You care not whether you falsely accuse and overthrow the rightful Hezzan of the Dram-mune. That is intolerable. But to care nothing for the power now at your fingertips, the power to control the Firefish and thus the seas, and thus the world…that, for any man born with Drammune blood, is unforgivable."

She let the words hang in the air.

Tarvassa glanced at his fellow members of the Quarto. He clearly had no idea what to do next.

"Why don't you sit down, Minister Tarvassa," said the peevish Kank. Tarvassa sat. Kank turned back to Talon. "These men here gathered accuse you of Unworthy deeds."

"Shocking. But I have a proposal for you," she said. Talon watched Kank's eyes. Sool Kron's prediction had been accurate. Now that these bears had tasted honey, they wanted to own the beehive. They craved it. Kank believed they already owned it, that nothing could stop them. He had turned the government, and Tarvassa had brought him the Infiltrators, and Huk Tuth, apparently, the Glorious Military.

But Kank was wrong. They could be stopped right here, right now. All four men seated here before her, smugly claiming absolute authority over the land, offhandedly casting the life of a king to the winds, determining the fate of the Hezzan, would be dead within five seconds if she so chose. And no man in the room could stop her.

If she so chose, she would be a blur, executing a judgment sorely needed, these wrongs righted in an instant. Four men would be lying in pools of their own blood, while the nine remaining members of the Twelve would watch, and do nothing. Packer Throme would do nothing—he had forsworn the sword. Huk Tuth would attempt to stop her, but he was old and hunched and slow. So the two guards would go down next. And she had a two-shot derringer in her belt. That would leave her facing Tuth and the rest of these spineless weasels. The way she figured, she would have them outnumbered.

She relished the thought of it.

CHAPTER 16

Exchange

Delaney rolled out of the chute quickly, landing catlike on the floor. It took a grunting Father Mooring slightly longer. His toes reached downward for what seemed to him a very long time before touching solid ground again. He was glad for the feeling, though it seemed a tad too slippery for his liking.

Delaney took Packer's sword and scabbard from the tray where he had put them for ease of access, and started buckling the belt around him. "That witch, I swear," he muttered. "Leavin' us to shuttle up and down lookin' for 'em like we was huntin' quail."

In fact they had stopped here once before, looked around, heard nothing, saw nothing, and kept going. They went down to the lowest level of the palace, the cellar, where they smelled coal and lye and heard women chattering in Drammune. "Household servants," Father Mooring had whispered after listening for a moment. "Seems they heard a noise a while back, coming from this chute. But they have no key to open it."

In fact, all the doors of the hatchways were locked tightly, all but the one into the room in which they now stood.

"I'll kill her. I swear I will," Delany repeated.

"So you've said," the priest offered. "It may be they just ran into some trouble."

"I'll run some trouble into her," Delaney offered back. His belt rebuckled, he wiped his hand on his trousers. He stopped and looked at his fingers. He touched them, then sniffed them. He looked at both hands, front and back. He looked around, a wild question in his eyes.

"What is it?"

He reached out for one of Father Mooring's hands, pulled it up to his face, peering at it in the dim light. "It's blood."

"It's what?" The priest studied his own palm. Convinced, he patted himself, his chest, his thighs, his rump. "I don't believe it's mine."

"Nor mine." Delaney looked more closely at the chute. He wiped his hand across the wood just below the opening, looked at his darkened fingers. Now he could see it, spattered across the wood, the door to the chute, and under the lip of it. On the floor. His spirits sank. He spoke low and mournful as he said, "He hardly got outta there, afore she kilt 'im." Then his voice went high, cracking as he proclaimed, "Oh, Packer. What have I done to ye?" He looked at the blood on his hands. "Here's a stain shall never wash away."

"Now, let's not jump to conclusions," Father Mooring offered, his hand on Delaney's shoulder. "This might be Packer's blood, and it might not be. He's in God's hands. We must trust that all is working out as it should."

Delaney was not prepared to trust anything of the sort. All he could think was that for Packer to die here, like this, by the hand of Talon, was about the worst end imaginable. He looked around him. "All the glorious places where he coulda passed." His voice was low once again, his heart pierced. "Hangin's. Keelhaulin's. Battles thick with enemies. Even bein' et by a Firefish. Any a' those coulda been a wonderful end. But no, he gets it here, in a kitchen, throat cut from behind like a…like he was a pig for the pot." His chin trembled.

Talon chose not to kill the Quarto. Nor the guards, nor Huk Tuth. Though she was tempted to execute judgment on these self-inflated fools simply because she could, and because they deserved it, she realized that her small moment of satisfaction would undoubtedly prove very messy, making it impossible for her to focus on the real issue at hand. And the real issue was power. And the real power was in the Firefish.

So rather than kill the Quarto, she said to them, "I humbly request permission from the Quarto to present my proposal in peace, with a guarantee of my safety until such time as the Quarto rules."

Silence reigned as the men in question glanced at one another. They had no idea what shadow of death had just passed over them, and now they acted as though Talon were an irritant, keeping them from other, more important business.

"We need more information," Kank said testily. "What's the nature of this proposal?"

She ignored the disrespect. "I propose an exchange that will ease this transition. It involves the Vast," and here she nodded toward Packer, "and control of the Firefish."

"This transition...?" Kank's irritation evaporated. "You mean, a transition of power...from you...?"

"To the next Hezzan."

The Quarto now leaned in and spoke together in whispers. Their greed for power was transparent. Talon watched instead the face of Huk Tuth. He was impatient, his eyes narrowed under his protruding brow.

Their confabulation concluded, Pizlar Kank spoke. "The Quarto grants your request. You may speak freely."

"And my safety?"

Kank's look was sly. "After ruling on your proposal, we shall allow you to return to your current position, armed and hiding behind the king of the salamanders."

"And you speak in session, with one voice?" she asked.

Kank hesitated a moment, then said, "Yes."

"And the King of the Vast remains under my power?"

"Yes."

She nodded, lowered the knife, and stepped away from Packer.

Packer reached up and felt his neck, then looked at the blood on his fingertips.

"May I know what's going on here?" he asked Talon.

"Was that Packer?" Delaney whispered, his chin trembling again, but this time with joy. They had inched out to within a few feet of the closed door outside the Great Meeting Hall. He was sure he heard Packer's voice.

Father Mooring nodded, putting a finger to his own lips.

"He's alive, then," Delaney breathed out. He closed his eyes as

The Battle for Vast Dominion

relief washed over him. But now the stunning reality of Packer's deliverance threatened to overwhelm him, so he stood and walked gingerly back into the kitchen. There he silently closed the door behind him, went into a corner, knelt down, and sobbed.

Talon's eyes worked deep into Packer's. "You must be silent. I deserve not your trust, I know. But in the name of all you call holy, give me more time." Then she turned back to the group and said in Drammune. "I have asked him to be still, but he is Vast. His tongue will wag."

They laughed. Packer shook his head, quite sure he was the butt of some joke. He'd never felt quite so poorly used. In the barrel he had been afraid. Under Talon's torture he had been crushed to his spirit. Feeling her full destructive powers on the *Camadan* he had despaired. But now he was simply ashamed. He was a pawn in some game of chess he couldn't understand. They maneuvered around him, because of him, castles and bishops and warriors on horseback. He couldn't understand the language, much less the rules, much less the nuances of their strategies. He could take one step forward, only to retreat again. Everything within him told him to stand and fight, to play on the board not as a pawn, but as a knight, to face these people with honor and dignity, and with a sword in his hand. But all his choices, all his deepest beliefs, the very voice of God in his heart said, *Resist not.* Accept the shame. And he thought about the chessboard, and realized that the difference between a pawn and a king, between the moves those two game pieces are allowed, is slim indeed.

Talon took a breath, held it, then said to Kank, "I propose an exchange. The King of the Vast for the crown of Drammun." She saw nothing but puzzled looks, which was precisely what she expected. "You want my title, and my dominion. You believe you must kill me to take it. But I tell you I will give it freely. I shall serve the new Hezzan, and the Quarto, and bring you honor. I require three things in return: Packer Throme, the *Trophy Chase,* and the five ships that Sool Kron prepared for a mission to the Achawuk. Grant me this, and the authority to crew and sail these ships as I will, and I shall forswear my crown and pledge my loyalty."

"Absurd," Huk Tuth said.

"Commander Tuth," Kank responded sternly. "Do you have something to say?"

Tuth glowered at her.

"You now have permission to speak." Kank emphasized the word "now."

The craggy old man clamped his jaw. Then he said to Talon, "You are a traitor, and a coward."

"What do you have to say to these accusations?" Kank asked Talon.

"I remind Supreme Commander Tuth that I now own the dominions of Senslar Zendoda and the Hezzan Shul Dramm. I am yet the Hezzan Skahl Dramm. I will not countenance accusations with no proof. Such are punishable by death."

"Come kill me, then," he challenged. He showed her his teeth, in what on another man might have been interpreted as a smile.

"Have you proofs?" Kank asked Tuth, ignoring Talon's defiance and Tuth's provocation.

The scraggly supreme commander stared at her, his hatred overflowing. "I had the Vast in my hands. The entire nation was in my fist." He held his right hand out, palm up. "All I needed do was close it, and squeeze their blood from them." He closed his fist, and it shook. "But this...woman...stopped me. She did it through deception. She claimed to be the Hezzan Shul Dramm, whom I served." He looked to Pizlar Kank. "She is Unworthy of any title. She is not Worthy to live."

Talon walked toward Tuth. "The orders I sent you were written by the Hezzan's scribe, my scribe, and marked with the Hezzan's seal. Do you deny that such orders should be obeyed?" She stood before him.

Tuth said nothing.

Kank prodded him. "Commander Tuth, do you counter her claims?"

He glared up at her, tough as old leather, unmoving, feeling nothing but contempt.

"You have spoken false accusations against the Hezzan," she said. "The punishment is death." She drew her knife in an instant, its blade singing from its sheath, and had it at his throat before he could make more than a flinching move toward his own knife. "I ask permission of the Quarto to take this traitor's life."

He stared death back up at her.

Feeling flattered in spite of himself, for the Hezzan had requested his permission before killing a man, Kank spoke. "Commander Tuth, do you retract your accusation?"

Tuth said nothing. The members of the Twelve all shifted in their seats. They had seen Talon kill one of their own in this room before.

"Commander, unless you retract, the Quarto must rule. And we will rule according to the Rahk-Taa." Still Tuth said nothing. "Do not imagine that we hold your life in higher regard than adherence to the great Law of our people."

Tuth bared his teeth. "I retract the accusation," he said bitterly, and then he added, "though it is true."

"Well then, that's a personal matter between the two of you," Kank said simply. Talon did not move. Kank cleared his throat. "As there is no accusation on the floor, there is no reason for you to have your knife at the commander's throat, Madam Hezzan," he added. "Talon," he said again, as the pair continued a dance of death with their eyes. "I believe you have a proposal for us?"

"Yes," she said, stepping back, pulling the knife away as though her hand, or the knife itself, was reluctant to leave Tuth's neck. She looked at the blade. "Yes." She sheathed it, then turned her back on Tuth.

The instant she did, he lunged at her.

It was no contest. She sensed him coming at her like a jaguar watches the approach of a lumbering bear. She heard him stand, heard his knife come out of its sheath. He had his jagged dagger in his right hand, held with the blade downward. She knew this without looking; she had seen it at his belt, had watched him move for it, far too slowly, when she drew her own. She turned to face him now as he reached her. She saw the knife coming down and fell backward, grabbing his right wrist with her left hand to stop the blade, and then his vest at the collar with her right hand, and she pulled him toward her. Using his own momentum, she brought him down on top of her, and as she did she planted her knee firmly into his groin. Keeping his momentum going, she rolled on her left shoulder and, still pulling on his vest, yanked his head into the polished floor. It hit with a loud thud, and his dagger skittered away. Keeping his body moving, she rolled him all the way over onto his back, and then she was seated on top of him, straddling his chest. The point of her own knife was under his chin. But he was splayed out, spread-eagled under her, limp and unconscious.

She stood, looked around her, sheathed her knife. "So many men hear the words 'Mortach Demal' and think, 'woman.'" She saw Tuth's blade on the floor and picked it up. "They forget that the other word is 'warrior.'" The men present shifted again in their seats, destined not to forget either word very soon. She knelt beside Tuth, and put the knife point under his bare chin. She wanted to kill him here, with his own knife, but she felt the King of the Vast looking at her. He valued mercy, and she needed him. So instead, she cut off a hunk of his white, scraggly hair. Feeling no satisfaction from this, she stuffed it into his mouth. "The taste of my mercy is bitter," she hissed at him, too low for Packer to hear it. "Never forget it." She sheathed his dagger for him, then lifted one of his eyelids. She stood. "His head will hurt. He may walk knock-kneed for a day or two. But he will live to play the fool again."

And then she walked slowly back toward Packer as she spoke, leaving the Supreme Commander of the Glorious Drammune Military to come around in his own time.

"I propose," she said, as though nothing much had happened, "to sail to the islands where the secrets of the Firefish are known. To the Achawuk Territory. Where the Firefish feed. I have knowledge from our Archives, which Sool Kron has presented to the Twelve. With the help of Packer Throme, who has sailed into these waters before, seen the beasts feed, and returned, I will learn their secrets. I will bring back to Drammun the knowledge that will be our means for dominating the world."

"Why would you do this?" Kank asked, perfectly prepared now to ignore Huk Tuth. If Talon had killed him, he would have behaved no differently. He had seen her mind work before. He had seen her kill before. He finally understood what had drawn the Hezzan Shul Dramm to her. She was a weapon well worth wielding. But he pushed these thoughts away, quite sure they were Unworthy. "Tell us why you would give up your crown to sail into this danger, and then bring your hard-won knowledge back, only to give it to your successor."

"I would do it to prove the Worthiness of the Drammune."

Huk Tuth moaned, then opened his eyes. Immediately he rolled over, pulled his knees under him, intending to stand. But he couldn't. The pain was too great. So he stayed on his knees, head on the floor, spitting his own hair out of his mouth, fully conscious of his abject humiliation.

The Battle for Vast Dominion

239

"If you return with such power," Tcha Tarvassa now asked, pulling his eyes from Tuth, "what's to stop you from taking back the Crown by force?"

"I sought the Hezzan's dominion," she answered, "and so you believed me to be greedy for power. But I requested the Ixthano not for my own sake, but for the sake of my husband's vision. I believed I was the only one who could execute it. I claimed he was Unworthy, for the sake of that vision. But I confess to you now that I believe his vision was utterly Worthy. For this vision to come true, Drammun, not Talon, must dominate the world. I desire to prove my Worthiness."

Tuth finally stood. He wobbled. "She cannot be trusted," he said through gritted gray teeth across which white hair still clung.

"Nor can she be defeated, apparently, even when attacked from behind." Kank said it dismissively, and the others chuckled. The fire in Tuth's eyes flickered briefly toward Pizlar Kank. "Commander..." Kank said, and stopped himself. "No, excuse me, Chief Minister, what do you know about the Achawuk islands? She claims the Fire-fish feed there."

Tuth sat carefully. He pulled the stray hairs from his mouth, wiping his fingers on his vest. "The Vast have assembled a fleet to slay the Firefish. They intend to return to the feeding waters within the Achawuk islands."

"How do you know this is true?" Kank asked him.

Tuth glared at him, insulted to be questioned. He could not decide who he hated more, Talon or this smug, self-satisfied quartet. But then he composed himself. "Prince Mather of the Vast revealed all to Fen Abbaka Mux, who told me. It is true."

Kank found it impossible to trust Talon. And yet, if they wanted to take the power of the Firefish from the Vast, a better plan was not likely to be found. And at any rate she would be gone, leaving the door open for Pizlar Kank.

"Will the King of the Vast agree to help?" Tarvassa asked.

"He lives at my whim, and dies when I decide. But he believes I am drawn to follow his God. He will help me."

Kank nodded, appreciating the deception. "Do you have any other terms?"

"I have three terms, all spoken. This king is to go with me, and his great ship, which I shall captain, and the five additional ships that Sool Kron prepared. But I also have one request."

Kank shook his head. But he said, "Speak it."

"There are two salamanders listening to these words behind that door. They have followed me here. Arrest them, but do not execute them. I will need them both on my journey."

Delaney had finally dried his eyes and composed himself, but he took so long that by the time he returned to the corridor, it was just in time to watch Father Bran being taken into custody by two big guards. He pulled his sword, but the priest's urgent appeals kept him from using it. "Surrender your sword, Delaney! Surrender it!" Bran's voice was a command. "All shall be well. They have decided...we will sail with Packer Throme!"

The overwrought sailor had no idea how that could be, or why the priest was so confident, but under the circumstances he allowed himself to be swayed.

A few minutes later he sat by himself in a dark, cold, windowless cell with no bed, no toilet, no food, no water, and no explanation. And he regretted his decision bitterly. What was wrong with him, that he allowed his country's enemies to lord it over him? And what was wrong with his countrymen, that they kept insisting that he do so?

As agreed, Talon put the knife back to Packer's throat as the Quarto discussed her proposal. They spoke in whispers, but Tcha Tarvassa was obviously adamant on several points. Finally, Kank nodded his agreement. Then he nodded at Talon. "Very well. The Quarto grants all three of your terms. You will be high commander of the mission to the Achawuk. Take the King of the Vast, the *Trophy Chase,* and the five ships, and crew them as you like."

Talon did not lower the knife. She sensed there was more.

"But we add one term of our own. You say the Vast have prepared a fleet to hunt the Firefish among the Achawuk. We will send a dozen more warships with you. These will help protect our...investment."

"I accept this additional term," she said warily.

"Among these ships," Kank continued, "will be the *Kaza Fahn,* commanded by Huk Tuth."

Tuth shot up from his chair, wincing. "Do not ask me to serve under this woman!" He pointed at her with his weapon.

"Be seated, Chief Minister. We have ruled. You must prove your Worthiness."

He did not sit; his eyes bored holes into Talon. She watched him in return, but took no satisfaction. She understood quite well the danger he would pose. She should have killed him, she thought.

"Be seated now, or you will be found Unworthy."

Tuth sat, and closed his eyes. His humiliation was complete.

"Your new chief minister knows the Vast quite well," Kank told Talon. "And he can certainly command a score of ships. Under your guidance, of course. Now, take this ragged king of the salamanders, and go. Prepare your mission. You will have all the resources of Drammun at your disposal. Huk Tuth will see to that."

But she had questions yet. "You have made no ruling as to my title."

"You shall maintain your title," Kank answered coolly. "You are the Hezzan Skahl Dramm."

She watched his eyes. "And I shall sail as such?"

"Oh, yes," Kank answered. "Most definitely."

"And I have the protection of the Quarto?"

"Until you sail."

"And the King of the Vast, he is protected as well?"

"Until you sail."

She nodded, finally lowering the blade from Packer's throat. She sheathed it, thinking that sailing was becoming a more dangerous trade with every passing minute.

"I bid you good day."

After Talon had left the room with Packer Throme, and Kank was sure she was far out of earshot, he turned to Huk Tuth. "We have proclaimed the woman Talon Unworthy of her title."

Tuth raised his head.

Kank continued, sounding impassive. "This is not to be known outside this room."

Tuth pondered this. He nodded. She had the highest price on her head they could have named, and he would be the only one on the voyage who knew it.

"Do you understand me, Chief Minister?"

He did.

"We want to know how to command the Firefish. She is quite right about the power such ability represents. The Vast cannot be allowed to keep such knowledge to themselves. But we do not want the woman Talon to return. You, Huk Tuth, must bring this knowledge of the Firefish back to us. Bring it here, and bring Talon's head with you, and there will be a throne for you atop this palace."

Tuth stood. His humiliation could yet be turned to honor. He bowed in spite of himself, and took his leave. But on the way out, he despised in his heart the men with whom he had just dealt. They were foxes, not wolves; hyenas, not lions. And yet they sat in judgment as to who was Worthy in all the kingdom? Sool Kron had done this.

But if they were foolish enough to make him Hezzan, then the Quarto would learn what price was paid for dishonoring Drammun.

"Can he defeat her, do you think?" Kank asked aloud.

"He cannot outfight her," Dorn Rodanda answered. "That is plain."

"He won't outwit her," the bookish Zekahn Irkah added.

Tcha Tarvassa grinned, his lizard eyelids half-closed. "It doesn't matter," he assured them. "While they are gone, we shall have both his power and hers. The government and the military. Whichever one returns shall find a very different kingdom, and a different set of rules."

"Unless we proclaim Tuth as Hezzan," Irkah warned, "as we have promised."

"But did we promise him that?" Kank asked. "I remember only promising a throne on the rooftop of this building. And I do believe we could find a privy up there somewhere, given time."

Their laughter was cold and smug. And heartfelt.

"Now there's somethin' I thought I'd never see," Mutter Cabe said to Delaney. They were once again in the rigging, feeling the *Chase* move, heel a few more inches, accelerate a knot or two with every few square foot of canvas they unfurled.

"Aye," Delaney said. His hands worked the lines as he dropped a glance to the quarterdeck. "If I'd a' never seen it, I'd a' died a happier man." They spoke of the leather-clad figure, sword at her hip, knife and pistol in her belt, standing at the quarterdeck rail of the *Trophy Chase*. "*Captain* Talon."

"Is it true she's the Hezzan?" Cabe asked.

"Nah," Delaney said with a shake of his head. "Even the Drammune got more sense than that."

"The priest said she is."

"But he don't know. She talked like she was Hezzan, sure, but it was just a lie. Just so she could put a knife to a king's throat and save her own skin. That's all."

Cabe nodded. That sounded more like Talon.

"If she don't sail us to ruin, it'll be by God's own grace," Delaney assured him.

Mutter looked behind them at the seventeen crimson vessels trailing them, surrounding them, astern. And when he thought about their destination, he had a hard time disagreeing.

"This is God's business," the dark priest said in a whisper to the servant girl. "I must get a message to him."

"There are guards there," she whispered back.

"May I come in?" he asked, glancing up and down the street.

"I don't think so…" She was alarmed even to be having this discussion. The girl lived in the palace and worked in the hospital, but her parents lived here, a few blocks away, outside the Old City walls in a dilapidated part of town. Father Usher Fell had followed her here.

Now he closed his eyes, feeling the opportunity slip away. He stepped closer, and she backed up involuntarily. He placed his hand inside the doorframe, so she could not suddenly close the door on him. He tried to look kind. She was a plain thing, seventeen, though she looked younger. Her hair was a light, dirty brown, almost the same color as the weather-stained wood of the door she held partially open. Several pimples marred an otherwise milky complexion. "Dear girl," he purred, "you believe in God, don't you?"

"Of course," she said, feeling a bit accused.

"Then you understand that in this world, believers will have tribulation."

She nodded, not liking the direction this was headed.

"When the Church is held in high esteem, everyone claims to believe. But in times of persecution, believers pay a price for their faith. Nearing Vast is entering such a time."

"But…the queen believes—"

"The queen is persecuting the Church, dear girl! She offers pretty smiles and warm words, but she has arrested the High Holy Reverend Father and holds him captive in her palace! He will be taken to prison when he is well enough, and then he will be out of reach, unable to direct the Church of God. I ask only that you get a message through to him, one of the utmost importance, and bring his response back to me."

She looked like she was going to cry. "But the dragoons never leave him."

"That may be. But the dragoons do not eat his meals." He held up a note, a parchment folded into a square half the size of her palm, sealed with blue wax. "Put it in his bowl and cover it with porridge. He will find it."

Curious, she took it and examined it. "But…won't it…you know, get ruined?"

He raised an eyebrow. "I've seen the porridge you serve. It's thicker than boot paste."

She nodded. She knew that was true. "But what if I get caught?"

"You won't."

"What if I do?"

"Then run to the seminary. You will find refuge in the chapel, as all those who flee to that place will."

Somehow, this made her feel better. She looked again at the note from his hand.

"Now, here's the important part. Are you listening?"

She nodded.

"He cannot write his answer. If it is no, he will turn his bowl upside down. If yes, he will lay his spoon upon his fork in the sign of the cross. Can you remember to look for those signs?"

"But how will he know to do that?"

Father Fell blanched. Then he said slowly, "It's written in the note."

She nodded again, smiling now, appreciating the cleverness of it.

"Will you do this?"

She smiled. "Yes."

"Very good. Now bow your head." She did, and he touched her forehead. "God go with you," he said. Then he hurried away.

Dayton Throme awoke with an odd feeling in his stomach. He sat up, felt dizzy, and laid his head back down on the woven mat that was his bed. He groaned within as it dawned on him that he was ill. Bad timing, he thought. They were already on edge, these people, watching him like a hawk. He'd caught a cold once, and they set a vigil to assure themselves of early notice, should a sneeze become the precursor to cataclysm.

He sat up again, this time more slowly. If he couldn't walk, what would they think? He put his head between his knees, waiting for the dizziness to pass. It didn't, and his stomach grew more unsettled. He lay back down. Now he began to wonder if he had a fever, too.

Very bad timing.

Delaney saw the beast rise. It wasn't his watch, and he should have been in the forecastle sleeping, but he couldn't, and so he wasn't. He was thinking too much. He hated it when so many thoughts came and went so quickly. He was never any good at controlling them, like some people seemed to be, and when he couldn't sleep it was worse.

He had thoughts of Marcus Pile, whom he missed terribly. He had thoughts of Scat Wilkins and John Hand and Talon, who was now his fourth captain on this ship, and he hoped her end would come soon, too, like the others. He thought of Andrew Haas, who had captained this ship for a while and lived, because he was a good man.

And he thought of Firefish. The feeding waters. He remembered that amazing sight, so wondrous he could hardly now believe he had really seen it, except there were so many other witnesses...that one Firefish rising at the bow, and Packer speaking to it, and it attacking the Drammune. That was a joyous thing. And he thought of John Hand killed by the same beast because he was unable to command it. That was not so joyous.

And he thought of Achawuk warriors, swimming out to attack him in the black darkness of the night. They would kill him and die at his hand, just to claim the *Trophy Chase*. And they would zoom in and out of his mind.

How could any man sleep with such things behind, and such things ahead, and all of them winging like a swarm of bats in and out of a cave? So he walked up to the forecastle deck under the moon, where light clouds flew past like they were in some great hurry to get somewhere. He saw Father Mooring standing at the bowsprit, deep in thought. And Delaney looked out over the sea to port, to the west, and wondered about Nearing Vast.

And now he thought of Panna Throme, and how she had said he was delightful. And he let that thought linger a while. But it flitted out sooner than he wanted, and he thought how an intricate woman like her could become queen, even though she was born in a fishing village, and then he thought how Packer had become king. And he was content to be a small part of it, in a world where such great and wonderful things could happen. And he knew God had set him down right in the big middle of it all, because who else could have made him be friends with a stowaway who became a king? No man. And he was thankful.

And that's when he saw it. Off the port rail at two-hundred-and-forty degrees, Delaney saw the outline of a head, the head of the beast. It was motionless, watching, and then it sank down into the water. Delaney sprinted to the quarterdeck, found Andrew Haas there.

"Sir, it's the beast. It's out there. It's still watchin'."

"Whoa, sailor. What's watching? A Firefish?"

"No, not any Firefish, the same one. The one Packer commanded!"

"That one's dead, Delaney. Admiral Hand killed it with a lure."

Delaney felt like he'd just been shaken awake. "Aye." He looked out over the sea again. "But I was sure…"

"How could you tell? How far out was it?"

"Five hundred yards, maybe."

From behind him a cold voice dripping with scorn said, "Five hundred yards! In the dark?" Delaney spun around. It was Talon, there beside Haas. Where had she come from? Out of the shadows, out of darkness. "And you recognize it as different from all other Firefish?" she asked.

"I jus'…I jus' felt it was the same one." He looked away from Talon, spoke to Haas. "Why else would it look?"

"Why?" Talon asked, remembering her encounter in the shallop, when she had fed Monkey to the thing to save herself. It had risen up and peered over the edge of the boat. She remembered its eyes, its intelligence. "They stalk before they strike."

"Don't I know that?" Delaney exploded, wheeling on her. "Who don't know that!"

"You will speak with respect to your captain, sailor," she said, her eyes narrow and her voice a cold blade. Andrew Haas could see how she enjoyed skewering him.

Delaney put a hand to his sword, the cords of his neck bulging with anger. Talon's eyes flashed.

"Delaney!" Haas thundered at him. "Get back to your bunk; this isn't your watch!"

But Delaney had locked eyes with Talon, and did not back down. Her hand went to the hilt of her sword.

"I gave you orders, sailor!" Haas bellowed, trying to save his life.

Delaney pulled his eyes away and acknowledged Haas again. "Aye, aye. Sir." He glanced at Talon. She looked amused. He looked away. "Anyways," Delaney said to Haas, hooking a thumb toward the port rail, "we got company."

"Thank you, Delaney," Haas said, still keeping an eye on Talon. "We'll signal the other ships to stay in tight formation."

"And I will awaken the king," Talon announced. "So that he may command this beast." She strode off before Andrew Haas had a response.

Delaney seethed. "'I will awaken the king,' my right cheek. Sir, permission to follow, to see she don't stab him in his sleep?"

"Permission denied. And don't expect me to step in and protect you again. Next time I'll just let her kill you."

Delaney was stung. "Who says she kills me? I got a sword, too, ain't I?"

"You got nothing, Delaney. Not against her." Delaney stared hard at him. But Andrew Haas had compassion underneath the words, and would not back down. "We need you. The king needs you. Don't get killed over being too stubborn to know your place. Which, right now, is in the forecastle."

Reluctantly, Delaney obeyed.

Packer was not asleep when she walked in, but rather lying in his hammock reading Scripture, a lamp burning on the wall over his shoulder. He was reading in Matthew's Gospel, contemplating once again those most difficult of words: "Ye have heard that it hath been said, An eye for an eye, and a tooth for a tooth: But I say unto you, that ye resist not evil…" He knew the time was coming when every bit of what he knew, and who he was, would be tested. He knew that all the trials he had seen up until now were but the preparation for this voyage. He knew it in his soul.

Talon did not knock.

"Well hello, Captain," Packer said. "Please come in."

She was already in, but she left the door open behind her. "A Fire-fish has been sighted. You will come with me, and command it."

Packer lowered the book. "Talon, what is it you want from me?"

"To command the Firefish." She stared at him, but he was waiting for more. "And to teach me these secrets."

"I have told you. It is all the Lord's doing, not mine."

"Then come show me," she answered without a pause.

He closed the leather-bound book. He put a hand behind his head, in no hurry. "You can take this ship prize. You can take me and all my men prisoner—"

"I have already done so."

"But you can't capture God. You can't control Him. You'd have more success putting manacles on the wind."

"And yet the sails of this vessel even now harness the wind. Do not suppose I am stupid. I understand you better than you understand me."

He blinked. That might well be true. "Then you know I didn't seek power. I became king before I even knew it."

She looked at him oddly.

"Mather Sennett saved my life by claiming the Ixthano, just as I was to be hanged by Fen Abbaka Mux."

"Then you are a citizen of Drammun."

He stared at her, unsure if she was following the logic here. "The point is, I was given a gift, Talon. Someone died in my place. And if you understand me, then you know the same was done for you."

Talon's flesh crawled. "Who told you this?"

He held the book up again.

"You will not find my story in there," she sneered. She saw his sword, lying in its scabbard in his open locker, returned there by Delaney. She walked over and picked it up. "It was the Hezzan Shul Dramm who died for me. He stepped in front of arrows meant for me." She unsheathed the blade, examined it. She ran her fingers down its length. "Pyre Dunn," she noted, approvingly.

Packer nodded. She was following him, surely. She did not seem so anxious to go find the Firefish, and that made him hopeful. She found this conversation important. "But your story actually is in here," Packer said, holding the book up. "It's the story of a king's dominion. He died to give all He has to us. He claimed the Ixthano, and it was granted. All we need to do is accept it."

"No. If the Worthy dies for the Unworthy, that is not an Ixthano."

"In the Kingdom of Heaven, it's the only Ixthano."

She was silent.

Packer looked into those steely eyes. He sat up, hopped out of the hammock, stood face-to-face with her. He ignored the sword in her hand. "Talon, I don't know what God might grant you. But if you'll trust Him, He won't disappoint you."

"Because He cares for me."

"Yes."

"As He cares for His own Son."

"Yes!"

She stepped toward him and he backed up, suddenly feeling vulnerable. But she did not raise the weapon. "Then tell me the meaning of these words: 'My God, my God, why hast thou forsaken me?'"

Packer took a deep breath, and let it out, feeling punctured.

"He *does* forsake those who serve Him," Talon said. "Yes, even His own child."

"Well, there's a little bit more going on there—"

She sneered. "I'm sure there is. And yet, this is your Scripture. So I am to trust with my child the God who abandoned His own?"

"Yes." But he swallowed hard, and she saw it.

She kept pressing. "As Senslar Zendoda trusted this God, and abandoned his own child?"

Packer was confused. "Senslar Zendoda had no children."

She looked at him now, eyes glittering and hard as diamonds. "You are wrong."

Packer stared back at her, wondering how she could possibly know anything about a man she had met only once, when she had killed him. A man who had left Drammun thirty years before.

Talon waited, as though expecting Packer would figure it out.

Thirty years...His eyes went wide. Talon unsheathed the sword in a flash, had the point of it at Packer's throat. As she saw the realization dawn in him, he saw the satisfaction grow in her. Without lowering the sword, and without taking her eyes from Packer's, she tossed it, a flick of the wrist, and it stuck horizontally into the wall, just above his locker. "Senslar Zendoda offered himself up to your God. I was forsaken as a result."

Packer could only stare and shake his head. "No," he started. But he understood now how she saw it. "No. People do bad things. But not Him. He will never leave you or forsake you. He has promised that."

Her look turned sad, and her eyes grew distant. "If He forsakes no one," she asked, "then why is there a hell in your religion, as well as a heaven?"

Packer opened his hands, not to embrace her, but to explain. To plead. *Just come to Him and see,* he thought. But she cringed, stepping back as though he were attacking, as though she feared him.

And she did fear. She feared the light she saw in him once again, the compassion, those hands open, arms spread wide to engulf her, to destroy her. But she caught herself, hardened herself against the attack. She straightened up, held her chin high. Talon faced him down, absorbing power, absorbing, if she could, his essence, even as she rejected his words. "We sail into the source of all power, Packer Throme. The power to control the world lies with the Firefish, and they live among the Achawuk. When we arrive, we shall learn about power."

"Power given from above is the only true power," he told her.

"Then show me that this is so, Packer Throme. Command the Firefish."

CHAPTER 17

Fire

"Your pardon, Highness." Millie Milder, kind and elderly, now served Panna as something near to a personal valet. Not that Panna had much choice in the matter, unless she wanted to fire her, or lock all doors behind her. Millie would be hovering, doting, fretting, to make sure everything was just so for the young queen. "You have a visitor."

The queen looked up from the stack of papers on her desk. She was constantly amazed at the sheer number of documents that flowed through the palace, demanding her attention. But when she looked up at Millie, she saw an odd expression, partly deep concern, but partly mirth.

"Does the visitor have a name?"

"Miss Marlie Blotch," she said, and stepped aside as the girl stepped in.

Panna knew her. Marlie was a hard worker, and shy. She worked in the hospital, serving the sick and injured. "What is it, Marlie?"

The girl trembled like a willow in the wind.

"You can come here," Panna said easily.

Marlie walked closer, then held up a small, folded scrap of parchment. The seal was broken.

"Is that for me?"

She shook her head. "No, ma'am. I mean yes, it is now. I mean, it was for the high holy man."

"The High Holy Reverend Father. Where did you get it?"

"A priest. Told me I should put it in his porridge."

Panna paused, as the implications of this statement rolled through her mind. "And did you?"

She lowered her chin until it almost touched her chest. She whispered, "Yes, ma'am."

Panna again paused, but did not ask for the note. It wasn't addressed to her. "And why are you bringing it to me?"

The girl still held the parchment in the palm of her hand, and now she opened her hand wide and stretched out her arm, as though it were dangerous and she wanted it far from her. "It's against you."

"Against me? In what way?"

"To hurt you."

Panna nodded. "I'm going to take this and read it, even though it isn't addressed to me. I'm doing that because you are telling me it may have information about a plot against this government. Do you understand that?"

"Yes, ma'am."

Panna took the note, unfolded it, and read it silently. "Do you know the name of the priest who gave this to you?"

"No, ma'am."

"Who else knows about this?"

"No one." She swallowed hard, her eyes wide. Panna waited for the truth. Marlie did not disappoint. "Well. Me. And the priest. And the High Holy...him. And now you."

"And who else?"

She paused. "My mother."

"And did your mother send you here with this?"

"Yes."

"She did the right thing."

"Yes, ma'am. Am I in bad trouble? He told me I would be safe."

"Safe? In what way?"

Her chin trembled. "He said the Church would protect me. I could run to the chapel and kneel at the altar, and no bad thing would happen. I don't want to go to prison." And with that she broke into sobs.

Panna let her cry for a moment, until Marlie looked back at her, and saw the patience, the concern in her queen. "In this kingdom, there is always sanctuary at the altar of the seminary chapel. But that is for criminals. And you are not a criminal, are you?" Marlie shook her head, eyes pleading. "And you never should have agreed to take a note to a man under arrest. You do see that now, don't you?"

The girl nodded.

"And are you sure that Father Stanson, the High Holy Reverend Father, read this note?"

"Yes, ma'am. He made the sign it says in there, putting his fork across his spoon."

"All right." Panna folded the note. "You will not go to prison, because you told me this. So long as you do good from now on."

"I'll do whatever you say!"

"What I say, Marlie, is that you must learn to do the right thing, always, no matter what anyone says. But here's what I want you to do right now. I want you to stay here for a little while. I'm going to bring in the Sheriff of Mann to talk to you."

Marlie's eyes went wide.

"I only want you to tell him what you told me. He'll ask you other questions. Okay?"

"Okay." She had something else on her mind. "Your Highness?"

"Yes?"

"My mother wanted me to ask…is there some reward?"

"For bringing me this note?"

"Yes."

"No, there is not. Tell your mother that the reward is that you will keep your job, and not go to prison."

"Yes, ma'am."

"I'm ordered to my bunk for the night," Delaney said, pausing at the hatch.

Father Mooring nodded. The priest had seen the sailor's outburst against Talon, and wanted to talk. "You have a hard time seeing God at work in her, I know."

Delaney dismissed that thought with a wave of his hand. "God ain't at work in that one, sorry to inform ye."

The priest looked thoughtful. He had been soaking up the peacefulness of the evening, when Delaney's shouting had roused him from his meditations. "Stumbling blocks, trials, temptations, and suffering," he said gently, ticking the words off with his fingers. "Those are the four plights. We are promised in Scripture that we must endure them all until our Lord returns."

Delaney tugged on his tattered earlobe. "Bit of a meager table, if ye ask me."

"Talon represents three of the four plights. But that means God will also bring to us at least three of the four promises." He waited for the other man to respond.

Delaney did not disappoint him. "What are the promises?"

"Wisdom, endurance, deliverance, and peace. The promises match the plights."

"Yeah. Well. I'd like to promise her a few plights. Good evenin' to ye."

Delaney started down the hatch, but Father Mooring had more to say. "We who know the truth must suffer in order to show God's grace to those who do not."

Delaney stopped and pondered that. "I heard somewhat like that before."

"Your anger can never show Talon the way."

Delaney's face went dark. "It can show her the way somewheres."

"And yet, dear brother, she, too, is created in the image of God. She, too, may yet be redeemed. You cannot know God's plan for her."

"Mebbe not. But I got this tidbit a' news for ye. If God plans for the likes a' her to waltz into heaven, after doin' what she's done on this earth, then He ought be up there makin' a different plan."

"The evil in your heart is no less dark, friend."

This stunned Delaney. "She's a murderin', lyin', cheatin' deceiver! I hardly ever lie and I don't cheat no more at all, and I only ever murdered once! That's it! And then repented of it."

"At heart, Delaney, I am a murdering, lying, cheating deceiver, too," the priest said.

Delaney looked at the priest like he'd gone mad. "You? Nahhh."

"Yes, and so is Packer. And so is Panna. And so are you. To stand against God in even the smallest way is..." and here he struggled with a phrase that might reach Delaney, "it's like dipping His whole creation in a bucket of tar and kicking it down a hill." Judging by Delaney's reaction, Father Mooring felt he had been successful. "Vengeance is mine, I will repay, saith the Lord.'"

Delaney shrugged, and descended the stairway without saying good night. He was feeling off balance, and he had to get away and think a bit. Was he standing against God somehow? Sure, he'd like to dip Talon in tar and kick her downhill. Who wouldn't? How could a righteous God who could judge the whole world not want someone to take her out of it, for good and all? "Created in the image of God," was she? Maybe, a long time ago. But she'd skewed that around so bad it couldn't ever be made right. Could it?

He climbed into his bunk and lay awake again, thinking again of Talon, and of Firefish, and of Achawuk. And buckets of tar, and God. He began to pray, and almost immediately his muscles seemed to turn to lead, and his mind pulled him down into the darkness.

He fell into a deep, dreamless sleep.

Talon and Packer stood together at the prow of the ship, Father Mooring their only companion. But God did not grant that anyone would command the Firefish tonight. The beast was seen no more, not that night, nor the next day, nor all the way to the land of the Achawuk.

For the next several days running, Usher Fell returned to the same doorstep and knocked. Each day he got no answer, and each day he grew more concerned. Then finally, on the fourth day a woman of thirty-five or so, haggard and wan, answered his knock. "Marlie ain't here. She's workin'." Her demeanor was antagonistic.

"Did she leave a message for me?"

"No."

"Thank you. I'll come back later."

"Don't," the woman said gruffly. "She ain't doin' no more of your sneak work."

Now he grew quite alarmed. "My dear woman! I would hardly characterize—"

"Well, I don't care what you would hardly do. Askin' my little girl to break the law is sneak work, and she's the one who'll go to prison for it."

"I understand your concern for your daughter—"

"Good." And she slammed the door.

Usher Fell stared at the door, then knocked again. Hearing nothing, he guessed the woman was still standing on the other side. "I will give you a gold coin if you will help me."

There was no answer. He knocked again. He turned, started to shuffle away when the door creaked open behind him. He turned back to find the woman leaning against the door jamb with her hand on her hip. She looked no less irritable.

"Sign of the cross," she said bluntly.

"Excuse me?"

"I said, sign of the cross. The silver."

Usher Fell was confused. The silver...the cross...the idea popped into his head that she was trying to make some reference to Judas and the pieces of silver he was given to betray Him. "I'm sorry, I don't understand..."

The woman grew angry. "Fork and spoon, fork and spoon! The note said, if the answer was yes, he was to cross his fork and his spoon!"

Finally he understood. The *silverware*. "Ah! The Supreme Elder's answer! Your daughter did get the message through. Well, bless her then. And bless you, ma'am!"

"Yeah, yeah. I'll be plenty blessed if I never see you again. Where's my money?"

He handed her the coin. She studied it, hefted it in her hand, then slammed the door on him once more. Usher Fell walked away relieved. He had a plan, and now it was blessed by his superior. Which meant, for all and good, that it was blessed by God.

The woman leaned her back against the closed door. "We'll take this coin for our troubles," she said to Marlie, who looked up at her from a bowed head. "But the queen is right. Don't you do that no more."

"He was a priest," the girl said. "How did I know what's right to do when it's priests that asks?"

"Well, it's a mite confusin', I admit." The woman looked at the coin. "But now we know which side is right, for sure. The worst men, Marlie, those who do the darkest deeds...they always pay the most for sneak work. Don't forget that."

"Yes, Momma. I won't."

And Mrs. Blotch slipped the coin into her apron.

When Dayton Throme awoke, the villages were burning. He saw the fire from where he lay on his side. Smoke, and flame. He picked his head up, and it swam around in circles. He put it back down on the mat. It swam some more. He shivered. He looked again at the village. Billowing black smoke poured upward. It seemed to him that huge buckets of ash and soot were being emptied from the earth into the sky, poison flowing upward. He smelled it. It made him want to retch.

He shivered again. With great effort, he sat up. The world spun around him, but this time he felt warm hands on his arms, his neck, his head. He lay his head back and relaxed into something, into a dark dream of motion and comfort and textures, wool and leather and satin and sand. He opened his eyes. Skins and blankets covered him. Blank faces, painted with bright colors, vermilion, ultramarine, emerald. He recognized several elders. Zhintah-Hoak was here. They were all here. They were silent. Watchful. And then they disappeared, and darkness enfolded him.

And then he was looking out to sea, over the mayak-aloh and its pure blue waters, and past it to the horizon. He was not on his own small hill, but somewhere else. They had brought him to some high point above the islands. They had propped him up here, looking out. His face felt cool, bare, oiled. He felt it with his hands. They had shaved his beard. They had painted his face.

Dayton closed his eyes as the realization came home to him. His sickness. The smoke, and the fires. The war paint.

Tannan-thoh-ah.

They thought the end was near. He felt the world spin. He shivered and then fell back to sleep.

"That's a lot of gold." Dirk Menafee hefted the bag.

Princess Jacqalyn just laughed. "That? Heavens." She had ten times as much in the dresser drawer not three feet from him.

The part-time brigand, longtime bounty hunter, and onetime hero of the Battle of the Green stroked his grizzled beard, then poked his finger around in the small sack. "How many coins is this?"

"Twenty," Usher Fell said. "That's half. The other half when the job's done."

He shook his head. "You're askin' a lot. A man gets hanged for a job like this. They never quit huntin' you."

The princess walked around the small table. They were seated in a lavish private parlor adjacent to her bedroom, here in the dark inn where Usher Fell had moved her. It was the same inn to which Talon had taken Panna in preparation for the assassination of Senslar Zendoda. The princess was not familiar with this place, though she had heard of it. But now she found it very much to her liking. Standing, she moved her chair next to Dirk's. She scooted it in close, then sat down to his left and put her left elbow on the table, right in front of him. She looked him in the eye. She was dressed down, for her, but she was still dazzling.

"My dear man," she cooed, her every movement smooth as oil. "Let us examine the situation. You are being asked to do a service for your government and your Church, and you will have the protection of them both. And," she tapped the bag of coins in his hand, "you are being paid quite handsomely for it."

"It's just somethin' a man needs to think about, long and hard." He looked in the bag again.

She ran a polished fingernail softly down his cheek. He looked up, startled. She caught him with her eyes. "When it is done, the queen of all the land will hold you in the highest possible esteem."

"Yeah? How high?"

Her eyes took him in, swallowing him whole. "The highest esteem. What do you think, Father Fall? Perhaps a dukedom for our dear Dirk?"

"Oh, at least," the priest said with assurance. "But let's get the work done first." He unrolled a map across the table. "And it's Fell, by the way."

They saw the smoke before they saw the land from which it rose. It filled the horizon, gray at first, then black and thick. As they drew nearer, the *Trophy Chase* went silent, her crew watching with grave concern.

"Looks like the whole blazin' sea is burnin'," Delaney offered, awestruck.

"It's more than one island," Mutter replied.

"How does that happen?" Delaney asked, not illogically. "All the islands at once. Fire can't jump water."

"The blazes were set." Mutter said it with his usual sense of dark conviction.

"Who would want to go burning Achawuk islands?"

"The Achawuk."

"Nah. Why?"

Mutter watched for a long time, his jaw muscles clenching, releasing, as though in a spasm. Then he said in his darkest, lowest voice. "Because we come."

"Smoke, dead ahead!" came the cry from the lookout, high above the *Marchessa*.

Moore Davies peered through his telescope at the horizon. Sure enough. He expected his Firefish Fleet, as it was now called, to raise the Achawuk islands within an hour or two. That smoke would be coming from about the right spot. But what was burning?

Davies commanded the full flotilla again—all but the three ships that had perished at the hands of the Drammune. Gone were the *Gant Marie,* struck amidships, *Forcible,* brutally assaulted, and *Windward,* burned to the waterline. His fastest ships were in the lead, full of huntsmen and lures, sides of beef and beef blood. In addition to the *Marchessa,* these included *Rake's Parry, Danger, Candor, Campeche, Swordfish, Wellspring,* and the *Poy Marroy.*

The slower ships were decked out for the processing of Firefish: *Gasparella, Black-Eyed Susan, Homespun, Bonny Ann,* and *Blunderbuss.* They had been returned to their former inglorious forms, their main decks cleared of cannon and refitted as flensing floors, where the flesh of Firefish would be cut from bone, the meat cut and packed. The foredecks would be for experienced lemmers, where organs, bone, and teeth would be separated, boiled, and cleaned. The afterdeck was for tanning, rigged now with heavy clotheslines on which the hide could be cured before being packed in salt and lime.

The ship's captains remained the same, even the skipper of the *Blunderbuss,* a man now honored for his wisdom in the skirmish against the Drammune. All the captains, though they sailed in no particular formation now, had lookouts assigned with standing orders:

watch the *Marchessa,* mark every signal, and call it out. When such signals were commands, these sadder, wiser, but much quicker captains now obeyed. Immediately, and without question.

The men aboard who had sailed against the Drammune were eager to prove themselves in an arena in which they were far more confident—the commerce in which Nearing Vast now led the world. Their mood was light, but focused. They had a difficult job to do, and though it might not be so glorious as winning wars, still, the bringing home of acres of impenetrable Firefish hide was a great and patriotic duty, and would contribute mightily to the glory of Nearing Vast. They were proud to do it.

But not all the crew were the same men who had sailed to defeat in war. Not all were men. Not all were even sailors. Fully one-third of the souls who manned the processing ships were women, skilled in the ways of fishing and of whaling, tough as gristle, and just as eager to prove the worth of Nearing Vast as any man or any sailor.

But now there was smoke ahead…that was never good. The mood aboard the ships grew grim as they sailed closer and closer to these storied islands and wondered what tales would be told of them, once their work here was done, for good or ill.

The elders stood in a semicircle around Dayton Throme, their stricken rek-tahk-ent. The smoke from the fires below filled the air and the sky. They looked not at Dayton, but strained to see through the haze, out to sea. Then one of them pointed silently. The others peered through squinted eyes, until a gust of wind cleared a path, and they all saw: white sails on the horizon, surrounded by red ones.

"Shehab-ba denho-kah," Zhintah-Hoak said. *Douse the flames.*

Immediately, two of the younger men ran down the steep hill, the rugged mountain path and its switchbacks, through the trees, and toward the water.

"Now that's right odd," Delaney said, watching the smoke. "Ever see a forest fire just go out? All by itself?"

"No," Mutter said. The two were still clinging to the rigging high above the *Chase,* doing little but watching the islands approach. The thick black smoke had ceased rising now, and the air was clearing. Gray smoke still hung close to the water. "That was no forest fire."

Then from just above them, the lookout bellowed, "Firefish!"

Delaney and Cabe turned in unison to see the sailor pointing over their heads. "Firefish, dead ahead!"

Their necks swiveled, along with every other neck aboard, and they squinted into the sun, shaded their eyes, scanning the whitecaps ahead of them. And then the lookout added, "And she's runnin'!"

Delaney pointed. "There, see it?" Its head was underwater, but its dorsals churned the surface, creating a series of waves that might easily be mistaken for more whitecaps, except that they were so narrow and so evenly spaced.

"And it begins," Mutter Cabe said. There was no time left to puzzle on it anymore. Both men were in motion even before the bosun could call out orders. They knew what was coming. They had been holding the great cat back in deference to their Drammune escorts, but those tubs didn't matter now. They had come here to chase the Firefish, and now it was time for the cat to roar, and to leap, and to pounce.

"All hands!" the bosun cried. The ship's bell clattered below. "All hands a' deck! Drop the main full! Maintop, full! Fore, full! Mizzen, full! All others, steady as she goes! Hull speed, boys, hull speed for the *Trophy Chase*, and all stand back in awe!"

And then, as the men until now off duty poured up from their bunks in the forecastle, the bosun called again, "Starboard watch, to battle stations! Achawuk islands, dead ahead!" and the ship's bell clamored out a warning.

Any man aboard whose heart wasn't already in his throat found it there now. The armory was unlocked, muskets and pistols were distributed, cannons were primed and loaded with grapeshot.

They were hunting the Firefish, and would follow where it led. And right now it led straight into and among the Achawuk islands.

Huk Tuth stood on the quarterdeck of the *Kaza Fahn*, watching the great ship pull away from him. His own sails had been hauled, her sheets tied to maximize the draft and billow from the wind. But he'd done all he could. Anything more and he risked laying his ship over on its beam ends, and capsizing. The *Chase* would be caught only when she wanted to be caught. He had felt angry and powerless this entire voyage, but now he felt simply diminished, left behind as though he didn't matter.

He watched in silence, hating Talon as only a vengeful man can hate. He ran his hand through the scraggly hair that hung from his helmet. He felt the cut ends at his right ear, as though that lock were a limb he'd lost. He tasted again the bitterness of the hair she'd stuffed into his mouth while he was unaware.

"I want round shot in all cannon," he murmured, a rumble barely audible, to his first mate. "I want grappling hooks on deck. Signal the *Hezza Charn* to do the same."

"Aye, sir," replied the mate, and he went to make it so.

Dayton Throme sat up, his eyes clearing as the haze drifted away. He felt better; his fever had broken. He looked around, and realized he was alone. The elders had finally let him be. They had felt his forehead, surely, seen his peaceful breathing, and understood he was getting well again.

He stood, wobbly at first, feeling his heart pound in his chest and in his head. But he could stand. Where was he? On the side of the highest craggy hill, a mountain that overlooked the blue-on-blue mayak-aloh, and beyond it, the endless sea. He had never been to this spot, but he had seen it from below, a jutting perch among the crags. He felt dizzy for a moment, and his vision blurred. He looked around the calm blue waters below. The fires were dying out. Smoke still drifted on the waters. But the great, black plumes were gone. That was good. Surely the Achawuk had decided that Dayton's illness was not the sign of the cataclysm. Perhaps they all went back to their business.

But as his vision cleared, he looked more closely, and his spirits sank. All around the water, the beaches were filled with people. Jammed. Thousands of them. Tens of thousands. Not just men, but women and children, old and young. Their faces were all painted, and all carried spears. And not just on this island, but every island, every shore below him that ringed the mayak-aloh.

And they were busy preparing something. They passed torches among themselves. They damped the fires, and they piled up the ashes. They brought canoes out to the water's edge. The entire Achawuk nation lined the shores ringing the mayak-aloh, preparing.

They gathered as though readying for the start of some great hunt, some great battle, some great event. But what?

Dayton looked out to sea, under the clouded sky. Now he saw the ships. His head swam and pounded again, and he sat down. The illness was not through with him yet after all, and his stomach threatened to come up again. After a moment, he looked back out. There it was, the white sail of a Vast vessel, being chased by the red sails of a score of Drammune ships. The Vast ship was fleeing for safety. He closed his eyes and offered up a desolate prayer. Drammune behind, and Achawuk ahead. That ship didn't have a chance.

And then he scanned the seas, and saw to his right, to the west of these ships, more ships. These were all Vast. His heart pounded. How many? He counted them...there were thirteen. Fourteen Vast ships against...seventeen Drammune. They could help. But they were so far away. He looked back to the single white-sailed vessel, leading the red Drammune ships. She kept running. How could she escape?

And only now did it dawn on him—she would flee into the mayak-aloh, and she would lead the rest in here as well.

Dayton looked again at the Achawuk lining the shores below. The spears, the canoes...how many Achawuk were needed to destroy one ship? A thousand warriors? How many Achawuk were there in all...a hundred thousand? Two hundred thousand? How many ships were there? Thirty-one, all told. The math favored the Achawuk. As it always did.

He put his head back as a chill ran through him once again. He pulled the blankets over him. Not only would he not be rescued, but the coming battle would be thirty times worse than anything he had yet seen. Casualties would be horrendous. Women without their mates, children without fathers. Even a victory would be catastrophic.

It would be a cataclysm.

It would be the *tannan-thoh-ah*.

CHAPTER 18

Smoke

"Amazing creature," the priest said, delighted with the sight. "Just amazing." Packer and Talon had joined Father Mooring again, who stood in his usual spot, staring out at the sea, absorbing his first real look at the beast. "And very large."

Talon cut her eyes to Packer. "There it is." Her tone suggested that her next statement would be *Command it!* But she said nothing more.

Packer said nothing at all, but watched the thing swim, now about four hundred yards in front of the ship. He saw the dorsal fins cut through the water as it undulated, like a series of dark gray paddle-wheels all but submerged, one in front of the other.

The day had turned overcast, but it was not raining. The humidity could be felt on the skin, the smell of rain in it. The sun was obscure overhead, yet somehow threatened to peer down through the clouds at any moment. Ahead, the Achawuk islands filled the horizon, the nearest ones less than two miles away. A haze hung over these, cloud or fog or smoke, it was hard to tell. This Firefish was headed straight into the midst of them, heading for a gap between them.

A dark sense of misgiving enfolded Packer as he looked at the islands ahead, remembering the terrors of this territory. "Talon. We can't follow. The feeding waters are in there somewhere, and so are the Achawuk."

She looked at him blankly. "And yet you have been here before. With but a single ship. This ship. And you prevailed."

"I didn't prevail, Talon. I presumed. I never should have brought us here then, and I never should have brought us here now."

She laughed. "But you did not bring us here. I did. Look behind. This is a Drammune expedition. You are captive." She watched him wrestle with his role, then she said, "These doubts play across your heart like the shadows of clouds over the sea. Yet look, the sea is unchanged. Where is your God, Packer Throme? Has He changed? Does not He shine down regardless of your doubts?"

Packer closed his eyes. She was teaching him now?

"We gain on the beast," she said.

Packer looked, and saw it was true. The Firefish was a little more than three hundred yards away. Seagulls careened above it, as though it would provide them scraps of something they could eat. The *Chase* should not be able to outrun a Firefish. Was it slowing? If so, why?

Talon watched Packer's eyes, saw his turmoil.

She watched him. "You fear the Achawuk," she said, as though this were a revelation.

"I've fought them."

"And won."

It was useless. "Talon, God will do what He wants. And I don't know what He wants here."

She shrugged. "And what do you want?"

The question stunned him. It was the right question, the one he needed to have answered. Did he want to fight? Or to have God fight? "I don't know," he said honestly.

"Then ask Him for the power to command the beasts." And she walked away, back toward the quarterdeck, where a captain belonged.

"Amazing creature," Father Mooring said again.

Packer looked hard at him, afraid for a moment he was speaking of Talon. But he stared dead ahead. The monster was less than three hundred yards away. Packer looked up, behind him. The rigging was full of sailors, all looking down at him. Watching. Their faces were blank. He felt judgment in every stare, even Delaney's. Especially Delaney's. And he realized they all wanted him to lead, to do something heroic. They wanted him to be king. To command the Firefish. He looked back out to sea. The beast kept churning, and the *Chase* kept gaining.

"I don't know what to do, Father," Packer confessed.

"I will tell you your heart's desire," the priest said easily.

This snapped Packer's head around. Not even Senslar Zendoda had been able to do that.

But Bran Mooring spoke as though it were the simplest thing in the world, as he watched the Firefish dance through the waves. "I've seen it in you since I've known you, Packer Throme. Since you were a student sketching Firefish instead of listening to my lectures. And I still see it." Now the priest turned his head and looked at Packer. "You want all things to be right, and good. You want things to work out for the best, for all men. All women. All the world."

Packer felt his chest heave with a single pain. "I do want that. But doesn't everyone?"

Father Mooring continued. "You wanted things to work out for your father. That's why you followed the Firefish. You did it for him, so he would be remembered for the man you knew him to be. You wanted to make it all work out for Panna. And for the fishing villages."

"I'm not that unselfish."

"Of course not. You have dark motives, too, as do we all. There are monsters inside us, as well as in the world. Most often, we run from them, and believe they don't exist. If we have courage, we fight them, to conquer them. If not, sometimes we are destroyed by them. But God uses them. If we go to Him, He tames them where we can't. 'When I am weak, then am I strong.' Those monsters, the ones out there, the ones in here," he tapped his chest, "they all serve His purpose."

"To make it right."

"Yes. Packer, you are weak. And you are a fool. And I mean that in the very best sense."

But God hath chosen the foolish things of the world to confound the wise; and…the weak things of the world to confound the things which are mighty. "Thank you, Father. That's exactly what I needed. Thank you."

The priest shrugged, and turned back to watch the Firefish. "It's what I do."

Packer took a deep breath, smelled the ocean air, the salt spray, for the first time this trip. It filled his lungs, it opened his mind. He felt the wind in his hair. He looked out over the sea, and now he saw the beast submerge. The Firefish was gone. Packer leaped up onto the bowsprit for a better view. Suddenly, cheers filled the ship. He looked up above him and behind, and then he laughed. All those faces, a moment ago looking down in judgment, or so he felt, were now filled with energy, excitement, and amazement.

"Packer at the prow!" they called. "Packer at the prow!"

"Packer Throme!" and "Lookee there, the king!"

"Cheers for the king!" and then, "For the king, the *Chase*, and Nearing Vast!"

And the crew, ever ready to find a chant-worthy phrase and wring every last ounce of life from it, shouting it until they were hoarse and the syllables had no meaning, now picked up this one line and ran off the gangway with it.

"For the king! The *Chase*! And Near-ing Vast! For the KING! The *CHASE*! And NEAR-ING VAST!"

And now Packer felt it.

He felt it well up from deep within, and then he felt it overflow. He felt joy flow through him, as though the sun had been covered by rain clouds for years, decades, ages, and now it burned through with a sudden glory, so brightly that it illuminated every man, woman, and child on earth, every bone, every muscle, every tissue, every rock and tree and speck of sand. He was riding the *Trophy Chase*, pushed by the hand of God into...whatever God had in store.

Talon saw Packer on the bowsprit now. *Yes,* she thought. She could feel it, too. Here was the power she had sought. Packer stood, one foot before the other, his arms up, his hands clenching the guy lines for support. That was him, the young man who had dropped his sword and spread his arms, overpowering her with nothing but the fire of God within him. And that's what had overpowered her. That was what had given her the Hezzan, and then his child, and then his throne, and now would bring her power even greater. Packer could do this because he believed. There were many other explanations in the world, many other beliefs besides the Vast and their One True God. But Packer believed this way and he could find the power, and channel it, because of what he believed. She would own this power, if she could. If not, it would undo her. And she would undo all else.

"Ships!" the lookout called. "West sou'west! Port astern!" He was high atop the *Trophy Chase* as he called out the words, but they were lost, drowned in the chanting that still echoed up from the decks and down from the masts and spars and fled across the seas.

"Vast ships!" he tried again. Delaney heard him this time, peered astern, saw sails on the horizon. "Shut yer yaps, ye blowhards!" he screamed to the crew. "We got ships!" He pointed.

His tone more than his words finally drew some attention. The cheering slowly died away, and a buzz began. *Vast ships? Did someone say Vast ships?*

The lookout shouted the message again, and silence reigned. All eyes scanned the seas to the southwest.

The sailor in the crow's nest peered long and hard through the scope. Talon stood at the quarterdeck beside Andrew Haas, assessing this new threat.

"A dozen ships at least!" the lookout called. A long pause ensued, as all eyes strained to count the dots on the far horizon.

"It's the *Marchessa* in the lead!" the lookout shouted at last. He had waited until he was absolutely sure. Cheers erupted again. The *Marchessa*! Many of these men had sailed with that ship and with the *Camadan* for years. This was one of the *Chase*'s storied escorts. And now their old friend had appeared out of nowhere, and just in time, with a fleet of help in tow. The *Marchessa* was a Firefish ship if ever there was one. These events could only bode well.

Talon stewed, pondering her best move. These Vast had come to hunt the Firefish. Her Firefish. She looked astern, to the south. The Drammune ships followed the *Chase* yet. Though they had lost much ground, they were still closer than the Vast by a half a league. But the Vast had a better heading in this wind. They would move faster across it than the Drammune, who sailed with it.

By her reckoning, the Vast would meet the Drammune just about where the *Chase* was now. And then Huk Tuth would need to contend with the Vast, and the Vast with Huk Tuth.

And while they fought, the *Chase* would have the Firefish to herself.

Huk Tuth pondered his own options. They were few, and he didn't like any of them. He saw the Vast ships before the *Trophy Chase* did, and he had already sent his men, every man aboard every one of his seventeen ships, to battle stations. They all now watched the white-sailed ships approach. He and Tchorga Den were in the lead, the *Hezza Charn* five hundred feet ahead of him off the starboard bow, the rest of the Drammune warships arrayed behind.

He looked ahead of him. The *Trophy Chase* had not turned, was not turning, but instead continued to pull away. And as he watched, he saw the flagman aboard the *Chase* send the signal. Talon was ordering him to fight. And he was itching to do just that. But she was headed for the narrows to make her escape. He would be left behind. With that ship under her, he might never see her again.

Tuth swore. He spit. Then he swore again, remembering again the bitter taste of his own hair. It was seared into his memory. And that was her purpose, that was why she did it. He hated her with an intense hatred, more even than he hated the Vast.

Every instinct was alive within him. He wanted to fight. But which enemy? The Vast, or his own Hezzan? He pondered one more minute, and then made up his mind. "Signal the Armada," he said. "Tell them the *Trophy Chase* has been overthrown, and they are to ignore any orders from that ship."

This was true enough, he believed.

Moore Davies lowered his telescope. He stood on the bridge of the *Marchessa*. His first mate looked at him, awaiting orders. So did the bosun. So did the helmsman.

"Is it a fight, Captain?" the first mate asked. "They're after her, for sure."

"They'll never catch the *Chase*," the helmsman said, putting into words what all were thinking.

"Those red ships are supposed to be our allies, ain't they?" the bosun asked.

"Supposed to be," Moore Davies replied. "And sailors are supposed to be in church Sunday mornings on every weekend pass. Battle stations, men."

Talon had a vision, as she watched the Vast ships approach the Drammune vessels, as she saw the inevitable clash unfolding. It was a vision larger than this battle, bigger than two nations at war. In her vision, the old ways had returned. The ways of piracy, before the Firefish, when she and Scatter Wilkins had terrorized the seas. But this time, she was captain, and Packer was her right hand. He was her

Talon. The Hezzan of the Drammune and the King of the Vast would defeat the navies of the entire world. He would send the Firefish to attack on her command. Then the Firefish, the beasts that put an end to those predatory days, would become the means to return again, and in a far fuller, far more powerful way. She would rule the seas, and the men who sat in thrones around the world would bow down to her. It could happen. It had to happen; all was moving toward it, everything she'd ever done had put her here. She would find a way to turn Packer Throme.

Unlike the rest of the crew, Packer had not turned to look at the Vast ships, nor joined in the celebration. But he had heard. He knew the Vast Fleet had arrived. He prayed, and kept on praying. He burned within, his spirit rising up, it seemed to him, like a sacrificial offering. He would not turn now, neither to the right nor to the left, until all had been accomplished. Until either his prayer had been answered or he was standing before the throne of God, asking Him why not.

Talon looked at Packer standing at the prow, head back in prayer, arms up as he clenched the guy lines, as though invoking the Almighty. *Yes,* she thought, *pray to your God. Call on His power.*

She watched from the quarterdeck, standing close to Andrew Haas. "Ignore the Vast ships," she said in a voice so low it was almost a whisper.

He was shocked by the tone, the hiss, as much as by her message. "But ma'am, the feeding waters. We need a ship like the *Marchessa*—"

"Pursue the Firefish. Those are my orders."

"Full pursuit!" the bosun called out. "Back to business, men!"

The cheering died away again. The sailors looked at one another. Could they have heard him right? They weren't going to wait for the *Marchessa?* They all had visions of that streaming, golden pack, that horde of Firefish under the surface pursuing the *Trophy Chase.* The *Marchessa* and ten other ships decked out to kill them…that was the whole point of a Firefish Fleet. And yet the *Chase* was going it alone.

"Firefish, dead ahead!" the lookout called out once again.

Packer opened his eyes and saw the beast headed toward a narrows between two jutting fingers of nearby islands, swimming into what appeared to be the open sea beyond it, though little was visible. A light gray smoke hung low on the water like a shroud of fog, obscuring what lay beyond. It was a strange gray vapor, blowing gently across the water, thick here, thinner there. It seemed to come from land out onto the sea.

The dorsals of the Firefish undulated through the narrows.

"Steady as she goes!" the bosun called, relaying Talon's orders from the quarterdeck.

Moore Davies scanned the seas ahead, gauging speed and distance. The Vast Fleet and the Drammune flotilla sailed on a collision course. Both followed the *Trophy Chase*, and that ship had now disappeared between two islands, through a strait too narrow for more than one ship to pass at a time. The Drammune ship *Kaza Fahn* was approaching fast. It would be close, but Moore Davies believed he would arrive first.

"Stand by to fire," Captain Davies said evenly. The bosun relayed the message, and cannon were primed with powder. Lamps were held near touchholes. Musket and pistol hammers clicked across the decks.

Huk Tuth surveyed the readiness of his ship. His men were well armed, their crimson hauberks and helmets in place. They lined the rails. They stood by the cannon, muskets loaded, pistols ready, polished swords in scabbards. And they watched the salamander ships with hunger in their eyes.

"Hold your fire, men," said Tuth aloud, "unless one of these Vast vessels makes any move to threaten us. Signal the other ships the same."

Talon did not take her eyes from the calm water ahead. It was almost glassy compared to the open seas they'd just left behind. The smoke was a mist on the surface, drifting steadily, as though its only purpose was to obscure all vision. It made eyes water, and caused more than one fit of coughing. But she just sniffed at it suspiciously, as though she didn't trust it.

Moore Davies maneuvered the *Marchessa* into the strait just ahead of Huk Tuth's *Kaza Fahn*. Both ships bristled, two hedgehogs with quills extended, each waiting for a prick from the other. Vast sailors took aim with muskets and cannon as their ship turned to port. The *Marchessa* showed the Drammune her stern not a hundred feet from the prow of the *Fahn*. They awaited orders with fingers to triggers. Tuth and his Drammune warriors aimed right back, waiting for the same.

Discipline held on both sides.

With their lead ships now sliding into the narrows, the following ships did the same, alternating Vast and Drammune, then Vast again, through the passage.

And so the Firefish Fleet of the Vast and the squadron of Drammune warships entered the Achawuk waters, pouring into the mayakaloh.

Up on the rock ledge high above, Dayton Throme saw it all unfolding. He saw the smoke drifting from the fires on every shore, saw the breeze pull it across from the far shores, sliding it over the water like a blanket. He saw people on every shore tending fires, dousing flames with water, coaxing out smoke and steam by laying green leaves on burning piles of wood. He saw them spreading coals, piling up ashes.

Out in the middle of this enormous expanse, he watched the great ship sail. From above, he could see its sails, its lines. Even in the mist he could tell she was different, long and lean. Now the ship came out into a bit of a clearing, where the smoke was lighter; the heaviest smoke behind her. Yes, this was the same ship, the one that had escaped. He had seen her only in darkness. But this was a stunning craft, not to be forgotten. Most ships, even the most elegant, still looked like static, upright things that the wind could topple. But this one, this ship seemed elastic somehow. Mobile, as though she were flesh and blood rather than wood and canvas. And she moved like nothing Dayton had ever seen. She didn't seem to be sailing. She seemed to flow. Like a pebble dropped through oil, smooth and sleek. And fast.

Behind this one came another white-sailed ship, and then a red-sailed one, and then white, all angling through the narrows, following the great ship into the smoke. He understood why they followed. The great ship was a true prize, a leap forward in design, the sort of weapon over which nations go to war.

His heart felt heavy again. She had returned. No ship ever survived these waters. And none of these ships would survive. Not now, not here.

"Heave to, Mr. Haas," Talon ordered. She could not see the shore. She could trust her own blind dead reckoning for a while, but she couldn't trust it forever. She had to stop, or take a chance that the *Chase* would run aground. And the Firefish had disappeared again.

"Soundings, Captain?" Haas asked.

"No!" Talon responded harshly.

"We could cast anchor," Haas said, baffled. "These are calm waters. Could be shallow enough here."

"That would be deadly, Mr. Haas."

No, he thought, *that would be prudent, to prevent drift. Refusing to wait on the* Marchessa, *that would be deadly. Sailing blind into smoke, that would be deadly.* But he said nothing. She was in her own world, seeing everything through some dark lens, making judgments only she could understand, contrary to the obvious. This was just how he remembered her. Her whole demeanor made his skin crawl.

Haas looked to the bowsprit, and there was Packer Throme. The king. Doing nothing. Looking small and pitiful, bowed down. *That,* he thought, *is not what's needed just now.*

Talon looked toward the prow as well. Packer Throme's head was, in fact, bowed. His arms were up, hands holding the guy lines, but his elbows and knees were bent, with one foot in front of the other. She sensed no power there. He looked like the dead and crucified Christ, the empty husk of a body, not the powerful image that had met her on the *Camadan.* In front of Packer, smoke drifted across the water. Something was badly amiss, she feared. The eerie quiet, the danger. Perhaps they had already sailed from the living world into the Dead Lands.

"Keep this ship hove to until I say otherwise," she ordered. "And get me Mutter Cabe. Send him to the prow." Then she walked forward.

When she arrived at the bowsprit, she found Packer very much alert. His head was not hung down in sorrow nor in pain nor in grief nor even in prayer. He was staring down, down deep into the waters. She looked over the rail, saw only blue water.

"What do you see?" she asked.

He didn't answer.

"What do you think you see?" she asked.

He closed his eyes.

Mutter Cabe dropped to the decking. "Ma'am?"

"Shela-hanth," she said to him.

He blanched, then turned red. "Aye," he answered.

"Tannan-thoh-ah?" she asked him. "Araha?" *Here?*

"Araha," he answered. "This here's what they call the mayak-aloh."

Talon saw Packer look to the heavens. She continued. "Yes. The Achawuk believe in a spirit that moves the world, and that spirit will lead them to a great slaughter right here. The tannan-thoh-ah."

"You've known this?" Father Mooring, standing alongside, asked her, eyes probing hers.

She thought of the warrior she had questioned, and from whom she had finally won the secrets of their beliefs. It was a shame he had not survived to accompany them here; he could have been quite helpful. She shrugged. "It's not your religion."

Father Mooring's reaction bore all the earmarks of surprise, an expression quite unusual for him. "So you're riding the beliefs of two different faiths to this place?"

She said nothing, but walked to the rail and peered over, down into the sea.

"And you're hoping one of them can teach you the ways of the Firefish."

"It is wise to have counsel when traveling to the very source of power in the world."

Now the wind picked up. Smoke swirled. And then suddenly the haze cleared, and the clouds above parted. The sun shone down, a shaft of clear, bright light that dazzled them. Packer squinted against it, held up a hand to shade his eyes.

"Dear Lord," Father Mooring said, looking down into the waters beside Talon. "Dear Lord, we are in a pot of worms." Mutter came to the rail as well.

Packer heard, then stared down into the seas. The waters below were clear and calm, like a crystal lake. The sun reflected off every object, illuminating everything, right down to the seafloor. And the seafloor teemed with movement. Father Mooring had been speaking literally. There were hundreds of them, little snakes, sliding around and among one another, not much bigger than worms. But the priest had been incorrect. Packer knew what they were. And when one rose up briefly, and circled, and then settled back down, they all knew.

These were Firefish. Hundreds of Firefish, deep below them.

CHAPTER 19

The Crucible

The seminary was bright and sunny, its lawn manicured, all its cottages restored and repaired. Panna arrived in a white carriage that pulled up to the front of the library, a stone building not much bigger than the Throme cottage in Hangman's Cliffs. She was helped down by Stave Deroy, who then, with several other dragoons, helped Hap Stanson down from the same carriage. They gave him his cane, and assisted him the few steps to the library.

Inside, the librarian, a young man with a kind but faraway look, bowed deeply, welcoming the queen and the head of his order. He stood alongside Father Usher Fell. They had both been expecting these guests. "Follow me," the librarian said. He picked up a lantern and walked to a spiral staircase.

"I'll stay up here," the High Holy Reverend Father said. "I'm afraid in my condition I cannot navigate stairs well. But I will await your findings with great interest."

Panna nodded. "Chunk, will you follow Father Fell? I will follow you."

"Yes, ma'am."

Hap watched as the four descended. Then he hobbled back outside. Two dragoons, leaning casually against the carriage, straightened up. They gripped their pikes. "You're not to leave," one said to the priest.

"Of course not. I just require a moment next door." He pointed at the chapel. "I have been unable to offer my accustomed prayers. You are welcome to accompany me."

They both shook their heads. "You're not to leave."

"Are you not Christian men?" he implored. "It is a chapel. I will kneel and say my prayers, that is all."

They gripped their pikes tighter.

"Let him go," a voice said. All three men turned to find Ward Sennett standing alongside, holding a large leather binder in his hand, full of parchments.

"All right," the more senior dragoon agreed. "But we're going with." And so, flanking him, they walked into the sanctuary.

Deep below the ground floor, the library archives went on and on. Rows and rows of books, scrolls, and boxes filled the musty space. Clearly this was not simply a basement, but a part of the tunnel system beneath the Old City. The single lantern lit almost nothing. "Back here," the young priest said. "Follow me."

They followed him to a small brick doorway, an arch no more than two feet wide. The librarian turned sideways, slipped inside. He walked to a wooden table, on which was laid out several sheaves of paper, slightly yellowed . "Here are the records which you seek."

He turned back to find Father Fell standing by his side, and a big dragoon struggling to force his bulk into the space. One arm and one leg were all he could manage. He pulled himself back, and looked at Panna, embarrassed. "I'm sorry, Your Highness. I'm too big."

"You're just the right size, Chunk. The doorway's too small. But it's all right," she said. "You wait here."

"Ma'am, no…you stay here with me. Let 'em bring the stuff here to you."

Usher Fell hesitated momentarily, then said, "Certainly," He picked up the papers, and brought them back out. "So long as we don't take them upstairs, we can look at them here. The ancient scrolls, however, must be handled delicately."

Panna read the documents expecting to find the proof of Packer's innocence she had been promised. "These hint that Packer was removed from school for more than just cheating. But they don't say what his offenses were."

"But they do," Usher Fell said, standing beside her, pointing to a spot near the bottom of the second sheaf. "Right here. It says, 'According to the records the elder Throme now quotes freely, referring to the Deeds of Mission Achawuk led by Father Dorndel Botts, it is deemed unwise to continue the younger Throme's association with the seminary. The incident within Father Fell's cottage provides the appropriate vehicle for his dismissal.'"

"But what are these 'Deeds of Mission Achawuk'?"

"Ah. It is an ancient document. The record of that historical mission reveals that the Firefish, or something that sounds like them, were sighted, feeding, near the Achawuk lands. But those documents are not necessary. This clears him, right here. It is an official document that says his father was running around quoting church records, and that is the reason Packer needed to be expelled."

"I don't see that this clears his name. It doesn't say what happened in the cottage. It simply creates a greater mystery."

Father Fell frowned. "I'm disappointed. But...I'm not sure how to clear that up. Certainly, only Packer and the girl were there with me."

"Where is the girl now?"

"Deceased. Very unfortunate accident."

She glared at him. "Unfortunate for her."

"Well, I'm sorry you came down here for nothing."

Her eyes narrowed. He was a clever man. "What else is in that document?"

"Which one?"

"The Deeds of Mission Achawuk."

"Oh, nothing. Nothing really."

"I would like to see it."

Fell looked a bit forlorn. "I don't think it's necessary, but if that is your wish..."

"Yes, and also my command."

"I'll bring them. No, wait. Those must be read within, and your dragoon cannot enter. Perhaps you could find a slightly...smaller guard?"

"Heavens. I'll go in. Stave, wait here."

"But ma'am..."

"Wait here!"

And she followed Usher Fell into the records room. The old priest laid a scroll out on the table. The young priest held the lantern. Panna leaned over, and began to read.

Then, as if on cue, Dirk Menafee stepped deftly from the shadows, grabbed Panna's hair with one hand and put his pistol to the back of her neck with the other. He cocked the hammer.

The sailors were tying canvas, having furled most of the sails, keeping the ship in place. Now they stopped, the sunlight illuminating the sea. They saw the Firefish below, more Firefish than they had dreamed existed in the world. The beasts swam around and among one another, like eels poured into a pot. Hundreds. Maybe thousands.

"We're cooked," Delaney said as he looked down into the teeming mass. He got the sick impression that the *Chase* was floating on top of them, that the ocean had turned to monsters. They all looked small, but he knew they were not. Some were bigger than others; some were very young. But most were fully grown, fully formed, and fully capable of destroying a whole fleet of ships the size of the *Trophy Chase*.

"Tannan-thoh-ah," Mutter Cabe said. He looked around the shores, and saw the men entering the water, swimming out to the *Chase*.

"What will happen?" Talon asked him.

"I don't know much. Just stories from my youth."

"What stories?"

"'The Mastery,' they call it. When everything changes. In the next world, man becomes the glory of the beast."

"What does that mean?"

He shook his head. "It means we won't see the sun rise on this world again."

From his perch, Dayton Throme also saw the sun break through, saw it illumine the *Trophy Chase*, dazzling the sea, and then he saw what was below, under the water. The whole bottom of the sea was illumined as though through a crystal lens. The Firefish were dark gray, but the scales caught in the sunlight gleamed golden yellow. More of them than he had ever seen before. Across the entire bottom of these still waters, masses of them. All the Firefish in existence, he

The Battle for Vast Dominion

thought. Enough to destroy every ship on the ocean. Enough, perhaps, to destroy the world.

And as he watched, the first of many human waves entered the water, men with painted faces swimming out, their spears on loops of leather or twine around an arm, or around their necks.

"We're done here. Come about," Andrew Haas told the bosun. "We need hard port rudder and matching sail. We're goin' back the way we came."

"Aye, aye," Stil Meander answered, relief flooding his eyes. And then to the crew he boomed, "Stop yer gapin', ye sheet-slittin' slackdogs! We're comin' hard about!" And he began the ordering of the sails.

The men aboard the *Chase* turned from the fearful sight of the Firefish to their duties. Delaney and Mutter were among those on the foremast who loosed lines they had just finished tying, and unfurled canvas they had just furled, and did it gladly.

Talon looked at the quarterdeck with blazing eyes, up at the masts with bared teeth. "Belay that order!" she shouted, but her voice did not carry to the topmost yards, and judging by the lack of reaction from the sailors, didn't carry to the lowest, either.

She leaped down to the foredeck in one bound, then cleared the rail and landed on the main deck in one more. Sailors who couldn't seem to hear her watched in wonder. She was up the stair to the quarterdeck with her sword in her hand. Andrew Haas had just enough time to unsheathe his own blade before Talon disabused him of it. Hers flashed once and his flew over the rail and splashed into the sea.

But she did not quit coming at him; she pressed forward, and he backed into the cabin wall behind him, the edge of her blade against his throat, her left elbow pinning his shoulder to the wall. "Belay that order!" she hissed at him, "or die a mutineer!"

Haas remained silent.

"Belay that order!" Stil Meander boomed, waving his arms frantically, trying to save the first mate's life. "Belay it *now*!"

Talon saw the action cease above her, and let Haas live. She pulled her sword away, but did not step back. "You had your orders."

Frightened as he was, Andrew Haas still did not back down. "Kill me if you want, Talon. We're all dead anyway if we stay here. There's too many of the things. Can't you see that? We need out of here, and we need out now. Sailing into smoke! The Achawuk are out there somewhere. And the Drammune! It's a trap—it's all a trap! We can't survive it."

"Those are opinions, sailor, and should be stated as such to your captain. Who wanted to take soundings here? Who wanted to drop anchor here? Was that me, or was that you?"

"Why me, a' course."

"And who said it would be too dangerous?"

"You did. Ma'am."

"And what would have happened if we had taken soundings, or dropped anchor down onto those beasts?"

He swallowed hard.

"So who was right?"

"You were. Ma'am."

She released him. "I know what you do not. Why does this smoke not choke us?" She looked up at all the men, addressing the entire crew. "Answer that! How can we breathe smoke?"

No one said a word.

"It does choke...a little bit," Delaney offered in a whisper. Only nearby sailors heard him.

"Wood smoke blinds and stings and gags! This stuff...it is more fog than smoke. It is made by the Achawuk! Not to blind us! It is what keeps the Firefish below the sea. The beasts want to come up here. They want to feast on you, Mr. Haas." She turned away from him. "And every one of your putrid carcasses." She glared up into the rigging. "But they will not do so unless we behave like prey, so that they cannot resist. Do you want to behave like prey, Mr. Haas? With hundreds of predators watching from below? Do you want to run, and invite attack?"

He shook his head. "I didn't think—"

"You didn't think! Mr. Haas, I relieved you of your sword that you might not oppose me with it. The next time you disobey, I will relieve you of your head, and for the same purpose. Do you understand me now?"

"Yes, ma'am."

She looked above and around her. Satisfied they were meek enough, she turned back to Haas. "Now, heave to once again."

"Heave to," he managed, nodding at Stil Meander.

The Battle for Vast Dominion

"We're heavin' to!" Meander called out.

"Yeah," Delaney said darkly. "We're heavin' to. We're heavin' idiots to obey the likes a' her." And he took another look at Packer, who hadn't even turned around from his perch on the bowsprit.

"He knows we're powerless here," Mutter Cabe said, climbing back up to work alongside Delaney. He was clearly relieved to get away from the decks, and farther away from both the Firefish and Talon. "The king has given up."

"Packer? He's done no such thing. He's prayin', that's all." But Delaney wondered.

Dayton saw still more Achawuk wade into the waters. Thousands upon thousands of warriors, faces painted dark blue or crimson or green, spears tied to leather thongs draped over shoulders. On each leather thong a chunk of blackened cork was fastened, flotation for the spear and, if required, for the man. Tens of thousands went, and more waited their turn. When they were all in the water, it would be enough to choke out the surface of the mayak-aloh, to assure that no ship could sail, or move. Enough to assure that no ship's boat could be lowered, except into their waiting arms, and that no ship could be abandoned, except into their spears.

All these ships were doomed. Cattle to the slaughterhouse. He had been away from Nearing Vast for many years, and he knew his mind no longer worked along their paths. But why would these ships come here? There was nothing here. No rum here. No gold. No one from whom to steal. These were islands lost in time, a place of sand and water, sun and wind, of slow and peaceful life and sudden, brutal death. Firefish and Achawuk—those were their only assets. Both were deadly, and unmerciful. Why come here at all?

And why come to the mayak-aloh? If they had navigated through these waters two islands over, even one island away, they would have passed through the entire chain unmolested. Every Achawuk alive was gathered here, right here.

And still they came. One or two ships were still angling to enter. It seemed to Dayton as though the hand of God must have brought them here for judgment, or that the devil lured them all here to their destruction, to the one place in all the world they could never possibly escape.

It was a prophecy, after all—the tannan-thoh-ah. All of it was true.

And now there was nothing left in all the world to do but to stand and watch the slaughter.

"And now, they come," Talon said softly, under her breath.

The sudden spike of sunlight was retracted back into the heavens. Clouds rolled back in, covering everything. The mist, or smoke, or whatever it was grew heavier. Andrew Haas stood by his captain's side, watching the *Marchessa* appear from the haze astern, floating silently except for the slap of lapping waters on her prow. And then, well back, the Drammune ship *Kaza Fahn*. Haas was thankful there had been no fight between them as yet, but sorry they had come here at all. A fight in open waters would have saved at least some of them. The Firefish would not stop until all were destroyed.

"Their numbers…you believe to be in the thousands?" Talon asked.

Haas was confused. Then he looked where she was looking, over the port rail. She had not been talking about the Drammune, nor the Firefish, but the Achawuk. But he saw nothing, nothing except gray haze. "Where?"

"Look at the surface of the waters."

All Haas could see were ripples coming toward him, out of the smoke. His heartbeat quickened. These tiny waves rode atop the larger ones, insignificant, the kind that might be created by two hundred pebbles strewn across two hundred yards of sea. Then he heard the gentle splashes, the sort children might make in a bathtub. These froze his heart.

The ripples grew denser.

"Battle stations," Talon commanded quietly. "All hands. Your standing orders, Mr. Haas, are to heave to, and to fight like demons." She looked him in the eye. "I trust you will find no reason to disobey."

Haas shook his head. "No, ma'am. I won't."

She watched his eyes, studying him, impassive as a hawk.

He spun on his heel and called out, "Battle stations! Achawuk, port side!"

Stil Meander added his own booming voice. "To arms, ye blaggards!" he called out, "The savages have come to feast!"

Sailors dropped down from the rigging like coconuts from a palm tree. Talon walked among them as she went back to the prow of the *Chase,* once more to check on her prize, Packer Throme.

As she walked to the prow, she heard gunshots astern.

"Your Highness!" Stave Deroy shouted, pulling his pistol. But by the time he aimed it, the only person he could see was Panna. The gunman was behind her, using her as a shield.

"Do it!" Usher Fell hissed, barely above a whisper. "Why are you waiting?"

Dirk Menafee bared his teeth, but did not pull the trigger.

"Kill her! You will have your reward!"

Dirk swung the barrel of the gun toward Father Fell. "You have all the proof you need?" he asked, not at the priest, but into the darkness behind him.

"Yes, quite enough, Mr. Menafee." Two deputies and the Sheriff of Mann stepped from the shadows. The deputies grabbed Father Fell by the arms and began to manacle his hands behind his back. The sheriff, a young, square-jawed official who radiated the integrity of competence, was a protégé and staunch admirer of the late Bench Urmand.

"This is outrageous!" the priest started. But then, after glaring once at Dirk, he thought better of protesting.

Dirk holstered his pistol. "Sorry, ma'am, if I scared you at all."

Panna straightened herself. "You were…convincing. But no harm done. Thank you." She turned to Usher Fell now, looked at him as she spoke, watched his expression slide from anger to dismay. "Your actions are punishable by death."

"Persecution," he said to her. "Martyrdom. Your retribution will only strengthen the Church of God." Then he turned to Dirk Menafee. "And I'll want my money back."

"Not likely."

Aghast, the priest asked him, "Do you have any idea what you've just passed up?"

"No, I don't," the grizzled one replied. "And see, that's the problem. This queen here, she does what she says. Like it or not. But that one you serve? She's likely to do or say anything to get her way. I think she's out of her screamin' mind, frankly."

Fell could not disagree, and so spoke no more as he was led away.

Huk Tuth heard the roar of gunfire, too, but he ignored the sound. The blasts came from behind him in the haze. Drammune were attacking the Vast, just as he was about to do. Tuth had not seen the momentary shaft of light that illumined the beasts below. He had eyes only for his chosen prey. The great ship had slowed to almost a stop. He did not spend a moment worrying about why that might be.

"To port," Tuth ordered, "fifteen degrees, all speed." He glowered at the banner of the Vast flying high above those cloudy billows, above the ship that had become his nemesis. The *Marchessa* would provide protection for that ship on her starboard side, the weather gauge. Fine. The *Fahn* would attack from port.

"All hands to the lee rails! Ready cannon! Ready grappling guns! I want the *Trophy Chase!*"

The gunfire came from behind the *Kaza Fahn* from *Rake's Parry*. The Achawuk had let the *Fahn* go, but now the warriors arrived, thick and dense, corks bobbing, spear tips up, as the Vast ship came to them.

The captain of the *Parry* ordered his men to open fire. Like the *Marchessa,* his ship carried huntsmen. They could shoot, and now they did. A hundred weapons fired, a hundred Achawuk ceased swimming and sank beneath the surface. These warriors, the first names written on the role of the dead within the mayak-aloh today, were pushed down under the surface by their brethren, who followed in their bloody wake without a word.

As the warriors neared the ship, their spears were in their hands, their solitary objective clear in their minds. When they reached the hull, the hammering began. Spears bit deeply into wood. Crewmen froze. They'd heard all the stories. They knew that sound. Their officers called out firm and unflinching orders, while unsteady fingers reloaded warm and empty weapons. The few cannon remaining after the refit barked futilely, like watchdogs chained to a post. The Achawuk were too close, too dense, too many. Sailors fired down on their foes from the rails, lightning lashing out in anger. But more foes came. For every swimmer shot, two more reached the hull. For every two shot on the hull, four climbed up behind. In the time it took the men to reload once, another rung of spears reached up the hull, a scaffold of destruction, a trellis built slat by slat, climbed by living vines, multicolored in shades of red and green and blue, growing upward at a deadly rate in some horrible dream.

The *Parry* would be boarded. She would be overrun. She was lost.

"The blood is in the water," Talon said to Packer, listening as the firing continued astern. She stood on the deck just behind him, looking up toward him. "You must command the beasts. To save your men. To save your ships. You must command them to attack your enemies."

He did not look back at her. He kept his eyes closed. He had been offering himself up alive, ready to die or live within God's power. Her words were a hot knife down his back, pulling him away, drawing him toward her, toward a course that was as reasonable as any he could imagine in the world. But it was not his chosen course.

"They stir," she said, and pointed down at the ocean floor. Her voice, more than her words seared him.

Packer's eyes opened on their own, and were drawn down into the sea. Another shaft of light, not so strong but strong enough, filtered down to the ocean floor. The crawling movements of the beasts were something more than that now. A pattern had developed. They aligned themselves. The Firefish were circling. Slowly now, clockwise, like a whirlpool forming.

And then he saw the yellow glow begin.

"Yes," she whispered. "They come alive. They rise." The Firefish below the *Chase* were in fact rising. They were changing, turning from dark gray to yellow, growing larger as they came closer. The blood was in the water. They could not resist.

Fear rose in Packer. It was a physical sensation, like a cold sword blade in his belly, up through his chest. His knees and feet tingled, his joints felt loose, as though he were hanging out over nothing, a thousand feet up, and the ground was turning far below. He was a powerless puppet perched on a stick of wood above a lair of monsters, with another monster behind him.

He knew what Talon expected.

Do not forsake me, Packer prayed. But his heart melted. His hands and arms shook.

Talon saw the tremor and leaped up on the bowsprit just behind him. She whispered in his ear. "Where is your God?" she asked.

The Battle for Vast Dominion

"Where is His power? Does He yet hold you in His hand? Or is He gone?"

Resist not evil...Those words came to Packer. And they crushed him. He was ordered not to contend with Talon, and yet the power he trusted to save him was gone.

His mind relaxed, his head fell backward. He could not defeat her. He was in God's hands. He was in her hands. And he could not tell the difference.

She grabbed his hair and held his head tight against her cheek. "You *have* the power," she hissed into his ear. "*You*. God has given it to you. Use it! Do you think He wastes such gifts? No...He *wants* you to use it."

"Look at him now," Mutter said as Talon whispered to Packer. He and Delaney had descended at Talon's command to the foredeck and stood at the port rail. Mutter gestured toward Packer. "Where's all his big talk? He's not so cocksure now."

Delaney furrowed his brow. "Packer's never been cocksure."

Mutter shook his head. "Walkin' to the prow like some holy man. He ain't so big. Turns out he's just a fisherman after all." Mutter clearly took satisfaction in what he saw as Packer's comeuppance.

Delaney tried to understand this. He and Marcus had heard the confessions, seen the torment of Packer's soul. But what if someone never knew what was going on inside of Packer Throme? What if there had been no window into him? Could it be that Packer would seem confident, even arrogant? Yes, Delaney concluded, it might be possible.

"Firefish," Cabe said suddenly, looking into the sea, over the rail. "Comin' up now."

"Achawuk!" another sailor said, and all looked up at the haze, saw the first faces appear from the mist, dark masks of death.

"Drammune!" another shouted from the stern. All looked to the *Kaza Fahn*, now sliding up on the port side.

Delaney almost felt thankful. At least there was something to fight. He looked at Packer once again. Nothing. The woman who had become their captain was still drawing the man who was supposed to be their king into her spell, whatever it was. Delaney checked his pistol one more time. "Hope you got plenty a' ammunition, Mutter. We're on our own now."

"Look," Talon was whispering in Packer's ear. "Look down. Look deep. You will command them."

Packer's heart and mind gave way, and both sank, as though he were asleep. His heart was stone, a stone sinking now through dark, cold waters, falling, failing. There was no light here. No warmth. His mind…he felt his mind collapse, as though crushed by the cold, by the pressure of falling so far, so deep. His body quaked, and he let go, tumbling down into some place, some cold and stony place he'd never been.

And it was there he saw the vision.

This was not like Talon's vision, of domination of the seas, and thereby the world. Nor was it like the one he'd been given before, when kneeling on the deck of the *Trophy Chase*. Then God had taken him to the cliffs to speak to him, that he might remember.

God was not in this place. This was a place of darkness, and Packer knew he was falling into that realm where souls go to be abandoned, where spirits without hope fall and remain forever.

In his vision, Packer stopped falling when he hit the deck of a ship. The ship was aflame. He landed face down, and his right hand went through the decking, through the planks of the ship. He pulled it out, and his hand was missing. He had a stump of an arm, just below the elbow. He looked up and he saw Talon, dressed in black. He now recognized this place. It was the quarterdeck of the *Trophy Chase*. The *Trophy Chase* was burning. Talon wore her robes, the robes of the Hezzan, but here they were all black. Her hair was wild, long, and loose, blowing slowly in an unseen, unfelt wind. Her eyes, though, were cold and calm. Before her was an iron cauldron, sitting amid the flames. In it, something steamed and boiled.

The witch, he thought.

Or perhaps he heard the words. That appellation, that nickname, that accusation…it was the one she never could escape, that followed her from ship to ship and shore to shore. And now it had caught her. She watched him, distant, predatory. She held his eye, then looked into the cauldron. Packer rose, and walked near, and he looked into the cauldron, too.

A mist floated across it, a steaming poison, dark gray, like soot. She blew on the mist, and it vanished. Underneath, clear waters boiled. In the boiling waters he saw snakes. Serpents, alive and angry, hundreds of them swimming under the surface, chaotic, frenzied.

They stir! she said. She was looking at Packer. *They rise!*

Now Talon dipped a wooden ladle into the pot, and she stirred. The beasts moved around in circles, and the water moved, and they all swam in unison, clockwise, faster and faster, until a whirlpool dropped down in the center of the cauldron. She let go of the ladle. As he watched, the wooden spoon spun into the center of the maelstrom. But it was not a ladle now; it was a ship. A ship with tall masts, white sails, a long, lean ship with a deep, deep keel. And men were on that ship. He saw one man standing atop the bowsprit, clinging to the guy lines, looking down into the water, watching the serpents as they circled.

Huk Tuth saw the yellow hair standing at the prow, with Talon behind him, as the *Kaza Fahn* slipped smoothly up beside the *Chase.* He knew what this pair was doing. He'd seen this before, had seen Packer at the prow of this very ship when the *Rahk Thanu* and then the *Nochto Vare* had been destroyed.

The yellow hair would command the Devilfish. And Talon, the Hezzan, would command the yellow hair.

Tuth snarled his disgust. He opened his mouth to shout the single word that would teach them both respect for the Worthy Ones. His men could open fire and end this. But he didn't give the command.

Instead, he heard the knocks, the hammering. Spears like teeth biting into wood. And on his port side, where he had positioned no men.

He spun around. He peered into the mists as he ran to the port rail, now fully aware of his error. The warriors were thick, and covered the sea, choked it with painted faces, bodies, spears, floating blocks of cork, covered it fore and aft, like a thick wool blanket.

They were halfway up his hull. Halfway to the deck.

As the *Marchessa* slid slowly even with the *Chase,* just off her starboard rail, Moore Davies saw, as all his sailors did, Packer at the prow, Talon behind him on the beam, her hands now clamped on top of Packer's hands, as he gripped the lines. She was whispering to him. His eyes were closed. He seemed limp. Talon, dressed in black, hunched over Packer, and all but wrapped around him—she seemed to Davies like some kind of cancer, a tumor growing on him.

Beyond the *Chase,* off her port side, Davies could see the *Kaza Fahn,* could see the danger she posed. As the *Marchessa* pulled even,

Davies hailed the *Chase*. But he had no more than called out the "ahoy" when the rapping started. The Achawuk, swimming from the farthest shore, were on his starboard hull. They had emerged from the mists. They had surprised him just as they had Huk Tuth.

The Vast captain on one ship and the Drammune commander on the other, each flanking the *Trophy Chase* for a different purpose, protected the great ship between them from the Achawuk. Each captain gave the same command at almost the same time, and for precisely the same reason.

"The Achawuk, starboard!"

"Achawakah! Thantach!"

"Fire at will!"

"Charnak!"

Drammune and Vast sailors released their ammunition, lightning and thunder down the rails, clouds of smoke leaping out in an angry hurry, then rising slowly, calmly. Each pistol and each musket was aimed true by a trained marksman at a target much closer than those used on Drammune or Vast shooting ranges. Almost every shot found its mark.

The cannon was even deadlier. The Vast started with grapeshot, and after one round of cannon balls, the Drammune deck guns spewed canister across the water. Far less accurate but far more effective. Many more living swimmers became casualties, turning the water red. And yet more Achawuk pushed them under. Wounded or dead, it didn't matter. If they could not continue, they were submerged beneath a canopy of those who could.

And they kept coming. Too many. Too many. The Achawuk boarded the *Marchessa*. They boarded the *Kaza Fahn*.

Dayton Throme's heart withered as he watched. The mists were clearing as those who had been stoking fires, creating the smoky fog, now left to join their brethren in the seas. The Achawuk were now a solid mass within the waters.

The ships had followed, nearly all of them now, one after the other into the mayak-aloh. They had made it through the narrows, into the mists, only to find the Achawuk within that fog, deadly and waiting. After the first three ships arrived unscathed, the next six were simply overrun. And now all would be overrun.

He watched the brutal drama play out, remembering his own experience, the panic, the dread, the pit of fear into which he plunged as it came to him that there would be no way out, no way but death, and that this savage people could not be stopped.

He prayed for mercy for those aboard those ships, just as he had prayed for mercy for his companions six years ago. It was a mercy that had not come then, and he knew in his heart would not come now.

The crewmen of *Rake's Parry, Danger, Candor, Campeche,* and *Swordfish,* fought, and died, with honor.

They had erred against the Drammune, and had come here to seek a pardoning glory in these waters. And here they found it, at the cost of their lives. More than one man, swinging a sword, or the butt end of a musket he had no time to reload, looked up into the rigging, saw the limp sails, and prayed for wind. But that storied miracle, the one that had saved the *Chase,* would not be repeated here today. The Achawuk were strong. Their spears were sharp, and bloody. A blind and mindless dedication drove them. And they were just too many.

These sailors would fight a losing battle here today. Blood would flow from earnest veins onto the decks of good, true ships, and then into the waters of the mayak-aloh. And their blood would mingle there with the blood of their enemies, of Tchorga Den, and all the sailors of the *Hezza Charn,* and then those of the *Ganda Flez, Chammando, Herza Ko*…all Drammune ships with storied pasts, now silent as the grave, their sailors driven from this life at the point of a spear. And their blood would mingle with their enemies, the Achawuk. What Achawuk survived the boarding of these ships would move quickly on, returning to the sea to swim to the next ship, red or white, it didn't matter, and continue their trek toward the tannan-thoh-ah, the final destruction, the Mastery, the end of the world.

And all that blood would mingle, and seep downward, and dissipate, and raise the ravenous hunger of the Firefish.

In Packer's dark dream he watched the small beasts swim in circles under the surface of her boiling cauldron. The little ship now spun, turning at the center, at the mouth of the whirlpool.

The blood is in the water, Talon told the serpents.

Then Talon had in her hand a wooden cup, and she poured red liquid from it into the waters. She poured and poured, and it turned the boiling liquid a dark and murky crimson. But the cup would not be emptied. And the liquid drove the serpents mad. They writhed, they rose, they swam at faster and faster speeds. As she kept pouring, Packer saw writing on the cup. He peered at it, stepped closer. He could read the words.

These were names. Many names. Packer saw them; he read them as she poured. He recognized them. Fen Abbaka Mux, John Hand, and Scatter Wilkins. Lund Lander. Jonas Deal. Ned Basser and Duck Tilham. Mather Sennett. Bench Urmand. Senslar Zendoda. Will Seline. There were many other names he knew, Cane Dewar, Seval Carther, Ricks Goodfellow…he recognized them from the roll of the dead he'd written after the last Achawuk battle. And then there were many names he didn't know. Vast names. Drammune names. And Achawuk. Soldiers, sailors, men of war. Men with families and friends, with fortunes great and small, with homes and possessions and pasts and dreams, men with everything but futures. Men who had killed other men, and had done so with all the strength that they could muster. Talon poured their blood into the cauldron.

The serpents in the water glowed bright, bright yellow, bright like liquid gold. The blood turned the waters black, but it turned the snakes to gold. They swam, their eyes ablaze, their mouths agape, their golden teeth bared in their ravenous desire to devour, all wanting more. And she gave them more. The more she poured, the more frenzied they became, swimming in circles, angry, hungry. The more they devoured, the more they wanted. And Packer knew they would never be satisfied. There was not enough blood in the world to sate these golden beasts.

"Stop pouring," Packer said to her. His voice was far away, and slow.

Talon looked at him as though she didn't understand, couldn't comprehend. "But you are the one who pours," she said to him. "You have done all this."

Packer looked at the cup again, and the hand that held it was marred, and scarred, and bore a signet ring. It was his hand, his right hand. He looked down at his arm, and it was still severed. He tried to drop the cup, but he couldn't. Her hand was on his, covering his, holding his as he held and poured the cup. She just laughed, cold and present, in his ear. "You command them. I command you," she said.

"No, God!" he cried.

"No God?" she asked. "That is correct. No God has given you this gift. It is yours alone. Yours to use. You have renounced the sword, and taken up the Firefish. A greater weapon, greater by far. And it is not possible to renounce this weapon. You must use it. It is yours to *use*."

And then he saw the ship, the small ship at the center of the whirlpool, go under. It sank to the bottom, and was attacked by the serpents.

And then the Firefish rose.

Dayton saw it. So did the Vast aboard the *Trophy Chase*. So did a handful of Drammune. So did a thousand warriors in the water, near enough to watch the beast, to see its massive, knobbled head, its yellow, glowing scales, its fiery eyes.

It rose to the bowsprit. And there it stopped, its eyes even with those of Packer Throme. It looked at Packer and at Talon. Talon saw into its eyes. She saw the question there, the hunger.

And then she saw its rage.

"Command it, Packer Throme!"

But Packer did not move. Nor did he open his eyes. Now Talon looked into its maw as its great jaw unhinged. As its huge mouth dropped open, she felt its heat. She saw along the jagged row of teeth a single tooth that protruded through a Drammune helmet, crushed and pierced.

"Command the beast, Packer Throme!" she cried. "Command the beast!"

Packer heard the words, felt the command, the urgency in Talon's voice, but he heard all within his dream. He watched a golden serpent within the cauldron. And the cauldron itself had changed. It was golden now, and the liquid within it was golden. It was not a cauldron, but a crucible, and on the surface collected dross, every impurity. And still the golden serpent watched him.

And then it cocked its head to one side. And then it leaped toward him, flying from the crucible, its golden teeth bared, its golden skin alive and liquid, to devour him. Packer cried out, and opened his eyes.

There beside him was the Firefish, aglow, mouth open, eyes ablaze. It saw him, locked its enormous eyes on his, and cocked its head.

And Packer's heart leaped within his chest. He knew this beast. This was his Firefish, the one who knew him, the one that longed to speak and couldn't speak.

This was the very beast he had commanded once before. And it was awaiting his command again.

CHAPTER 20

The Presence

John Hand had thrown the brass box, the lure, into that gaping maw. It had struck the back of the beast's mouth, triggering a reflex that brought its jaws down hard, snapping at the morsel, releasing the lightning that shattered the bowsprit that killed the admiral. The Firefish had then submerged, enraged, intent on circling back below, to rise again to the attack, to kill the darkness that strangled Deep Fin, that sucked in all the light, and that had now thrown this false food into its mouth.

But a terrible thing awaited it beneath the waves. It was that stench, that horror. It was that poison in the water. The burning! One of these storm creatures had released the poison! It was the same terrible wretchedness that had caused it to flee once before, when the great pack of storm creatures killed that small one, the straggler. Then, the beast had lost its appetite, and had run with all haste as far away as it could run.

And so that same poison made the Firefish run again. It turned and fled, seeking to get as far as possible from this noxious, toxic venom. And as it ran, it gagged, and as it gagged, up came the offensive, tinny morsel.

Behind it, as the beast fled through the seas in sickness, it felt a shudder, and then an aching, crashing, crushing boom, a wave under the waves. It hit the beast, hurt it deeply, and drove it to run in panic, faster, farther. And then in anger and in fear, sickened both with poison and with pain, it ran deep. It descended once again, deeper now even than before, into a coldness and a pressure so encompassing that all things turned black and empty. Here, its own heartbeat echoed throughout its body, every beat slicing, pushing from within as though striving to get out. And then it waited as the pulsing slowed, and slowed, and slowed until its very sense of being faded, until it was a current in itself, a flow within a flow, cold and slow and hardly conscious.

It stayed there, alone, near death, near life, until the drifting currents far below the sea surfaced it slowly, over many days. It came back to the warmth. Back to the light. And as its grogginess departed, it found that it was well, and healed.

And it was hungry.

Food it could find; whale and shark and eel and schools of fish. But the Deep Fin it could not find. Deep Fin was gone again. The old ache returned. The gnawing need that could not be satisfied, the emptiness that would swallow all the seas.

Until, one hunt not long ago, it spied a school of storm creatures on the surface of the sea. Out ahead, running ahead, was a fast, sleek creature, with a long, deep ventral fin. And yes, yes! It had that skin, the skin of the Firefish. And so the beast swam closer, close enough to see.

But not too close.

The memory of the poison, and the painful boom, the memory of the dark presence, the meaty little lump with the cold predator's face, there where light and joy should be but were no longer, that memory kept it away. And so it watched. It swam along, watching from far away, not daring to hope. It was unseen, except for once, when tiny eyes along the side, just two small eyes had seen it, and it had submerged, escaped.

And when it went closer in the night, when no one saw, it found there at the head, where the face of the creature should be, no face at all.

And yet, there was a presence. At night under the stars, a sense of light shone yet. It emanated, though it was not the same. There was a warmth at the head of the creature. And it was good. But it was not the presence the Firefish longed for and remembered.

And it did remember. It recalled the joy it felt, flying below, then leaping up! Up into the nothing, into the Great Light! Like a flying creature, arcing high above that source of light! Yes, it remembered well the master...and it sought the master.

And then, as it swam along beneath Deep Fin, with storm creatures all above, a strange thing occurred. Another Firefish, swimming in the same direction, came alongside, too. A sense of desire, a pull, a wanting came with it, a yearning toward a place the Firefish knew, somehow, but did not remember. And so the Firefish went along. And then more Firefish came. They traveled deep, deep under water where no surface creatures ever saw. And up above, Deep Fin swam. It not only swam along, it led! Deep Fin was leading, taking Firefish to the place they must go.

And other Firefish joined. And then many more. And then the beast grew worried. These others circled underneath Deep Fin. They hunted. And so the beast felt it must protect. It must keep them from Deep Fin. So the beast gave off its clicks and sounds, it warned the others. This was not their prey! And the others heeded.

The Firefish felt strength. And soon it led the school of Firefish, as Deep Fin led it, to the warm compelling place, where it had never been. It ran on ahead, ahead even of Deep Fin, leading where the Deep Fin led. And all the beasts then followed into these great, still waters.

And there within the place, the Firefish gathered. And the beast now understood. Now it remembered. It had been here, long before. Long, long ago, when it was very young, and water itself was new, and the feel of the sea on its skin was like lightning and light...there was a place, this place...

And here the great beast found comfort among its kind. Deep Fin above, its own below. And prey, much prey, other storm creatures, swam above. Feeding would be plentiful. This was a good place.

Until...the hunger and the poison came at once. The scent of blood changed everything. It drove deep into the great beast, into all the Fish, the red spike in the belly, but with it, poison at the surface, seeping down. Not poison like the burning, not the deadly sickness poison, but bad enough, enough to keep them all away, uneasy, restless, unwilling to attack or kill, and swimming in a great circle, a hunting circle, waiting.

Then the storm creatures came throwing lighting, thunder. And then the blood came, blood and blood and blood, with poison keeping them all away, holding them all back.

The Battle for Vast Dominion

And then the madness came. At first it was a high and thin whine, a frustration, then a grinding of teeth and stinging barbs into the skin…And then a spike into the belly that reached up to the brain, and it seared, seared with desire, desire that could not be fulfilled. The heat of the kill, fresh meat to eat, blood in the water, poison on the surface, thunder and lightning…

They would attack. They would all attack. The one Firefish knew this, and it watched Deep Fin. But Deep Fin was now surrounded by the pack. A storm creature on either side, and blood, fresh meat, flowing, pouring down with poison…the other Firefish would not wait. They would attack Deep Fin.

And then the morsels began to rain down on them. Oh, the feeding! The feasting! Oh, it must begin. It must!

The beast flew in circles like the others, maddened, but it had one more desire. A desire the other beasts did not, a desire that opened in its mind like the Great Light streaming from above. It circled underneath its master, circling and circling, not to attack, but to protect. It would keep all others away. It clicked, and dove, it lunged, it bit…

But the madness, the madness grew!

The beast could not protect Deep Fin.

And so it rose. It rose with yearning, wanting that light, wanting to warn, to comfort, to find comfort. It rose from the water into the nothingness, and there, there where the presence ought to be…it was!

But wait.

There was another presence here. Another face. A darkness worse than all the darkness in the meaty little lump. A great, great darkness.

And the darkness contended with the light.

"Speak to it! *Command* it!"

Packer saw the beast, the Firefish, watching, waiting. But he did not speak to it. He thanked his God, and closed his eyes and prayed. He prayed again the prayer he'd been given, the good prayer, the simple prayer that was given to him. And this was it: *God, reveal Yourself. Show Your power. Make all things right.*

In his mind now, as he prayed, he saw the cup again. But now his own hand no longer poured it. Talon's hand was gone as well. A light shone down, all around, and no ship burned, no cauldron boiled. The crucible was water, red from blood that poured, but turning clear. Another hand now poured the cup, a hand pierced through, scarred jagged by a spike. And on the cup the names were gone, and instead there was an inscription. The words were in Drammune. The first was large, carved deeply into the wood. It said, "Ixthano." And then three words Packer did not know, smaller, were carved beneath:

"Anochter Nem Omas."

And the blood that poured calmed the waters. The blood turned the dark, stained water clear, and pure. And the beasts settled to the bottom, scattered, and disappeared. The blood cleansed the water.

Talon screamed with rage. "Command it, now!"

Packer turned to Talon, his hands sliding easily from under hers as he stood balanced on the bowsprit. She stepped back. Her eyes were wild. "What are you doing? Command it!" Spittle flew.

He looked at her calmly. She was not in control of herself. And at that moment he knew, absolutely, that he could defeat her.

He turned toward the beast.

Then he turned back to her. He held up his hands, held them out by his sides, palms up, balanced on the bowsprit. "No," he said, and shook his head. "Only God will command this beast."

Without a conscious thought, her knife was in her hand. "You will!" she ordered him.

Packer felt sorrow. "I will not."

Talon saw the pity. It enraged her further. She raised her knife backhanded, bringing her right fist to her left shoulder; she paused for only a moment, the idea flashing in her mind that she would kill her path to power. But now she knew he would not provide that path, and she would need to find it on her own.

"*Fool!*" she sneered. And then she swung the blade at his throat.

Packer saw Talon's blade, like a musketball let fly, like an arrow shooting from a crossbow. He saw it coming, but he did not back away. He raised his head, exposing his neck. He closed his eyes, obeying not Talon, but God. Resisting neither God, nor Talon. Understanding now precisely what it meant to turn the other cheek. To wait on God, to persevere, to live by faith. To die by faith, faithful to the end. To humble oneself, even unto death.

Packer felt the sting of the blade. It was a deep cut, as a mishandled paring knife slices through a finger to the bone. He heard a tear, a garment ripping, and a gasp. He opened his eyes. Talon stood before him, her eyes wide, locked onto his, as though accusing him of some horrible crime. She held her blade out to the side, in her right hand, point up. He looked at it. It dripped his blood. Packer put his right hand to his neck. He felt the warmth of his own blood cooling on his fingers. And then Talon looked down at her belly.

Packer saw the blade of a sword, a stained and marred broadsword, red now, protruding from below her ribs, below her heart. And then it disappeared.

Talon dropped her knife. It tumbled to the waves and was swallowed silently by the sea. She put her right hand on her open wound. She cupped her hand, and it filled with blood.

"Eyna tchomal," she said, her voice a breath escaping. *My child.*

At that moment the ship was rocked. A Firefish struck the *Trophy Chase.*

The beast did not strike to destroy, not with the light shining. It would not destroy, not even with the darkness swallowing the light. But in that moment, wanting the master's light, needing the Deep Fin to flee, it reacted. In frustration it flicked its tail, and struck Deep Fin a thundering blow.

And the presence fell. The morsel of light plummeted downward. Immediately, the beast followed.

Under the water, the beast smelled the blood.

Talon fell onto the deck, landing with an ugly thud on her back. She lay in agony, her face contorted, her eyes tightly closed. Father Mooring knelt beside her, his hands already at the wound, ripping away the leathers. Delaney stood at the rail close by the bowsprit, red sword in his hand, peering forlornly overboard at a few small bubbles, a pocket of smooth water and, below the surface, the scaly skin of a Firefish disappearing underneath the ship.

"I believe the blade has pierced your kidney," the priest told her gently, his calm voice near her tortured face. "But it missed your womb."

Her pain seemed to subside some. She wondered how he knew about the child. But of course, she had cried out. Talon opened her eyes, saw Delaney turning toward her from the rail. His look was grim, and deadly. She'd underestimated him. No, no, she had not.

He was fully capable. She knew that. But she had given him the opening. She had been distracted. A lapse in vigilance.

She almost laughed at herself. She had wanted all the power in the world, the weapon that would rule mankind. And she had forgotten, for one moment, the damage one idiot could do, one fool with a single blade. And now he had done it. And he had undone it all.

Delaney loomed over her, bloody sword still dripping in his hand. She saw no mercy in his eyes, no regret.

"Ye stupid witch," he said. "You've kilt the king. You've kilt us all." And with that he pulled his pistol.

"Not here, Delaney," Father Mooring said, looking up from the fallen woman's wound. He pushed the barrel away with a stubby finger, so it was no longer aimed at Talon's head. He waved him away backhanded, as though shooing a small child.

Delaney grimaced, but relented. "Missed her heart, and that's a pity," he said, wiping the blade on his pant leg. "Size of a butter bean anyways, I wouldn't doubt." He stuck his sword back in his belt. He was content to let her die slowly.

As Delaney went back to the rail to look again for Packer, Father Mooring ripped the hem off his own robe, tore that in two, and folded each piece into a cloth he could press against her bleeding wounds, front and back.

Talon closed her eyes, and nodded as this strange little priest of the Vast God administered mercy where it was least deserved.

The pack could not be stayed. It attacked now, almost as one. Drawn to the blood that poured from above, from Achawuk, Drammune, and Vast, maddened by prey that beckoned and poison that repelled, the Firefish gave in to frustration and their need to feed. One flew upward, then another, and then they were all on the attack, each one a predator lunging at its prey like a falcon diving on a lamb in a pasture.

A hundred Firefish flew upward, and in their ravenous madness, they went straight for the strength of the pack, the heart of the herd, eschewing the stragglers, attacking both Drammune and Vast where ships were gathered thick and close. They flew straight up. They angled upward, streaks of yellow fire. They drove for their prey horizontally. They hit hulls amidships. They struck fore, they struck aft.

They came cracking up through decks. One after another they hit in rapid succession, each strike a crash of thunder, booming across the waters. They were cannon firing, fireworks throwing off sparks and debris, one, two, three, four, then two at once, then three at once, then half a dozen simultaneously, then too many to count.

They ravaged what was left of *Rake's Parry, Danger, Candor*, destroying decks already picked clean of souls by the Achawuk. They demolished the bloodied and deserted decks of the *Hezza Charn*, and *Ganda Flez, Chammando, Herza Ko, Devah Lak, Zoray Dando*...all ghost ships already, now ground to splinters. They struck *Campeche*, and *Swordfish, Wellspring*, and *Poy Marroy. Gasparella, Homespun, Bonny Ann. Zuka Lohr, Exandam, Fendo Maron*. All had come to prey on the beasts, and all were destroyed by their quarry. Men leapt from decks, seeking safety. But there was none.

A dozen Drammune warships, mighty vessels, were churned to flotsam in this mad rush for satiation. The Firefish struck and kept on striking, sailing through canvas, flying into the air amid the rigging, snapping masts, flashing lightning and throwing off a hail of wreckage that rained down even as the beasts did, crashing back onto decks, through hulls, into dark, agitated waters. Their return to the seas threw off walls of foam and liquid, thick with blood and men and ruin.

The beasts consumed the dead; they inhaled the living.

Dayton Throme watched, an overwhelming sense of horror finally settling into bleak, dark misery, a despair from which he felt his heart would not recover. His fever, he knew, had returned. But he was not hallucinating.

He had predicted this, somehow. He had been the harbinger. He was in truth the rek-tahk-ent. The foreteller, the one who comes before. This was his prophecy, fulfilled. Somehow, as he watched, he felt this was his doing, as though, if he had but died, if he had not been spared when all others aboard were killed, this would never have happened. If he had not fought. If he had not pulled the tooth and wielded it as a blade, he would have died, and none of this would have come to be. If he had listened to his wife. Dear Netessa, his beloved. She had tried to tell him. His fellow fishermen. Dog, a wiser man than he'd known. If only Dayton had never sought the Firefish...

He closed his eyes. Nothing could repair this damage. No grace could cover such great tragedy. The world was indeed ended.

Delaney turned to watch as the seas erupted, mesmerized as a hundred streaking missiles battered the ships astern, flying through them into the air, echoes booming across the sea.

"What's all that thunderin' racket?" Stitch asked, raising his head from his bloody work. The old surgeon had joined Father Mooring's thus-far-futile effort to stanch Talon's bleeding. The entry wound was wide and ragged. Delaney's blade had ripped her open from behind, pelvis to ribs, as it sought her heart. Stitch had stuffed his pile of rags into the wound, but there was little left to do.

Delaney's voice was low, resigned now to defeat. "That, sir, is the sound of the end."

"The end of what?"

"Well, of everything, I reckon."

The beast trailed the morsel of light, watching as it bobbed under the storm creature, underneath Deep Fin. And the morsel trailed blood. All its instincts warred against all its greatest desires. This was prey. This was food. This was the Presence. This was Deep Fin. The beast came close, drawn by every base impulse to devour. But the closer it came, the brighter the sense of the Presence.

It saw the attack begin. Firefish from below were flying upward. It swung its head downward, eyes scanning, scanning, looking for the Firefish that would dare attack Deep Fin, dare accost the Presence. And one came...a smaller one, young, separating itself from the pack, not wanting to compete for meat, thinking Deep Fin a straggler. It was quick and nimble, streaking toward the belly of the great storm creature. This little one sensed the morsel, smelled the blood, and veered straight for the Presence.

Angered to fury in a moment, the great beast propelled itself with one enormous arcing of its body, and circled to intercept, gaining speed in a fraction of an instant, now coiling, now striking out horizontally. It met the small one, caught it in its great jaws, caught it just behind the head. The smaller beast's bones crushed easily. It came in two.

And then the big beast turned again, looking upward, seeking once again the tiny, light-filled creature. The Presence floated, facedown. Many swimming morsels, other tiny creatures, now surrounded it.

Delaney looked down into the water, saw the Achawuk approaching. They were finished with the *Kaza Fahn*. A few Drammune fought on, but not many. The Achawuk were on the move. Ignoring the destruction astern, they were intent on their next victims. The *Chase* had drifted away some, but not enough. The warriors were in the water, a solid mass of them headed toward her. They were almost on her hull now, swimming hard.

Now, finally, Delaney saw Packer's back as it rose to the surface, saw his friend and king floating face down. The Achawuk would reach him in a moment. He pulled his pistol, aimed at the nearest one and fired.

"Get me a line!" he called. "Packer's down there!" And he climbed the rail. If he could jump in, he might save Packer, if someone could fish them both out quickly.

But Mutter grabbed his shirt. "Ye ain't goin' down there, Delaney."

He looked around the decks and saw only blank, dark looks, sailors torn asunder within by the scale of the destruction astern, the demise of their king, the devastation of the Achawuk off their rails. There was no hope in them. No one shouted any orders. Andrew Haas was not on deck, nor was Stil Meander. Those who had kept their senses fired down into the Achawuk. Those who had not, watched, or knelt, or wept, praying for the end.

Delaney looked back down, and saw the Achawuk overtake Packer. They pushed him under. Just another body, another small nuisance. They swam over him, swarmed over him.

Delaney's heart cried out. His king was gone.

The hammering of spears began.

"Knowed it!" Delaney complained morosely from the rail. Still with one leg hooked over the gunwale, he reloaded. His eyes swam, his fingers trembled. But he, at least, would go down fighting. "Knowed it, knowed it, knowed it. I blame knowed we'd lose as soon as Packer started listenin' to that witch." He rammed a ball home, his anger bringing him out of his darkness. He considered putting this musket ball right through Talon's skull. He saw her eyes closed tight, her body trembling. He would not cut short her agony. *Hezzan, aye, sure*...he thought. *'Bout as much Hezzan as me.* Then he aimed over the rail, squinting through bleary eyes, and pulled the trigger, sending the ball through the brain of an Achawuk warrior. He began to reload again, straining to see. He would shoot until they were on him, and then he'd fight until his sword arm gave way. And then he'd see Packer in heaven. The sooner the better.

But Packer was not in heaven quite yet.

He floated, barely conscious, aware of the life flowing from him. Talon hadn't taken his head as she had intended. She had paused for some reason. She had hesitated long enough for Delaney's sword to find her. But the wound was a razor cut, and it was deep, and it was clean. Blood flowed. He could not stop it. His heart would pump his own blood into the water until there was nothing left for his heart to pump.

Just a moment more, he thought. Just one calm moment more, and then he'd struggle for his last breath. For Panna's sake he would not easily abandon this life. For Nearing Vast, that they would not lose another king. For Delaney, and Marcus, and Cap and Hen and Dog and all the rest. He would struggle one more time.

Then Packer saw the flash, felt the tingle of dissipated electricity. Through the murk he saw the severed head of a Firefish slowly rotate away astern, its eyes still open, its mouth agape, its teeth prepared for a kill. Blood, or something like it, floated from its neck in the water. Then he saw the severed body follow along like a writhing snake.

Now the Achawuk reached him, jostled him, surrounding him. A strong hand on his back pushed him under. It was not an unkind or heartless act, he felt. It was firm, and knowing. This was the warrior's duty. Packer held his neck with both hands, feeling the water wash through the gash, stinging from the salt, pulling it open. His hands shook as they clung to his own neck, as a solid mass of warriors enclosed the surface over him, cutting off the light. Then spears echoed, striking the hull of the *Chase*. To struggle for life now, fighting upward against the Achawuk, would be fatal. To do nothing would also be fatal. But there was nothing left for him to do. He closed his eyes and darkness overtook him.

The big beast's momentum took it far behind the *Chase*, and then it turned, looked down, scanning for more predators. Seeing none, it swam back, looking upward, searching out the Presence.

The Presence was gone, only the other morsels remained…had the light gone away?

But no, there it was, descending, separating itself from the morsels. With a flick of its tail the beast was face to face with the Presence, looking up at it from below. But the Presence would not look. Its eyes were closed. Its fins were not moving. The blood was thick. And suddenly, the beast knew…the Presence was dying.

Packer opened his eyes as he let out a lingering breath. He felt no need for air. He felt only peace. Perhaps he had already drunk in the Sea, he thought. This was a peaceful death, this drowning. Through the bubbles, through the murk, he saw. There was the beast. His beast. That face. It was huge, filling his vision. Its misshapen head, its jaw jutting spiked teeth, its skin glowing yellow—none of these were frightening now. He knew this creature. He knew this face. The questioning, the yearning. The joy. And now, the sadness.

Packer stretched his hand down toward it, to comfort it, and the beast moved closer in an instant. It flicked its tail again, and the gap was closed. It lowered its head, and pressed its triangular fore-head into Packer's hand. Yellow fire moved around his hand, needles of electricity shot through him, but they were warm, numbing, even pleasant. He put both hands on its head. The scales were soft, somehow, almost silky, amid these fiery needles.

He closed his eyes, pleased to have been given this moment, here, now, just at the end.

The touch of the Presence!

Those little fins, they were unlike any other the beast had ever known. They were alive, intelligent, as though each one had knowledge dwelling in it, as though they were smaller creatures within the small creature. All that was the Presence shone through those fins, came through that touch. A strange joy rose within the beast. Here was the Master. Here was the One it had sought. This was the One it would love and serve forever. Those fins were made to touch the Firefish, and the Firefish was made to revel in that touch.

Packer's hands went limp as the bulbous head pressed up into his chest. In the darkness he felt needles go through him, painful, warming. The beast was pushing him up, up toward the light. He let go of all claims, and ceased his struggle. He rested now as the light engulfed him. He saw Panna here, in the light. He saw her face, and he heard her laugh. He touched her hair. He held her, kissed her gently on the cheek.

And then the light overwhelmed him, and Panna was gone.

He was dreaming now. He must be, because now he saw his mother. She was young, and radiant. She sat on a beach, on a big blanket in the sand. The sun shown down warm, illuminating the radiance of her face, and he walked toward her. No, he rode toward her. He was on his father's shoulders, holding tight. He was a small child with his little arms wrapped around his father's head, his tiny hands pressed into his father's forehead as the great and laughing man beneath him boomed and bounced and rose up out of the sea. He carried Packer high, and now little Packer laughed, the sun shining down, the breeze cool on his skin, his mother waiting happy, laughing on the beach, her eyes bright. Packer tasted the salt sea, smelled his father's matted hair, and rested his chin on top of that great, strong head. And the world was utterly right and perfect. Nothing was missing. Nothing was broken. All was in place, just as it should be. Joy filled his little heart, his mind, his lungs. And he laughed.

Here, finally, this was what he longed for! This was what he sought. Just this, and nothing more. All good. All right.

The beast rose from the water.

Achawuk warriors made way, sliding away, swimming backward in sudden panic. A man with the Firefish. Rising from the sea. Rising with the beast.

The Achawuk were stunned. They ceased attacking, and stared.

"Tannan-thoh-ah!" one cried, halfway up the hull of the *Chase*, his foot on one spear, his hand on another. Delaney shot him through the neck. He tumbled to the water. No warrior took his place, as all now watched man and beast. Delaney turned to see.

The beast rose higher.

Packer rode high in the air now, the breeze cold on his skin within his sodden clothing. His eyes fluttered open. Where was he? He was on the Firefish. He was holding it tight, his arms around the crown of its head, his hands on its forehead, his feet against its dorsal fins. He

The Battle for Vast Dominion

kept rising, ten feet, twenty. The fire from the beast…he couldn't feel it now. But he felt alive, awake, and alert. But surely it was a dream.

The Presence!

Oh, the Presence rode high now, in honor! A crown of glory!

A thrill went through the beast. The light was strong again, the Presence was powerful. The Firefish carried the Presence on its head, just like Deep Fin had done! And within the Presence, draped around the beast, filling it, was all the strength of light and all its joy. And now, here, wrapped around its head, this tiny morsel seemed not small at all. It was enormous, as large as all the sea, as great as all the world, brighter than the Great Light from above. The Presence, it now knew, should be raised up, must be raised up. It must be raised as high as Deep Fin raised it.

And so the Firefish, its body undulating below the waters, rose still higher.

And it reveled in its moment.

The man had become the glory of the beast.

And the Achawuk knew it.

"Tannan-thoh-ah!" cried another warrior. This was Zhintah-Hoak, the elder. He could see it. He could feel it. The beast gloried in the presence of the man. "Tannan-thoh-AHH!" he called, a ringing cry this time, his voice clear and full and pristine. The thunderous sounds of the Firefish attack on the Vast and the Drammune faded away behind. The rampage of the beasts had ended. Silence engulfed them all, silence except for the single phrase that echoed across the mayak-aloh.

And now every Achawuk warrior on the hulls of the *Chase,* on the *Marchessa,* and on the *Kaza Fahn,* every warrior who saw, ceased climbing, ceased fighting. Instead, they dove back into the sea. Every warrior in the water, on shore, all who heard, swam toward Packer and the beast. Every one of them repeated now the phrase.

"Tannan-thoh-AHH! Tannan-thoh-AHH!"

Packer watched as the phrase was spoken, shouted, repeated, rippling outward, turning every head, focusing every eye on him, and on the beast.

Dayton Throme saw it. He heard the chant. He stood. He felt

The Battle for Vast Dominion

309

dizzy. He sat again. But he did not take his eyes off the scene below. Dayton Throme, the rek-tahk-ent, knew exactly what this meant to the Achawuk. The beast rose, stately, as though it knew precisely what it was doing, and why. This was the Mastery. The master-knowing.

On the beach he saw warriors lighting torches. He heard them repeat the words, the phrase, the master-knowing. They had seen it; they were witnesses. They spoke the words, not in a chant, but each man, each woman, each child reciting it alone, isolated, but merged together into a murmur, a fluid, lilting, lyrical sound that was almost a song, but was not quite. And as they did, they took their torches into the canoes. They sat, one man, or one child with a torch in each canoe, canoes already laden with that black substance, so full they barely floated. They paddled these canoes out into the waters, taking the fire with them.

Those left ashore took burning branches, logs, anything ablaze, down to the water's edge, and there they doused them in the mayak-aloh.

And the Achawuk swam, they all swam toward the man, and toward the beast. And they spoke the phrase. They invoked the end of the world.

But the other Firefish, Dayton wondered...where did they go? They had ceased their merciless attack. They went back under the surface. But why? Dayton Throme worried. They would not be gone for long. Nothing stopped them when they fed, until there was nothing left on which to feed.

Huk Tuth lay prostrate and dazed on the defeated decks of the *Kaza Fahn*. An Achawuk spearhead protruded from his skull behind his left ear, still attached to two feet of shattered wooden shaft. He had been cut or nicked in twenty places before one warrior had buried a spear in his shoulder, stopping him just long enough for another to deliver this one to his head. Tuth had fallen to the deck unconscious, just as a Drammune sailor severed the Achawuk warrior's head as penalty for his misdeed.

Huk Tuth, however, was as hardheaded as any man alive, and had lived through horrors that would have killed six other men by now. He was not ready to part with life just because a spear had pierced his skull. He opened his eyes, and looked dimly out over the sea from where he lay. He was tired, bone-tired with a deep exhaustion to which he longed to give himself. But before he could, he had to know the outcome. What had happened? Did Talon live?

He saw the yellow hair. He saw him riding atop the Firefish. The commander closed his eyes. He opened them again. He saw the same.

Knowing the import of this, understanding in a primal way the devastation such a thing would wreak on his homeland, the Vast commanding Firefish, he forced himself awake. He spat out blood. He sat up, wheezing, wincing in pain. He felt the weight on his neck, something pulling on his head. He found the spear with his hands, pulled it from his skull. He looked at it, saw blood on the blade. He tossed it aside. He held stubby fingers to the wound. Fighting dizziness, he looked through the rail, saw Achawuk swimming toward this King of the Vast. They were lauding this vile, simple, ignoble youth who tormented Huk Tuth's very spirit.

Tuth turned his eyes to the great Vast ship, the *Trophy Chase*. He blinked, and winced. It seemed to be listing, angling toward him. But few sails were set, and those that were set, luffed in the breeze. *Good riddance*, he thought. He blinked blood from eyes he could no longer trust. He scanned the *Chase*'s decks for Talon, but he did not see her. Dead, he hoped. But somehow he doubted.

He looked around his own decks. Drammune and Achawuk bodies lay scattered. The few living were all Drammune, and now they gathered, limping, bleeding at the rails, watching. The Achawuk had not finished the job.

"Charnak!" Tuth mumbled, blood and spittle dripping from his lower lip. He was surprised at his own lethargy. Why was he so tired? Why couldn't he get his mouth to work? And why didn't his men shoot the yellow hair? "Charnak," he said, trying to speak more loudly. But it came out more softly yet, barely a breath. No one heard.

He lowered himself back to the deck as black spots flooded his vision, growing into deep, empty holes. Dizziness overcame him. *Charnak*, he thought. He put his forehead on the deck, and a dark, warm rest washed over him.

The feeding frenzy started just astern of the *Chase*, where the severed head of the Firefish floated to the surface. It started with a single splash, water churning as it might if several children played tag near a shore. A Firefish tail flipped up, then fell, and then great jaws took the head, and pulled it under.

And suddenly, chaos erupted.

The smell of this new blood, the blood of one of their own, brought the other beasts in a mass. It stopped them where they were, ended their attack on the storm creatures. The beasts that had attacked the ships and had then wallowed in their wreckage and their tatters, that had crushed and crunched these storm creatures, that had strained the surface of the meaty morsels, were not yet sated.

And now, this scent drove them to a higher plane of frenzy.

CHAPTER 21

Ashes

Father Stanson entered the chapel, and limped quickly to the altar rail. He felt almost giddy. He was safe now. Not even the queen would dare to pull him from this place. He had sanctuary! He had escaped. He knelt, and put his elbows on the rail. He bowed his head.

Someone coughed, a sick sound, full of phlegm. He looked to his right. There at the rail, tucked in next to the wall, was a young man in a ragged priest's garb. No, it was a student's green robe.

"Son, are you all right?"

The young man raised his head. He looked with hollow eyes. "I've done it, Father. No food, and little water. Much prayer. I have fulfilled my mission."

"What mission was that?"

His eyes searched Hap's. "The one you gave me."

Hap furrowed his brow. "The one I gave you?" He shook his head. The young man was clearly not in his right mind.

And now the boy's look caved in, as though a great sorrow took him. "The burning forest. I...drank bad water. I walked until I couldn't walk...I crawled. I prayed for hours every day. I have eaten nothing. I have spoken to no man. Am I...purified?"

Hap Stanson looked around him, hoping some priest would appear to help rid him of this crazy person. He doubted now that the boy was even a student here. "Well, bless you in your hour of need." Hap bowed his head again, to pray in thanksgiving that he had been rescued, had found sanctuary.

The boy coughed again. He laid his cheek on the altar rail. "Have I fulfilled my mission?" he croaked.

"Only God knows," Hap said sweetly.

And then Lester Mine collapsed, rolling onto his back. His breathing was labored. The High Holy Reverend Father and Supreme Elder stood, glanced around, then walked to the boy. He knelt over him. And now, finally, the memory came back. The boy who had come on horseback, with the message that Packer Throme had ascended to the throne. The one who fought on the Green for Packer. Stanson hardly recognized him as the same young man. "Poor wretch," he said. "May God have mercy on your soul."

He thought about going to find help, but he could not leave the altar. Only at the altar was there sanctuary for him. As he looked at the young man, he felt for the first time that he might be somewhat accountable here. But instead of calling out for help, he prayed for the soul of the boy, hoping in a quiet, darkened place deep in his heart that Lester Mine would simply die, and release them both from his suffering.

There were hundreds of the beasts at the surface, hundreds more below. And they all rushed now for this new feast. As they did, they jostled for position. One bit the carcass, another fought it for a share and bit into the first one's hide. The first one turned to bite and gashed a third. And as they all converged in hunger, then in anger, they also joined in the fight.

There were Vast and Drammune sailors still alive in the water. They had been there, panicked, terror-stricken, waiting for the tail or the teeth that would end them, and then suddenly they were unwanted. The Firefish left them. The Achawuk ignored them, swimming away. They had no fight in them, nor had they been ordered to fight one another even if they had. Re-energized, they swam for all they were worth for shore. Any shore.

The beast with the fair-haired crown of glory saw the melee

The Battle for Vast Dominion

begin. It looked past the three storm creatures still afloat, past the great Deep Fin. All its instincts told it this new danger was unlike any other. Here was Firefish against Firefish. Nothing would be safe. They would attack the beast. The Presence would be in danger. Suddenly the beast felt vulnerable. The Presence should not be here. The Deep Fin, that's where the Crown belonged. And so the beast moved forward in the water, rose, and approached the head of Deep Fin.

It rose up to the bowsprit. Packer leaped easily. His body felt light as a feather, hard as granite. He landed with easy grace on the jutting prow, grasping the guy lines for balance. His head was clear, his eyes sharp. He turned, and the beast looked at him one more time, eyes wide. Packer saw both joy and sorrow there. He reached out his right hand and touched the beast once more, a stroke between its eyes. It bowed its head, moved it back and forth against his hand. He felt no needles, no sting, just warmth. Packer pulled his hand away, and the beast sank down, disappearing below the waves.

Packer stood again at the prow, but this time there were no cheers. Most of the sailors did not see him. They were gathered at the stern, watching the brutal display of the feeding frenzy. But some aboard did see. Delaney. Stitch. Mutter Cabe. And of course, Father Mooring. These all stared at him. They would forever swear that he glowed with the fire of the beast, that his skin blazed just as bright and golden as any Firefish scales.

Delaney, pistol still in his hand, sword stuck in his belt, watched with his brow furrowed into crags, shaking his head. But when Packer caught his eye, Delaney grinned. It was him—it was Packer after all, and not some apparition. "Welcome back," he said.

Father Mooring stood up, hands bloodied from his work on Talon. He beamed up at Packer. He walked close, looked up at Packer's neck, pointed a red-stained finger. "You've found healing, there in the water."

Packer touched his own neck. The wound was there, he could trace it with his finger, but it was closed. It was not bleeding. As he stroked the fatal wound that was no longer, he realized his right hand moved freely, easily. He looked at it, opened and closed it quickly. The hard mass of scars across his palm had softened, and was now almost invisible. He could feel the inside of his fingers. The round, white circle at the base of his hand remained, the only visible scar.

"The Firefish," he said aloud. "The fire in its scales…" He trailed off as the full wonder of the beast overtook him. Meat, hide, teeth… these were relics of its life, artifacts of death that had great value to men in war. But alive…the power of the beasts alive was so much more, so much greater. The power to heal.

Packer looked at Talon now, still on her back, the surgeon hovering over her again. Packer leaped down from the bowsprit. He felt the deck solid on his feet, felt the slap of it through his soles. He was strong, but already the warmth was leaving him, that feeling of easy power and fluid calm. "She's alive, then," he said. Talon was breathing with difficulty.

Stitch looked up. He blinked at Packer. "Aye, so far at least. But I never saw anyone ripped up this bad who made it."

Packer knelt by her side. He put a hand on her forehead, and her breathing eased.

Delaney grimaced, shook his head. "Best let her die as God intended."

"Has she spoken?" Packer asked.

Father Mooring looked at him as though that were the oddest question. "Yes, in fact. We've had a bit of conversation in Drammune."

Packer wanted to speak to her himself. Instead he asked the priest, "Father, what do the words 'anochter nem omas' mean?"

Father Mooring stared hard at Packer. Something was very different about him. He looked healthy, remarkably so, and calm as a woodland lake. But it wasn't that. It was his eyes. They seemed to see into things, as though he looked deeper, somehow, than the priest remembered. "It means 'one death, once, for all.'"

Packer nodded.

Now Delaney put a hand on Packer's shoulder from behind. "Well, ye're all soakin' wet, so I guess ye ain't a ghost this time, neither."

"No, not this time, either," Packer told him, gently.

He stood, looked at Delaney for a moment, then watched the water rise behind the ship, foam and flesh in the beasts' wild, terrible battle. But though the carnage was very real and very present, it seemed distant to him. He looked out over the port rail toward the *Kaza Fahn*. He watched the Achawuk still swimming toward him and the *Trophy Chase*. They came from all sides now. The seas were filled and crowded. He could see them leaving the shores, too, canoes with torches, women, children, old and young. Many had already gathered in the water around the ship, but though they treaded water far from shore, not one tried to climb the spears. The ladder up was empty. They just waited, watching. A multitude, expecting a miracle.

And now he noticed that the canoes they paddled from the shore were loaded with something, weighted down, riding low in the water. There were hundreds of these, rowing out toward him, toward the center of the mayak-aloh. They came from every shore. And as he watched, the canoes begin to sink. As each one reached a certain point, as though predetermined, hands reached out and pulled it under, its contents blackening the waters. Packer pondered this.

Then he walked astern. Delaney followed. As the men saw him, they made way, tapping others on the shoulders, until every eye watched the king. He climbed to the afterdeck, and walked to the stern rail. He looked regal, but the fiery glow was gone now. Any shock the men felt now at seeing him alive after they thought they'd lost him, dissipated quickly. It was right that he was here. Talon had tried to cut his throat, and then he'd fallen into the sea. Sure. But this was Packer, Packer Throme, King of the Vast. He had returned alive and well. That was as it should be.

He said nothing now, but looked out over the sea. This was a spectacle more hideous than the one he'd seen in these waters once before. There were more of the beasts here, more by far. And it was a furious attack, counterattack, with each Firefish gouging, being gouged, turning and gouging, biting, huge jaws clamping down, razor teeth slicing into meat and tail and bone and fin, scale and skull, any part of any other Firefish that any jaw could reach.

The water had turned to foam, and now to pink froth. The melee rose ten, twenty feet above the surface, a hill of reddish whitewater, five hundred feet across, pushing the *Chase*, the *Kaza Fahn*, and the *Marchessa* away. Beyond this battleground was the wreckage of a score of ships. Men swimming for shore.

It saddened him. The scale of death and destruction in this place was enormous, hellish, like a judgment of God in the Book of Revelation. And yet, even those much greater scenes of violence and death were foreordained. Packer remembered Marcus Pile's prayer as though the young man spoke the words aloud. *I figure Thou couldst care less about whose heart is still beatin' in his chest, but Thou carest a whole lot more about whose soul comes to life.* This devastation, this reaping of so many lives, was heartrending. And yet, who was Packer to question it? Talon contended with God. Packer and Panna and Father Mooring and Will Seline fought against such powers, against principalities. To hope there would be no casualties in such a war seemed naïve.

Delaney shook his head in wonder. "The fight's gone from men now," he said in a tone of benediction Packer had heard him use only once before. "Now it's in the hearts of beasts."

Packer looked around, and saw that it was true. Achawuk no longer attacked, Drammune were beaten and quiet, the Vast watched silently. Only the Firefish now preyed on one another. It seemed that all the dark forces of the world had been pulled back, death and destruction had fled the hearts of men and had run to the Firefish, concentrating their fury here. Demons cast from men to beasts.

"I think that God is doin' somethin' here," Delaney noted.

Packer smiled, for the first time in what seemed forever. "Yes. I think so."

"But we hardly ever do know what, do we?"

And Packer nodded.

"So...now we pray?" Delaney asked. He was thinking of Marcus; it's what Marcus would have done.

Packer nodded. "Now we pray." The two friends knelt at the rail. They bowed their heads together. One by one, the rest of the crew dropped to a knee, many to pray, many others simply content to follow their leader, now that he was once again leading.

And the melee subsided. Before a word of prayer was said aloud, more quickly than it started, it was over. The mound of frothing water settled, and was gone. The sea before them went dead calm. The soft slap of water against the hull, the creak of a mast, a line going taut, a distant seagull, suddenly these were the only sounds.

Delaney looked at Packer with eyes as wide as saucers.

The poison came. It came in power, and it would not stop. A wave of horror, sickness, driving all other thoughts away. The burning, the stench...It stung the eyes and filled the head. And so the Firefish swam, blindly away, away, as far and fast as they could.

The poison from the canoes, soot and ash, stopped the melee in an instant. Every beast turned toward the open sea and fled, searching for pure water, water it could breathe.

The Battle for Vast Dominion

Talon struggled in the dreamy darkness, fighting the currents and the cold. She bobbed to the surface, desperate for air, and when she did, there was the priest. He was gentle and warm as the sun, and she found some rest from her struggle.

He spoke to her. He spoke in Drammune, as he had before. But now she could not follow the words. They made no sense. He spoke of forgiveness and redemption, things that had no meaning for her. But she took comfort in him. His voice, his strength. It was calm and yet powerful. And her child, she thought, was safe here, in the light, with him. She wanted to give this strange man her child to hold for just a while. He could protect it while she fought. He would keep the baby safe, and she could fight this darkness that pulled her under.

And then the light faded and she entered the clammy darkness once more. Deep beneath the surface, swords were drawn. Her sword flashed, and sang. A hundred stood against her, then a thousand, then ten thousand. They came at her all at once. She fought. She would fight until they died or they surrendered. But they surrounded her, suffocating her. They were a single dark mass of swordsmen, and she couldn't move, couldn't breathe. And then one stabbed her through the middle, and then another, and another, a hundred blades, a thousand, and in a panic she rose into the light, to the surface, out of the darkness. And she heard the voice again, the priest's calm, gentle voice.

She opened her eyes. There he was again, the little man. So kind, as though she were the child. He held her hand. He touched her forehead. He spoke comforting words. He wanted good for her. He cared. But why? She search his eyes, and asked him.

He spoke of mercy.

Mercy…humility…weakness, these were a path to power with the Vast God. This was logical. Give up your own power, and absorb the power of the universe. But she had never shown mercy, not once that she could remember. And so why should she be granted it?

"'Not by works of righteousness which we have done,'" the little priest spoke from amid the light, "'but according to his mercy he saved us.'"

She opened her eyes again. "But He cannot save my child." Pain shot through her abdomen.

"Yes, of course He can," the priest assured her.

"She will be abandoned." She felt as she said the words a great tearing, a rending of herself, so deep it was neither anger nor sorrow, but some rending of the soul underneath both, underneath all, in that place where a husband abandoned her, a father abandoned her, a mother sent her away. She did not want the same for her own child. She would not abandon this baby, not even to God.

"He will save the child," the priest said. "Perhaps, not in this world. But in a better one."

She struggled to comprehend this, but she couldn't. He was sure of it though. Perhaps that was enough. But no, no—she would die, and then her child would die. She would die a hundred times, a thousand deaths, the cruelest of all deaths, just to save her only child. Why didn't God understand that? Why did He crucify His only child?

But then she knew. It came to her like a single shaft of light shining down from parted clouds. God Himself had died for all His children. He would die a thousand deaths to save them. The cruelest death. Just as she would gladly sacrifice herself to save her child. As the Hezzan had died for her.

Now she asked for mercy, not for herself, but for her child. If she could not be lifted up into the light, perhaps God in His mercy would take her child. And so she offered, finally, her child, and with her child all her hopes, to God.

Talon knew now that her own life was over. When she went below again, she would not surface. She had nothing more to fight for. She would have liked another chance to understand this mercy, this prize that one could never be worthy to receive. But she knew it would not come. She'd been given another chance. She had made her choices. She had few moments, mere seconds now, as the darkness rose and her will to fight, ebbed away. But she had one more thing she must give up.

"I have a message for Packer Throme," she said. "You must tell him."

"He's here. I'll get him."

"No. You must tell him. After I am dead."

Father Mooring felt a great stab of sorrow. She was an earnest woman, and so fearless. He held her hand tightly, so she'd know that he was there.

"Tell him..." She closed her eyes as pain shot through her once again, this time searing, tearing her away, ripping her from the world.

She fought back one more time, struggled to the surface, opened her eyes. Her lips trembled. She must say it; she wanted to say it. "Tell him…" and here she faltered. Then she said, "I know who shall rule."

The darkness swept over her like a torrent, and she went under.

And then her eyes stared out into daylight, at the sun, the ship, the sky, but they would see no more on earth forever.

"Your Highness," the voice said from behind Packer. "Excuse me."

Still kneeling, Packer turned away from the suddenly calm sea. The crowd of kneeling sailors looked at the first mate, Andrew Haas. He stood before the king now, on the afterdeck, holding a dripping cap in his hands. Pain etched his face. His clothes were soaking wet and filthy, his hair matted, grime all in the pores of his skin.

Packer stood. "What is it? What's wrong?"

"Don't mean to interrupt your prayers, sir. But I have news. Sorrowful news."

"Speak it."

"We tried to stop it, sir. We used brace timbers…jacks. Did all we could." His voice cracked.

Packer waited, not comprehending. He looked beyond him, saw a similarly bedraggled troop below on the quarterdeck. Ten, fifteen hands, as wet and morose as Andrew Haas, all watching him. He looked at the decks, and noticed now their angle. He looked up at the sails. There was no wind, no sails were filled. He looked out at the Achawuk, gathered below. They seemed nearer now, as though the ship was lower in the water. Packer looked back at the ship's first mate and searched his eyes. "Say it plainly, Mr. Haas."

"That Firefish, the one that bumped us? Snapped the hull planks. Broke timbers. Amidships, just above the keel, port side. And…well, sir…there's nothin' more to be done." He swallowed hard, knowing he had not yet spoken plainly. But he couldn't say the words.

"You mean we're sinkin'," Delaney said, his voice not much more than a gasp.

Haas nodded at Delaney. He wiped at his eyes. Then to Packer he finally said the words. "Sir, the *Trophy Chase* is goin' down."

Packer turned away, a sharp stab to his heart. It was just a ship.

He fought against it as though it couldn't be true. He wanted to order them all back down, to try again. But they wouldn't be here now if there were any hope.

And then Packer remembered the vision...and a cauldron, and the small ship within it, spinning in the maelstrom. It had disappeared. While his own hand had poured the blood of men, the ship was there. But when his hand was gone, so was the ship. The ship had been the ladle. The ship had stirred the pot. To turn the oceans clear, he realized, to cleanse them, to calm them, this must be. And Packer longed more than anything to see the oceans cleansed and calmed.

He turned back to Andrew Haas. "How much time do we have?"

Haas looked around, at the decks. "Ten minutes. Fifteen at most."

"Thank you, Mr. Haas. You did all you could." He walked to the rail, spoke to all the men now gathered, the whole crew, many still kneeling, many more standing. They waited for some word that might make this right.

"Thank you all," Packer said to the men. "You've been a worthy crew for a great, great ship. You have served her with dedication, and with passion. No men on earth could have done better. Your country and your king are deeply grateful, and will remember your service always." He paused, looked around him. Then he said, "The story of the *Trophy Chase* ends today, but she will never be forgotten."

They gazed at him, and at the sails, then at the decks in shock. A few wiped at the corners of their eyes. But they did not move from where they stood, where they knelt.

So Packer said, "You have one last duty. I trust you will do it as well as you have every other duty. Lower the boats." He took a deep breath. "Abandon ship."

The men moved slowly, but with purpose. They carried out their final orders with a sense of ceremony, preparing the jolly, the shallop, the longboats. They gathered up gear, they loaded up guns and ammunition, food and water. Ale and rum. And as they worked they touched the *Trophy Chase*, her rails, her masts, her lines. Not one in ten of them would have known what to say, or how to act, had they been at a funeral for any man or any woman. But here, at the passing of their ship, they were at peace with one another, knowing precisely what needed doing, what needed saying, and how to say it.

They spoke their goodbyes as they worked, a phrase here, a word there, a rare full sentence. But strung together, their plain words provided a simple eulogy that expressed the very spirit of the *Chase*. And these men were her spirit, speaking as they departed her, never to return.

"She's a great, great ship."

"Best there ever was."

"Or ever will be."

"Aye to that."

"She bested 'em all, one way or another."

"Achawuk, Drammune..."

"Pirates."

Quiet laughter.

"Scatter himself couldn't sink her."

"No, no man could."

"Only the Firefish."

"She killed a passel of 'em, though, afore one got 'er."

"Tamed 'em, too."

"Just a tap, is all it was."

"Like it was her time."

"A knock on the door."

"Time to go home."

"Aye. Like a knock on a door."

"We'll miss her."

Silence.

"Aye. She'll be sorely missed."

"There never will be another like her."

"She'll never be forgotten."

"Never."

"Never."

"Aye to that, lads. Aye to that."

There were no dead aboard the *Trophy Chase*, no casualties at all, save for the great cat's final captain. While the men loaded the boats, Packer, Delaney, Father Mooring, and Andrew Haas carried Talon's body, wrapped now in sailcloth, to the captain's quarters. They laid her on the bunk built for Scat Wilkins.

"Should we put her sword in her hand, sir?" Andrew Haas asked solemnly.

Packer shook his head. "She's laid aside her sword forever now." Delaney sniffed.

Packer bowed his head and said a prayer. "Take her, dear Lord. And in Thy mercy, have mercy on her soul…and take her unborn child quickly and painlessly, we pray. Unite that child with its grandfather." He paused. "Unite all those whom You have loved, and who have loved You. Thy mercy is deeper than the sea, higher than the sky. We don't understand it, Lord. But have mercy, we pray. Lord, have mercy on us all. Amen."

No one moved, and Packer knew why. They waited for him to speak. "Talon," he said softly, "was the daughter of Senslar Zendoda. She carried in her womb the child of two Hezzans of Drammun, and the grandchild of a great Swordmaster of Nearing Vast."

Delaney stood with eyes wide open, staring at the wrapped body, as the others filed out. Father Mooring paused, put his hand on the Delaney's elbow. "You couldn't have known," the priest said gently. "She told no one, no one but Packer."

"You knew," he said, a trace of accusation in his voice.

"Only that she was with child, and only because she cried out after…you wounded her."

He searched the priest, looking for hope, for understanding. Father Mooring saw the depth of anguish there. "You saved Packer Throme."

"But dear God," Delaney said, "I didn't mean to kill no child."

Father Mooring nodded, but could say nothing. Delaney had been bent on death, and had shown not the least bit of compassion. The priest watched now as the sailor crumbled all within. Delaney turned back to the body, then dropped to his knees in front of the bunk. His shoulders began to quake.

"I didn't mean to kill no child," he whispered. And then he hunched over, his face in his hands. "Not no little baby, Lord…"

Father Mooring heard the sobs as he stepped silently just outside the captain's quarters. There he waited patiently for the sailor to find the dark bottom of his own soul, and there to find forgiveness, yet again.

Not all the crew could fit into the boats. Shuttles began, taking those who preferred it to the *Marchessa*. Nervousness about the Achawuk gave way as the warriors did, and a suddenly gentle people calmly parted, grave but hospitable, as these strangers went about their business. Stitch went with the first group. He would find more work aboard the *Marchessa* than he cared to think about.

Packer left for shore aboard the jolly. "They can't tread water here forever," he said, looking at the Achawuk. They were expert swimmers, and they seemed in no distress, floating easily. Their blocks of cork supported them, at least somewhat. But these facts did not lessen Packer's concern. "I don't know how to tell them to go back home."

And as he suspected would happen, they all swam after him.

He sat silently at the prow of the jolly while Delaney and the others hoisted the small boat's sail. He faced astern, watching the *Trophy Chase*'s last moments in the sun. The water was now mere feet from her port rails. She listed badly. She would be gone within minutes.

He remembered the first time he had seen this ship, from high above, from atop the Hangman's Cliffs. He had wanted more than anything to be aboard. And God had granted that wish, in abundance. He'd sailed aboard her from Hangman's Cliffs to the Achawuk islands, from those islands back to Mann, from Mann to Hezarow Kyne, and then back here. As he watched, he understood now for the first time why captains went down with their ships. He felt the loss keenly, as though he were abandoning a friend in time of need. But Talon was there, and she was her captain. He hoped that she had finally found peace.

And then suddenly the sails of the great cat dropped full. The sun caught them, and the breeze popped the canvas. Men cheered. Packer stood, his heart leaping up. Would the *Trophy Chase* live after all? Could she outrun even her own demise? But no, no, the men had climbed up into her rigging one last time, to unfurl every sail.

Full sail. That was the *Trophy Chase*. That was how she had roamed the seas, and that was how she would go down. He loved his men for knowing this, for this final honor given her, directly from their hearts. He put his hand over his own. And then he stood erect and he saluted her. None of his men saw the gesture. They were watching their great ship, their hearts as full as his.

Packer sat again, then turned away and watched the shore

approach. He had seen her final, glorious moment. He wouldn't watch her sink into the sea. He wiped at his eyes.

All the Firefish ran, but they could not outrun the poison. It was everywhere.

The paths out to the deep seas were thick with it, blocked; more in the narrows than anywhere else. But the great beasts ran anyway, blind, sick, dying. Many found their way out. Many more succumbed, and sank slowly to the ocean floor.

One beast, however, slowed, and then turned back. It had run, just as the others had, away from the poison. It found waters that were clear enough to breathe, if only for a moment. There it stopped. It circled, as others swam past it, gouged and bleeding, terrified and sick, seeking in desperation any passage to deeper waters.

It waited. Deep Fin was still behind. The Presence was there. It had stayed with Deep Fin. The Presence and the Deep Fin were within the poison.

The other Firefish fled, and finally no more came. But Deep Fin did not come. The beast waited yet, the poison growing stronger. It raised its head into the emptiness. It looked around. And then it saw. It knew. The Deep Fin would not come. It was dying. It could not survive the poison either, being Firefish.

The Firefish waited, needing to leave, not wanting to leave.

It did not want to be alone again.

It did not want to go back to the cold and dark and deep, where the Presence was not. And so it circled once, and then once again, and then something within its brain, within its heart, clicked...an instinct, perhaps, but not an instinct for survival. A deeper pull. A decision that opened up its heart to the joy, the light of the Presence.

Yes. It would follow Deep Fin.

And so it flew back to the poison waters, back, back, at any cost, whatever cost.

Its eyes were blinded. Its head was filled with sickness. The stench was overwhelming. Still it swam.

And it found the Deep Fin, dying. It heard the creaks, the groans. It circled in the poisoned water, all but blind in pain and sickness, as the Deep Fin sank beneath the surface, and then floated down, and down. The beast swam among its wings, now swaying softly, gently in

The Battle for Vast Dominion

the waters. It swam around its outer skin. It felt the Deep Fin's scales against its own. It sank down, down with Deep Fin.

It searched for the Presence.

But the Presence could not be found. Deep Fin was dark, and cold. The poison settled down with Deep Fin on the ocean floor, and the Firefish settled with it. It wrapped itself around Deep Fin, wound itself all through its wings, its arms. And there it rested. It put its head on Deep Fin's head, where the tiny creature's face had been, where the Presence had lived and shone. Here it would wait. It would stay with the Deep Fin, in the dark, the cold, and it would await the Presence.

CHAPTER 22

Triumph

If victory in battle were always judged by the strength of the surviving forces, then Nearing Vast finished a distant second in the Battle of Mayak-Aloh. The Drammune clearly took the worst of it, suffering heavy casualties in pure numbers, but even more when those numbers were calculated as a percentage of their forces. Every Drammune warship had been sunk but one, and most all had been overrun by the Achawuk first.

The Vast fared only slightly better. The toll on their forces was almost as heavy in numbers, but when the last shot was fired and the last spear thrown and the last Firefish claimed its final victim, they had their flagship's entire crew intact, save only the fatal stabbing of a captain by a crewman—a captain, as it would be argued later in many pubs in Mann, who ought to be counted among the Drammune dead anyway. They had the *Marchessa* and almost half her crew alive, including Captain Moore Davies. They had outlasted their counterparts on the *Kaza Fahn* because they were not caught quite so off guard, and because they had a mission to fulfill, and a tradition to uphold. The Vast had never lost to the Achawuk. And as would become obvious to all soon enough, the Vast had one more ship yet, completely free of injury, suffering no loss or damage whatsoever.

Only when the battle was over did the rearmost ship in his majesty's intrepid Fleet manage to accomplish the extraordinary nautical feat of sailing between the jutting points of two adjacent islands. Having twice tried unsuccessfully to manage the strait, once misjudging the approach too far to port, and once too far to starboard, the careful captain of the *Blunderbuss* ordered that a third pass be undertaken much farther to the east, at the next entry point, which he hoped might provide a slightly wider passageway. It did, but by the time the slowest ship, perhaps the slowest ever built in Nearing Vast, entered the mayak-aloh, the Achawuk were swimming hell-bent for the *Trophy Chase,* all martial motives laid aside as they prepared their hearts and minds for the new age that had dawned among them.

Thus the *Blunderbuss* survived unscathed, once again.

The Achawuk, while suffering the heaviest death toll, also suffered the smallest percentage of dead and wounded. They certainly had overwhelming numbers still, as was evident to all when the survivors of the battle gathered on the shores of the mayak-aloh, beneath the rock outcropping that still bore their sick and dazed rek-tahk-ent.

But the numbers did not tell the story. As Dayton Throme knew, seated on his blanket-covered chaise, sweating and shivering, watching as the Vast ship's jolly approached the shore, the Vast had won the day. A small sailboat, more like a rowboat with a sail, made for the shore carrying the leaders of the victorious navy. Following it were several others, from the same sinking ship. And the Achawuk followed, too. Of course they followed, as thick on the water as lily pads on a shaded pond. The boat carried the Tannan-thoh-ah. The end of the world might not have actually come, but this man, whoever he was, certainly had. The Achawuk had witnessed the cataclysm. They had seen him bring glory to the beast. All had gone according to the prophecy except...except of course, that all these still lived. And what would they do with this inconvenient little fact? Would they think this man a god?

And who was he, really? What damage might he do, some Vast captain or admiral raised in a world where money ruled, trained to give orders, to take advantage of every situation, when faced with such an opportunity as a whole nation prepared to follow him anywhere?

Dayton saw a single boat now leave the lone remaining Drammune warship, following behind, as though not wanting to be left out on the waters. Dayton shook his head. Somehow now the Drammune would have to make their peace with the combined Achawuk and Vast.

Dayton felt tired, as tired as he ever remembered feeling. His strength drained away, as he thought of all that must now happen. It was as though he had been propped up from within, as though he'd forced himself to be awake and alert, holding sickness and fatigue at bay while the end of the world unfolded. And now, those props were gone. He sat back, put his head back on the rough blankets, pulled others up around him. And he shivered.

He could not get warm. But soon he was oblivious, sound asleep.

Packer left the boat and walked with his handful of Vast sailors, crunching up the beach to a rocky outcropping surrounded by sand on four sides, and there determined he would await some sort of council with the Achawuk. The jolly, too big to beach and too small to anchor offshore, was left with its prow in the sand and its stern in the waves, a bowline tied to a small tree. The men brought their duffels and small arms to the rocky camp, leaving the rations and water and ammunition behind in the boat.

The Achawuk came out of the water. They were not nearly so exhausted as the Vast might have expected. They saw the high ground the Tannan-thoh-ah had chosen, and gathered around the rocks, sitting one next to another in the sand.

And they kept gathering. They gathered, and gathered, and gathered until the sands were filled and the shoreline was obscured, providing the Vast with the rather discomfiting sensation that the waters had risen and now lapped around them, and the Achawuk swam in them yet.

When he arrived, Zhintah-Hoak was dripping wet but not even out of breath, as though expending energy in murderous mayhem and treading water for as much as an hour was not unusual for him. He walked through his people slowly, up onto the rocks, and directly to Packer. The Achawuk throng was deadly still. Standing two feet from Packer and looking him in the eye, he said with great gravity, in the slowest cadence any of the Vast had ever heard, "Taha tannan-thoh-ah." Then he stared, waiting.

Delaney bristled. "I don't like his tone," he said in a low growl.

Packer held up a calming hand to Delaney. And he waited.

"Taha rek-owa," Zhintah-Hoak said eventually, in the same even tone and slow cadence. But now he looked at Packer, his hair, his clothes. He reached out and put a hand on Packer's shoulder.

Delaney stepped forward. "He better keep his hands off of ye," Delaney said. "You tell him that."

Packer did not take his eyes from the warrior's face. He felt that would be disrespectful. But he said aloud, "Delaney, I don't speak Achawuk."

Delaney shot a hard glance at Mutter.

Cabe cleared his throat. "I do. A little," he said. "Long as they talk slow."

"Don't seem like that'll be a problem," Delaney offered.

"Ask him, 'Ahara?'" Cabe said.

"Ahara?" Packer's question was to Mutter, but the warrior answered Packer.

"Tannan-thoh-ah ahb rek-tahk-ent." He said it in a deep, rich, patient voice.

Packer looked to Mutter, who just scowled. Then he shook his head.

"You want him to say it slower?" Delaney asked.

"I know the words. Jus' don't make no sense."

"What's the words, then?"

Mutter sniffed. "He said, the end of the world meets the one who comes before."

"Comes before what?" Delaney asked.

"Before the end of the world," Mutter said. "I guess. It's that word what they all been sayin'. Tannan-thoh-ah. It's Achawuk."

"No kiddin'."

The warrior nodded at Packer, patted the king's shoulder. "Tannan-thoh-ah."

"Well, that explains that." Mutter grimaced, then raised his eyebrows. "Seems you're it, sir," he told Packer. "You're the end of the world."

Zhintah-Hoak kept his eyes on Tannan-thoh-ah. He did not like to look at the other Vast men. They seemed to him like small, scurrying creatures, moving with quick, frantic eyes and flashing hands. They chattered, their voices were scratchy and squeaking. They were chipmunks. But this man, the Tannan-thoh-ah, he was different. He carried purpose. There was fire in his soul. The spirit that moved the world moved in him. The Firefish knew. Zhintah-Hoak knew. "We have been waiting for you."

Packer was stunned. The man spoke Vast.

"Rek-tahk-ent...also Vast," Zhintah said.

Delaney whistled once. Andrew Haas and Father Mooring exchanged glances.

"He says the one who comes before is also Vast," Mutter offered.

"Got that, thanks," Delaney offered. "Sometimes, Mutter, I swear, you're duller'n a stonecutter's axe."

"Praise be," Bran Mooring offered. "I wonder if it's someone we know."

Packer's heart leaped, though he didn't know why. "I will go where you ask me to go," Packer told him.

Zhintah-Hoak waited a moment, unsure what all the conversation had been about. Then he turned and pointed upward, toward the stone shelf high above them. "Rek-tahk-ent ahb." It was hard to judge the distance, perhaps a thousand feet up, and a quarter of a mile away. Above the ledge, the mountain rose another thousand feet or more. Above that, a slate-gray sky with rows of low clouds, waves across an inverted sea, promised both rain that had yet to fall and the return of a sun that had shone only once or twice today. It might deliver either.

The Drammune boat from the *Kaza Fahn* now rowed to shore behind the throng of Achawuk warriors, crunching its prow into the sand a hundred yards from Packer. Several Drammune warriors leaped out, splashing through the waves, pulling their craft onto the beach and pushing their way, with little ceremony or concern for the Achawuk, toward the rocks where Packer and Zhintah-Hoak held their council.

All stopped and watched them approach.

Now a Drammune officer elbowed Zhintah-Hoak out of the way, positioned himself in front of Packer, and spoke gruffly. "Hezz Huk Tuth vare hezzan Vastcha tai taa," he said, gesturing toward his boat. He wore the insignia of a low-grade officer, and was in fact one of Tuth's lieutenants.

"Now, this one, I'm sure I don't like his tone," Delaney growled again.

Zhintah's eyes narrowed. These men were worse than squirrels. This one who pushed his way here, he posed like a strutting bird. He was a small, scared man who hid his fear behind aggressive action, like a child pretending to be grown. Any man carrying such behaviors deep into his grown days was dangerous.

All Vast eyes turned to Father Mooring, awaiting his translation. "Well. It seems Supreme Commander Huk Tuth wants to speak with Packer Throme rather urgently."

Zhintah now saw the priest for the first time. This man was no squirrel. He carried the spirit of the earth, the sea, the air within him. Zhintah's eyes danced as he watched the priest.

"I'll speak with him," Packer said. "Tell him he may approach."

"The nature of the request, sir…" the priest squinted, "was actually a demand that you go to him."

Delaney's eyes sparked, but he said nothing.

Packer sensed the resentment in Delaney, Cabe, and even Andrew Haas. "Ask him, Father, why the commander can't come here."

The priest did, then translated the response. "He's badly injured, Your Highness."

Packer nodded. The others relaxed. "I'll come speak to him."

"Packer," Father Mooring said. The tone of his voice caused all the men to look at him. His beaming face was gentle. "Before you speak with Commander Tuth, you should know the last words of his Hezzan."

Packer waited.

"They were, 'I know who shall rule.'"

"What does that mean?"

"I'm not sure."

Mutter did his best to tell Zhintah-Hoak that the Tannan-thoh-ah would visit the Rek-tahk-ent a little later, after pausing to speak with Huk Tuth, the commander of the Drammune. The Achawuk leader had nothing to say in return. Tannan-thoh-ah would do as he pleased. But he followed the party through the Achawuk to the red boat of these dangerous, strutting children.

The Drammune jolly was longer and wider than its Vast counterpart. With its rounded bottom and dark wooden hull, its single mast, sail now struck, it looked to Zhintah precisely like an enormous, inverted turtle shell with a pike driven through its belly. It did not give him any better feelings about these people. A wooden ladder led up to its lip, surrounded by Drammune sailors armed and in a mood to fight any who would attempt access to their commander.

"Don't think you're goin' up into that boat alone," Delaney warned Packer.

"Wait here," Bran Mooring said, before Packer could respond. Then the little priest walked past his escorts and straight up to the guards, said something in Drammune, and showed them the contents of his knapsack. The guards looked to their lieutenant, who shrugged. The priest had some skill at healing. Otherwise he was harmless. Father Mooring passed through them and climbed the ladder.

Zhintah-Hoak admired the little man all wrapped in brown. He moved quickly, like the others, but he did not jerk or chatter. There was a fluid peace that drove him. Like a small, deep stream, running between rocks. Serene and calm even in motion.

A few minutes later, the priest climbed back down the ladder, without his knapsack. "Unless God grants a miracle," he reported to Packer, "Commander Tuth won't see another dawn. In fact, I have no idea what's keeping him alive." Bran Mooring shook his head. "The head wound alone should have been fatal. His shoulder is badly wounded, and he's cut open in a dozen other places. He's lost a tremendous amount of blood. He's no danger to you."

Packer nodded, started toward the ladder.

"Wait, now." Delaney said, stewing. "Who else is in that boat?"

"I saw no one," the priest reported.

"I don't like it, Packer. I mean, Your Highness."

Packer studied the sailor. He said, "Thank you, Delaney. But you stay here."

Delaney kicked the sand, then stared up at the low-hanging clouds. Everything had gone skewed, he thought. Nobody did what made sense anymore. Either that, or Delaney had lost his mind completely. He wasn't sure which was true. Could be either.

Huk Tuth had been laid out on the planking of the boat's bilge. A canopy of sailcloth had been pulled overhead, braced on poles, to keep him out of sun or rain, whichever the sky ultimately decided to pour down. Packer blanched at the sight of him, almost retching at the smell. Flies buzzed. The odor of dried blood and rotting meat was heavy. The commander's breaths were shallow and labored. His skin was dry and white, almost the color of his hair. Both hair and skin were caked black with blood.

Tuth had heard the two men climb aboard, heard them sit beside him. Now his eyes searched for Packer. Finding him, they closed.

"Hezzan Skahl Dramm?" he asked.

"He's asking about Talon," the priest said.

"She's dead," Packer told him.

Father Mooring translated.

"She sailed from Drammun as Hezzan," Tuth said, with great effort. "But the Quarto had declared her Unworthy."

Packer said nothing. The old man struggled with each word.

"I pursued her here. To claim her dominion. But you took it."

"No," Packer said solemnly. "Her life was taken by my sailor."

Tuth closed his eyes. He breathed in and out a few times. Then he said, "On your orders."

"No," Packer started.

"Yes," Father Mooring interjected. "Delaney did act on your orders."

"No. I told him not to kill her."

"Unless she attempted to kill another. I heard you say it myself. He obeyed."

Packer swallowed hard. "Tell him yes, then."

Father Mooring did, and at the same time fanned flies away from the Drammune commander's head wound.

"You are Drammune, by Ixthano," Tuth said next. "By Fen Abbaka Mux."

"Oh, Lord," Packer said. Bran Mooring did not translate.

"By Ixthano," Tuth said, "you are now Hezzan of the Drammune."

Three priests came into the sanctuary, and found their High Holy Reverend Father kneeling at the altar. The body of a seminary student in tattered, filthy robes was laid out beside him, hands folded across his chest. Hap heard them enter, and stood slowly and painfully. They rushed to the fallen man, checking him for signs of life. They all three looked up at Hap, waiting for an explanation.

He rested a hand on the altar rail. Then he shrugged. "I found him here. Poor lad. I have given the final blessing. Do you know his story?"

But before they could answer, the doors opened again, and Panna Throme entered. Usher Fell was with her, the manacles on his wrists attached to a chain held by the sheriff, his deputies not far behind. Stave Deroy brought up the rear.

Stanson looked at Panna as though a ghost had just entered the room, then at Father Fell as though he were a disgrace to the cloth. He quickly recovered himself, however, and scowled officiously at Panna as she approached. "What is the meaning of this?"

"Harlowen Stanson, you are under arrest," the square-jawed sheriff said, "for conspiracy to assassinate the Queen of Nearing Vast."

Stanson sniffed. "The charge is nonsense. Besides, you cannot arrest me. I have sanctuary." His voice echoed in the chapel.

The sheriff noted the fallen boy, and blanched. "What's wrong with him?"

"He's dead," one of the priests said. They still knelt by the body.

Father Fell's eyes went wide as he peered at the boy's face. Then, unnoticed, a tall, lean shadow entered and sat in a pew toward the back of the chapel.

With a soft clatter of chains, the sheriff handed Usher Fell's reins to Chunk Deroy, then knelt gently by the boy.

"Who is he?" the sheriff asked Hap Stanson, who just shrugged.

"I know him," Usher Fell said. "That's Lester Mine. He was a pupil of mine. I last saw him when I sent him off with a message for his High Holiness." A trace of bitterness could be detected by all present.

"He's been starved and ill-used," the sheriff reported. "But I don't see any marks of foul play."

Hap raised his eyebrows. "Of course not. I sent him on a difficult mission for spiritual purification. He fasted and suffered, even unto death. He died to glorify God."

The sheriff shook his head. "I wouldn't know how to classify that crime."

Stanson rolled his eyes. "You're desperate. You're trumping up these charges."

Panna held out the folded parchment that Marlie Blotch had once hidden in Hap Stanson's porridge. "The evidence would indicate otherwise."

"I have no idea what that is," the cleric said, eyeing the parchment with suspicion.

"No?" From the pew near the back where he had been sitting,

Prince Ward now stood. He walked down the aisle, a thick leather folder in his hand. His gait was jaunty, his expression carefree. "Perhaps you'll recognize some of these?" He pulled a thick handful of papers from the folder.

Stanson narrowed his eyes. "The royal fool arrives to entertain us."

Ward ignored the remark. "I had a simple thought, after finding that little note from your augustness to the good father here. That last line, where you instructed Father Fell to burn the message 'as always'.. I thought, *What if that note was not the first message Father Fell had failed to burn?* And so I asked the sheriff to do a little digging. And sure enough, all of these were in Father Fell's apartments." He thumbed through them. "All written in your hand, your High Holiness, to your humble servant here. It's quite interesting reading, really. Certainly more interesting than the classes you taught at the academy." He pulled a page from the top of the stack and handed it to Panna. "Here's one you'll be interested in, my queen."

Hap Stanson was aghast. He looked Father Fell up and down as though the man might turn into a goat or a winged devil at any moment. "What have you done?" he breathed.

"Yes, yes, I know," Fell offered morosely. "I should have been burning them all along. But I know how you operate." He shrugged. "I have always feared that I might be the next one thrown into the lion's den. Frankly, I couldn't count on angels to stop their jaws. So I kept those instead."

"But...I have trusted you. All these years."

Father Fell now looked, for the first time, chagrined. "How was I to know? You seemed to trust a good many people close to you who wound up..." he trailed off, his eyes resting on the pitiful figure of the dead student.

One of the three priests now stood, and walked to Prince Ward. "May I have a look?" He was a senior priest at the seminary, almost as tall as Ward and Hap, with a dignified air, gray at the temples, gentle eyes.

"Be my guest." Ward handed him the folder, and the priest began leafing through the parchments under the careful eye of the sheriff.

Panna stepped to the front pew, and sat down. She had been reading the parchment handed her by Prince Ward. She spoke to Father Fell, her voice gentle, her hands shaking. "You sent Packer's father to the Achawuk islands. You told him he would learn all about the Firefish there. But you knew they would all be murdered."

"Martyred. It was a missionary voyage."

"You will also find a message in there," Ward added, "explaining precisely how the charges against Packer were used to cover over Father Fell's indiscretions. And one on how the young woman who swore Packer had cheated, subsequently died. You'll find the term 'accidentally' does not apply nearly so cleanly as these gentlemen would have the world believe."

Panna's shoulders drooped. It was so horrible, to have such injustice, such evil at the pinnacle of the Church, and for so very long. After a pause she said, "Isn't it odd." Her look was far away. "Isn't it odd that if Packer had been treated fairly, he never would have become a swordsman. He'd be a priest now. He'd never have gone to sea. Which means he wouldn't be the king. And I wouldn't be queen." Now she looked at Hap. "And you would still be high, and holy, and reverend. Instead of what you are..." and now her eyes focused crisply, "a criminal, soon to be on trial for your life."

"You think you have that power?" Hap raised one side of his upper lip in a snarl. "I am not under arrest. I have sanctuary here."

No one said a thing. They all looked at him blankly. The dignified priest who had been leafing through the notices looked sick. "Sanctuary was instituted for the poor and the weak, those like Lester Mine, who are ill-used by the powerful."

"And people like Marlie Blotch, who don't know which way to turn," Panna added.

"Vagrants, prostitutes, drunkards," Ward added.

"And even murderers," the senior of the three priests concluded, "if they come here to seek mercy and forgiveness. None who have come here for sanctuary have been turned away." He set the offending papers on the pew beside him. "But I would be ashamed to be a priest in a Church that abuses the weak and protects the strong."

"As would I," said the second priest, standing now beside the fallen boy.

"And I," said the third, staying on his knees.

"But the laws are the laws," Hap Stanson said defiantly. "I simply cannot be arrested here."

"I will not step outside the bounds of the authority vested in the State," Panna said. "I will respect the Church. But I would appeal

The Battle for Vast Dominion

to you three, as representatives of the Church, to set this matter right."

"What are you suggesting? I *am* the Church!" Hap insisted. "These mere priests have no authority here!"

"The authority of the Church," said the senior priest, "comes from God, and not man. And certainly not from one man."

"But you can't usurp my position in my own Church, in this chapel, in my seminary! I'll have your robes!"

There was a long silence. Then the senior priest said, "My robes are worthless if I protect this man, knowing what I now know. As a representative of the Church of Nearing Vast, I..." he looked at his two companions, "we rescind the protections of sanctuary he claims."

"No!" Hap raged, venom and spittle flying, his face contorted and red as a radish. The sheriff and a deputy immediately stepped forward. "You have no authority! I am the representative of God! He will smite you! I will call on Him and He will strike you down!"

In the pause that ensued, Chunk Deroy stepped forward. "I've heard that before," he said. He spun the clergyman around, and Hap cried out in pain. "My leg! You oaf!" But the dragoon dragged the cleric out the front door of the sanctuary without paying much attention.

The old Drammune warrior was serious. And the argument made sense. But Packer as Hezzan? It was ironic, even amusing. But it was meaningless. The Quarto would take away his title three seconds after learning he had won it. Probably, he had been declared Unworthy already, just to remove the Ixthano he'd been given by Mather Sennett.

"Talon knew this," Father Mooring added, as Packer pondered the idea. "This was the meaning of her final words."

I know who shall rule. Packer accepted the priest's assertion, but if he knew Talon at all, she had more in mind. Ultimately, titles meant as little to her as they did to him.

Suddenly Tuth had a knife in his hand. The old man's long, jagged weapon had been hidden under his thigh, awaiting this moment. He lunged for Packer with it, rising up from his deathbed, aiming for Packer's heart.

Packer saw it coming. He had seen it coming since he first climbed over the gunwale and saw the old warrior's knife sheath, empty on his belt. He had seen the withered hand fumble for it. He saw it coming at him like a ball lobbed from a father to a child. Tuth's move was painfully slow, embarrassingly clumsy, more writhe than lunge. Even had the weapon found its mark, it could hardly have been damaging. But it did not find its mark. Packer caught Tuth's wrist. Gently, he took the knife from his fingers.

The priest was alarmed, but he saw that Packer was not. He watched Packer ease the old warrior's hand back down to his side, and then slide the knife back into its sheath. Father Mooring then adjusted the bandages at Tuth's shoulder, applied pressure to stop the new bleeding.

"It was necessary," Packer explained to Father Mooring, "for his sense of honor. Tell him he has been a Worthy foe." Then to Tuth, "You are a Worthy adversary, and a Worthy warrior."

The priest translated.

Then after a moment, Huk Tuth spoke again. It took him a long time to say the words. But he was determined to say them, and he worked hard until all was said. "You defeated Fen Abbaka Mux. My superior. You defeated the Hezzan Skahl Dramm. She defeated me. Now you have defeated me also. You have won the secrets of the Firefish. You have conquered the Achawuk. You are Vast. But you are Drammune. You are the Hezzan Throne Dramm." There was a long pause, and then he said, "You have my allegiance."

Packer felt deeply humbled. Not by the title, which was worthless. But by this final act of an old warrior, and a sworn enemy. Huk Tuth had hated Packer, hated the Vast, hated all that they stood for, all they believed in. And yet at the end, unlike Scatter Wilkins, he was able to give honor to an enemy. Not just honor, but the highest honor, and to his greatest enemy. Here, surely, was an honorable man.

A society built on such honor would be, in fact, Worthy, Packer thought. If only the Drammune could humble themselves and delight in mercy as well as justice, weakness before God as well as strength before men. What an awe-inspiring people they could be. Far greater than the Vast.

Knowing somehow that a show of gratitude or even humility would be unbecoming, Packer said instead, "You are Worthy to command."

Tuth's breaths came deep and quick. It was precisely what a Hezzan should say.

"I am Vast, as you say," Packer now added, speaking as to a confidant. "The Quarto will reject me."

"The Quarto," Tuth answered, "...are fools. Pizlar Kank. A rabid dog. He cares only for power. They...will ruin Drammun."

Packer nodded. There was nothing much he could say to that.

Tuth looked up at Packer. He paused. He coughed, two small catches from his chest. Then he croaked, "I hate them." He closed his eyes, as though that explained everything.

And the more Packer thought about it, the more it did.

The path upward to the shelf overlooking the mayak-aloh began at a stone doorway. Or at least, so it was called in the tongue of the Achawuk. In fact it consisted of two large stacks of rocks, looking something like chimneys, each rising shoulder-high, between which people could walk two abreast. Beyond the stacks a single path led upward, winding through switchbacks, up through trees with long, waving fronds and large, tuberous roots that stretched out across the path. Packer, Mutter Cabe, Smith Delaney, and Bran Mooring followed Zhintah-Hoak through the doorway, and up the mountainside.

Zhintah led them solemnly, ceremoniously. Packer had plenty to think about, and appreciated the silence. The others sensed the king's mood, and kept their own counsel. Only Bran Mooring seemed cheerful. An occasional snatch of a hymn floated up from behind, as he brought up the rear.

As the party reached the summit, Packer was led to the painted wild man. The rek-tahk-ent was lying on a makeshift chaise, covered with blankets, wrapped up past his chin. His hair fell down around his eyes, and his eyes were closed. What could be seen of his face was bright blue, streaked and pocked by sweat. His body trembled. Father Mooring knelt beside him, felt his forehead, opened an eyelid. "Fevered. Bad case of the ague, I'd guess. Or influenza."

Delaney and Mutter Cabe took a step backward.

"He'll survive?" Packer asked.

"I believe so."

The man did not look Vast. His hair was long and dark, and where his skin was unpainted, his arms and legs, it was dark, too, browned like the Achawuk.

And then the man spoke. "Who's there?" he asked, his head lolling. His eyes blinked, and he opened them.

The image hung before Dayton Throme's eyes. It swam, as though he looked at a reflection in rippled waters. The face turned, spinning. But there could be no doubt. This was Packer. He was a grown man. The image was much like those Dayton had cherished in his memory. But this...this was more, somehow. It was not a memory. It was a vision. The face was concerned. It wanted something from him. There was joy there. The face spoke. It was a dream, it had to be a dream. And yet it would not go away. He reached out his hand as though, perhaps, just perhaps it was real. Perhaps he could touch that face, that blond hair. But the image reeled, careening into darkness.

The recognition came to Packer like a horse at full gallop. It wasn't a perception through the eyes and ears, but through every pore. He recognized this man with every fiber, top to bottom, soul and spirit. But then his father closed his eyes again. Packer feared he would never open them, that this brief moment was all he would be given.

"Father?" Packer fell to his knees by the man's side, a hand on his shoulder, shaking him. "Father, it's me; it's Packer." A door that Packer had closed and sealed had suddenly been opened, and not just opened but kicked in, shattered. All his sense of past and present seemed to slip away. Time, memory, hope, the reality of the moment, it was all jumbled now. He was riding on this man's shoulders. This man, huge and strong, was carrying him up out of the water. He was throwing Packer high in the air, and Packer was light as a feather in those big hands, laughing and laughing, wanting it never to end. And Packer was lying on the deck of his father's fishing boat, his father right beside him, looking down into the crystal waters, seeing his reflection as that big soft voice described every fish, and every plant, and every bit of coral below.

"Father. Father, it's me!"

And Dayton opened his eyes again, reached out his hand. Packer grabbed it.

"Son." The voice was thin, but it was sure. It was gentle, deep, and full of the light that was Dayton Throme.

"Yes. It's me."

Dayton closed his eyes for a moment, savoring the dream. But when he did, the image was gone. He opened them again. He looked at Packer, unsure now whether he was dreaming. He looked around. Zhintah-Hoak was watching.

"Packer is my son," Dayton said in Achawuk. "My only son."

The warrior nodded. "Your son is the master-knowing," Zhintah replied solemnly.

"Tannan-thoh-ah?"

"Atchah. He rode the Firefish. They rose as one from the waters. He is the glory of the beast. He is the master-knowing."

Dayton felt now he surely must be dreaming. That man, the captain, the Vast commander lauded by the Achawuk. It was Packer.

"And you are the one who comes before," Zhintah told him.

The one who comes before. Dayton understood now. Not the foreteller, but the *forebear.* He shook his head. "But seminary…"

"I was expelled, father. I learned the sword instead. And I went in search of Firefish."

Dayton looked at his son again, his heart welling up. It all made sense now. All the stray pieces, the threads of his life that had been cut short. Like Nessa's needlepoint viewed from the back. It was a mess, but now it had all turned around, and he saw the picture. It was beautiful. "And you've tamed the Firefish."

Packer shook his head. "I did nothing. God did everything."

"I'm glad, then. I know now that God will take care of these people. And you…you will lead them?"

"Lead them?"

"They have no king. But they will accept your leadership."

Packer didn't know what to say. How could he tell his father what had happened, all the events since he had disappeared?

"I'll try," he said. "With God's help…" And Packer put his forehead on his father's shoulder. His father, his own flesh and blood. He felt the warmth, the breath. Alive here on the earth, where Packer had no right to hope for such a thing. And God had done this. All the trials, all the sacrifice. All the troubles, all the pain. All the fears and all the failures. Through it all, God had been bringing him, inexorably, unstoppably, inevitably, *here.* To this place high atop a cliff. Overlooking the Vast sea. The infinite expanse, perfect in every detail. Everything made right.

The sun was low in the gray sky by the time the Tannan-thoh-ah returned with the Rek-tahk-ent. Four men carrying the fifth. Packer passed through the stone doorway, and the Achawuk murmured his new name. As they saw him, they sat, giving him honor.

The Drammune, on orders from Huk Tuth, put one knee and both hands on the ground, then touched their foreheads to the sand, honoring their Hezzan.

The Vast looked at the sight and shrugged at one another. Not to be outdone, they knelt before their king. The Achawuk bowed their heads in honor.

Packer shook his head. Then he looked back at his father. Dayton Throme blnked. "You've been busy, son."

Packer looked up to the heavens, then back down at the three nations now gathered under his leadership. He had only one thought now.

Panna is never going to believe this.

CHAPTER 23

Rewards

The moon shone down on the mayak-aloh, rippling its waters silver. Two fires burned on the beach. One of them had been built on the rocky outcropping where Packer Throme had held his first council with Zhintah-Hoak. Captain Andrew Haas sat here now with Smith Delaney, Mutter Cabe, Father Mooring, and a handful of others, talking quietly about the trip here, the trip back, the Drammune, the Achawuk.

The Drammune were camped nearby, gathered around their own fire.

The Achawuk had departed at dusk, disappearing into the woods like a receding tide, headed back to their villages. Packer had gone with Dayton, whose strength had returned in some measure, though the Rek-tahk-ent was nevertheless carried back to his little village and up the hill to the small lean-to at its peak. There the elder Throme hosted his son, wanting him to share his home. The younger was happy to accompany him absolutely anywhere.

Left on the beach with their stores of provisions, the Vast did what the Vast generally do with free time and free drink. They had managed to salvage the equivalent of two month's worth of ale and a month-and-a-half's supply of rum each, for all the men and women who would sail the two ships home. Their captain had opened the taps and bottles in order to bring the stores of drink more in line with the length of the trip ahead, for all those so inclined. Most of them were in fact so inclined, and these were now reclined, or supine, or recumbent, or prone, or simply splayed out face down in the sand. Most of them were snoring loudly.

But a few quiet souls were left, those less disposed to drown the day's grim memories or gin up a sense of celebration, talking, sipping a bit of ale here, puffing a pipe of tobacco there. And so, with the practical discussions having dwindled, Bran Mooring took the opportunity to relate a few tales most of these men had heard, but not in detail, and not from an eyewitness. He told of the Battle of the Green, and the Escape from Hollow Forest, and of Varlotsville. He was in his element, storyteller and teacher in one, thankful to be the chronicler of true tales from which deep meaning could be drawn, and without the usual forcing or stretching. At least such was his view. Morals and principles generally applicable to these fine and receptive students here gathered, were abundant.

Bran finished up the tale of Packer's negotiations with Huk Tuth at Varlotsville, demonstrating with a flourish how Packer had held the agreement in his hand, saying, "If you do not sign this, then you will learn all that we know about Firefish, and we will teach you out at sea, as enemies!" There were appreciative comments, and a low whistle.

"He knew. He knew he could command the beasts," Mutter asserted.

"Perhaps he did, deep down," Father Mooring answered.

They all thought silently, as the snores rose around them in a comforting cacophony. A suddenly sleepy Delaney yawned. "Makes a feller want to join right in, don't it?"

"Yes. And that's the hallmark of leadership."

Delaney was befuddled. "I meant the snorin'."

"Oh." But Bran shrugged. Delaney wasn't the first student to grow drowsy in his presence.

"Been a long, hard day," Andrew Haas agreed. He tapped out his pipe.

"Aye to that." Delaney rubbed his eyes with his knuckles. Then he stared distantly at Father Mooring. "I don't suppose I should stay awake worried about Packer wanderin' these woods without so much as a swordsman by his side?"

Father Mooring looked back at him. "No, I don't suppose you should."

Delaney sniffed. "Thought not. Then off to the land a' milk and honey for me." He rose, slightly unsteady, and took his leave. He glanced over at the other campfire. A few Drammune sat around it while others slept nearby.

Unlike the Vast, who felt no danger now from any party, now that their king was king of all, these warriors were vigilant. They had set a perimeter and they guarded it, walking it as though protecting a fortress. All the Drammune survivors were gathered within its few dozen square feet. Delaney counted fifteen, half of them wounded. Not one was face down in the sand with weapons and clothing and other belongings strewn about carelessly. They were not like the Vast, he concluded.

He was looking at their ship's boat, wondering how something quite so round could sail any particular direction, when he heard the flap of wings, and then saw a great bird rise up from it in darkness, moonlight painting its wings with silver. It settled on the tip of the mast, looking down from where it came. This was a falcon, fine and noble, and Delaney could see something tethered to its talons. And then it flapped its wings again, and hovered around in low, slow circles. The sailor wondered if this was that same bird, the one Father Mooring told about, that had brought a message from the Hezzan to Huk Tuth on the hostile plain outside Varlotsville. And then he figured, yes, it probably was. That was Huk Tuth's own bird.

It rose higher, then higher, and then under the moonlight flew off over the ocean.

Delaney padded down to the seashore, watching the feathered thing soar against the stars as it shrank away. Another message to...someone. But not to the Hezzan. The Hezzan was here. The Hezzan was Packer Throme. Delaney glanced again at the Drammune boat, and saw a lamp go out within it. He took off his hat. Then he watched the bird until it disappeared, a speck too small for his eyes to follow.

"I've spent so many hours here," Dayton Throme said, "looking out over that sea, into the setting sun. Praying for you and your mother."

He spoke slowly, Packer noted. He moved slowly, but his eyes were ablaze. He was the same man, and yet he had changed. "I wish you could know..." his voice trailed off.

"Know what?" Packer asked.

Dayton looked at him, surprised by the interruption. The Vast prized speed, he now remembered. He had been simply searching his mind for the right Vast word, the ripe berry ready for the plucking. "I wish you could know the peace of this place. I wish that Nearing Vast could absorb it. It would do you good."

"Maybe we can bring some of it back home with us."

Dayton thought for a long while. Then he shook his head. "No. The slow will always be overrun by the fast. That is the nature of things everywhere. Everywhere but here in these islands." He thought again, then said, "You must protect this place, Packer. These people will live on, but their way of life is already gone."

"But why should it change? They still have the Firefish."

Dayton looked at the foot of his hill, where there had always been a ring of spears. Now, there was nothing. No barrier. No protection. He looked at his son, sadness in his eyes. "The Firefish will not return. The Achawuk planned to take all the Firefish with them, into the next life."

"How...would they do that?"

Dayton nodded, seeing the knowledge as it entered his son. "The Firefish have been poisoned. The Achawuk have destroyed them."

Packer was aghast. "Surely not all of them?"

"The Achawuk," he said it as the people themselves did, "Hah-chah-WUK-ah," "they have developed many ways to control the beasts. This scent attracts them. That one repels. Mostly, it is blood that attracts, and mostly soot and ash that repel. The remnants of burning sickens them. But the ash of a certain tree, the bum-bay-lah, the one with the roots that overgrow the trails—it is deadly poison to the beasts. It kills Firefish."

"And that's what they used today."

"Today was the end of all things."

Packer shook his head, trying to understand the implications. His own Firefish then, was gone. It was a deep stab. "Surely there are other Firefish. Somewhere."

"Would you like to go search for them?"

Packer shook his head again. "No, sir. Not me."

"Nor I."

But Packer thought about this. He thought long and hard. The Firefish, gone. Their healing power, never to be known on earth again. Talon's quest for power, over. No more impenetrable armor, ever, in all the world. The Firefish trade, ended. The *Trophy Chase* had stirred the pot, but the pot itself, and the potion, that was Firefish. The Firefish venture, the war, the truce, all of it had led here. And now, all of it was over. When their world was discovered, when their knowledge became desirable by kingdoms of the earth, the Achawuk had simply taken the beasts away. The objects of Scat's dream of wealth, Mather's dream of power, Talon's dream of dominance. Gone. The Achawuk were wise. Wiser than perhaps even they knew.

Then he realized that the Vast were now essentially helpless. No Navy, and hardly more than a sprig of an Army. The Vast were powerless. But for the power of God.

After a long, thoughtful pause, Packer said, "Let's not tell the Drammune about this."

At dawn, Huk Tuth's body was burned on the beach in a great pyre. The new Hezzan praised the Supreme Commander, citing his honor, his courage, and his Worthiness. His audience was appreciative, focused, and prepared to embrace Packer as their new leader.

Then he prayed.

Father Mooring translated to a deeply puzzled audience.

By noon, a dozen more Drammune stragglers had arrived, survivors who had made it to shore on one island or another, and had now finally made their way to the campfires here. Preparations were already underway to sail their single ship back to Drammun. A few more stray soldiers would wander in, and one day later, when the *Kaza Fahn* set off for home, more than two dozen Drammune would man it.

The Vast prepared to leave as well. But Packer could not be convinced to depart until he was sure that the Achawuk were ready, and would not decide to follow their fallen brethren and their Firefish to a better place, completing the tannan-thoh-ah. This was a real consideration, duly deliberated at their high council. Packer participated, and Dayton and son did their best to assure Zhintah-Hoak and company that they were all alive for a very good reason, that the great river of life, which in fact was the One True God, had spared them, had sent the Tannan-thoh-ah, for just this purpose. But the Achawuk were unconvinced. If Packer, the Tannan-thoh-ah, planned to leave them...how then could he usher in a new era, a new world?

It was an impasse without an easy solution, and it was not to be resolved in one council. It would take many thoughts, many words, many days. Understanding the issue, and the importance of self-sufficiency, and the need to make the best use of all their free time, the Vast crew took it upon themselves to teach their new Achawuk friends all they knew about fishing. Fish were abundant, and easy enough to spear, but there were other ways. The Achawuk took very quickly to the highly agreeable technique of taking an entire day in a small boat with a jug of ale and a fishing pole, matching wits with the creatures. This method was particularly attractive to the Achawuk males.

But the women were quite adept at rope-making, and they were not nearly so keen on the new approach. So with Dayton Throme's guidance they began to learn the net-making art as well, leading to an entire fishing school that taught a more industrious method. The Achawuk were good students and natural fishermen, so Packer quickly decided that the jolly, the shallop, and the longboats from the *Chase* would be left behind to aid the island natives in their new fishing ventures.

But the stalemate continued. How could their Tannan-thoh-ah come, and then just go away again?

Finally, at a council meeting, a solution was found.

"I shall stay," Father Mooring suggested to Packer, "and speak on your behalf."

The validity of this was debated, but ultimately the day was won by Zhintah-Hoak, who made one crucial observation. "The spirit of the waters, of the air, of the soil, moves within the Tannan-thoh-ah. And this same spirit we have seen within his servant, the one called Brahn-Moh-Reen. That the words of the Tannan-thoh-ah shall come through his servant we know to be possible. We shall speak of this among ourselves, and we shall decide."

"Father Mooring," Packer said to his counselor, mentor, teacher, and friend, "I would never ask you to stay behind. Nearing Vast is in desperate need of your wisdom. And so is its king."

Bran saw the very real sorrow, and took Packer's hand in both of his. "From the moment these people laid down their spears, I knew I wouldn't leave them. I've simply been unable to break the news to you. My dear boy, look at it through my eyes. The Church has sent missionaries here for centuries, to no avail. Now, here is the Church, in the poor but very present form of me, and here are these people looking for a new life, a new world. Waiting to be ushered into truth. That, dear Packer, is an opening any man of the cloth would find hard to pass up."

But the Achawuk had terms of their own. There was one way that Tannan-thoh-ah would not leave the Achawuk, one way that Packer himself would not part company with them, even though he left the islands.

Zhintah-Hoak would sail along, to see the land of the Vast for himself.

And so the Vast, almost two hundred strong, stayed on the islands as guests, teachers, learners, and friends, for over two weeks, until finally they were restless for home. The *Marchessa* and the *Blunderbuss* were made ready. Food was easily gathered, as the Achawuk shared their stores with the Vast. Neither ship had suffered; few repairs were needed.

The Vast were quickly ready.

There were no ceremonies, as the Achawuk were not a formal people. But gifts were given in abundance, and given mutually. The Achawuk gave spears, and food, and face paints, ornaments and jewelry, paintings of Firefish, blankets, carved Firefish bones, and Firefish hide. The Vast gave knives, swords, pistols, fish hooks, rope, cannonballs, tobacco, and rum. They even gave of themselves. Romance had blossomed here and there between Vast and Achawuk. One woman, a flenser from the *Blunderbuss*, and two men, both sailors late of the *Trophy Chase*, decided they would stay.

The Achawuk used their new fishing boats to ferry the Vast to their ships, and then lined the beaches of the mayak-aloh once more, this time to say goodbye. As the Vast set sail from the crystal waters, Packer Throme stood on the quarterdeck of the *Marchessa*. They all waved at the shore. They fired cannon. The Achawuk chanted, and sang their song of the Tannan-thoh-ah.

"The Achawuk are a good, gentle people," was the watchword, repeated again and again on this voyage home. None could quite account for such a reality. And yet, it was true.

As the shore shrank away, all eyes turned downward. The sun shone brightly, playing across the sandy bottom. Moore Davies understood, and set the *Marchessa*'s course to pass over that spot, as best he could determine it, where the *Trophy Chase*'s masts and sails had last been seen, sinking beneath the waves. All the men wanted just one more glimpse of their great ship.

And they were not disappointed.

"There she is!" the lookout shouted, "Starboard bows, thirty points!" And hearts leaped, legs raced to rails, eyes scanned the seas.

Then hats came off.

The sun shone down on her, like rays from heaven. The currents billowed her sails like wind. She sat on the seafloor, keel already half covered in sand, heeled at an impossible angle. She flew, it seemed to every eye, even as she lay still. But more amazing yet was the beast. The Firefish was wound through her masts, draped across her decks, overhanging the hull like an oversized golden bunting.

"It's alive!" the word passed through the ship like lightning.

But as the *Marchessa* passed over, the excitement bled away. The beast lay still. And as they passed, the color of its hide grew dark again. The sun, somehow, had played along the scales, making them shine. The thing was dead. It was wrapped in death around the ship that had wrapped its legend around the beast.

In their final embrace, the Firefish had its trophy, and the great cat had hers. The chase was ended.

The *Blunderbuss* then tried to pass over the same spot, and for the same reason. The crew of the *Trophy Chase* had been assigned, for the most part, to the *Marchessa,* replacing crew that had been lost to the Achawuk. But a few *Chase* veterans had been ordered to the slower ship. These included Andrew Haas. The hope was that these good men could help to keep that ship from lagging too severely. It would prove to be a vain hope, and Haas immediately knew why. The slow ship's captain was quite sure, *quite* sure that the *Marchessa* had the coordinates all wrong, and that he knew precisely where the *Chase* went under. And, as captain, he would take his ship just there.

None aboard the soon-to-be-celebrated *Blunderbuss* ever saw the great cat lying in state, at her final rest, at the bottom of the sea.

But no one in Nearing Vast would ever know that.

The word, for once, did not get out about the return of the Vast seamen to their homeland.

The two ships arrived at the Docks of Mann mid-morning on an early summer Sunday. The place was all but deserted, as even the crustiest of longshoremen took off the morning of the Sabbath, if not to go to church, at least to drink to the health of those who did. And though the ever-vigilant dock foreman and the often-vigilant naval lookout had spotted the ships at sea, neither recognized them until they were all but in their slips. Then, rather than send word to the palace, both ran down to the ships to learn what news might be known, assuming nothing but the worst. Both were shocked into further silence to find their king aboard.

Packer descended the gangway first, an Achawuk warrior on one side, and a man who might have been Achawuk on the other. The king requested both a carriage and a horse. Both were brought immediately. Packer helped Dayton Throme, then Zhintah-Hoak, up into the coach. He assigned Moore Davies to ride along as company, and Smith Delaney to ride as guard, and he gave instructions to the coachman…take them through the city, that Zhintah-Hoak might see the capital, and then on to the palace.

Taking his leave, Packer Throme mounted the horse, a young gray mare full of spirit, hardly more than a colt. He turned her, shook the reins, touched his heels to her flanks, and bolted from the docks like he'd been shot from a cannon.

Panna sat alone in the upstairs drawing room, just outside the royal bedrooms. She sipped her coffee, then set it down on the table. She was prepared for church, dressed in a simple blue gown, her hair up off her neck. She was waiting for Millie to come tell her that the carriage was prepared. Now she stood, and walked to the open window that looked out over the gardens.

Sundays were hard. Her father, and all that Sunday meant to him, was gone. Packer was gone. Panna was queen, and as queen she had arrested the highest cleric of the Church. She would be ushered into the chapel, where she would sit in the royal seat, and then when it was over she would be ushered right back out. The priests brought in to speak had so far been hesitant, or angry, or afraid. It was hard to tell which. She had to admit she dreaded Sundays. Perhaps things would change, now that Father Stanson was being removed from his position. But for now it was painfully awkward.

The day, however, was gorgeous. Sunlight filtered down through the trees, dappling the grass, the flowers. Birds chirped pleasantly. She could see the pond, the same one where she once sat and read. The same one in her dream. It was a simple dream, one she did not wish to forget. In that dream, she saw children running and laughing, a boy and a girl. They ran through the gardens of the palace. They played in the pond where Panna at one time used to sit and read. They floated boats there, little toy boats with masts and sails, and they argued with one another about which was the *Trophy Chase*. And then, there was Packer, kneeling beside them! And then he knelt by the edge of the water, and he showed them how a tall ship sailed, where the captain stood, how the crew moved the sheets so the wind would fill the sails. And he blew on the sails, so they could see.

"Where do the Firefish jump to?" one asked.

"Anywhere God tells them."

"Is God on the ship, too?" the other asked.

"Oh, always."

"Where does God stand?"

"He's everywhere. In the sails. On the quarterdeck. At the prow."

And then an elderly man walked up, gray-haired and gentle, face weathered and worn and sunny. And the children hugged his legs and pulled on his hands until he sat down. And they called him Grampapa. And then Grandmamma came, and put her hand on his shoulder. And Panna looked down at her book. *The True Story of the Adventures of Packer Throme, King of the Vast, and his Great Ship, the* Trophy Chase.

Panna looked now through the wide, arched, open window, admiring the glassy surface of the water, imagining those toy ships, those tiny hands. She sighed. It was just a dream.

"Panna."

She turned around. And there was Packer. And not just Packer, but Packer from her dream. He stood tall and proud, and he radiated strength. His face was serene, and full of joy, and yet bore a depth of pain that made her heart cry out, as though it was not his pain he felt, but hers.

Packer walked to her, and took her in his arms.

"The battles are all over and won." He spoke the words gently, gently into her ear. "I'm back to stay."

So he was, for good and all.

EPILOGUE

Packer Throme reigned in Nearing Vast forty-seven years, with his queen by his side. Panna's dream came true just as she had dreamed it. Or almost. They did have two children, a boy and a girl. But then they had another boy, and then another girl. And then two girls. And then twin boys. And all of these reigned as princes and princesses in the palace, where the gardens were their battlefields, the ponds their oceans. Here they sailed their boats and fought their wars, and slew and tamed their Firefish, in forts and ships and palaces. Here they rode the seas and followed the winds wherever they would blow.

And they did everything—*almost* everything—under the gentle, watchful eyes of Grandpapa and Grandmamma, and they never did see one without the other. And when finally the day came that these two were lost to them, many years and many, many joys later, all the Thromes traveled to Hangman's Cliffs, the tiny town atop the cliff, the legendary place known now throughout the land. And Dayton and Netessa Throme were buried together in a clearing in the woods, not far from Will and Tamma Seline, where they rested in eternal peace.

The Drammune never did attack the Vast again, not while Packer reigned. Huk Tuth's message, sent by falcon, had assured the Quarto of the foolishness of such a move. According to the commander's final written words, not only would the Firefish swallow up whatever warships dared to cross an ocean and provoke their master's wrath, but should a war be lost, Packer Throme would claim his rightful place as the Hezzan Throme Dramm.

The Quarto burned the message, executed every returning sailor, and never spoke a word of it again.

And the Drammune attacked no other nations. After killing off two of his three fellow Quarto members, finding them not so Worthy after all, Pizlar Kank declared himself Hezzan. Under the Hezzan Pizlar Dramm, civil strife and violence grew. The rift between the Zealots and their opposition steadily increased, with violence more and more severe, lasting almost forty years beyond the inevitable assassination of Pizlar Kank. Discord and disharmony and rebellion were the hallmarks of Drammun during all the years of Packer Throme's life.

And all the strife within Drammun served to guarantee a lasting peace to all their neighbors, friends and enemies alike.

The Achawuk fared much better. Protected by the legend of the Firefish, no ships dared approach but those of Nearing Vast, and then only those sent by Packer Throme.

Packer himself returned to the mayak-aloh several times, the first trip within two years. He brought Queen Panna with him. She, in fact, had refused to be left behind, as she was the one who demanded that the trip be taken. The reason for her ardor was at root quite simple, but was overlaid by events long hidden, now finally exposed.

When Dayton Throme learned of the church archives below the library, he pored through the ancient documents, satisfying, finally, his long-suffering curiosity. He was searching for one last piece of information he could not puzzle out. That Firefish tooth, the one he had hung around his neck, the one that had saved him…how did it get to Nearing Vast? The woman who had given it to him, whom he knew only as Salla, had been found in an asylum. He had visited her only because he'd heard she spoke ceaselessly about the Firefish. The asylum was run by the Church, and she had been put there, she had said, by the Church.

Now, delving into the archives, Dayton discovered that Salla had in fact been born on the Achawuk islands. She had been brought to Nearing Vast, along with her parents, by "missionaries"—not priests at all but mercenaries. Her parents had died suspiciously, but for a while, it seemed that the young Achawuk girl would adapt to life in Nearing Vast.

She grew, was adopted, given the name of Salla, and eventually married. Then she had a daughter. But according to these records, Salla could not forget her childhood, and was drawn back to it in her mind. She began to speak openly of Firefish, and of the Achawuk. She became morose, darkened, and a danger to herself.

Her baby daughter was taken from her, and Salla was thereafter lost to the world and, committed to the asylum, she was heard from no more. Her husband disappeared, and then remarried. Her daughter was raised by an aunt. But that little orphan, the daughter of a full-blooded Achawuk mother, was Tamma Pottanger. Tamma, who married a priest named Will Seline.

Panna Throme, the Queen of Nearing Vast, was one-quarter Achawuk. She would see the homeland of her grandmother.

The legend of the *Trophy Chase* grew and grew, remembered in songs and stories and in the hearts of a seafaring nation. The sign of the Firefish above the tiny inn in Hangman's Cliffs was eventually replaced by the sign of the *Trophy Chase*. Packer Throme was on hand for the unveiling. Standing on a dais built for the occasion, he introduced a young man with hair like a shock of wheat, and a mottled, freckled complexion.

"Marcus Pile is the best carpenter's mate I've ever had the privilege of sailing with," Packer said to all. Marcus blushed as the crowd cheered. "When the *Chase* was beset by the Firefish, and our legendary Admiral John Hand was killed, Marcus was there. While many others in his position might have lost their nerve, he did not. To prove his valor, he plunged into the waters where the Firefish had been seen only seconds before. And he rescued this...the very image of the great ship, the great cat. The figurehead of the *Trophy Chase!*"

Packer pulled the cord, and the sheet fell, uncovering the lioness, claws grasping for invisible prey, jaws open for the kill.

The crowd took a breath, awed by the sight. And then it roared. Cap Hillis beamed, and as Hen nuzzled in to give him a hug, he pinched her, playfully. She slapped him, a bit less so.

No one noticed, or if they did no one cared, that one of the lion's paws had been replaced, and while the workmanship was fine, the proportions were somewhat suspect, both here and in the cat's reshaped hindquarters. Marcus had rescued the figurehead, and it was his to repair. But he was a carpenter, not a sculptor.

"And now I will ask Ensign Marcus Pile, a naval officer and a veteran of many great adventures of the *Trophy Chase,* to offer a prayer of dedication."

Smith Delaney's chest swelled with pride as his friend stood beside the king and bowed his head.

"Dear God our Father, who art in heaven," Marcus began. It was a good start, Delaney thought, and he glanced at Packer, who glanced back. They exchanged knowing looks, and Packer offered the smallest hint of a wink before closing his eyes.

"We are gathered here underneath Thee, who art high above over us all, to be reminded by this carved bit of wood of all Thy hand hath done." Here Marcus paused, and Delaney saw a dark look cross the young man's face. "But of course we knowest as Thou knowest— though not quite so well as Thou, of course—we know that no carved piece a' wood has life in her. I mean, in it. And while the *Trophy Chase* was sure a fine carved piece of wood, I mean as fine a piece of wood as ever floated on any stretch of water anywhere, she was but a thing after all, and without spirit in her. So, we would never worship her or anything or anything made by the hands of man, for we been warned all about that in Thy Scriptures.

"And so this little pouncing cat here made by mortal hands, and fixed by other mortal hands as best he could, here is the sign and figure of the *Trophy Chase,* now gone from Thy world forever. It is but a token, is all, and not a live thing as I mentioned, just a token of Thy grace and mercy that led so many of us, and mainly Packer who art the king, through the wilderness toward Thee. I mean the wilderness of the ocean. Which is water, but still wild, at least in many ways.

"And we hang her up here in memorial of Thee, like a testament, hopin' and prayin' that all who underwalk her and raise their eyes to gaze upon her...or rather, on it, because it is an 'it' and not a 'she'... we pray that all will remember Thee whenever they dost see it, and remember how Thou knowest all, while we hardly ever do know what thou doest. And help us always to remember that whatever Thou art up to, big or little, it's always a good thing. Though it may look a bit sketchy from where we stand. Especially when it's war and death and sea monsters and such. But even when it's just the bellyache or corns or other common though quite painful ailments, it's still of Thee, and Thou doest good in the world. Because that is who Thou art.

And so let us therefore worship Thee, as Thou deservest, and not this carved lioness, as that would become a stumbling block and a snare to our souls. For Thou art God, and we art not. And amen to that."

And all said amen, and all were satisfied, and looked upon the carved beast with a new sense of appreciation, and just a dash of apprehension, lest they might be tempted to worship it against their better judgment.

The *Trophy Chase* was remembered in other, more practical ways. One year from Packer's triumphant return from the mayak-aloh, Moore Davies took the king to the royal shipyards in South Barnes Mooring. The new admiral had a project underway that he wanted the king to see. Standing above the yards, where the shipwrights and carpenters worked day and night to rebuild the royal Navy, they saw the latest and greatest creations of the engineers of Nearing Vast. Not one, not two, but three full-scale replacements shone in the sun, like offspring of the *Chase*, built on John Hand's original plans, now come into the world fully grown.

One year after that, Packer sailed with Panna to the Achawuk islands on a ship almost identical to the *Chase*, this one called *Legend of the Firefish*. This was the first time Panna had ever sailed on a tall ship, and she spent the entire voyage, there and back, leaning over one rail or another, sick as a dog.

No one had to tell her, or Packer, that it was by God's grace she hadn't sailed with him on any of his previous voyages.

When the *Legend of the Firefish* pulled into the mayak-aloh, she sailed across the still waters just above the sunken, now caved and cratered ruin that was once the storied *Trophy Chase*. The sunlight shone down again, and illuminated the seafloor, but time and sand and currents had changed it all. A dull dust seemed to cover a disfigured heap. A few pieces of wood, masts or spars, it was hard to tell which, protruded upward from drifting sand. All canvas was gone, all rigging. But if one knew what to look for, one could still see a serpentine outline along the length of the wreckage. And at the prow, a huge skull was visible, enormous eye sockets empty, jack-o-lantern teeth bared in what might be mistaken for an eternal snarl.

The Achawuk gathered on the shoreline, cheering, as Packer Throme, their Tannan-thoh-ah, was rowed to them in the ship's tiny shallop. They called out to their much-missed Zhintah-Hoak, now returning to his homeland, when finally they recognized him. He was dressed in a suit, a bow tie under his neck, looking proud and pleased.

But Packer couldn't find his beloved priest among the Achawuk. He scanned the crowd, growing more and more concerned, until by the time his feet trod the sandy beaches, he feared the worst.

"Welcome, Packer Throme, my king," a sunny voice called out. Packer followed it to its source, and blinked. Yes, it was Father Mooring. But his hair had grown out, as had his beard. He wore no shirt, and his skin was tanned and brown as an acorn. He wore only what the other Achawuk wore. He stepped toward Packer, and embraced him.

"If I'd known you were coming, I'd have worn my best loincloth," he said with a grin.

Panna was immensely relieved to feel solid earth under her feet again. When she felt better, they toured the islands, meeting all of Father Mooring's new friends. A few had come to faith, just a handful so far, but Father Mooring seemed not the least bit discouraged. The king and queen worshipped with them in an open-air church two consecutive Sundays, on a solitary stretch of beach with a wooden cross erected in the shade. The services were conducted in Achawuk. Very, very slowly. They sang their songs of worship in the Achawuk tongue, to Achawuk tunes. The priest had decided early on that God had come to visit these people, not the other way around. After a two week stay, Packer and Panna sailed home to Nearing Vast. They would never again see Father Bran in this life.

After two decades, a town called Mayakaloh appeared as a small dot on the Vast Chart of the Seas. After two more the town became an established port of call. But it never did become a part of Nearing Vast. The Achawuk remained the Achawuk. Father Mooring lived out his days among them, revered as friend, and teacher, and as a faithful priest of the Most High God.

The House of Throme left many imprints of note, as it became more and more enmeshed in the heart and soul of Nearing Vast. On the first anniversary of Varlotsville, the people of that small town gathered at noon, and knelt in the square, surrendering once again to God and thanking Him for the victory over the Drammune.

On the second anniversary, word had gotten out, as it almost always did, and the king came to participate. The occasion then spread throughout the City of Mann. By the fifth anniversary, it was a national holiday, known as Kneeling Day, and everyone left off whatever they were doing, mostly leisure activities now, picnics and parades, in order to bow the knee at noon, and surrender once again to the God who defeated enemies. By the twentieth anniversary, pubs opened at nine in the morning and didn't close until well past midnight. A century later, most of the kneeling done that day was in shrubs by those who had overimbibed. But the day was remembered, nonetheless.

Much of the Western Wilderness was settled during Packer's reign, in no small part due to the storied handiwork of two grizzled men who ventured west, the Hammersfold brothers. They overcame giant bears and giant men, driving them yet farther west. Or so the legend went. And the kingdom expanded.

The House of Sennett, true to its checkered past, found a mixed place in history. The former king and queen, Reynard and Maeveline, made their peace with Packer and Panna and lived out their days, if not happily, at least peaceably within the Mountain House. Prince Ward wandered back and forth from rake to valued confidant, until finally his excesses wore him out. He put away the ale for good, married, and then lived a quiet life of civil service. He happily and capably led projects large and small, and helped rebuild the honor and the strength of Nearing Vast.

Princess Jacqalyn, by contrast, went to prison, where she railed at everything and everyone until she drove herself quite mad, after which she lived in relative comfort in an asylum among the trees, now regrown, not far from the Hollow Forest.

Mather Sennett found honor in death that he had never earned in life. Having revealed publicly his indiscretions, neither Packer nor Panna would ever say a word against him again. He was "my honored predecessor," and though he was king for but a day, Packer always pointed out that it was a truly glorious day in the history of the nation. Mather forever showed the spirit of the Vast, a spirit of sacrifice, and of love, and of humility. And as such he was an example for all generations.

The Church prospered once again, under new and humbler leadership. Usher Fell and Harlowen "Hap" Stanson, stripped of all their titles, left this world side by side, their exit gate a trap door in the gallows on the Green. It was a grim and searing lesson for the many witnesses on hand, but one that carried with it the knowledge that in Nearing Vast, at last, power and prestige could not substitute for upright character, and evil deeds would have evil consequences.

Dog Blestoe returned to Hangman's Cliffs, but not to his fishing boat. He had no grip left in his hands. But once or twice a year he was summoned to the palace and asked for his advice. He always grumbled, as he fingered the coins in his pocket, coins he sorely needed. "The kingdom will come to ruin," he'd say aloud, to any who'd listen to him there in Cap's pub, "when kings pay that kind of coin for nothing but half an hour of idle talk with old fishermen." But he not would abide another soul to speak ill of the king.

Smith Delaney was immediately and forever hailed a national hero to the Vast, the man who finally slew the assassin Talon, the evil Hezzan of the Drammune, and saved the king from certain death. Delaney could not be bought enough mugs of ale, or hailed often enough in the streets, or patted on the back too much by total strangers. Far worse, he discovered to his chagrin that suddenly, many intricate women seemed to find him quite, quite delightful.

"I'd be pleased if ye just kept me assigned to ship, and not to shore," he told his king in confidence. "I wasn't made to be so toasted a man as it seems I've now become." The king understood, and assigned his faithful friend to the *Legend,* the spitting image of the great cat they both loved, captained now by Andrew Haas. So Delaney sailed the rest of his life through. And when he had finally sailed his last, he was buried among the Thromes and the Selines, with all due honors, high on Hangman's Cliffs.

Then finally, one perfect spring day when the songbirds sang and the smell of new flowers, honeysuckle and lilac, drifted through the palace, Packer Throme, now ancient and infirm, breathed his last. Panna held his hand, her chair pulled up close, her hands brindled with age but firm and sure and comforting. The king's children, and their children, and their children yet again, gathered around his bed in the royal hospital, doors and windows thrown open wide, hearts thrown open wider yet. Tears rained. Small voices asked, "What's wrong with Grandpapa, Momma?"

And older, gentle voices answered, "He's gone to heaven, dear one. He's gone on to see his King."

"He has a king?"

"Oh, yes. Our King Packer serves a great and noble King, much greater than he ever was. As do we all."

And Queen Panna laid her head down on her husband's shoulder, and her frail body shook. Then the family melted away, leaving her with her Packer, her one true love.

"Sleep well," she told him, stroking his scarred hand, the noble signet loose on his forefinger. She touched his peaceful face, his cheek, his beard, now white and thin. "Rest. And then rise, young and strong again. And hold a place for me." For this world had suddenly grown very small, and cold, and distant. "I miss you already." And her tears flowed.

And when her aged eyes had seen a grateful nation pay its last respects, when throngs of mourners, hearts afire, trailing the royal bier as though each one had lost a father or a grandfather or a great-grandfather, when her hands had clenched the dirt in the small cemetery high above the seas, and she had scattered the fragrant loam that was the final blanket drawn up over a king's last bed, when all her sons and daughters, and all their sons and daughters, wives and husbands, and all their children had comforted their Grandmamma as best they could, then Queen Panna of Nearing Vast lay down her toils, and released her spirit, and joined hands once again with her beloved, the two of them now young and strong and vibrant again, forever.

And the Firefish? They never did return to the mayak-aloh. They were never seen again.

And yet, they never quite disappeared. Even many, many years later, when these remarkable events had dimmed almost to darkness, distant names and dates for Vast schoolchildren grudgingly to recite, an occasional flame still flickered. Something was seen in the water here, far under a bottomless lake. Something lurked in the ocean there, where a ship had strangely disappeared.

And then the children's eyes would widen, and their hearts would race.

The End.

About the Author

George Bryan Polivka was raised in the Chicago area, attended Bible college in Alabama, and ventured on to Europe, where he studied under Francis Schaeffer at L'Abri Fellowship in Switzerland. He then returned to Alabama, where he enrolled at Birmingham-Southern College as an English major.

While still in school, Bryan married Jeri, his only sweetheart since high school and now his wife of more than 25 years. He also was offered a highly coveted internship at a local television station, which led him to his first career—as an award-winning television producer.

In 1986, Bryan won an Emmy for writing his documentary *A Hard Road to Glory,* which detailed the difficult path African-Americans traveled to achieve recognition through athletic success during times of racial prejudice and oppression.

Bryan and his family eventually moved to the Baltimore area, where he worked with Sylvan Learning Systems (now Laureate Education). In 2001 he was honored by the U.S. Distance Learning Association for the most significant achievement by an individual in corporate e-learning. He is currently responsible for developing and delivering new programs for Laureate's online higher education division.

Bryan and Jeri live near Baltimore with their two children, Jake and Aime, where Bryan continues to work and write.

Be sure to visit his website at www.nearingvast.com.

∼ TROPHY CHASE TRILOGY ∼
George Bryan Polivka

BOOK ONE: *THE LEGEND OF THE FIREFISH*
Packer Throme longs to bring prosperity back to his fishing village by discovering the trade secrets of Scat Wilkins, a notorious pirate who now seeks to hunt the legendary Firefish and sell its rare meat.

Packer begins his quest by stowing away aboard Scat's ship, the *Trophy Chase*, bound for the open sea.

Will belief and vision be enough for Packer Throme to survive? And will Talon, the Drammune warrior woman who serves as Scat's security officer, be Packer's deliverance...or his death? And what of Panna Seline? In her determination not to lose Packer, she leaves home to follow the man she loves, but soon she is swept up in a perilous adventure of her own.

BOOK TWO: *THE HAND THAT BEARS THE SWORD*
In the midst of their joyous "honey month," newlyweds Packer and Panna Throme are once again thrust unwillingly into high adventure.

Pirate Scat Wilkins, no longer in command of his great ship, has returned with evil intentions for Packer as the *Trophy Chase* sets sail for deep waters once again.

While Packer is away, Panna, his bride, faces danger at the hands of the lecherous Prince Mather.

And a deadly peril has arisen across the sea. A new Hezzan in the Kingdom of Drammun now has diabolical designs on Packer and the Firefish trade, which catapults all of Nearing Vast into the horrors of war.

BOOK THREE: *THE BATTLE FOR VAST DOMINION*
Packer Throme, determined to demonstrate that power comes only from above, leads his people in a war against the dreaded Drammune. The evil Hezzan of Drammun will kill without remorse for the secret of the Firefish...and so will dark forces lurking within Nearing Vast.

As army faces army, and navy faces navy, all are drawn inexorably to the source of the epic struggle...the feeding waters of the Firefish within the Achawuk Territory. One final surprise awaits Packer Throme there in the foreboding place where the struggle for the dominion of the world will be settled at last.

To learn more about Harvest House books
or to read sample chapters, log on to our website:
www.harvesthousepublishers.com

HARVEST HOUSE PUBLISHERS
EUGENE, OREGON